The
Gilly
Salt
Sisters

Also by Tiffany Baker

The Little Giant of Aberdeen County

The Gilly Salt Sisters

TIFFANY BAKER

DOUBLEDAY LARGE PRINT HOME LIBRARY EDITION

GC

GRAND CENTRAL
PUBLISHING

NEW YORK   BOSTON

This Large Print Edition, prepared especially for Doubleday Large Print Home Library, contains the complete, unabridged text of the original Publisher's Edition.

Grand Central Publishing
Hachette Book Group
237 Park Avenue
New York, NY 10017

Printed in the United States of America

Grand Central Publishing is a division of Hachette Book Group, Inc. The Grand Central Publishing name and logo is a trademark of Hachette Book Group, Inc.

ISBN 978-1-61793-831-3

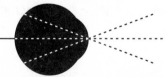

This Large Print Book carries the Seal of Approval of N.A.V.H.

For Edward

And the eye cannot say to the hand, "I have no need of you."

—1 Corinthians 12:21

The
Gilly
Salt
Sisters

Prologue

It was the season again for fire in Prospect, a time of cold and ice but also an occasion for rising heat and smoke. A moment for salt and prophecy, when the future met the past and the old ceded to the new, for better or for worse.

This year, as usual, it had taken the good men of town a full week to make the pyre for the municipal bonfire. For seven days Claire had kept tabs on the rising stack of timber growing in the middle of Tappert's Green, largest logs on the bottom, spread evenly for air to pass, and more delicate sticks leaned up against those in a giant incendiary tepee. The men eyed her as she drove slowly past them on her way to deliver salt in town, pausing in their toil, red-cheeked and burly in the cold, their eyes suspicious under their hat brims. None of them waved, nor did Claire expect them to. She knew that if it weren't for her sister and her, no one in town would have any reason to cinder anything at all.

Claire's family had never really been welcome at the celebration, even if they were the reason behind it. Their role was purely functional. First, the oldest person in town lit the bonfire, and then either Claire or her sister, Jo, stepped forward, a packet of salt in hand, ready to toss it to the flames and see what it said. It was the simplest kind of divination: two elements colliding. If the fire flashed blue, it meant the town would prosper in the coming year. If it flared yellow, some kind of change was on the horizon, and a puff of black was too terrible to contemplate.

The first time Claire ever threw salt

to the fire, it did indeed turn black. She was six and so little she had to reach up before she could scatter the salt to the flames. There was a sizzle and a pop, and then came an acrid swirl of undeniable pitch smoke. The towns-people behind her drew in their breaths and clutched their children closer, then shuffled into the shadows, their eyes probing as owls on the hunt. The circle of space around Claire, her mother, and her sister grew larger and colder.

Jo had put her hands on Claire's shoulders and leaned down to whisper in her ear. "Step away from the logs now. The salt's spoken. You can't change what's been cast. Take my hand and come with Mama and me."

Claire had frowned. "We don't get to stay?" she'd asked. All that autumn she'd heard about the festivities from her classmates, how there would be music, and dancing, and boys stealing kisses by the glow of the flames.

Jo shook her head. "Never. I ex-plained that, Claire. We're just here to show the future, not partake in it." And before Claire could protest further, Jo had taken her by the arm and started marching her back to the quiet of their marsh, refusing to meet anyone's eyes, not even Whit Turner's, the richest, most charming boy in town, and her sweetheart. Claire saw Whit's mother, Ida, sneer in her direction as they passed, as if they were no better than the ashes beneath her shoes.

Every year after that, walking home down the sandy lane and hearing the rising revelry and the squeals as people threw their own little packets of salt to the fire, Claire used to chafe under the habitual exclusion, protesting to Jo and her mother that they were just the same as anyone else, that in spite of their salt the Gillys should be dancing round the fire, too.

But that was back when she was innocent, before love came along and stroked her heart with one of its sooty fingers. You never really recovered from a touch like that, and maybe, Claire thought, that was as it should be. No one slipped through life perfectly unscarred, after all, and if someone did, how unlucky, for surely there must be a hotter fire waiting in the afterlife when that was the case. And Claire would know. Once she'd been . . . not free of sin, exactly, but free of its implications. Her past had not yet caught up to her future. But eventually it did, of course. That was what it meant to be human. Oddly enough, it had taken a man of God to make Claire see this mortal truth.

For years she'd wanted nothing to do with the salt. Jo had cast it by herself every December's Eve and borne the consequences of what it foretold, until Claire had put a stop to the whole pagan nonsense. No bonfire. No salt. She turned her back on the whole tradition. But certain elements would not be ignored. Claire learned that lesson the hard way—that you cannot scorn the ground from whence you came, for the body rises from the earth just as it goes back to it.

But that was years ago. Now she was a woman tipped to the far side of middle age, and the entire town was gathered together like naughty children let out after curfew, and Claire was among them, if not a part of them. Jo, too. Claire could feel Jo's solid presence behind her, steadying her for her task. The townsfolk stood with their hands clenched under their chins in anticipation as a wizened Timothy Weatherly put the torch to the wood. There was a crackle, and then Claire could smell the smoke: a mixture of alder wood, elm wood, pine, and pitch. At first the scent was scratchy and rough, but as the flames picked up heat, they burned sweeter, pulling oils out of the wood and dispersing them into the stark winter night. The odor rose and built, scorching away the past year's sins and regrets. Claire inhaled again and caught a whiff of something almost like cinnamon and then, unexpectedly, a clean ozone flare, and she knew that it was time to step forward with her packet of salt.

The night was wondrously clear, Claire saw. The sky was as star-strewn and gaudy as some of the gowns she used to wear in another life. The happy cacophony of the crowd—a child's shriek, the off-key wail of a flute, a group of teenage boys performing one of their football chants—faltered and died as she took her place and held up the salt for all to see. And then there was a sudden and terrible hush as a glare of yellow burst forth.

Yellow for caution, for possible danger. Claire met Jo's eyes and shook her head. Maybe a death, maybe ill luck. Something unexpected. *Who will it fall upon?* Claire wondered as she felt Jo reach for her hand. Mr. Weatherly, with his creaking hips and rusty tools? Pretty Hope Fell, due to begin college in two months' time? One of the town's young mothers, still plump and tired from pregnancy? Before Claire could think further, however, the thread of the flute started up again, knitting the night back together, and soon there was a burst of laughter, more shrieks, and another baby's wail as she and Jo faded into the darkness and began making their way home. Because life went on, even in Prospect, even in spite of what the salt might say.

Just never quite as one imagined.

Chapter One

When all was said and done, Jo supposed, she would simply call hers a story of salt. Parts of it were bitter on the tongue, parts of it were rocky, and over the years parts had even melted clean away. What was left were the concentrated bits, the crystals that cracked and sparkled when crushed between her teeth. "Grit," the people in Prospect called it, but it was far more than that, Jo knew. It was regret given weight, history made tangible. It was everything she and her sister should have said to each other and then never did.

But fate worked like that. It was sneaky and a little underhanded, wasn't it—springing something new on you right at the moment you needed everything old in your life to snap into focus. In Jo's case that something was a letter from Harbor Bank in Boston, the envelope as plain as anything, the words inside it even starker. They went something like this: Long ago, predicting better times, Jo's mother had taken out a second loan on the family's salt marsh. Jo knew that much. She'd been paying the loan off for years, and those better times had never come. Instead, to Jo's surprise, the loan interest was about to increase drastically. If Jo wasn't good for that difference, the bank wrote, she'd soon be finding herself stranded on dry ground. Why didn't she give them a call?

Well.

Judging by the impressive amount of gilt on the bank's letterhead, listing all its branches up and down the eastern seaboard, Harbor Bank was nothing like Prospect's humble and friendly Plover Bank, where Jo and everybody else in town did their everyday business. Of course, that also explained why Jo's mother had gone to Harbor Bank to beg money. No one who knew Salt Creek Farm would willingly sink his hard-earned dollars into the place.

Jo was tempted to pick up the phone and try to share her side of the story, then gave up and left the receiver in the cradle. Whoever had mailed the letter from Boston would neither understand nor care that if Salt Creek Farm vanished from this narrow lip of Cape Cod, the rest of Prospect might follow in short order, for the fates of the two—marsh and town—were intertwined. No one could remember anymore why or how, just that it had always been so, ever since Jo's ancestors had first shaped the land with hoes, spades, and their own crooked backs.

Jo shoved the letter into the kitchen junk drawer, then thought better of it and took it out and smashed it into the trash. Truthfully, it didn't much matter what she did with it, she suspected. The bank would just mail another one until the day they decided to quit being polite and sent the sheriff instead.

People in Prospect blamed Jo for her salt's strange ways, as if she could control a substance that solidified on its own time and dissolved at the slightest opportunity. This attitude didn't dispose her kindly toward the town in return. After all, they were the ones who'd chosen to put themselves at the mercy of the salt every December's Eve during Jo's youth, when she used to have to step up to the town bonfire and toss a packet to the flames to see what the future would bring. Jo didn't know what kind of science made the salt color the fire, only that it happened and was none of her doing.

She wished she *could* control the future. She'd work a spell on the anonymous clerks of Harbor Bank and make them cancel out her debt. But the clerks were obviously not interested in the miraculous alchemy of the Gilly salt. What they cared about was arithmetic. As long as there was a plus sign on their side of things, Jo knew, nothing else much mattered. It was a hard logic to argue with.

But they didn't see what Jo did when she walked out onto her front porch. Their eyes didn't automatically travel to the rows of collecting basins to see if crystals were forming. They wouldn't have been able to pick the treasures out of the trash in any of the junk heaps behind the barn, and they certainly wouldn't have had the faith Jo did in her battered pickup. It didn't look too pretty, that was true, but it still ran fine. She climbed into it and started the engine. In spite of what the bank was saying, it was her delivery day and she had rounds to make, meager though they were.

As she jostled and bumped down the rutted lane into town, past the tiny church of St. Agnes, she fretted about how much longer she might have on the only land she'd ever known. One month? Four? Maybe a whole year if she were lucky?

"We would prefer a mutually amicable solution to this situation," the bank's letter said. *"Please contact us."* Jo

snorted and jammed the engine into third. She could just imagine their reaction if she dared to stroll into the bank's headquarters in person with her swath of scars pickling the right side of her face, her glass eye thick as anything, not to mention the sight of her clothes, stiff and pale from years of working the marsh in all kinds of weather. On the other hand, maybe that wasn't such a bad idea. Maybe the very sight of her would startle the bankers into clemency.

She looked up, surprised that she'd arrived already in town. Misery loved company, and Jo was no exception. She was pleased to note that if Salt Creek Farm had been having a tough decade, so had all the rest of Prospect. The library was open only three days a week now, and the post office only in the mornings. Mr. Friend's hardware store, dusty and jumbled with rows of outdated tools, still stood on the corner of Bank and Elm right next to the five-and-dime, but the barbershop was shuttered, along with the diner. Three years ago Mr. Hopper, the establishment's former owner, had died of a stroke, leaving the stools empty and the men in town hungry as all get-out.

Naturally, Prospect blamed the scourge of Jo's salt for their decline, but Jo wasn't having that. She knew exactly who was behind the town's demise: her little sister, Claire. She was the one who'd upped and fled Salt Creek Farm a decade ago—turning nature on its head and leaving Jo short a pair of extra hands. Growing up, Jo had worked the marsh alongside her mother and Claire, and while it wasn't much, they'd always managed. But when Claire had married and Jo's mother had died, Jo found out how hard it was for one woman to do the work of three. In fact, as evidenced by her skimpy salt yields, it was proving impossible.

Lately, whatever Jo did around the farm seemed to carry negative consequences. If she chose to scrape the delicate surface crystals off the ponds, for instance, it meant she wasn't repairing the broken sluice near the weir. And if she then turned around to fix that, it meant she wasn't dredging the channels that had started to silt up. This year she'd had to let a full third of the evaporating basins fill with mud, leaving them fallow and unproductive, and she was also forced to ignore the attic's leaking roof, overlook the warped wooden gates in the smallest sluices, and make do when all her metal tools started rusting. Of course her productivity had fallen way off. She needed new equipment, repairs on the truck, and to patch the farmhouse porch, but she had debts to repay. Ones she hadn't even been aware existed.

There was another lurking problem with the marsh that the bank in Boston didn't know about, however. The truth was, it didn't matter how little salt Jo was making, because sales were slim in Prospect. And that was her sister's fault, too. Claire had frightened almost everyone off from buying it except for the local fishermen, who found it handy for keeping their catch and bait cold. Without the business of men like Chet Stone, the uncle of Claire's first love, Jo had a bad feeling she'd be sunk deader than the fish stowed in his trawler. When

Claire didn't like a thing, Jo knew, she didn't like anyone else to like it either. In that regard she was like a bad-tempered child, scattering her toys before anyone else could pick them up and use them, consequences be damned.

Jo remembered how the grocer, Mr. Upton, tried to refuse carrying the salt his first summer in town. She'd been very young, barely at her mother's knee, when they'd marched into the shop with a sample for him to taste. "No thank you," he'd said, putting up two palms, and Mama hadn't fought with him. Instead she'd smiled, sweet as pie. "Fine," she'd said. "That's just fine." And she waltzed Jo out the door. It hadn't taken very long for the salt to work its magic. By the next week, all Mr. Upton's meats had turned rancid and there were flyspecks in his fresh butter. A shelf of canned beans collapsed against Mabel Arch's arthritic hip, the fishmonger suddenly refused to deliver, and the sliced loaves of bread grew mold underneath their clear plastic wrappers. Jo's mother had waited two more days, then gone back and discovered that Mr. Upton had experienced a sudden change of heart. He would stock the salt after all.

He was one of the few in Prospect who still did stock it now, but he kept it low and behind the counter, on a shelf so dusty and shaded you practically needed mining equipment to find it. And whereas he used to have bags and bags of the stuff readily available, now he kept only one or two at a time—enough not to cross the charm of the salt and bring back the rancid meat and flies, but not so much that it was a regular commodity. Whenever Jo went in to see if Mr. Upton needed more, he'd avoid her eyes and shake his head apologetically. "I really can't right now," he'd say, closing his cash register. "Maybe next month." And Jo would gnash her teeth and want to bury Claire up to her neck in a pile of the salt she hated, leaving her there until all Jo's old customers came back.

But there was only so much blame Jo could heap on Claire. If their situations were reversed, Jo suspected, if Jo were the one married to Whit and living in that big Turner House, and if Claire were the one stuck all alone in the marsh's mud, she no doubt would have found a way to make everyone from Provincetown to Falmouth crave the salt. Jo's truck was rickety, but it still drove. Jo should have been rattling up and down the Cape, looking for new customers, she knew, but that was easier said than done, what with the way strangers stared at the bouquet of scars fanned across her cheek, and besides, who was supposed to mind the marsh if she went gallivanting all over God's green earth?

Speaking of, she'd arrived at the end of it. That is, she was at the docks, where Prospect's last few fishing boats bobbed like dilapidated corks. What with OPEC and the ongoing energy crunch and gasoline getting so expensive, more and more captains were deciding to fold their hands and give up life on the sea. It was a shame, Jo thought, and not just because it meant she was losing business, but also because without the traffic in the wharf the docks looked rattier and more weathered than ever—sagging in dangerous directions, missing crucial planks, rotted away in other spots. Here, more than at any other spot, the town's recent decline was apparent. Jo stepped with care down the main dock and approached Chet Stone's boat.

"Hello, sailor," he called when he saw her coming, his ironic greeting for her due to the fact that no matter how many times the men asked her to come aboard, Jo would never so much as tap a toe on any of their boats. He had a transistor radio going, blaring something about the American hostages held in Iran. Chet frowned and shook his head. "What's the world coming to?" he asked, reaching his arms out for the bag of salt Jo had brought. "People don't stay where they ought anymore. Good thing you're still around." He grinned and hefted the sack down at his feet. "My fish stays cold, and my boat stays safe. But those poor suckers"—he jerked his thumb at the radio—"well, I'm afraid they might be goners."

Without a word, Jo took the money

he handed her, but she was thinking that if Chet Stone knew about the letter in her pocket, he just might say the same about her and decide to quit the sea, too, and then she'd be in a proper pickle with her most loyal customer gone. She cleared her throat and shoved the bills into her coat pocket. "Don't worry," she finally said, "I'm not going anywhere fast."

"Let's hope not," Chet answered, turning back to the bait he was chopping, "or we're really going to hell in a handbasket."

———o-o o-o———

As she drove back through town, Jo was thinking so hard about her exchange on the dock that she almost plowed right into a ladder planted in front of the old diner. She parked her truck and got out, approaching the dusty window.

"Hey," a square-jawed man whom Jo had never seen before snarled, "watch where you're walking." Startled, Jo looked up to the top of the ladder, where a pudgy teenage girl was perched on the highest rung, trying to hang a crooked sign. THE LIGHTHOUSE DINER, it read. Jo blinked. She hadn't heard there was a new owner for the place. Her heart fluttered a little at that fact. New blood in town meant new customers. Hoping they hadn't met her sister yet, Jo put her hands on her hips and readied herself for an impromptu sales pitch.

She studied the man, then looked up to the girl again. The age spread was too big for them to be anything other than father and daughter, or maybe uncle and niece, Jo thought. The man had a half-gray crew cut and liver-spotted hands, and the girl was a rounded-off version of him. Plump cheeks, plump nose, and eyes just a little too close together for her to be really pretty. In Prospect, Jo knew, girls like this either ended up pummeled into ribbons by early marriages to rock-fisted men, or they survived and turned into fishwives with chiseled mouths and hearts to match, but there was still time for that in the girl's future. Right now Jo had selling to do.

Strangers never took easy to the

salt—or to her, for that matter—so it didn't surprise Jo when the man and the dough-faced girl frowned as they took in her scars. Almost thirteen years had passed since the fire that had burned her, but Jo still wasn't used to some of the looks she got. She supposed her insides hadn't yet caught up with the state of her exterior, but she also thought that was pretty much true of everyone. Most folks just didn't show it. The man in front of Jo didn't appear as if he had that issue, however. He looked like the kind of person who wanted those around him to fall in shoulder to shoulder and give a salute.

"Tip it to the left!" he was shouting at the girl. "The left, damn it!" The girl sighed but then did as he said before climbing down from the ladder in an awkward, flat-footed way, as though she'd had all the opinions beaten out of her early on. Then Jo noticed the way the girl rolled her eyes when the man wasn't looking and saw that she was wrong. The girl had opinions, all right. She just knew to keep them to herself. Jo waited for the girl to plant both her feet on the ground before she told her, "You should have tipped it to the right."

The man frowned harder, then stumped over and held out his palm. "Cutt Pitman," he said. "And that's my daughter, Dee." He flicked his fingertips toward the girl. "Diner's not open just yet."

Jo didn't bother to shake his hand. "Joanna Gilly," she replied. "I'm not here to eat. I brought you some salt." She took a sample bag out of her pocket and put it in the man's callused hand. "Call me when you're about to open, and I can deliver you some more. We can talk about price. I'll be in town next Tuesday."

She turned to walk away, but the man stopped her. "Why would I buy salt from you when I can get it by the pound in a box?" he asked.

Jo folded her arms and licked the scars blistering the right side of her mouth. "If you don't buy from me," she said, "no one will eat here."

Cutt smirked. "Says who?"

Jo fixed him with her good eye. "That's the funny thing about this town," she said. "No one will come out and say so. They just won't show up. I'll be back next Tuesday." And she spun on her one good heel.

"Pesky old bat," she heard the man mutter as she trudged away, and then he waved a hand and ordered his daughter back up the ladder. "Tip it to the right. No, the right!" Jo heard him yelling.

So they didn't want her salt just now, but that fact didn't surprise her. How were they to know any better? To them, Jo reflected, it was probably about as common as house dust, and maybe about as useful. But it didn't worry her, their refusal. She just had to give them time—that was all. Patience was its own reward, she told herself, putting the ancient truck into gear and pulling into the street, and it was a good thing, too, because currently patience was about all she had.

———o-o o-o———

By the time Jo returned home, the sun had started to set, but the afternoon was still pleasant, quite so. Instead of gray shellac, the sky above hung more like burnished wood, the air swirling all golden and mellow. Jo was a great believer in the sky. For one thing, it was about her only companion, and for another, it never lied. When trouble was galloping in her direction, the wind and clouds let Jo know it right quick, maybe because she'd been born in a storm. Weather had brought her into this world, and when the time came, Jo expected it would carry her back out. She just hoped she would get a fair warning first. She scanned the marsh, running her eye over the swirling order of it: the main channel that cut from the beach, the inundation pools, the smaller ditches, and, finally, the evaporating basins themselves, tucked in rows in the middle of the whole operation, the marsh's eternally shrinking and expanding heart.

This time of year, the mud was so alkaline it grew vivid with microorganisms: bright purple, copper green, and the single basin that was bloodred. That was Henry's basin—Jo's twin brother, who'd drowned at the age of eight. Every year Jo ended up heaping the crimson salt onto his grave. She didn't know what else to do with it. She couldn't sell it like that, she knew, and she didn't want to use it herself. It would have been like eating the flesh of her family.

Past Henry's pool was the salt barn, and next to that was a grassy clearing where the Gilly family graves lay. Only boys were buried in the marsh's cemetery, which long ago had been specially consecrated to receive them. *Because death circles life*, was the way Jo's mother had explained it to her, but surely, Jo liked to think, life circled death. Otherwise what was the point of enjoying a good Sunday roast, or the sound of birdsong on a summer's evening, or Christmas carols, or any of it? But maybe, Jo mused, she could say that by virtue of coming through the fire the way she had. For her, everything had grown sharper after her accident: the burn of air on her wrinkled skin, the shift of the seasons. The colors of budding spring flowers could just about knock her socks off, and the autumn . . .

well, the autumn always got her so for-
lorn and chilly she just about wanted to
weep when the wind swept down and
claimed the leaves for its own. When
Jo felt like that, she would come out to
the graves and sit her bones down for
a while. It sounded backward, she
knew, but she found the spot to be the
perfect pick-me-up when melancholy
grabbed her by the throat. It cheered
her to remember that there was something even colder and harder in the
world than a Cape sky turning to winter.

Claire, of course, didn't have concerns like these. She was a Turner now,
and for the Turners things were always
a sight better. All you had to do was
look at their monstrosity of a house,
squatting on Plover Hill with all its
crooked porches and bowed windows,
to know that. Over the generations the
Turners had built themselves the Cape
version of a castle. The damn place
had so many rooms in it that Jo couldn't
imagine what Whit and her sister did in
them. But that was the Turners for you,
always grabbing up more than they

could wrap their arms around. Lately things hadn't been exactly smooth for Whit and Claire, Jo happened to know, but she figured they were a mite better off than she was. They still owned the rocky hill their house sat on, for one thing, and they owned the sand dunes that edged along the lane. They owned a portion of Drake's Beach, and they owned the pier in town, not to mention much of the town itself. About the only thing they didn't own in the general vicinity, in fact, was Salt Creek Farm, though it wasn't for an honest lack of trying.

You may believe in curses or not as you will—and Jo would—but there was no denying that bad blood and worse luck ran between the two families, a string of ill will that went all the way back to the first Turners and Gillys. It was a spat of flesh and soul, for if the Turners were the mercenary heart beating in the center of the town, pulsing money through the place, the Gillys were its spirit—untouchable, unknowable, and above the worldly smut of Turner dollars. And just as the heart sometimes wars with the body even as it relies upon it, so, too, did the Turners and Gillys resent one another's presence in Prospect, for while the Turners needed the magic of the Gilly salt for the town to prosper, the Gillys needed the Turner businesses to keep them solvent. The only thing the families really had in common was that the townspeople resented them both equally.

That being said, Jo had never blamed Claire for her poor choice in marrying Whit. When Whit learned he couldn't have Jo, he'd simply turned around and done what Turners do. He'd stolen in kind from Jo the one thing he knew she loved the most, the way he'd pilfered gumdrops from the five-and-dime when they were children and then eaten them, one by one right in front of the store, not caring a fig who might be looking and certainly not bothering to share, not even with Jo.

———o-o o-o———

Before she lost a sister, Jo lost a brother. She and Henry were born during a wicked nor'easter in March of 1942. According to Jo's mother, the world had stopped for three days. No phones worked. The electricity was knocked out up and down the Cape, and the roads were as closed as the churches and shops. The hospital doors in Hyannis even froze shut, but since no one could get out there anyway, it didn't much matter.

In the little church of St. Agnes, the storm also famously stripped the face off the west wall's painting of the Virgin. "Oh, it was a terrible thing, child," Father Flynn told Jo when she asked him about the incident. He squatted down and gazed evenly into her eyes. "I was away during the storm, conducting parish business in town, and when I returned, I found the windows smashed to the ends of the earth, the front doors blasted open, and Our Lady touched by the hand of God. I keep her this way as a reminder of the Lord's power." He paused and frowned. "Well, that and we've never had the funds to fix her, but one day soon, perhaps. One day soon." He bent down and cupped Jo's head, smiling a little. "Let's start with your catechism, shall we?" He paused again, and Jo thought he was going to say something more, but he did not, and she hung her head with disappointment. Apparently, for Father Flynn, the specifics of her origins began and ended with Our Lady.

As Jo grew older, her mother told her the fuller version of the story, sparing her nothing—or so Jo thought. By the time she discovered what a skilled storyteller her mother had been, however, Jo, too, would be an expert in the art of lying. Each night, as Jo settled down to sleep, her mother would perch on her bed and break her off another piece of family history as she deemed Jo ready to hear it. It took Jo until she was a teenager to digest the whole unpretty account.

On Salt Creek Farm, Mama said, the storm had done what it could with the little bit the landscape offered. Clumps of pickleweed had transformed into veins of ice. The salt basins, drained for their spring clean, had filled with snow, and waves lashed so far up on

Drake's Beach that ten years later people were still finding odd nubs of driftwood buried in the dunes.

Jo's mother had given birth by herself, but considering Jo's father's habits, she explained, it was better that way. He was trapped in town, sheltering with friends, downing beers and telling filthy jokes while Jo's mother filled the biggest pot of water she could find, boiled it over the fire in the hearth, and ripped a perfectly good bedsheet into strips. She fetched twine and a pair of scissors, threw as much wood onto the fire as she dared, stacked more nearby, and then squatted by the flames to wait.

When Jo's father finally made his way back after the storm, he didn't go straight inside. Instead he hesitated on the front porch, surveying the damage from the gale. Jo could just picture it. Maybe a scrub pine or two had uprooted and blown into the lane like tumbleweeds. For certain, shingles would have lain like broken birds, and broken birds themselves must have been sunk in the drifts like stones dropped from heaven.

There would have been no trace of the underlying salt. For once their land would have been indistinguishable from any other in Prospect. Maybe it was because of that, or because the cold walk home had sobered him, but Jo always believed that the clouds that normally filled her father's mind parted at that moment and he was able for the first time in a long time to imagine a life beyond Salt Creek Farm. Jo suspected he would have taken off running right then had the farmhouse door not squeaked open, letting out a blast of heat. There stood Mama in her dressing gown, clutching two babies instead of one: her brother, as ginger and freckled as all the Gillys, and Jo, as sooty as the mountain of ash piled in the grate.

The clouds in her father's soul clapped together again. "Tell me at least one of them is a boy," he'd said, and Jo's mother had nodded and held out Jo's red-haired brother.

"Praise the saints for that," Jo's father had answered, and pushed past

Mama to the bottle of gin he kept stashed in the broken hall piano. Two deep swallows for two babies. As long as she ever knew him, Jo's father had seen double on a permanent basis.

Yet if her father hadn't been a souse, her mother never would have gotten married. She informed Jo of this with a veneer of calm regret.

"Why?" Jo had asked.

"It's the salt." Jo's mother had sighed. "People are spooked by it. No sober man in any direction is going to marry you or Claire without a shotgun pointed at his head—and maybe not even then."

According to Mama, Jo's father didn't start off on the wrong path. He was an able mechanic who'd managed to eke out a living fixing up decrepit autos and turning them into something that would run. When World War II broke out, he'd tried to enlist in the army, figuring he could work wonders on jeeps and tanks, but the military wouldn't take him.

"Bad heart," the fish-eyed recruiting doctor had informed him during his physical, the man's mouth stretching wide on the vowels. "Very bad. You'll be lucky to hit thirty, much less forty."

Jo had always guessed that that's when things had gotten muddy for her father. That's when he'd started drinking, figuring if he was going to croak, he might as well do it nicely oiled. When he'd ended up married to Jo's mother, his life had turned to mud for real, fulfilling his worst prophecies. Mud out the front door as soon as he put a foot down. Mud roiled in the bottom of the drainage channels, mud in the salt itself, coloring it an alien gray. All of it he blamed on Jo's mother and the brine she reaped.

"Are her feet cloven?" his friends used to taunt him as they fell out of Fletcher's Tavern on their regular night, tripping over their bootlaces in an alcoholic tangle. "Does she drink the blood of spring lambs?" Jo knew perfectly well what her father's gang thought of the women of her family. They were the stones strewn in their roads, the scary shadows combing their walls when they couldn't sleep. The Gilly women knew

their futures. Spying Jo's mother waiting outside the tavern with the truck,
one of his pals would yowl, "Why'd you
do it, Tommy? Why'd you go and marry
that witch?"

"It was the salt," Jo's father would
answer, and that would shut everybody
up good, for if the men in Prospect
were silenced by anything, it was the
threat of Gilly salt, which flashed every
year on December's Eve and whipped
plain butter to cream and could heal a
wound on contact or open it wider, and
no one ever knew which.

"Yes," Jo's mother said, snapping off
Jo's bedroom light. "It was the salt.
That's true. The thing is, I never know
what it will do either."

Jo snuggled under the quilt and tried
to fall asleep. As always, Mama was
right. The Gillys never really could figure what the salt had in store. Otherwise, Jo thought, her existence surely
would have been very different. If nothing else, she would have made sure her
brother had lived.

—○-○ ○-○—

The summer Henry drowned, he and Jo were eight years old, it was August 1950, and it seemed like what wasn't wilted in the world was already halfway to fried. Going into Prospect with Mama for supplies and eyeing the town children in their pretty bathing suits and sandals was a special kind of torture for Jo that year. Not only because of the heat, but because it was the first time she could remember keeping a running tally of the difference between other lives and hers. It didn't bother her, exactly, but she noticed it. Her peers were heading out with their mothers for a day at the beach, their hair nicely plaited, plastic pails in their hands, and Jo was heading back to a world of hot mud, flies, and sweat rags for garb.

She had no time for toys. Instead of a sand bucket, she had a wooden bowl and a barrow to push from the ponds to the barn. She did have a dented metal pail, but it was for clams or catching snails in the garden. Standing in the cool aisle of the grocery store, she wondered what it would be like to have a mother with tender fingers, who wore

flowery dresses instead of men's trousers, whom all the other mothers smiled
at when they saw her coming. But that
never happened. When Mama stepped
up to the counter, townswomen tucked
their daughters closer to their sides and
turned their faces. "Don't mind them,"
Mama would whisper, and then hustle
Jo home to the very substance that
caused all their problems in the first
place.

That August it was so hot and dry
they were getting twice as much salt
as usual. Jo's mother scraped the evaporating basins clean every evening, but
she simply couldn't keep up with the
labor—not even with Jo by her side.
Jo's father wasn't any help. For one
thing, he was a man and therefore
barred from working in the ponds, but
also lazy by nature and scarce around
the place. It was only half his fault,
though. The salt was for women's hands
alone. Jo's father might rake the mud
from the ditches at the beginning of the
season or shore up the earthen levees
that separated the collecting basins,
but it was Mama and Jo who gathered

the crystals from the ponds, especially the delicate and pure flakes that floated on the surface of the otherwise coarse sludge.

"Men are too used to pushing and shoving their way through the world," Mama told Jo as she folded her fingers around Jo's on the handle of a wooden rake and then guided the instrument out over the evaporating pond, pulling the crystals toward them without wetting them. "Women know better how to get what they want without making ripples."

"Henry's not pushy," Jo said, squeezing the rake handle. If anything, she thought, her brother was the opposite of what boys were supposed to be. He was as soft and retiring as the inside of a mollusk. Even from birth they were nothing alike. For starters, Henry had the copper hair and freckles of their mother and Jo got the inky skin and eyes of their father.

"It's the Portagee in you coming out," her mother always said, as if Jo and her father were the last survivors of some foreign tribe instead of decent

Europeans. Mama's family, the Gillys, whose last name she'd kept out of sheer stubbornness, were Irish through and through, all the way down to their freckled feet and their luck with cards and dice. Jo didn't inherit those traits either. Her feet were nut brown, and she had the steady temperament of a train running down a track—unsuitable for games of chance but perfect for life in a salt marsh.

Her brother, on the other hand, would have been better off in a library. Weak-kneed and nearsighted, he learned to read at the freakish age of three and would spend hours lolling on the front porch, his nose in the old books left over from the Gillys who'd gone before them. Jo would come up from a day in the flats, and Henry would start babbling about the life cycles of mice or describe the different categories of clouds in alphabetical order. Jo liked to picture the two of them crammed together in Mama's belly, him floating in a haze of distraction, her already taking care of the particulars, dividing up the food that came sliding their way so he wouldn't forget to eat.

Her mother interrupted Jo's day-dreaming, scraping another load toward the little mud platform by the side of the basin and working it into a neat pile at her feet. "No," she agreed. "Henry's not pushy at all." Her hands stilled a moment, and she got a faraway look in her eyes. "Maybe that's going to be his saving grace."

"What's mine?" Jo asked.

Mama looked down at her, as if surprised to find a whole daughter sprung up on the land. "You don't need one. It's only boys the salt's got a wicked taste for."

Jo wrinkled up her face. She didn't like the sound of that. It sounded like another excuse for girls to do all the labor. "What do you mean?"

Mama shook her head, as if scattering flies from her hair. "Nothing." She took her hands off Jo's on the rake. "Try it on your own now. Put a little more shoulder into it this time."

Jo took great pride in her new skill, showing off to Henry the small rake her mother gave her, but he just shrugged and rolled his eyes. "Why are you happy about having to do more work?"

"It's not work," Jo corrected, straightening the strings of her new canvas apron. "Mama says it's a craft, and you can't do it. You're a boy."

Henry shrugged again. "Then lucky me." He had no idea of the ins and outs of the farm, and no interest either, so Jo took on the extra chore of scraping the basins without much more thought, the way she added an extra scoop of potatoes to her plate in the evening. The work filled her up, even if it wasn't exciting. She thought about what her mother had said about the salt having a wicked taste for boys and wondered if Henry was less lucky than he knew, or if maybe the salt was just more powerful than either of them imagined. It never occurred to her that maybe it just had history on its side.

Every dawn that August, Jo's mother sent her down to the muddy channels to check on the water levels of the basins. If they were almost dry, Jo scraped off the grayish sludge lurking at the bottom of them and then reflooded the depressions, unwinding sluice ropes and lifting the gates on their pulleys, letting water rush in from the holding pool. She would think about her brother then, tucked like a snail in the comfort of his bed, and feel sorry for what he was missing: the gurgle of the rills at his feet, the line of pelicans hovering on the horizon, precise as a squadron of bombers. It seemed to Jo like the world was putting on a show just for her.

As the heat intensified, Jo's mother worried more about the water levels dropping, and she began to send Jo into the marsh two, sometimes even three times a day. It still wasn't enough, though. The salt was coming so fast that none of them could keep up. Finally, on a day so hot that Jo would have sworn an egg yolk could have bubbled on her forehead, Jo's mother pushed her hands through her hair and gave in, deciding to buck convention.

"Fetch your brother off the porch before you check the water levels," she said. "That way if you need to open the gates, there'll be two of you. Get the work done twice as fast, and then come help me bag salt." Jo scowled at this idea. Henry, she was certain, would be no help at all. She was the only one who knew how to unwind the ropes and lift the gates on their pulleys, and the only one who knew just how much water was enough.

"Are you sure?" Jo asked, biting the side of her lip for her insolence. "Can't Daddy help instead?"

Jo's mother cast a weary glance back at the house, where Jo's one-year-old sister, Claire, was napping and Jo's father was tinkering with the shell of an old car tipped in the weeds, occasionally pausing to take a long swig out of the bottle at his feet. "I don't think so," she said, her mouth tight. "Go release more water into that first pool, but stay away from the weir."

Jo did as her mother asked and fetched her brother, then led him through the marsh. Henry trailed her over the levees, kicking at the dried mud, hands shoved in his pockets, sullen at being pulled away from his book.

He watched while Jo knelt in the mud by the main channel. She untied the sluice's ropes and tried to crank the rack and pinion, but the gate's cogs wouldn't turn. Something had gone wrong with the mechanism.

"Help me," she said. "See if something's caught in the gear." Her hands were slippery with sweat and seawater. She couldn't get a tight-enough grasp on the sluice's handle. Water rushed and pushed on the opposite side of the partition like a crowd of prisoners intent on freedom.

Jo looked up, but her brother was gone. He'd wandered farther down the channel to the weir, which formed a barrier between raw sea and the beginning of the marsh. Time and time again, Jo's mother had warned them not to play near it, for though the water looked calm on the surface, it was mean as a dragon beneath, capable of sucking little children like them into the underworld without even a breath left behind.

"Henry!" Jo called, but he wasn't listening. "Don't step in the water," she cried, but it was almost like he'd been told to go straight in. It was hot, and he wanted to cool off. She watched him bend down, his hair dipped toward the surface, and then, just as her mother had warned would happen, he jerked suddenly—Jo couldn't tell why from her vantage point—and toppled under the water. She charged over to him and was about to dive in herself when fear and total panic froze her muscles, sticking her to the spot like a rabbit under floodlights. "Henry!" she cried again and again, but there was nothing. She willed herself to wade into the frothing water, to make a rescue, but dreaded the idea of being sucked under like Henry. Who would save them then? She waited for ten breaths, but Henry didn't come up. The dragon had swallowed him whole. Jo quit breathing herself, unsure what to do, before she finally came to her senses and ran to find her mother.

Jo would never forget the look on Mama's face when she ran into the kitchen alone and told her what had happened. She was expecting a blaze of terror, or anger, maybe, but when she choked out the story, her mother just put her hands over her face and breathed into her palms, as if she'd been waiting her whole life for news this bad to hit her, and now that it had, she could finally exhale and let it all out.

By the time Jo's parents pulled Henry's body out of the water, he had started to bloat and turn a strange chalky white—already more a creature of water than land. Jo stared while her parents hauled him onto dry ground, appalled at the sight of what salt water did when it bit down to a person's bones, horrified at what *she* had done by not going in after him. Her mother saw Jo looking but didn't move to comfort her in any way, and so Jo hugged her infant sister for comfort instead, understanding that the first chapter of her childhood had just slammed to a close. Claire squirmed and fretted, but Jo held her tight, terrified that she might run toward the water as Henry had, and knowing that if she did, it would be Jo's fault all over again.

The days after Henry's death turned even warmer, with air so still that it was almost evil, the salt piling up in little hillocks on the surface of the evaporation basins. One by one, the pools dried up completely, and when the wind returned and began to blow the salt away, Jo and her mother saw that the mud in the pond closest to the graveyard where they had buried Henry had stained itself the color of blood.

Her family was used to the basins changing colors. At the end of every summer, when the ooze in the bottom of the ponds was at its mineral thickest, algae would bloom into purples, greens, and russets, making the marsh into a patchwork quilt. But none of them had ever seen anything like this. "Good God in heaven," Mama said, crossing herself at the basin's edge and shifting Claire on her hip. "It's never going to end."

"What isn't?" Jo asked. They were the first words she'd spoken in three days, and her voice sounded like cat claws scratching wood.

Her mother put an arm around her and drew her tight to her side. Ever since the accident and her initial coldness, Jo's mother had been finding any excuse to touch Jo, which was both a comfort and an agony for her. She knew she could never take Henry's place. "Never mind," Mama said.

In the distance Jo heard the porch door slam. The hunched shadow of her father stepped out the door. He was choosing to mourn the old way, wearing proper black, refusing meat, and speaking only under duress. He'd given up music, poker, and Wednesday-night drinking at Fletcher's, but he couldn't forgo gin. In fact, he wasn't even bothering to hide his bottle inside the hall piano's broken guts anymore. He just left it sitting on top of the instrument, and Jo's mother let him.

"Where's Papa going?" Jo asked, for she noticed he was holding a case in his hand. He started down the sandy lane toward town, his silhouette growing smaller and smaller. Jo's mother smoothed a hand over her hair. She and Jo and Claire were dressed in black, too, but Mama's grief was subtler than Jo's father's. She didn't need all the formalities of mourning. It was as if the currents sucking along the weir were trying to tug her soul out to the violence of the sea, where she could roil and seethe, if she could only get there.

"It's going to be just us girls now," she said. "I don't know why I thought it could ever be different." She watched Jo's father disappear down the lane, and then she stepped over to the red pond and scooped up some of the salt. "Open your mouth," she told Jo, putting a pinch of the bitter stuff on her tongue. "Now swallow."

Jo did as she said, surprised that the salt didn't taste any different in spite of its color. Life, it seemed, would go on, the same as it always had. But that wasn't her mother's intended lesson. Mama knelt down and looked in Jo's eyes. She put another pinch of salt into Jo's mouth. "You have to root your feet to the earth and become one with the land," she said. "You're a true Gilly. You and Claire will have to carry our name now. Remember that, Jo. They'd have to turn you inside out to get the salt out of you."

Jo licked the last fleck of brine from her bottom lip and curled her fist around the smooth pebble she'd been carrying in her pocket since Henry's death. She and Henry had always played rock, paper, scissors before bed, and she had always won.

"Paper covers rock!" she'd yell, smothering his fist with her open palm, and Henry would fight back tears. Now it seemed Jo had won again, for here she was with her pebble, and her brother was dead. Stone was stronger than salt, salt was stronger than flesh, and flesh sank like iron underwater. It felt awful. Jo flung her pebble into the pond and watched it disappear.

"What was that?" her mother asked.

"Nothing," Jo answered. Jo's mother scowled at her and then turned to go back to the house, empty now of both Jo's brother and her father.

"Don't go putting things in the salt that don't belong there," she said, "unless you're prepared for the worst to happen."

"What could be worse than Henry

dying?" Jo asked, and dabbed her eyes.

"Plenty," Mama said. "You just aren't old enough to guess that yet."

Jo waited until she was sure Mama was back in the house, and then she tossed another pebble into the pond, watching as it sank into the red sludge, where it might linger and stay down in the earth with her brother's bloated remains, a token of her sorrow, the only one she had to give.

———o-o o-o———

On the day of Henry's funeral, the townswomen of Prospect crammed the pews of St. Agnes, filling the church with the competing scents of lavender water and gardenia perfume, not to mention plenty of rustling whispers.

"Sit up straight, now," Mama instructed Jo before the service began, adjusting Claire on her lap. "Others are watching." *And talking*, Jo wanted to add but didn't.

It was muggy in the sanctuary, and Jo was tired. Somewhere behind her a fly buzzed, and then the double doors banged open and Ida Turner, of all souls, the undisputed first lady of Prospect, marched up the center of the tiny church, the beady eyes on her fox stole the perfect counterpart to her own. Her presence gave Jo a bitter sort of comfort. If anyone was more unpopular than they were in Prospect, she knew, it was Ida. It was just that everyone was too scared of Ida to say it to her face. She was pulling her six-year-old son, Whit, by the wrist, and seeing him reminded Jo all over again of her brother, even though Whit's hair was the color of a chestnut and his eyes were as brown as hers. She tried to catch them, but he stared down at his polished shoes, as if shamed by his mother's entrance. Something just came over Ida Turner whenever she walked into church. She got like a fire someone had stoked too high. Even Father Flynn, with his watery blue eyes and shaky fingers, avoided looking straight at her.

People in the church gasped now, however. In Prospect it was in the worst taste to approach an aggrieved family until after Mass was over and they'd had a chance to lay a bunch of wild herbs at the feet of the painted Virgin. Only then, after the family members had risen and made their way down the little aisle, would the mourning line form on the way out the door. Even Ida should have known better.

She didn't seem to care. She tugged off her calfskin glove, reached into her pocket, and stuck her bare hand out to Jo's mother just as Father Flynn opened the door from the sacristy. He saw Ida and froze. When she had the floor, even God paused. In the dull light of the church, her hair was shining like an evil queen's, and Jo could see that underneath all her powder Ida was as dusky as a Gypsy. Against her breastbone a single pearl dangled from a silver chain, clashing with a ruby brooch, her diamond wedding band, and knotted gold earrings the size of small doorknockers.

Jo took her fussing sister out of her mother's lap. Without Henry next to her to distract her, she was seeing things she'd never noticed before: the way her mother's chin jutted forward when Ida came near her, the crocodile set of Ida's lips, the way the air almost crackled between the pair of women.

Jo thought maybe Ida wanted to shake hands with Mama, but Ida reached over to her instead and grabbed the point of her chin with her red-varnished nails, tipping Jo's face up so she could see it better. Startled, Jo let her arms fall open, and Claire scuttled out of her lap and over to her mother's, where she stuck a finger into her mouth and whimpered.

Ida leaned down so close that Jo could see the individual spikes of her false eyelashes quiver. She watched Ida lick her lips, as if she were savoring something delicious at a cocktail party. She looked like a woman on whom everything was polished, but when she spoke, her voice rattled like a stew bone on the boil. "It should have been you in that ditch," she said, low and hard.

Jo flinched, scratching her cheek on one of Ida's nails as her mother lunged forward, unwilling to let Ida have any word, never mind the last. "Remember, Ida," she spat, "salt is the essence of heaven and the measure of the soul. Even yours." She looked like she was considering which one of Ida's veins to tear open first.

Jo wondered what her mother meant by that, but she didn't dare ask. And anyway, Mama was full of platitudes. They were as worn and familiar to Jo as the breeches she donned to work.

Ida turned a shade paler under her makeup. "If I wanted to, I could take everything you call yours, Sarah Gilly, and make it mine today. You and I both know that." Her lips hung open for a moment more, as if she weren't quite finished, but then she clamped her jaw shut anyway, spun on one heel, and pushed Whit back down the aisle toward the church's double doors. He turned miserably to glance at Jo, his eyes meeting hers in silent apology.

She shivered and reached for her mother's cracked hand. "Could she really do that?" she whispered. "Could she really take away everything that's ours?"

Her mother's black scarf had slipped back, revealing her red hair, a bonfire roaring across her skull. She pursed her lips. "Don't be silly. I'd give both my arms away before I'd give an inch of anything to Ida Turner. Now, stand up. Mass is about to begin." Just then, mercifully, Father Flynn began moving toward the altar, cassock sleeves fluttering, his hands folded as though nothing unusual had just happened.

After the service, after the last wife in Prospect had finally greeted them with cool eyes and a cooler hand, after Father Flynn had blessed them and offered his own condolences, Jo replayed the encounter in her head as they traveled the last bit of the sandy lane toward the farmhouse, still unsettled by the fury in Ida Turner's eyes. The wealthy Turners couldn't abide the marsh-bound Gillys—everyone knew that—but Jo still felt as if she were missing something, some small detail that niggled at her like a vague cloud of gnats. She pictured Ida's jewels, ferocious as armor, and the tiny smear of lipstick that had feathered over one corner of her mouth.

It should have been you in that ditch.

It was a terrible thing to say to a child, but odd, too, Jo thought, for if Ida had meant to threaten Mama, why had she done it staring straight at Jo? She scuffed her feet in the sandy dirt, comforted by the stagnant air and the familiar odors swarming around her. Maybe Ida had been a little right. Jo was alive, and her brother was not. It certainly could have been her caught in the weir, and maybe it should have been. Jo just couldn't tell anymore. When it came down to her family and Salt Creek Farm, even she had trouble recognizing where things began and ended, and over the years, much to her frustration, that line wouldn't grow any clearer.

Chapter Two

The first time Dee Pitman ever looked upon the mangled face of Joanna Gilly, she thought for sure the devil had sprung to life and come to snatch her soul. She'd been warned about Jo's appearance, of course—how she was burned all up and down the right side of her body—but no one had cautioned Dee that Jo's spirit was still smoldering hot under those wounds. She was the kind of person Dee wanted to trust but didn't dare, in case Jo burst back into flames and took Dee up with her in smoke.

It was Dee's first week in the Cape village of Prospect, and her father had just bought himself a diner, even though he wasn't a restaurateur. The pair of them weren't really ocean people either, and Dee was still trying to get over the rush of nausea she got every time she looked out at all the water swirling on the horizon. She'd never seen the ocean in person before and wished it would just keep still, but wishing never made anything so, something Dee knew all the way down to the little pockets of marrow in her bones.

Between the two of them, only her father, Cutt Pitman, had ever spent any time on the sea. Dee's natural habitat was Vermont, but her father had been a cook in the navy during the Korean War, and then for a little while after before returning home and becoming a father unexpectedly late in life. To hear him tell it, a person would have thought Cutt was Sinbad the Sailor or something, but in reality he never saw much of the ocean. He'd spent most of his time in the stinking belly of a warship, getting mashed from side to side with boxes of powdered eggs, sacks of half-green potatoes, and tins of unidentifiable meats. When the navy finally let him go and Cutt found himself back on a mountain in Vermont, it was like he'd never left, he said, and that just didn't sit right with him, but what was he going to do about it with a wife and a new baby to look after? He took a job in the local hospital cafeteria, got his land legs back, and that was all that.

But then Dee's mother got cancer and died when Dee was seventeen. Losing her seemed to make Dee's father restless again. He'd go on drinking binges, and at the hard end of them he'd ramble on about freedom and the sea, weeping into his nicked hands. He didn't exactly plan to move them to Prospect, Dee knew. He'd just unrolled a map one day, jabbed a pencil point down somewhere on the Cape, and then told her to read the name of the town out loud to him.

"Prospect," she said. It sounded strict and biblical to her ears, not a place she wanted to rush straight off to. Cutt put down his bottle, staring at it like he'd never seen it before, then looked around the living room with the same expression.

"Well, then, I guess Prospect it is," he said. "Eastward ho." Like he thought he was being funny or something, when the truth of the matter, Dee knew, was that their hearts were about as heavy as two balls of tar. There wasn't a single laugh to be had between them.

———o-o o-o———

As they drove up the Cape, it quickly became apparent that they were arriving in a summer region at the butt end of the season, which made Dee feel even lonelier. The closer they got to Prospect, the more crowded she watched the other side of the road grow with station wagons and little sports cars, all of them full of families and couples heading back to the mainland and their real lives. Dee stared out the car window and wished she were going with them, but instead she was trapped with her father in their sweat-box of a sedan, entering into a low landscape of scraggly bushes, ugly grasses, and, of course, the ocean. Right off she could just tell it wasn't for her. The creepy way it swirled reminded her of a snake twisting. She couldn't say if it was coming at her, fangs ready, or slithering away, having failed to bite.

It was so muggy she fell asleep, her head pressed against the car window's glass, and when she woke up, a string of drool was hanging from the corner of her mouth down to her chin. She sat up and realized they'd stopped and that she was alone, so she wiped her face and took a hard look around. As far as she could tell, they'd gotten not just to the end of the road but to the end of life as she knew it. They were parked in front of the diner her dad had bought, on a street so oyster gray that Dee automatically squinted. There were no green mountains to make her dry eyes feel better, no farms with dumb happy cows, no granite ponds. Just a one-street town stuck on the lip of a bay, a bunch of blank-eyed buildings with their shingles all cracked, and so much damn water she didn't even have to dip a toe in it to feel like she was drowning.

Her father materialized in the diner's empty doorway. "Are you coming?" he shouted over at her, seeing she was awake. "Bring the suitcases. Work's waiting." She looked around for any sign of life but didn't see any, so for once it seemed reasonable to listen to her father and do his bidding.

They were to live over the diner, as it turned out. Cutt hadn't told her that part of the plan, and as she climbed the rickety staircase in the back of the building, Dee wondered that she never thought to ask. But grief had turned her indifferent to life's big decisions, even while it made the tiniest choices impossible. Dee never knew what to eat in the morning, how to fix her hair, or what to say to her father. As a result she ate everything, gained weight, left her hair in tangles, and went days without letting two sentences fly out of her throat.

At the top of the stairs, she found a series of rooms so dingy she wondered what they'd been used for. Storage, maybe. They had the closed-up and dusty feel of an old person's attic, but Dee thought she could make her room nice enough. It had a dormer window that looked out over the town's main street, and the sloping ceiling made it feel cozy. She slid the window open, moved the sagging iron bed frame underneath it, and started putting her clothes away in the beat-up bureau leaning in the far corner. There wasn't any closet, but that was okay. Dee barely had any clothes.

After she put everything away, she went for a walk and discovered that Prospect had the bare essentials: a post office, a library, a bank, and a store. At the far end of Bank Street, there was a wide-open circle of patchy grass called Tappert's Green. There were still a few families picnicking on it and some greedy gulls nosing around for leftovers, but in spite of the surface cheer the place still had a bad vibe to it. Dee couldn't put it into words, but she noticed that a couple of town dogs crossed the street when they streaked past it. In the middle of the field, Dee made out a charred circular outline in the grass. She shivered. It seemed like the kind of place where witches would be burned if Prospect got the opportunity, and then she found out the town still had a living pair and that when it came to fire, they weren't to be trusted at all.

———o-o o-o———

On their third day in town, Cutt hired a man named Timothy Weatherly to do some renovations in the diner. Dee found herself looking forward to having an eyeful of muscles around the place to ogle, but when Mr. Weatherly arrived, she saw he was a stringy old man in saggy overalls and a faded baseball hat. He was about as appealing as a day-old serving of Cutt's meat loaf. Cutt didn't seem to mind him, though.

"I want to theme the place," he told Mr. Weatherly. "You know, make it nautical. Boat pictures on the walls. Brass lights. Nets, buoys, and ships' wheels. The whole nine yards. Think you can handle that?"

Mr. Weatherly just worked his mouth in a tight circle and Dee could tell he was thinking that those trimmings might thrill the tourists, but they wouldn't do squat for the mood of the locals. "Aye," he said. "Whatever you want." And he went to fetch his tools from his truck.

While they reupholstered booths and sanded down the counter together, Dee listened to her father grill Mr. Weatherly on everything from how cold it got in the winter to where to buy the freshest eggs.

Mr. Weatherly answered his questions with patient monosyllables, and then, without warning, he suddenly stared straight at Cutt and asked, "You set yourself straight with Jo Gilly yet?"

Dee observed as her father put down his sandpaper and wiped his forehead. "What?" he said, a little tremor of annoyance creeping into his voice.

A funny look crossed Mr. Weatherly's thin face. Not fear, exactly. More like a case of minor nerves, Dee thought. Like he was going to say something he hoped no one else would overhear, and since there was nothing she liked better than some juicy gossip, she leaned forward to catch his words.

"There's a marsh about a mile outside of town in that direction"—he jerked his thumb behind him—"out past the church of St. Agnes–by–the–Sea. Place belongs to the Gilly sisters, or it used to until the younger sister almost burned the older alive in the salt barn and left the place behind."

Dee inched closer to the conversation at the counter, forgetting her broom and pan in the far corner of the restaurant. Mr. Weatherly took off his cap and scratched the side of his head slow like, the way he did everything. "This was, oh, twelve years ago, I'd say, in '68. Crazy time, right? Even out here in Prospect. Hippies rolling through in their pot-filled vans, the damn war in Vietnam making folks argue when they met one another on the streets. My brother lost his only boy over there, you know. Sad times."

Dee's father, who was a veteran of those kinds of times, nodded, and she said a little prayer that they wouldn't veer off into man talk about battles and presidents and all the things no-good politicians hadn't done for the common citizen. She was in luck, it turned out, because Mr. Weatherly scratched his head one last time, jammed his cap on again, and got back on point. "Times were better then out there on Salt Creek Farm," he said. "Tough, but better."

Unconsciously, Dee nodded and saw her father give her the snake eye. She hustled back to her broom but managed to sweep her way close to Mr. Weatherly again.

"Joanna's a solitary kind of soul," he was saying. "Not like her sister, Claire. You're not going to see Jo in town much, but when you do, make sure you treat her nice. She's the one who lives in the marsh now, and our fortunes tend to flow with her salt. You'll find that out soon enough."

"I thought your luck would depend on the sea," Dee said, ignoring the glare from her father.

Mr. Weatherly shook his head and bent to his sanding. "Nope. On the salt. And by the way, don't let Jo's appearance scare you none. Remember, she was in that terrible fire. Just treat her nice. And if she offers you any salt, you best say yes and accept it. Her sister won't like it—she tells everyone it's tainted—but I know better and keep some around on the sly anyhow. Mark my words. You won't be sorry."

Cutt scowled. He was still a navy man and didn't take his threats lying down, Dee knew, especially not ones from a wrinkled-up woman who didn't have anything to scare him with but salt. "We'll see about that," he muttered, whacking a nail into the counter. "We'll just see."

What about the other sister? Dee wanted to know. *What happened to her?* But Mr. Weatherly, sensing Cutt's foul mood, pulled his cap down low and shut up for the rest of the afternoon, and all she had to entertain her was the never-ending *rasp-rasp-rasp* of sandpaper followed by the hot stink of fresh varnish on old wood.

———∘–∘ ∘–∘———

Joanna Gilly—craggy, weather-beaten, and boasting the surprise of a glass eye—arrived at the diner two days later, just as Mr. Weatherly had suggested she would. But Cutt didn't spring for the salt, even though they were opening the next day.

Morning rolled around, and Cutt and Dee unlocked the front door, but just as Joanna had predicted, not one person took up a seat on the barstools. Nobody sat in any of the booths either. The weather was still nice, and the streets were plenty full of late tourists, but it was like the diner had some weird force field pulsing around the door. At the end of the week, Cutt finally turned off the grill in disgust and closed the place early.

"The old girl was right," he muttered, crashing pots and pans, and Dee kept her distance. Her father hated it when other people were right.

"Well," she pointed out from the safety of the other side of the kitchen, "at least if we take her up on her offer, we know we'll get some business." Cutt's only answer to that was another crash from the stack of cookware and a fat scoop of silence. He hated it even more when Dee was right.

———o-o o-o———

Whenever Dee's father went and fouled things up for himself, he ended up turning to God. The time he drove over Mr. Dutton's pasture fence after a bender, for instance, put him in church for a straight month, but that was an extreme example. Usually Cutt popped in to Mass on a Sunday and fortified himself with a midweek confession. Dee sometimes wondered if her father was so devout because he messed up so much or if maybe it was the other way around. Maybe weekly salvation made it that much easier for him to sin. Whatever the case, she wasn't surprised when, on their first Sunday in town, Cutt decreed that they would attend church.

"It'll give us good faces around here," he said, straightening his only tie and giving her the once-over to make sure her blouse wasn't unbuttoned too low or her hair combed out too big. "We'll let all the folks know we're godly sorts. The kind that can be trusted."

Dee was surprised to find herself actually half looking forward to the outing. It wasn't that she loved church— she just wanted to get away from the diner. It had been only a week, but the cramped rooms over the top of it were getting smaller by the day for her.

If she was feeling shut in, she knew it was her own fault. She was only seventeen and should have been in school, but she'd forced her father to make a deal with her. If she came with him to Prospect, she made him promise, he would let her skip her senior year and work in the diner. If anything was more boring for Dee than church, it was high school, and she also didn't relish the idea of starting a social life over with a whole new pack of kids. "Anyway, it's not like I was ever Student of the Month," she reminded Cutt.

He poured an extra finger of drink when Dee pointed that out. "It's not what your mother would have wanted if she were here," he said.

Dee spread her palms over her plump thighs and forced herself to take a deep breath, but she couldn't resist sarcasm. "Well, then, I guess that's one good reason we can be thankful she's not."

She didn't see her father's hand coming, but the pain was nothing less than she deserved. Cutt got up and staggered out of the room, and they never spoke about the subject again, not even when they drove past the high school on their way out of town, where all the students were milling around out front before the bells rang, excited as a bunch of yapping puppies with new bones.

Dee would be the first to admit that in Vermont she didn't have the most sterling of reputations. In fact, her name hadn't just been dragged through the mud of her old town; it had chemically bonded to it. And not just the scummy topsoil either. She meant all the way down deep to the bedrock where the worms hung out.

Her father had no idea how she'd spent her weekends at home, and she knew that giving him that information wouldn't have done squat for her current quality of life. For all his bottle-tipping and foul-mouthed ways, Cutt wanted nothing more than to be a good servant of the Lord down in his guts where it counted, and he expected the same out of his daughter.

The thing was, though, Dee wasn't easy because she'd set out to be. It always just seemed to happen. Her first time was at a party when she was fifteen, with Dylan White, senior all-star quarterback. He'd taken her by the hand and led her upstairs to a spare room, where he fed her shots of rum, and before she knew it, the sweet liquid had entered her veins and turned her legs loose and her heart looser.

"Come on, baby," Dylan had whispered into her collarbone, his hips grinding slow ovals into her lap. "Let's go." He made it sound like he was inviting her on some kind of wonder cruise with an all-you-can-eat shrimp bar and a champagne fountain, and Dee was a girl who liked adventure, so she let him lay her back on the bed's mildewed pillows and peel the layers of clothing from her one by one until she was as pink and bare as a boiled prawn.

Four minutes later they'd docked, and seconds after that, they were back on separate islands. Dee was dabbing blood off her thighs in the dark, wondering if the stinging would ever subside, and Dylan was already halfway down the stairs, his shirttail askew in the front as if he'd just laid waste to a holiday meal.

If Dee had been a different kind of girl—a milk-fed cheerleader or the head of the student body—she would have gone right down the stairs after him, found him guzzling beer in the kitchen, and glued herself to him like a barnacle, batting her eyelashes at his friends but also digging the points of her nails into his forearm until everyone in that room got the general idea that they were a couple. Then she would have proceeded to make his life a living hell until graduation.

But later, when she thought about it, she realized she was still doing everything wrong, even in her imagination. For one thing, those kinds of girls never would have put out the way she had. They would have known better. And also, they had friends. If a boy like Dylan White had played loose with a cheerleader, the entire female population under the age of twenty would have known within three days that he'd not only fumbled the ball in the end zone but also completely missed the goalposts.

But Dee had left all that behind her, the way she'd also left the smell of pine sap, her sense of direction, and her mother's bones. As her father steered their car down the rutted, sandy lane toward St. Agnes, Dee cracked her window open and let the salty air brush her cheeks and forehead. The touch of it was gentle, almost moist, and she missed her mother's fingers. She used to smooth Dee's brow when she was sick. Now Dee wished she'd done the same once or twice in return, instead of spending all her time with boys who couldn't even remember her name. She closed her eyes and squeezed back her tears, and when she opened them again, they'd arrived at the smallest church she'd ever seen.

"Are you sure this is the right place?" she said, getting out of the car and slamming the door. The sanctuary was so plain it practically looked con- demned. Just a saltbox of bleached- out shingles and some arched windows with clear glass in them. No steeple, no crucifixes, nothing holy-looking at all, especially not the wild thicket of rose-bushes that choked the bottom half of the building.

But once they got inside, there was no question they'd found the right spot. There were ten rows of pews bolted to the wooden floor, a simple wooden al-tar with an even sterner crucifix, and along the far wall the oddest image of the Virgin Mary that Dee had ever seen.

"What do you make of that?" she asked, already moving toward it, but her father reached out and grabbed her arm, shoving her into an empty pew at the back.

"Just sit down for once in your life. Mass is about to start."

She took a seat on the hard wooden bench, still staring at the strange Virgin. Dee wasn't an expert or anything, but she certainly wouldn't have called the painting glorious. This Virgin was less a blessed mother, it seemed to Dee, and more a woman of the world. There looked to be a host of things wrong with her. For starters, a row of fish-hooks and lures was painted along the hem of her gown. And a single open eye was painted on her right palm, which stretched downward as if trying to haul up the souls of the fallen.

The painting's most striking feature, however, was her lack of them, for this Virgin had no face—just a blank spot chiseled into the wall's plaster. Her feet were dainty and painted in a pair of old-fashioned slippers, and in front of them a few votive candles flickered wistfully.

"Please rise," a wavering voice said, and an elderly priest started shuffling down the aisle, singing a slow and off-key hymn.

"Turn around to the front," Cutt snapped, but Dee was too stuck on the Virgin to pay attention to him. She was right in the middle of trying to imagine what kind of face an image like that would have, in fact, when the doors burst open and a woman arrived who was so extraordinary-looking she answered Dee's question without saying a word.

———o-o o-o———

All throughout Mass, Dee couldn't take her eyes off the woman. She was interesting from the back, but from the front Dee couldn't tell if she was pretty or just plain spooky. She was green-eyed, pointy-chinned, and had the palest skin Dee had ever seen. But it was her hair that gave the woman away, not just the color, which was an unholy red, but the way she had it all coiled and knotted, every strand sprayed and pinned as if her life depended on it. Women with nothing to hide didn't fasten their hair up like that, Dee knew.

The woman was with her husband, and if she was striking, he was just plain handsome and obviously rich. He looked a little older than the woman (there was a single streak of faint silver running through his hair), but not so old that Dee couldn't imagine him holding *her* arm instead of the woman's. He must have felt her eyes on him, because he turned his cheek a little bit, his gaze raking Dee's plump hips and the rest of her so hard that she turned about twelve shades of red and dropped her hymnal.

"What in the devil's name is wrong with you today?" her father said, giving her a pinch, and the handsome man across from her stifled a grin, making her blush harder. For the rest of the service, Dee took her father's advice and kept her gaze forward, even if she had to pretend she was in a military lineup to do it.

After the wheezy old priest gasped out his last amen, Cutt dragged Dee up to have a word with him. His name was Father Flynn. Up close, Dee saw, his face was droopy and kind, and all of a sudden she felt bad about the mean way she'd summed him up in her mind earlier.

"Cutt Pitman," her father said, sticking out his hand. "And this is my lamentable child, Deirdre."

"Everyone calls me Dee," she said, taking the priest's papery hand, and he smiled at her. She watched the red-haired woman hesitate for a moment by the queer picture of the Virgin, as if she wanted to touch it, but then she sniffed and turned on her heel, joining her wolf-eyed husband across the church.

"Who is that woman?" Dee asked as Mr. Weatherly stepped forward to join them.

Father Flynn and Mr. Weatherly followed her gaze, both of them looking surprised. "Why, that's Claire Gilly Turner," Father Flynn said. "Haven't you met her sister, Jo, yet? I would have thought she would have tried to bring you some salt by now."

At the mention of Jo, Cutt practically snarled, and he stuck his hands into his pockets.

"I see you've been introduced," the priest said mildly. "I know she looks frightening—she was in a terrible fire years ago—but she means no harm. Her family has worked the salt on the marsh just beyond here for generations."

"Doesn't she come to Mass?" Dee asked.

Father Flynn hesitated. "She is . . . somewhat of a recluse. She and her sister don't get along."

Dee looked over at Claire. "Yeah, I can see why."

Mr. Weatherly sighed. "You've heard some of the story by now, I see. Claire and Joanna haven't spoken in close to thirteen years. Claire was the one who caused the fire that injured her sister. Then, when she went and married Whit Turner afterward, it was the final break."

Dee leaned forward. This was getting good. "Why?"

Father Flynn looked uncomfortable, but Mr. Weatherly answered her question readily enough. "Because a long time ago Whit Turner used to be in love with Jo."

Dee stepped back, trying not to smile like a cat after cream. If there was anything she was good at, Dee knew, it was sniffing out when someone was pretending to be something she wasn't. It took one faker to know another. Her father grabbed her by the elbow, but Dee figured she should keep asking questions while she was on a roll. "And what's with the Virgin over there? Why is she missing her face?"

Mr. Weatherly's mouth tightened.

Suddenly he didn't look so friendly anymore.

Father Flynn took up the loose thread of conversation. "She's part of the Gilly story, too," he said. "The townspeople call her Our Lady of Perpetual Salt." His face darkened, and he folded his hands. Dee wondered about the painted fishhooks and the eye, but Father Flynn looked so downhearted that she didn't ask. She was tempted to reach out and hug the priest, or whatever you did to old people when they got mournful. He took a breath and shuffled his feet, impatient all of a sudden. "Lovely to meet you, my dear, but if you'll excuse me, I have to discuss something quickly with the Turners."

Dee watched him approach Claire, studying the way she shook his hand with just the tips of her fingers, and she wondered again if maybe Our Lady had the wanton soul of a redhead. It wasn't until Dee was outside the church that she realized that Father Flynn, the old goat, never did answer her most burning question, which was what had happened to Our Lady's face, and it made her twice as curious about this new town all over again.

———∘-∘ ∘-∘———

It was late September, but mild enough that Dee didn't need her jacket when she walked outside. She rolled up her blouse sleeves, appreciating the sun shining on her bare forearms. It was nice to have one thing touching her that wasn't her own self. She didn't miss the string of panting boys she'd broken off with, but every now and then it would have been agreeable to have a little company, if only someone to rub her shoulders at the end of a hellish day in the diner.

The church was located out on a little spit of land, farther along the bay from town. Dee could see the open ocean, and she could hear waves crashing. There were sand dunes right behind the church, and she longed to kick off her shoes, sink her toes in the grit, and see where her feet would take her. The other worshippers had all driven away, even Claire Gilly Turner and her handsome husband, and Father Flynn had shut the church doors and disappeared. The place was closed for business.

Dee turned to her father. "Let's take a walk," she suggested. Cutt looked up, surprised. Generally he wasn't a strolling kind of man. If Cutt was going someplace, he did it in the straightest manner possible, with no unscheduled breaks. He hesitated, and Dee held her breath.

"No, you go," he said. "I'm going to go over the inventory."

Dee exhaled a little. To be honest, it wouldn't have been that relaxing to have to march with her father down the beach to a fixed destination. She wanted to linger in the dunes and let the icy ocean water numb her feet. She wanted to get to know the sea with all her senses—her skin, her tongue—the way a real girl would and not like some miniature soldier on a battalion exercise.

She watched Cutt get into the car and slowly pull away from the church, feeling her chest grow lighter with every yard he put between them. Dee walked down to the shoreline and saw a beach after the Pilgrims' own hearts: colorless, flecked with stones, the waves a series of punishing blows to the land. She sighed, disappointed. In winter it would no doubt look even worse. What faint color there was—in the blobs of kelp, in the taupe sand— would be erased under a wet blanket of fog and sleet.

Near her at this end of the beach, there was a terrific pile of rocks tumbled one on top of the other, as if giants had played a game of dice and then gotten bored, and the land stretched out to a point. The church sat up there. Then, in the opposite direction, the beach scooped inward and laid itself out long and lazy to another point in the distance. It ended in another bank of dunes. Dee was curious about what was on the other side of them, so she put her jacket back on and started moseying down to see, her shoes in one hand, socks in the other, the dunes rising in a rolling bank to the left of her.

The beach was bigger than she thought. Her sense of direction had al-

ways been a little screwy, but in Prospect she was really hopeless at judging
how far one thing was from another. Finally she reached the other end of the
beach and climbed up the far set of
dunes. Her feet kept sinking in the sand,
making every one step feel like six, and
her thighs cramped and stung from the
exercise, but the ache of that felt good.
At least it was a distraction from the
stabbings she still got in her chest
whenever she thought about her mother
lying so skinny and white in her bed.

She didn't know what she was expecting to see from the top of the
dunes. More beach, perhaps, or maybe
another big pile of rocks or a road, but
that's not what she found. Instead she
saw that she was standing at the mouth
of Jo Gilly's salt marsh. A wide channel
of seawater separated her from the
dunes on the other side. It flowed into
what looked like a big pond, and from
there the channel got narrower and fed
into smaller pools, and then it spread
out into a confusing series of ditches
and squarish basins separated by
earthen levees. Dee thought it was the

strangest landscape she'd ever seen—busy but desolate, orderly but messy at the same time. It didn't look like a human kind of spot at all, but rather something that devious fairies might have built.

There were only two buildings in the distance. The closest one looked like some kind of storage shed or barn. It didn't look too old. But the second structure, all the way on the other side of the marsh, was ancient. It was clearly a house—not very big, with a generous porch and covered in shingles like everything else in Prospect. It had more windows than the barn but was just as plain in the end. Joanna's beat-up red truck was parked there, but there were no signs of life, and for that Dee was half glad. Joanna's scars had been scary enough in the middle of town. Dee didn't want to have to confront them in the middle of nowhere all by herself.

She hiked along the top of the dunes, taking in the watery spread of the marsh below her. The pools, which were really just shallow scoops with mud at the bottom of them, were the craziest colors: violet, rust, an iron green, and in one of the ponds the salt was bloodred. She'd never seen anything like it.

It was a little warmer once she got down level with the marsh. The dunes blocked the wind, and the air just felt odd down there, like it was heavier. Judging from the decades' worth of junk heaped around the place, the farm didn't seem like a place that change ever came to. She circled the barn, making sure no one was around the place first, and tried the double doors. They opened easily, but she didn't have the guts to slip inside. She just got a glimpse of shadows and some equipment, then a blast of air that was surprisingly dry. She breathed in, and the back of her throat tingled and burned. She shut the doors quickly.

On the other side of the barn, the side that had been hidden from her up in the dunes, she saw that there was a little graveyard—nothing like the formal gated cemetery where they'd buried her mother, but a few raggedy headstones of different materials and sizes, half hidden by the marsh reeds and grasses. Curious, she wandered toward them.

There were four of them laid out in a loose semicircle, and they all seemed to be boys or men. HERE LIES LYFORD GILLY, ETERNAL HUSBAND OF HEPHZIBAH, 1839, the first one read in severe letters on unpolished granite. SILAS GILLY, BELOVED SON, BELOVED CHILD, ANGEL NOW, read the second, but there was no date on it. The third stone was just a plain square of white marble, but the script carved on it was so full of flourishes that Dee had trouble reading it in the flat sunlight. SIMMS MASON GILLY DIED IN BRAVE BATTLE, 1918, it said. HERE LIE HIS REMAINS. MAY THE WOUNDED FIND ETERNAL PEACE. The last gravestone—another chunk of granite, but polished and thinner than the first one—was the most recent. HENRY SILAS GILLY, it said. 1942–1950. EARTH TO EARTH, DUST TO DUST, GIVEN TO THE SALT FOREVER. Dee shivered. On top of that grave, there was a small pile of the bloodred salt she'd seen earlier.

Suddenly she heard a bang in the distance. She jumped and looked over her shoulder at the farmhouse. Joanna Gilly was limping down the porch steps, and she didn't look happy. Dee stood up and started heading back toward the dunes, but then she saw a break in the grasses where the sandy lane scraggled to an uncertain end. She hadn't been able to spot it from the beach, but she figured it must be the same path that led from town and passed the church. It probably ran parallel with Drake's Beach on the other side of the dunes. At least she hoped it did as she sprang from the cluster of reeds and set off at a run back toward what now seemed like the lesser evils of her father, the diner, and the gray windows of Prospect.

——o-o o-o——

The next morning a strange and urgent kind of sound woke her before dawn. It was a pounding or drumming she couldn't place in her half slumber. She sat up in her bed under the dormer and pulled back the curtain just in time to see a huge white horse pass with a red-haired woman clinging to its back.

Dee let out a little cry and started away from the glass, though she couldn't say why. Claire wouldn't have been able to see her even if she'd cared to look, Dee knew, which she clearly didn't. She was crouched low over the horse's neck, her hair caught in a loose braid, dressed in nothing but a pair of breeches and a thin blouse. There was a light mist falling, and almost as soon as they appeared, Claire and her horse disappeared again into it and the street once again fell silent. Dee shivered and let the curtain drop.

She didn't say anything to her father about what she'd seen as they set up service that morning in the diner, but the memory of the vision distracted her, and she broke two coffee mugs before they even opened the doors. The second time a shard of glass caught her thumb, and she ended up bleeding in fat drops all over her apron. The color reminded her of the weird red salt she'd seen in Jo's marsh, and she almost swooned, but her father put an end to that. He slammed a fistful of napkins down on the counter and nodded at her to take them. "Damn it, Dee, that's a dollar fifty you just wasted before I've even unlocked the register." He sighed. "Go upstairs and see if Timothy Weatherly needs any help fixing the toilet up there, why don't you. You're just a menace down here."

She untied her apron and left it on the counter, stepping around her father the way she'd avoid a bear with a thorn in its paw. To be honest, she didn't really mind being banished to the leaky water closet with Mr. Weatherly. At least he wouldn't call her a stupid waste of a girl. In fact, getting him to say anything at all was like trying to pedal a rusty bicycle through gravel. He'd answer questions civilly enough, Dee noticed, but even then he used the least amount of words to do it.

He looked up at Dee when she entered the small bathroom and then down to his open toolbox. "Hand me that wrench," he said, jutting his chin toward the tools. "No, not that one. The big one."

She handed it over and watched him tinker with the pipes. "I saw something weird this morning," she finally said. Mr. Weatherly gave a savage twist to the plumbing but didn't respond, so she continued. "I saw Claire Turner riding her horse right down the middle of the street. It was almost like a dream. She just came out of nowhere and then disappeared again. Does she always do that?"

Mr. Weatherly held out the wrench, and Dee took it from him. He picked up a rag lying next to him and wiped his palms, but he didn't answer her question. "Now the pliers," he said. Dee rummaged in the toolbox, found them, and then squatted down on her heels and wrapped her arms around her knees. Talking to Mr. Weatherly was about as satisfying as talking to herself, she thought, which was to say not very.

"I walked out to Salt Creek Farm yesterday," she muttered. "That's sure a strange place. Why is the salt red in that one pool? And what about all those graves?" She wrinkled her forehead.

Mr. Weatherly stopped fiddling around with the pliers and fixed Dee with his flinty gaze. "You said you walked to the marsh. You didn't say you went down in it."

For someone who didn't reply to a thing she said, Dee thought, Mr. Weatherly sure did seem to pay a lot of attention to tiny details. She shrugged. "So?"

"Who told you to go down there? Did Jo invite you?"

Dee remembered Jo's lurching walk as she'd headed down the porch steps of the farmhouse. The woman had only one good eye, Dee knew, but it had seemed sharp-sighted enough. Dee blushed and shook her head. "No. No one asked me."

Mr. Weatherly picked up his pliers again and resumed whatever he was doing to the toilet. He stood up and bent over the tank, and though Dee couldn't see his face, his words rang clear enough. "Stay the hell out of that marsh if you know what's good for you. And tell your father to quit being so pigheaded and buy some of the damn salt already. This place isn't going to see a penny turn until you do, and it just might clear up all the trouble you're having with these pipes."

Dee stared at him wide-eyed, her thumb still oozing. "So it's true? Jo Gilly's salt could really curse our diner if we don't buy it?"

Mr. Weatherly looked at her like she was an idiot, a classification her father would have confirmed, Dee suspected. "Heavens," he drawled. "The stuff's not that toxic, no matter what nonsense Claire Gilly spouts off about it. I just meant to suggest you might want to flush the plumbing out with a little brine, that's all. It works wonders." And before Dee could say anything else, he collected his tools and went down into the diner's kitchen to see about the drippy taps, leaving her with her bleeding thumb, to pick at her wounds alone.

———o-o o-o———

Dee turned her eyes away when she told her father what Mr. Weatherly had said about buying Joanna Gilly's salt. He paused, his face coloring a faint pink, and finally he put his hand on the counter and said, "Fine. Next time she comes around, we'll buy her damn salt. But *you* do it. There's something about that woman that puts me off."

Dee didn't have to wait long. Jo showed up the next afternoon, her truck rattling and wheezing to a stop outside the empty diner. When Cutt heard it, his face flushed all over again, and he thrust a wad of bills at Dee, then stomped into the storeroom, where she knew he kept a spare bottle of something with a kick for situations like these. The bell above the door tinkled as Jo entered. Her right eye might have been glass, but her left eye was just fine, and it sized Dee up quickly. Dee caught her breath and tried to look busy with the ketchup containers as Joanna slung three small burlap bags of salt on the counter. "Are you ready to buy yet, girl?"

Dee felt in her apron pocket to make sure she still had the money her father had handed her. Without saying anything, she nodded. Joanna smiled, or at least Dee assumed that's what her mouth was doing. It was kind of hard to tell.

"Good. I knew you'd come around. This ought to be enough to last for a few weeks. Put some out on every table and the place will fill right up again."

Dee wondered if Jo was going to mention her sneaking around in the marsh. She'd run away before Jo had gotten in close, but Dee was sure Jo knew it was her out there all the same. She fumbled the wad of bills over to Jo, trying to keep her fingers from shaking. She didn't even count them. Jo did, though, and she gave Dee back a third of them.

"Salt isn't that dear," she said. "Not even mine." Dee folded the money back into her pocket. She'd keep it, she decided. It would be her personal fee for being forced to conduct this transaction.

Jo watched her closely. "You're going to put that money back in the register, right?"

Dee felt her face go hot. She was starting to think the townspeople might have a point when it came to Joanna Gilly. There was something about her that rubbed a person the wrong way.

"Sure," she said, taking her hand out of her pocket.

Jo nodded. "I thought so. That's a good child."

Dee scowled. If there was anything she hated more than being caught red-handed, it was being called a child. All her life she'd had features rounded with puppy fat that inspired old women to squeeze her cheeks and boys to grab her ass. She just didn't have the kind of looks that anyone took seriously.

She lifted one of the bags of salt now. It felt heavier than she expected it to, and lumpier as well. Jo watched while Dee opened the sack and stuck her finger in. The substance was coarse and grayish, like gravel crushed with quartz. It reminded Dee of the stone dust from the quarries at home. She brought her finger to her mouth, sucked the salt onto her tongue, and a wave of longing immediately swept over her for all the things she'd left cradled in the Green Mountains: her mother's memory, her childhood bedroom with the dotted-swiss curtains, the heart-shaped pond where she'd learned to swim. She closed her eyes to keep her tears pressed in. "The taste of it takes me back to something," she choked.

Joanna's voice was as gravelly as the salt. "Everybody says that."

Dee opened her eyes. "What is it?"

Jo scowled. "Everybody asks that, too. How would I know? You're the one who put it in your mouth. You be the judge." And before Dee could ask her anything else, Jo sailed out the diner door, slamming it so hard that the little bell almost choked itself, with ringing.

Chapter Three

If Claire Gilly Turner hated the salt, she had her reasons. As far back as she could remember, it had eaten up everything precious in her existence: her mother's attention and her older sister's time. It had stolen her brother and driven away her father. In fact, Claire's first proper recollection was simply the color white—but not an ordinary, peaceful white. She was talking a sizzling white like the tail of a rocket or the bubbly meat of a fried egg. A white that was so frothy and rich she craved its very touch even while she knew she couldn't have it.

She must have been about four. She was standing in the marsh, staring at the water, and it was high summer and high noon both at once, and in front of her the salt crystals were shining pure and loud. At the far edge of their property—so far that she looked like a wading bird—Claire could see Jo carefully swiping a long wooden paddle across the surface of one of the basins, a wooden bowl tucked next to her feet.

The rows of shallow evaporating pools had looked like tombs to her, Claire remembered—dead mineral pockets that froze in the winter, turned swampy in the heat, and became totally indeterminable in the spring. She only liked water that tumbled and thrashed, water that was free. Her favorite treat was to be allowed to scamper wild on Drake's Beach, dipping her toes in the icy froth of the Atlantic, then squealing when the ocean water gurgled over her ankles. She loved to fill a bucket with all manner of sea creatures she'd plucked from the rocks. She was fascinated with their alien biology, the slimier the better.

It had been so hot that day. Claire picked up a pebble from the ground and tossed it into the pond in front of her, sending a ripple under the crust of fine white salt and wetting it, something she was never supposed to do, for that commodity was precious. It came only a few weeks in the year, and while it was there, they were supposed to make the most of it. Claire's mother and sister worked long hours pulling those crystals in with their rakes, their faces turning into pink strawberries under their hat brims, their hands puckering inside their gloves, sweat drying in broad rings across their backs. Claire was too small to sweat, but she was sticky that day nonetheless. It was always sticky on the best salt days, the air so warm and full that walking through it was like pushing through mud.

But now she wanted her stone back. She stole a glance across the ponds to her sister. More, even, than throwing things into the basins, it was forbidden to step or reach into them, submerging the salt and polluting it. But Claire didn't care. Anticipating the suck and slime of clay at her fingertips, she scooted onto her belly and inched forward until her palm was almost touching the surface. She was about to sink her hand under when she heard a shriek, which she at first took to be one of the nasty gulls and then recognized as her mother. Before Claire knew what was happening, Mama was on her. "Ungodly child!" she shrieked, and gave Claire a hard shaking.

Across the marsh Claire saw Jo half turn in her direction, then drop her wooden rake. "Mama!" she cried. Her voice hadn't deepened yet into the smoky rasp it would become. "Mama, stop!" Jo was running then, skipping across the delicate network of earthen levees, but she was too late. Mama had hauled Claire onto her feet and begun swatting at her, smacking her legs, shoulders, neck, and cheeks. It was like being stung by a million irate bees. Claire put her arms up over her head.

"Mama, hush." Jo arrived. By then she was as tall as Mama, but dark. In contrast, Claire was her mother's mirror image: pale, redheaded, and with the same mulish jaw that some people in town said would prevent her from becoming beautiful and others called a sign of character. As quick as she started it, Mama stopped pummeling Claire. She put her fists up to her mouth, and emitted a strangled noise—a name, in fact. *Henry.*

"Claire." Joanna squatted down until the two of them were eye level, her wide hands spread like starfish on Claire's shoulders. "Don't ever step into the ponds. Do you understand?"

Claire nodded and pretended to be listening, but really she was focusing on the crash of waves in the distance. There was nothing she wanted in this marsh, she realized. Nothing at all. There was so little she wanted, in fact, that she even envied her missing father, for he had managed the greatest trick of all: escape.

For the next thirteen years, Claire dreamed of that, too. She desired only the signs of nothingness: a vacant bed, an empty closet, a suitcase ready to go. She didn't want the blunt points of wild irises blooming outside her window in the spring, or the food Mama scooped onto plates in front of her, or the swell of hips and breasts she started to sprout. She didn't covet friends or parties unless she could be the star. Most of all, she didn't desire love, at least not until it caught her by surprise, opening up a greed in her so gaping and huge that she became a thief just to fill it.

———o-o o-o———

Claire might have been estranged from Jo, but they were still family, she was forced to admit, still cut from the same piece of ragged cloth whether she liked it or not, even if Jo's side looked a little different from hers. Which was why when Cutt Pitman opened the diner, Claire wasn't surprised to find little dishes of salt sitting front and center on all the tables. In a way she was secretly pleased. Even when Claire wished for it, Jo could never be ignored.

In her adult years, Claire's distaste for the main substance of her childhood had grown even stronger. As a youth she had been powerless in the face of the stuff, but once she was the wife of Whit, the tables had turned in her life. If she didn't like the salt, Claire knew very well, she could persuade others to get rid of it. But hatred bears hatred and sadness more sadness, and with the salt it was no different for Claire. She started out with an aversion to the matter, but over the course of her married life, as one grief heaped itself upon another, she began to fear the salt rather than simply dislike it.

She had never consciously planned to imply to the town that the salt was tainted. That tactic had come to her in a flash of irritation the day after she and Whit returned from their honeymoon. Claire had woken happy that morning, stretching luxuriously in her marriage bed with its satin coverlet and lace pillowcases, and then she'd dressed and marched down Plover Hill and over to Herman Upton's little store.

"Hello, Claire-Bear," he chimed as she stepped through the door, and then he blushed when he saw the heavy, familiar rings on her left hand—Ida's rings. "Goodness, it's . . . it's just so hard to believe you're all grown now," he stammered, fiddling with his collar. "How was the honeymoon?"

"Lovely," Claire said, and simpered a smile. "I'm here to open an account."

Mr. Upton's face brightened, and he bent down to retrieve his ledger. "Of course." He laid the book on the counter. "Mrs. Turner—that is, Ida—had one, too, when she was still with us. Why don't we just replace your name for hers?"

Claire frowned. "I'd like my own, thank you very much."

Mr. Upton paused and examined her over the tops of his glasses. For a moment his eyes looked almost sorry, Claire thought, and then he got busy flipping pages. "Of course you would," he said. "But naturally."

It was cold in the store, so Claire folded her arms close into herself and looked at the selection on the shelves. Everywhere around her were all the goods she'd grown up consuming. Boxed potatoes. Canned chili when they could splurge on it. The soap flakes that Mama used for both laundry and dishes. And, of course, sacks of her family's salt, huddled front and center of the store like a row of impertinent beggars. Claire scowled.

"Just sign here," Mr. Upton said, pointing to a blank spot at the bottom of the page. "Shall we send the bills on over to Whit?"

"Yes, that will be fine." Claire scribbled her new signature, her hand still unsure with the crosses and lines of her married name. Once again she was aware of Mr. Upton's eyes examining the rings on her left hand. The diamonds looked too big on her, she knew, a nineteen-year-old local girl. She sniffed and hid her left hand, pointing at the shelf in the front of the store with her right one.

"If you only knew what was really in that stuff," she said, her mind spinning out the words just a beat ahead of her mouth, "you'd never put it up in front of your shop like that."

Mr. Upton turned a shade paler and looked nervous. He'd never really gotten comfortable with the salt, only accustomed to it. "What do you mean?" he asked, and swallowed hard.

Claire played with the end of her long red braid. She might have been a married woman, but she still had the hairstyle of a schoolgirl. The effect must have been unsettling for Mr. Upton, who'd known her since her birth, and she was perfectly aware of that. She fluttered her eyelashes. "I never said anything until now, but let's just say I've seen that salt eat right through metal over the course of a season. I'd hate to think"—and here she gave an artful little shudder—"what all might be leaching into the dirt on Salt Creek Farm. You've seen the piles of junk out there, not to mention the family graves." Claire pointed at the bags, leaned forward, and lowered her voice. "What do you suppose makes my brother's salt turn bloodred?"

Mr. Upton's eyes followed her finger to the bags. "But . . . but," he stammered, "they need to be there. You know that."

Claire smiled and fiddled with her

ring. "Do they? It seems like you might want to use that spot for other items, more expensive ones, for instance. Now that I'm a Turner, I bet I'll be spending more money than practically anyone in this store. It seems like you'd want to make your best customer happy."

She watched poor Herman Upton pale, then tremble, then finally concede, his narrow shoulders slumping as he walked to the shelf and started taking down the little burlap sacks. He held each one cradled in his palm for a moment, the belly of the bags bloated, then moved them to an inconspicuous spot lower on the shelf. "Maybe these would fit down here," he said. "I think they would. I suppose it wouldn't hurt to carry some other kind of salt from time to time."

"That's better, isn't it?" Claire said, all sunshine again. "I'll see you in a few days. I don't actually need anything today." And she sashayed out the door. *I'm a proper Turner now*, she thought. *Why, I could buy the whole store up if I wanted.* The idea was so exhilarating it made her physically dizzy. She almost had to grab the doorframe for support.

The girls who'd teased her throughout grammar school because she'd worn stained work clothes to school would never see her in anything but silk or cashmere now, she vowed. The boys who'd called her a witch would have the kinds of jobs—at Moe's garage and the filling station, at the country club in Wellfleet, managing the department store in Hyannis—where they would have to call her "ma'am," and the old ladies who'd gossiped about her red hair and family would come begging for donations to their charities. Even Father Flynn, who'd given Claire her catechism and First Communion, would have to kiss her hand on Sunday and wait for her to be seated before he could begin Mass, just as he'd always done with Ida.

And like Ida, Claire would take over as the queen bee of town, flitting from group to group—at the country club, at charity meetings—dropping hints everywhere she went that the salt the women made their children gargle with when they had colds and sprinkled on their husbands' pot roasts might not be so good for them after all—that it might in fact be poisoning them from the roots up.

Best of all, she'd never have to touch the stuff again if it didn't please her, and it didn't, not even half a hair. Claire knew that her mother had coerced Mr. Upton to stock it in the first place. Mama used to tell the story before Claire fell asleep—about how he'd refused at first, then lost his customers before watching all his meat turn rancid for no good reason and his produce rot and spoil.

"If you go against the salt," Mama had said through her jumble of yellowed teeth, "it will go against you. Remember that, girl." Claire would watch her mother smooth the covers, her hands two white spiders, and she'd get the shivers so bad that Mama would have to add another blanket.

Was it then Claire decided she wanted nothing to do with the salt and its ominous workings, or did that come later, after marriage and after a string of losses so tangled it made even her into a believer of fate? She supposed that by the time she married Whit, it no longer mattered very much. She had already done all the worst things she could think of. She'd burned down the barn with one careless flick of her wrist and changed her sister's life forever, and then she'd turned her back on Jo and her mother. Most terrible of all, though, were the sins she'd committed in the name of love. She'd cut the boy she adored out of the flesh of her heart and told herself it was for the best.

Sin did that to you, though—made it easy to carve yourself into pieces, each of them singular and more estranged from the next. Claire had left the farm, it was true, and she didn't stop there. She'd married Whit Turner, but she didn't do it out of love and abiding affection. Instead she'd married him out of thirst, pure and simple, and then she'd set about making sure the rest of Prospect thirsted with her.

Thanks to Claire's rumors, Mr. Upton had suddenly found it difficult to move any Gilly salt. Almost immediately flies began hovering again around his meat counter. By the month's end, he was stocking only dry goods. He grew gray and hunched, and when Jo came in, hoping to make a sale, he'd simply wave his tired hands with resignation. "Not this week," he'd say, shooing her out the door. "Maybe soon, though."

Mr. Hopper removed the salt bowls from his diner at the request of the locals, who were suddenly concerned about their sodium intake, and after a few seasons even the promise of half-priced meals couldn't lure them into his place. Each time a business slumped, another local household banished the salt from within its walls.

Only down at the harbor did the salt still flow. Without it the docks would have iced over so hard that no one would have been able to walk across them and fish would have spoiled at sea before the men could sell it. Following the lead of Chet Stone and his dour brother, Merrett, the boats bought a few extra crates each month, keeping Jo—and the rest of the town—afloat.

"Someone's got to use the stuff to

keep the luck of it flowing," Chet said with a shrug when Jo tried to thank him. "If no one else wants to, it might as well be us."

The fishermen's leniency infuriated Claire when she found out about it. She couldn't understand the pull that the marsh held over the town. Why, even Whit was obsessed with the place, asking her from time to time if her mother had a written will and if she was in it. And then, when her mother died not even a year into Claire's marriage, how angry Whit had been to discover that the whole farm belonged to Jo!

"Who cares?" Claire had asked. "You took me out of the marsh, remember? Why do you all of a sudden want it now?"

She hadn't liked the answer he'd given. Neither did she like, over the next few months, his multiple offers to Jo to buy the place. Each time her sister refused, Claire was secretly relieved, for the burden of the marsh was not one Claire wished to carry. She would have sworn that it was sinking a bit more each day, and that was fine with her.

Better than fine, in fact. If she couldn't destroy the marsh with her own two hands, she figured, then she would just watch it slide into the bowels of the earth on its own volition, and if the moment ever came to give it a little shove, why, she'd be right there, ready and waiting.

Chapter Four

The morning after Joanna Gilly made her first official delivery of salt, Dee set out small serving bowls of it—one per table and a few on the counter—the way Jo had told her to. When she was finished filling the last bowl, she stuck her finger into the grains and licked them onto her tongue, where they fizzled, sending little sparks from her mouth to her brain, waking her up but also making her dreamy at the same time. When her father wasn't looking, Dee sprinkled some of the salt onto the potatoes he'd fried for lunch. He didn't seem to notice, although he did have seconds, but Mr. Weatherly winked at Dee and nodded his approval.

"I see you took my advice and bought Jo Gilly's salt," he said. "Wise move. Claire's been saying for years that it's impure. She's scared off most of the town from it, but I've never seen any evidence of the stuff being bad. Things will pick up now. You'll see. Might take a day or two, but folks will start wandering in for sure, even if they maybe don't reach for the salt." He wiped his long fingers with a clean handkerchief. He was finishing the repairs on the shingles out front, but inside, the diner already looked a different place. Cutt had kept the black-and-white-tiled linoleum and the maroon leather booths and stools, but he'd varnished the baseboards and window frames darker while he lightened the wainscoting with cream paint and hung up a bunch of pictures of ships he got cheap from a motel near Wellfleet that was closing.

He and Dee had driven out to a salvage yard and picked out brass lanterns for sconces and found glass buoys and some old fishing nets. The glass balls had looked cloudy and mysterious to Dee, like fortune-tellers' orbs. She rolled them carefully into the trunk of the sedan, securing them with netting, and wondered what her own future held. Everything around her was low and open—the swaths of beaches, the miles of rolling dunes, and of course the sea itself. This was a place Dee couldn't keep the future out of if she tried. It would just blow on through with the incoming weather.

She shivered and looked out the big front windows of the diner. The wind was turning a tiny bit colder every day. This afternoon it had pulled some leaves off the town's few trees and was batting them around in the bored and cruel way cats played with mice. The papery crimson of the leaves was about the only spot of color. Dee could see how it would become completely miserable here in the off-season. In Vermont the winter days had been so blue and bright that the sky practically vibrated. People would whip out their skis, little kids would ride their sleds, and there was a

winter carnival with hot cocoa, snow-
ball wars, and ice-hockey competitions.
Dee couldn't begin to imagine what
folks did to entertain themselves in wet
and colorless Prospect. Depressed,
she leaned on the counter and rested
her fork on the side of her plate. "So,"
she asked Mr. Weatherly through a
mouthful of fried potatoes, "what do
people do out here for fun in winter-
time anyway?"

Mr. Weatherly scowled, and it occurred to Dee that she was probably
asking the wrong person. Mr. Weatherly was so stiff and crotchety that she
bet he hadn't had any legitimate fun
since he was young. He'd probably
grown up going to sock hops and dancing the old-fashioned way in boy-girl
pairs. But no one did that anymore, not
even in Vermont. It was all strobe lights
and disco beats. Mr. Weatherly wiped
his thin lips with a napkin. "Are you asking about the December's Eve bonfire?"
Dee said she guessed she was. Mr.
Weatherly balled up his napkin. "We
have a bonfire on November thirtieth—

December's Eve. The whole town shows. That's it."

Dee sighed and scraped her fork through the ketchup on her plate. "Where is it?" Sometimes, if she kept Mr. Weatherly talking, he'd drop a nugget of juicy information right in her lap. He'd never explain it—just drop it and watch her struggle to make sense of it.

"Tappert's Green."

Dee pictured the wide circle of shaggy grass she'd crossed on her first day in town. She couldn't imagine standing around there in the wind and snow. "Do Claire and Jo go?" she asked, and Mr. Weatherly tugged at his cap brim.

"They used to," he finally said, avoiding her eyes. "But they never stuck around."

Dee noticed that whenever she asked Mr. Weatherly questions about the Gilly sisters, he took an extra beat to answer, as if he were weighing his words in his head.

Just then the bell above the diner's main door jingled and a gaggle of women stepped inside, laughing as the wind gusted their skirts this way and that. Dee leaped up from her stool and grabbed her plate, straightening out her apron.

"Dad, we've got customers!" she called into the kitchen. Their very first customers. Damned if the salt wasn't working. Dee grabbed a bunch of laminated menus and headed toward the women, but she soon stopped short. Perhaps the salt had worked too well, she thought, for standing in front of her was none other than Claire Gilly Turner—red-haired as a fox, wrapped in a scarlet coat, and from the looks of it in absolutely no mood to have the likes of dumpy old Dee waiting on her.

—o-o o-o—

Dee led the group of women—they were five in all—to a corner booth and handed out the menus while the ladies honked away about some town committee they were all on. Something to do with the library, it seemed. Dee noticed how the women waited for Claire to take her coat off first and choose where she wanted to sit in the booth. All but Claire accepted the menus.

When Claire waved hers away with a bored tip of her hand, Dee saw the tiny ripple of panic that that caused around the table. One of the ladies slammed her menu face down on the table, and another just handed hers back to Dee with an abashed look.

"Five coffees, please," Claire said, not bothering to look Dee in the eye. "And I take mine with extra cream." Her voice was deeper than Dee expected, almost chocolate in its smoothness. It wasn't exactly an order Dee needed to write down, but she did anyway, out of nerves. Face-to-face like this, Claire made her feel like a puppy—all paws and fuzz. Her heart froze as Claire suddenly scowled.

"What's this?" The women around the table froze as well, their lipstick smiles stuck halfway between grimaces and grins. Dee looked down to the dish of salt that Claire was pointing at, full to the brim, the gray grains clumped together in irregular clusters. It didn't look that appetizing, Dee had to admit.

Claire reached one of her thin arms across the table. The inside of her wrist was paper white and flecked with delicate blue veins. Dee had never seen anyone with hands that white. They reminded her of a Victorian lady's. She stared, fascinated, as Claire plucked the bowl up with her spindly fingers and transferred it to the tray in Dee's hand.

"Take this away," she said, jutting out her sharp chin. "You know, this stuff is absolute poison. And bring us something sweet. I think the ladies would enjoy a little bite after all." Gratitude lit up the faces of the women around the table, and the plumpest one of them licked her lips, smearing her raspberry lipstick. Claire raised an eyebrow and Dee recognized it as a signal to hustle. At the counter, however, she lingered, observing the table.

"What are you doing?" her father said from the kitchen, putting his hands on his hips. "You should be serving, not slacking." Dee slid the plates he gave her onto her tray and lifted it up onto her shoulder. He was right. Hard work was its own balm. It erased everything else.

When she returned to Claire's booth, balancing five mugs and some plates of coffee cake, she found that the women had spread clipboards and folders out all over the table, so there was nowhere to put the food. She hovered awkwardly, not sure of the best way to interrupt.

"Do you think the first week of August or the second?" the plump woman was asking, knotting up her forehead like she was doing some kind of advanced science, but no one said anything. Claire had her chin cupped in her hands and was gazing out the window, and when she finally answered, it seemed to Dee that she was so bored she could barely think straight.

"The first," she said, but then changed her mind right away. "No, wait. The second." And all the ladies had to erase what they'd just started penciling into their calendars. By the time they were done, there were little pink eraser shavings littering the table and floor. Only Claire hadn't made any notes. She didn't have a single sheet of paper in front of her. She looked up and finally decided to acknowledge Dee's presence.

"Oh," she said. "You're back." She waved the flag of her hand. "Just put it anywhere, really." And Dee knew without a doubt that Claire wasn't even going to taste the cake her father had risen at dawn to bake. She'd ordered it as a test, to watch what the other ladies would do, to see who would be so weak as to eat a morsel of it and who would close her lips to temptation. Looking around the table, Dee thought she could predict who would pass the trial and who would miserably fail, and she was right. The plump lady sighed and immediately reached for a piece. Claire's eyes narrowed. "Agnes. My goodness. At least take a fork."

The woman turned as pink as her lipstick. She folded her hands in her lap and hung her head. "Oh, I'm not so hungry after all," she said. "Someone else can have my slice." Naturally, there weren't any takers—not after that little display—and so when the ladies got up in unison and left forty minutes later, letting Claire march them out the door in her scarlet coat like she was heading a parade, there were five full slices of cake left over and a smaller tip than Dee would have expected from *the* Claire Gilly Turner. She collected the plates and empty mugs and watched Claire cross the street, her hips swinging like a baton while her shoulders barely moved.

"Why do you think Claire Turner bothered staying in a town like this?" Dee mused out loud, bringing the tray up to the counter.

Cutt snorted. "People like her are never going to be your concern, Dee. Just take her business and be glad for it. Did she leave a tip? Give it here."

Dee sucked her teeth but handed him the coins from her pocket. *It's a free country*, she thought viciously. *I can wonder what I please.*

Her father glowered at her. "You better mind your own beeswax if you know what's good for you." He handed her a rag soaked in ammonia. "Now go wipe the table clean."

She swiped one of the pieces of cake from the tray, shrugging when Cutt snickered and told her it would make her fatter. "Waste not want not," she said. Knowing what was good for her was never one of her strong suits.

———o-o o-o———

After that initial visit, Claire started eating breakfast at the diner almost every day. If she'd been out riding, she came in a little after sunrise, leaving her horse tied out front as if Prospect were the Wild West, stepping through the door while she smacked mud off her breeches and her tall leather boots. On the days she didn't ride, she arrived in town in a ruby convertible, driving the same way she rode her horse: like she was fleeing the flames of purgatory, the top peeled back to the elements. Each time Dee was ready for her. In fact, it became almost like a game. Claire would prance inside, and Dee would pull out the menu. Before Claire would sit down, she'd wait for Dee to remove the salt dish from the table. Only then would she fold herself onto the maroon leather and ask, "What's good today?"

Depending on the day, Dee would

have a different answer. Tuesday was a hash-brown special, and on Friday they did a pancake meal, but it didn't matter, because Claire would always order the same thing: a boiled egg on white toast and coffee with extra cream. At first Dee wrote it down, but after a while she quit bothering. She'd walk back to the kitchen to put in her order and wonder why a woman with hair that red and eyes that green ate such boring food. Could Claire maybe be right when she said the salt was toxic? Nothing she ordered was flavored and Dee never saw her reach for salt on the table. Maybe there really was a good reason she wouldn't eat it.

Dee got to be familiar with the kinds of colors Claire liked for her clothes—blues and greens—and figured out that if she had her hair pinned up really tight, it meant she was in a raging bad mood. After Claire was finished eating, she left her napkin folded in thirds and a laughable tip. For a rich lady, Dee thought, Claire was pretty tight with the coins. Other than ordering, she never said anything, not even thank you. She just sat there like the Sphinx, with her legs crossed at the knee, the front page of the newspaper held open, her eyes stuck to the print. *You don't know me, but I'm learning all about you*, Dee would think, sliding Claire's plate across the table. She saw how raggedy Claire's cuticles were and figured Claire was a nail biter, just like her.

From the post office clerk, Dee learned that Claire hadn't received one personal letter in twelve years. "Only mail that comes through here is for her husband, Whit," said the matron, pushing Cutt's bills over to Dee. "Imagine that. Not even a magazine. Nothing. Even the invitations are addressed to both him and her. You'd think that boyfriend she used to be so crazy about would write her now and then, but I guess with him being a priest and all, that's not such a good idea." She shook her head. "Still, what could be the harm in sending a Christmas card or two? But I guess Mr. Turner wouldn't like it."

Dee gathered the envelopes into a neat bundle, her brain buzzing. There wasn't much to discuss in a place the size of Prospect, so Claire made a natural talking point. She was like one of those bad girls from the Old Testament, Dee thought: Bathsheba, maybe, or Jezebel, or Rahab, with her red rope hanging out the window. Those weren't girls who were just plain trouble. Those were women who had themselves some serious *plans*.

"What boyfriend?" Dee asked, trying to keep her voice casual. The postmistress blinked at her. People in town were forever having to stop and explain things to Dee—why she couldn't park her father's sedan on the left side of Bank Street on Tuesday, for instance, or the number of ships that had sunk right there in the bay.

The honking voice of the postmistress broke into her thoughts now. "Why, Ethan Stone," she was saying. "He was Claire Turner's first love, the one we all thought she'd marry, but dang if that boy didn't pick the priesthood over her pretty red hair and break her heart. She married Whit Turner soon after that, and it's worked out real nice for her, as you can see, but"—she leaned across the counter and dropped her voice to a whisper—"she's not fooling me. She's still a Gilly, and that won't ever change. She can leave the salt behind, but it's never going to leave her, Turner riches or no, and that's a damn fact." And with that she slammed the latticed brass grate down behind the window and broke for lunch.

———o-o o-o———

It took a while for Dee to adjust to the idea of Claire as a heartbroken wretch, but after a while the theory started to make some sense to her. Just as a block of ice sometimes still had a liquid center, Dee thought, maybe Claire did, too.

After Claire ate breakfast, it was her habit to run errands. If the diner wasn't busy, Dee would sit at the counter and watch her flit in and out of the bank and the post office. It seemed Claire couldn't go anywhere without at least three of her snobby friends stopping her so they could eye up her outfit and purse and find out which parties she was going to that week, and the men in town were even worse. Old, young—it didn't matter. When Claire walked by them, they stopped in their tracks and smiled like dogs being thrown a bone.

Even surrounded by admirers, Claire moved like she was in a private bubble. Dee observed her on Sunday after Mass, crowded in by a gaggle of old ladies, not listening to a thing any of them said. It was odd, Dee thought. Even though everyone in town seemed to hate Claire for her good looks, her good luck, and the way she stared down her nose at them when she talked, they seemed to love her for it, too, the way peasants in a fairy tale flocked around the feet of their queen, not because she was nice or did good deeds or anything but simply because she was *theirs*.

Dee understood that sentiment better than anyone. After all, she'd just lost the most important person in her life. Instead of the press of her mother's fingers against her cheek, instead of her voice whispering good night and the sound of her singing in the kitchen, Dee had only the bearish grumbling of her father and the impersonal clatter of the diner. She was in a strange town, cast loose in a blurry landscape of dunes, grasses, and undulating waves. Nothing felt certain to her.

Maybe that's why she started waking earlier each morning, her nerves trembling to hear the beat of horse's hooves, her heart thumping in time with them. When the instant finally arrived, she'd peel back a dingy corner of curtain and hold her breath, watching Claire's graceful back arch and bow over her horse, her loose hair flaring around her. And in that moment, Dee would find herself wishing more than anything that Claire could be hers, too.

———o-o o-o———

The very first time Dee ever waited on Whit Turner, he told her she had an ass so fine she should sit it on a plate and serve it to him hot. Then he ordered himself some breakfast. "Two eggs fried, coffee black, white toast, and by the way," he said, handing her the menu with a wink and a dazzling smile, "I'm Whit Turner."

Dee stuck her order pad in her apron pocket and looked him right in the eyes, trying to decide if Whit was one of those men who wanted a girl to blush and squirm when he talked a loose streak or to look him in the eye and answer him back. Given the leer he had pasted across his mug, she decided on sass.

"I know who you are," she said. "Your wife was in earlier. And you'd better watch it. I have family, too." She tossed her head in the direction of the counter. "That's my father up there."

Whit drank in her breasts and hips as if he were sipping on bourbon. "You don't look like the kind of girl who worries about what her father thinks," he finally said. "In fact, you seem to be the exact opposite."

It wasn't the first time Dee had heard something like that. Her mother always claimed that Dee had just busted open at the seams when she turned thirteen, and there was no stuffing her back. It was true, too. Old men, young men, even little boys tended to gobble her body up with their eyes—and sometimes their hands, if she didn't watch it.

She got pinched in line at the movies, wolf-whistled at in parking lots, and groped at high-school parties. By the time she was fifteen, Dee could sit in church next to her father and count the men who would run their fingers up under her blouse given a chance, and by the time her mother died, she'd become the kind of girl who would let them.

Whit Turner wouldn't necessarily have been one of her calls. For one thing, he sat so square-jawed and proud in his pew on Sundays. For another, his clothes were too fine, and he lived in that big house on the only hill in town. Also, he was married to Claire. That right there was enough of a basis for him to keep it in his pants, in Dee's opinion. Claire seemed like the kind of woman who wouldn't wait to serve her revenge cold.

Dee left Whit alone to eat his meal. It was late for breakfast in Prospect— nine o'clock—and the diner was empty. People in town seemed to like to eat at regular hours, which meant the diner was packed at seven in the morning, again at noon, and sometimes around six o'clock in the evening, and then it grew pretty quiet the rest of the time. Dee wondered if Whit had picked a down hour for a particular reason and, if so, what that reason might be. Perhaps a row with Claire? Claire had eaten by herself at the crack of dawn, as usual, Dee remembered, but she hadn't seemed upset about it. On the other hand, it was difficult to tell what state of mind Claire was in most of the time.

When Dee came back with the check, Whit wiped his mouth slowly. He flicked his eyes to the counter, making sure her father couldn't see, and then reached out and circled her plump wrist with his forefinger and thumb, rubbing the spot where her pulse beat under her skin. A charge went through her, a jolt of pure energy running up her veins, and she knew right then she was sunk.

"Let's do it again," he said, sliding a bill—a five—into her apron pocket. He was a much better tipper than Claire.

She should have returned the money, of course. She knew that even then. She should have pulled her wrist out of the delicious circle of his fingers and hung her head like she was ashamed or embarrassed, the way small children did when they were shy. But her skin tingled where Whit touched her, and her brain started ticking through the colors of lipstick and eye shadow she could buy with five dollars, not that her father would have let her wear any of that stuff. She always had to put it on after she left the house. She licked her bottom lip with the tip of her tongue and bit down just enough to make her mouth that much pinker. Then she leaned forward, close enough to inhale the leather-and-pine scent of Whit's aftershave, and she whispered "Okay" into the tender part of his ear.

Most men would have jumped, or shivered, Dee knew, or at least flinched, but Whit gave away nothing, and that's exactly how he hooked her. He crumpled up his napkin like she wasn't even there, and then he slid out of the booth. "Thank you, sir," he called to Cutt as he passed the counter and breezed out the door, ringing the little bell above it and leaving Dee rooted in the back of the diner, her mouth hung half open in a stupid and confused way. She watched him glide past the diner windows to his car (some model that was heavy, black, and very luxurious to her eyes), and then she watched his car disappear into the distance, feeling the whole time as if a long string inside her were unwinding faster than she liked.

Her father's rough voice tied it back up again. "Now, that man's a gentleman," he said, slamming the cash register closed. "Wealthy as hell, but honest as wood."

Dee didn't say a thing.

———o-o o-o———

They served meat loaf for lunch that day—hot and filling—and it was their busiest service yet. The counter was packed, and so were half the booths. Dee didn't have time to think about Whit or Claire or anyone else, and that was a blessing, but after the service, business fell back to nothing again, and the fidgets crept over her. Dee hung her apron and headed out.

The day had turned moody and gray. Clouds had piled up on the horizon like trucks in a traffic jam, and a nervous wind was swirling down low and then lower. Dee wrapped her scarf tighter around her throat and jammed her hands into her pockets, not bothered at all by the day's turn for the worse. In fact, it suited her mood just fine.

A minute's walk had her at the end of Bank Street, where the water stretched wide and colorless on one side and Tappert's Green spread itself out on the other. Today there weren't any picnickers or tourists, just a group of insolent crows nosing around in the dying grass for grubs. Dee shivered and stamped her feet to scare them, but they just turned their blank eyes toward her and opened their beaks and screamed. If they were dogs, Dee thought, they probably would have tried to bite her.

Plover Hill began behind Tappert's Green, and right before the ground tilted up, there was a single pear tree stuck in the ground, surrounded by thick shrubbery. Although Mr. Weatherly hadn't told her very much about the tree, now that she was there, Dee saw why he didn't need to. If there was one thing she could always identify, it was a local make-out spot, and she'd clearly just hit Prospect's jackpot in that department. Behind the tree the earth dipped into the shrubs, creating a private hollow. The trunk of the tree was as notched as a totem pole, carved everywhere in hearts and linked letters pierced through with arrows. Dee ran her fingers over the initials and lines, some of them finer than others, and wondered which of the couples had lasted the ages and which were as doomed as the rotten pears on the grass.

A blast of wind rattled one of the tree's last leaves past her face, and she peered up through the branches at the gables and porches of Turner House, crouched on the top of Plover Hill. For its bulk it should have been a prettier structure, but too many Turners had tried to one-up each other over the ages and none of the pieces of the place went together too well. It was a grand house, all right, Dee thought, but at the same time it tried too hard.

She leaned against the tree, imagining what the rooms inside Turner House looked like—if they were cozy and cluttered with books and rugs or more formal and filled with crystal and lots of silver picture frames. She couldn't figure how Claire had made the leap from the jumble of junk lying around Salt Creek Farm to the shingled monstrosity looming above her, and then she thought how much more ill-fitted Jo, with her scars and clumsy accent, would have been to the place. Probably the right sister had married Whit Turner after all.

What would she do if she lived in such a house, Dee wondered, and were married to a handsome man like Whit? Another gust of wind whipped dust into her eyes, and she blinked, turning away from the tree and setting off in the opposite direction, back toward the diner, trying not to linger too much on the memory of Whit's hot fingers looped around her wrist and what kind of delicious trouble they might mean.

Chapter Five

Harbor Bank was in a communicative mood, it turned out. Its second letter arrived on Salt Creek Farm as plain as the first, but this time the words were more colorful. *"Second Notice,"* a heading read in big red type. *"It is urgent that you contact us immediately regarding the status of your loan,"* the smaller text said. *"Failure to do so will result in legal action."*

Double well.

This time Jo did what the letter suggested and picked up the phone. It was rare that she ever called anyone, and her fingers shook as she dialed out the number. On the third try, she got it right.

"Harbor Bank," a bored female voice answered, "how may I direct your call?"

Jo thought she would stick with the bare facts, the way the bank had. "This is Joanna Gilly," she said. "From Salt Creek Farm out on the Cape. I need to talk to someone about the terms of my loan."

"One moment." The bored lady sighed and transferred her to a Mr. Monaghy.

"Gil Monaghy," he said, and his voice was far from bored. In fact, it had a whole circus going on in it. "What can I do for you?"

"You can explain to me why my mortgage payments have gone up," Jo barked with no preamble, "and what you want me to do about it."

It turned out that Gil Monaghy had exactly the right kind of voice to explain that when Jo's mother had taken out a second mortgage on the marsh, she'd done it with the agreement that after a set number of years the interest would dramatically increase if the loan wasn't paid off. Now it had come time to pay the piper. "It's not that you've fallen behind on your rate of payments," he explained, "it's just that you've had a new amount due for several months, and you've fallen behind on the difference."

"How much do I owe?" Jo asked, and Mr. Monaghy stated the number into the phone as if he were talking about lemonade money.

Jo's heart clattered around while she searched for the right response. "That's a lot," she finally said. "What if I don't have it?" The truth was, she thought she could just about cover it. She had a nest egg socked away, started by her mother, but this would wipe it clean out.

"Then, regrettably, we have to take action."

Jo knew what that meant. It was code for a bunch of suits coming to take possession of the marsh. "What if I can pay the difference in back payments but I can't keep up with the new balance every month?" Jo asked.

Mr. Monaghy sighed. "Then we will start this process all over again. I highly discourage it." His voice gentled. "Perhaps," he suggested, "it may be time to think about selling the property. Have you considered that?"

Jo snorted. "Trust me, it's not an option. No one wants it." *Except Whit Turner,* she thought, the last soul on earth to whom she'd ever sell. And without further ado, she hung up on Mr. Monaghy and his suggestions.

There were some things Jo just knew you couldn't pull off: upending a stone, for instance, once it was sunk in the earth, or trying to wake the dead. Most of all, when it came to Gilly salt, you had to take it as it came.

Maybe, Jo thought, if she got lucky, the bank would also learn that lesson in time.

—∘-∘ ∘-∘—

Given that she had already ruined her day in conversation with Mr. Monaghy, and given that winter was lurking around the bend, Jo decided to go ahead and make things fully awful for herself and drown the last clutch of the marsh's feral kittens. It was a monstrous business, she knew full well, but there was an art to dousing the creatures that most people weren't aware of. When it was done right, the poor things didn't suffer.

Mama used to dump them pell-mell into a hole she'd dig any old where, scatter the lime, and be done with them, but after she passed, Jo started taking more care, because it was just her out there and she could. She had a special spot she liked to take the cats out to, near the graves. Even the dead needed new blood around them occasionally, Jo figured, and this way the cats at least served some sort of purpose. It made the whole business a little easier to bear. Jo could take a creature dying—she could even take it expiring in the palms of her hands—but she did despair at the stupid waste of it.

This litter was smaller than usual. Jo tied the cats into a large feed sack. It was the kind she didn't think got sold anymore, with red and white words stamped across the burlap in block letters. Then she fetched a tin washtub, filled it with icy water from the hose, and carried the kittens and her equipment out behind the barn.

She worked quickly, trying not to think too much about what it was she was doing. As she went, she curled the little bodies side to side with their paws tucked and their tails wrapped around them. They were very young, these kittens, barely into fur, and their still bodies looked even tinier wetted down in the chilly air.

Just then she heard a squeak behind her, too loud to be feline. She startled and turned, amazed to find Dee Pitman, that nosy child from town, standing right there behind her, stuttering and stammering like a cornered titmouse. "What . . . w-what are you doing?" Dee yelped, and Jo sighed and rose, remembering how horrified she'd been the first time she'd watched her mother do the job. She'd been six.

"Can't we keep them as pets?" she'd asked, watching Mama submerge cat after cat. "Can't we keep just one?"

Mama had simply squinted at her. "Sometimes the biggest kindness sits on the back of cruelty," she said. "The sooner you learn that, the better." And then she'd made Jo finish up.

Jo smacked her hands together now and eyeballed Dee. "They didn't have a chance in hell," she said, ignoring the mewing coming from the last kitten in the sack. "They're feral. The mama cat's gone, and they're too little to live on their own yet." Dee didn't say anything, so Jo continued. "Every year there's more of them. They're a curse and a plague, make no mistake." She nudged the sack with her toe. "Damn place is going to hell."

Dee found her voice. "Because of the kittens?"

Jo was confused. Who would be dumb enough to think a bunch of cats could cause the kinds of problems she was facing? Obviously, Cutt's daughter wasn't the brightest girl if she couldn't figure that out. Then again, Dee didn't know the full extent of Jo's worries with the bank and all. No one did, and Jo wanted to keep it that way. She narrowed her good eye. "How's the diner business?" she asked to change the subject. "Is the salt doing you fine?"

Dee blushed and avoided her gaze. "Actually, that's kind of why I'm out here. Um, it turns out we won't be needing as much salt as we thought. The diners aren't really eating it. They prefer the store-bought kind. They say yours is . . . tainted."

Instantly Jo pictured one of Claire's bony hands plucking a salt bowl off the diner's counter and then imagined her saying in the calmest way, almost as if she were sorry to have to do it, *If you only knew what was in this stuff, you'd never eat it again.* Jo sighed again. "Don't tell me. My sister swanned into your father's diner and made you think twice."

Dee looked uncomfortable. "It wasn't a big deal," she said, keeping her face turned away from the three kittens. "But maybe it's better if your salt's not right out in the open."

Jo let out a harsh bark of laughter. "With my sister, Claire, everything's a big deal. You'll see. But mark my words, if you stop serving the salt, the Lighthouse will fall right back into the ruin that you found it in. You best tell your customers that there's no truth to Claire's tales."

"How do you know?" Dee asked.

Jo shrugged. "If I were in your shoes, I'd pick the side of the salt, that's all."

This advice didn't seem to make Dee feel any better. She looked down at the row of inert kittens. "What do you do with them after?" she asked as Jo knelt again and reached into the bag. Dee turned her face away as Jo pulled out the last squealing kitten.

"Lime and a deep hole," Jo said, and plunged her arm into the washtub.

Dee fled over the bank of dunes to Drake's Beach without another word, the image of limp kitten corpses no doubt lingering in her mind. The after-noon was starting to bunch up on it-self, and the light was dying. Cutt would probably be parading around in the diner's kitchen, Jo thought, snapping a dish towel and wondering where the hell his daughter was, and soon folks would start trickling in for the dinner special, not as many as for lunch, but some, and in the middle of it all would be the spaces where the dishes of Jo's salt should have been waiting to work their magic, the pale circles of them as blank and mysterious as so many little moons.

———o-o o-o———

She really shouldn't have tormented the girl like that, Jo conceded to herself after Dee left. After all, she knew better than anyone what it was to be taunted. For the entire year following her brother's death, her mother had dressed her and Claire in scraps of black so they'd stood out wherever they'd gone, marked by their grief. Jo had been only nine years old. She was too young to understand the adult silence that fell when she and her mother and sister walked into the bank or the pharmacy in town, but at the same time she was too sorrowful to fit into childhood anymore. Her clothes had rings and mud on them from her working in the marsh before she came to school, and her lunch smelled of boiled cabbage. The other children started giving her a wide berth, picking up and moving their lunches when she approached their tight little groups, making up rhymes about her that they'd sing in the coatroom.

She'd never been popular to begin with, but she had never really minded because she'd always had Henry to eat with, Henry to go on the swings with, and Henry to explain to her the words she couldn't read for herself. When there'd been two of them, the town children left them alone, but now that Jo was singular, all her oddities were magnified, even to her.

For comfort she turned to Our Lady. Every Sunday she trailed her mother to church, Claire's toddler hand folded in the pleat of her own, and stared at the Virgin throughout Mass, her missing face a blank riddle that Jo couldn't solve, the cracks in the paint catching at the edges of her imagination, reminding her of her own small sins.

"There's more to adoration than plain love," Mama would tell Jo before bed, her flat voice echoing in the darkness. "Remember that. There's a pain involved you can't imagine."

Jo started paying better attention to the particular kinds of things the townswomen left for Our Lady. The Gillys always deposited their salt, but Jo discovered an unspoken language of offerings. Girls aching for love left fresh flowers, and girls who'd been betrayed left dried. Women worried about their children left sugar and honey, and women with money problems slipped quarters under the bottoms of their votives. And when it was time for confession, everyone without exception would take two fingers and slowly trace the empty arc of the Virgin's face, as if they preferred to confess their failings to her instead of to the Lord.

Father Flynn despaired of it all. "I'd like to remind everyone not to leave parcels of food or other items sitting out in the sanctuary," he would sometimes be reduced to announcing before his sermon. "It only attracts rats. If you'd like to engage in private worship, the votives are kept under the last pew, and a nickel donation is appreciated." But the women of Prospect roundly ignored him, keeping their own counsel about how and to whom they should pray.

"Why?" Jo pressed her mother.

But Mama never answered. "Go to sleep," was all Jo ever got.

When she got tired of staring at Our Lady and her plethora of offerings in church, she'd move her attention over to Whit Turner, who sat in the pew across from her and who, though two years younger, made her laugh with the faces he pulled behind his mother's ramrod back.

Every week it was just Whit and his mother, Ida. His father, Hamish, wasn't a man of religion and so didn't attend services. Ida, on the other hand, had been born poor and Catholic, and though she was no longer poor, the Catholic part had stuck good and hard, the way it was supposed to.

Before she was Ida Turner, she was Ida May Dunn, a dirty-kneed girl squatting in her drunken father's fishing shack with her half-witted sister, wholly dependent on the Catholic Temperance League for clothing, pantry staples, and basic morals. It was amusing for Jo's mother to watch Ida mince into St. Agnes all buttoned down and proper, because as a girl, Mama claimed, Ida had run as wild as the crosshatch of tides along Drake's Beach. Some of those currents, Jo knew, could suck a body under, and some of them would only roll a person's bones around a little, and woe to the poor soul who didn't know which was which.

The same caution applied to Ida herself. Halfway through church she'd sense Whit squirming and turn to catch him mid-grimace, two fingers stuck in the corners of his mouth, waggling his eyebrows at Jo. "Whittington Turner," she'd hiss audibly, pinching his earlobe in between her varnished fingernails, "if you look to that Gilly girl one more time, I'll blind you." That would sober Whit up. Jo would watch him straighten his back as tight as Ida's and fold his hands on his lap, and she'd marvel at how he could slip those stiff Turner airs on and off like a pair of socks.

After Mass, when the weather was fine, Mama would set Jo free on Drake's Beach with instructions to come home with something for the dinner pot. The Depression and war years were well over, but life for locals was still lean-toothed. For the most part, people in Prospect took their sustenance from the sea: fish, snapping lobsters, kelp, clams dug from the shore. But things were slowly changing. The new Mid-Cape Highway was finished (sometimes Jo liked to fantasize that her father had run off to work on it), and every year more people were trickling into their little village. Near Hyannis the wealthy frolicked in their family compounds, even added onto them, and every summer pastel cars adorned with fancy grilles and fins clogged the roads. Stuck behind them in traffic, Jo would squint and be reminded of the box of petits fours she'd once seen Ida pass around after Easter Mass that her mother had refused to let her eat from.

"We don't take from Ida Turner," she'd snapped, slapping Jo's hand back down to her side. "We're scant, but we're better than all that."

Thanks to Ida, lots of people in town were scant.

"I'm out of chops," Mr. Upton would sadly tell them from May to August.

"I'm out of fillet, chuck, and hamburger, too." So it was liver, shanks, and oxtail for Jo and her family. They listened as the strains of big-band records and the rattle of cocktail shakers floated down Plover Hill and watched as the Turners had the clapboards up and down Bank Street painted a pearly gray, trimmed back all the hedges in town, mended the pickets around Mr. Upton's market, and instituted a fine for any shopkeeper who didn't keep his windows clean.

"Pretty soon the Turners are going to have us all in uniforms," Mr. Upton grumbled to Jo's mother when she delivered salt to him. "Lately you can't spit without hitting something new they've bought. I hear they're even eyeing properties over on the mainland now." Jo's mother's eyes would darken at these revelations, but she wouldn't say anything, just hand over Mr. Upton's salt with a frown. They had their own worries, Jo knew. Each summer they were selling less and less salt. The summer people, it turned out, preferred their salt fine and white. They didn't see the point of the Gillys' lumpish stuff.

Given that their bread was buttered on opposite sides, Whit and Jo should never have become friends—there were better than a hundred and one reasons against it. Ida hated Mama, for starters, and Mama hated Ida back with a passion she reserved for the marsh's feral cats.

"Sluts, every one of them," she'd sniff, toting another sack of kittens to its demise. "Loose as a boatload of drunken sailors. Leaving poor innocents to starve. Strutting around with her tail stuck up in the air." (Sometimes it was hard for Jo to tell if her mother was cursing Ida or the cats.)

Maybe the enmity between their mothers should have fueled similar high feelings between Whit and Jo, but it turned out they both had the same ornery streak painted down their spines in red. His was more obvious, but Jo possessed it, too, and so instead of repelling each other, they clicked together like magnet and metal, each the material the other needed. And for a while—for many years, in fact—nothing managed to pull them apart, not their mothers, not the fact that he was a wealthy Turner and she was a dirt-scraping Gilly, not the two-year difference in their ages.

But it couldn't have lasted forever, and not for all the usual reasons people in town flapped their gums about—not because of the fire, or because of Jo's and Whit's reverse stations in life, or because Jo's sister was always the prettier Gilly. In fact, as with most small-town scandals, the real reason for the split between Jo and Whit was far simpler and bigger than most folks thought to consider: Death came between them. And even though she would never like to admit it, and despite all appearances to the contrary, in her heart of hearts Jo had some very good reasons for thanking the lucky stars that it did.

———o-o o-o———

The first time she made the proper acquaintance of Whit, Jo was seven and up to her elbows in wet sand on Drake's Beach. If she had enough time and if the weather permitted, she liked to forage a little after church, running a line

out into the surf to catch fryers or gathering a cluster of kelp, but mostly she
dug buckets of clams: gristly and small,
but rich enough when her mother
stewed them. For the Gilly women, a
bucket of clams meant that another
day's grocery money got to stay put in
the jar in the kitchen. Jo had her head
tucked down and was concentrating,
and so she was startled when she
heard a boy's voice ask a question.

"Where do they come from anyway?"
She stopped digging and turned.
Usually she had the beach to herself,
but there stood Whit Turner, immacu-
late in his church pants and a pressed
oxford shirt.

"What?" she said, confused. She'd
never seen Whit out by himself before
that afternoon. His mother usually
whisked him off to lunch at their country club.

Behind Whit the panicked shadow of
his governess appeared like a hovering
insect, but Whit ignored her. "I mean,
they don't have mothers and fathers,
and clams don't lay eggs—or do they?"

Jo had never thought about it before.

To her, clams were free food. That was it. She dug them up and her mother steamed them, end of story. But then, Whit didn't have the personal relationship with hunger that she did. Only people with full bellies questioned where their food came from, Jo knew. The rest of humanity just bowed their heads and thanked the Lord for his bounty. She shrugged and shoved her spade back into the sand. "Not everything's got a mother."

Whit frowned, considering what she'd said, which was new for Jo. Usually Mama told her to be quiet and get back to work, and Claire just prattled at her. Whit bit his lips. "Everything has a mother. Even Jesus."

Jo thought of the chipped outline of Our Lady, faceless in her eternal vigil, and shrugged. Whit sank down in the sand next to her, his shoulders bowed over the hole she'd dug. "Sometimes I wish I had a different mother," he mumbled, tracing a pattern in the wet sand with one finger. "Mine's not that nice."

Just then the eavesdropping shadow of his governess came to life. "Whit

Turner," she scolded, hauling him up by his elbow. "You know you're not supposed to be down here, and you're certainly not supposed to be telling tales on your family. You're a Turner. You have to act like one. Now, come on, we're going to be late for tennis."

Whit rolled his eyes and grinned at Jo. His hair was tousled, like Henry's used to get, and she had an urge to reach out and smooth it. It wasn't that she missed Henry's company, exactly— for he had led his brief life with his nose buried in encyclopedias and books, his weak heart fluttering like a restless canary in his chest. It was more that she missed the possibility of it. She looked at Whit and then, knowing that her mother wouldn't like it one scrap, threw out an invitation. "If you come back tomorrow," she said, pointing down the beach with her spade, "I'll be over there. I know where there's sand dollars."

Whit's governess started dragging him away, but before they got too far, he turned and yelled, "If you find out where those clams come from, let me know!"

Instead she got an earful about Ida Turner that evening when she told her mother about the encounter. "I'd make another friend if I was you," Mama said, slamming a bowl of mash and peas on the table.

Jo pouted. "But why?"

Mama snorted. It was a stupid question. Even Jo recognized that. She braced herself for a lecture. "Because," Mama declared, "no matter what you do, you're never going to get the mud out of your clothes, the brogue out of your voice, or the brine out of your blood." She stuck a spoon in the potatoes and peas and kicked her chair away from the table. "Ida is scared of sinking, even though she's squatting up on Plover Hill like a big old crow. But trust me, Ida knows plenty about scraping bottom."

Jo sighed and bent her head to her plate, taking a bite of the clams. For the first time, she found the taste of their salt unpleasant. "I bet the Turners don't eat like this," she said, pushing her dish away.

Her mother regarded her coolly. "The

less you worry about the Turners, the better. Now, hush up and eat the food God's given you." Claire started squalling, and Mama shushed her. "Not you, too," she said, dipping a crust of bread into some milk and handing it to Claire. "Don't tell me there's another one in this house complaining about the order of things."

Jo bit her tongue and tried to swallow the rest of her meal. Had she been complaining? She didn't think so, but it was hard to know how Mama would take things sometimes. Jo looked out through the kitchen window, across the marsh. Beyond it, just over the dunes, lay Drake's Beach and the memory of her afternoon with Whit.

"Did you hear me?" Mama said. "After supper the far ponds need scraping. Take your sister with you, but don't let her wander none."

Jo sighed and looked at Claire, who blinked her wide toddler eyes, her flame-red hair gnarled in fierce little curls. "I won't," Jo promised, but under the table she had her fingers crossed.

She couldn't promise the same for herself.

———○-○ ○-○———

The next week Whit surprised her, screaming down the beach on a motorbike. It was ridiculous. The bike was too big for him, and he wobbled like a punching clown, but there he was, flying down the shore, a wicked smile plastered on his mug. Right before he got to Jo, one of the tires caught a stone and the bike pitched sideways, throwing Whit off and spraying sand in an arc.

"Are you okay?" Jo said, running to help him.

Whit stood up, grinning like a hyena, and brushed off his jeans. "Nice, huh?"

Jo put her hands on her hips, her heart pounding. Ever since Henry's death, she'd been shy of accidents. "No, it's not." An awful thought occurred to her. "Did you steal it?" Although why Whit would have needed to steal anything was beyond her.

He smirked. "The Weatherly brothers lent it to me."

"What?" She knew the Weatherly brothers—Tim and Hank. All the girls in town did. They were a senior and a sophomore in high school and famous for their pompadours, the packs of cigarettes they kept rolled in their T-shirt sleeves, and their motor vehicles. The Weatherly brothers were Prospect's pet grease monkeys. "Why would they give a bike to a little kid like you?"

Whit shrugged. "Dunno. Why do people do anything?"

"But look. You scratched it." It was true. Along the back fender, there was a four-inch gouge in the red paint. Whit crouched down to have a look. "You're going to get it now," Jo said, unable to keep from gloating. "You know how the Weatherly brothers are about their transportation."

Whit sat back on his heels. "I don't think so."

"You don't think what?"

"I don't think they're going to mind."

Jo gaped at him. "Are you crazy? Of course they're going to mind. Timmy almost knocked Hank's head off last spring when he crashed their jalopy."

Whit rubbed his thumb over the scratch. An uncanny adult look settled on his face. "Yeah, but I'm just a little kid. What can they do to me? Besides, if I come home beat up, they'll have to explain to my mother why they loaned the bike to me in the first place, and you know as well as I do that Timmy and Hank aren't such great talkers."

His logic was impeccable. Jo was impressed.

"I'll just tell them it was there all the time," he said. "They won't believe me, but what choice will they have? They'll end up blaming each other, and that'll be that. Now, come on, help me push this thing upright."

It was the first inkling Jo ever had of the kind of man Whit would eventually turn into. The seed was there inside him the whole time, but that day she was blinded by the optimism of the cloudless summer sky, tricked by the easy breeze blowing on her neck. She was barefoot in the sand, and the heat seeped through her arches into her calves. There was something about Whit that filled up the empty spots in

Jo's bones. When she was with him, she felt like she had a little piece of Henry tethered back on the earth. "All right," she said, and knelt to help him. She giggled. "We're partners in crime."

Whit did something then that she would never forget, a gesture that seemed innocent at the time but would later infect her, the way a rose thorn buried in flesh could fester. He pushed the hair back out of his eyes and took his hands off the bike. "We're partners in everything," he said, spitting in his palm and holding it out.

"Partners," she said, spitting in her own palm and pressing it to Whit's. Neither of them said anything for a moment, and the spot where their hands were joined grew warmer.

Jo stood up. "Come on. Let's go back. I bet the Weatherly brothers will be wanting their bike."

Whit said something unexpected then. "I heard my mother saying she wanted to buy up your mom's place," he said, "but don't worry. I'll make sure your salt stays safe." Jo took a step back, stumbling over a rock. Her temper wasn't like Claire's, who at age three could already throw a howler of a tantrum, but now she felt a tingling travel up her spine and settle at the base of her brain. She remembered what Ida had said to her at Henry's Mass. *It should have been you.*

Jo stepped forward and gave Whit's shoulder a shove. "Shut up, Whit Turner. You don't know what you're saying." She spit thick saliva.

Whit shrugged and started heading back toward the dunes without her. "Suit yourself," he said. "I'm just telling what I heard." He paused and held out his hand. "Are you coming? I'll give you a ride on the bike before I take it back."

Jo hesitated. In the house, she knew, her mother would be pouring cool glasses of milk and setting out cold biscuits, squinting at the clock and wondering where she was. But there was Whit's hand, hovering in the air, an open invitation. Jo took it.

"Don't worry," he said, pulling her along as if he'd been doing it forever. He moved with all the grace her brother never had. "All that stuff is for the grown-ups. It's nothing to do with us."

"Sure," she answered, knowing full well she was lying as only a true Gilly could.

———o-o o-o———

Whit was the first, last, and only friend Jo ever called her own. Theirs was a backstairs friendship, conducted on the sly on Drake's Beach, only in fine weather, and only when it was the two of them. Skirts got wide, then straight, and then short, and Elvis broke into music with his greased-back hair and crazy hips, but Whit and Jo's private universe stayed steady.

She taught Whit to fish, skip stones, whistle with two fingers, and whittle, and he taught her to waltz, smoke, and swear in French. Perhaps if they'd gone to the same schools or mixed in any of the same circles, they wouldn't have remained friends, but as it was, their differences served to lace them tighter instead of pull them apart. They knew not to expect too much from each other and so year after year, as soon as the lady's slippers bloomed, they took off to the shore and picked up where they'd left off before the snow started to fall.

"Hey," Whit would always say the first time he saw Jo after a long winter, "you've been a stranger."

"But not as strange as you," she'd snap, and they'd both crack up. Whit had a way of laughing—all the way from the bottom of his belly—that made Jo want to join in with him. Back then she thought it was because his pranks and antics were so outrageous, but in time she came to believe it was because he had the kind of laugh that was either with you or against you, the type of noise that made you realize that in spite of all Whit's congeniality, you still had better choose carefully around him.

They became blood friends over a frog when Jo was eight and Whit was six. Normally the two of them frolicked on the beach, but in this instance he dared her to take him into the marsh. Ever since the first time she'd shown him the place, he'd been insatiably curious about it.

The frog was a throaty, barrel-chested

specimen, squatting in a cluster of eel-grass. Whit held him while Jo marveled at how human his knobby toes looked. "Let's name him," she suggested. "Let's call him Sir Greenheart." Since Henry's death she'd been the one poring over his books about knights and pirates.

Whit looked at her askance. "It's a frog, Jo. Not a prince. But you're welcome to try to kiss him." He thrust the frog toward Jo's lips, but she didn't scare so easily.

"Let him go." The poor thing was bucking and twisting in Whit's palms.

"What? Are you crazy? Do you know how much I could scare my governess with this?"

Jo put her hands on her hips. "I'm serious."

"I am, too. Just picture it. She peels back her covers tonight, and voilà! She has company in her bed!" The frog lurched again, and Jo found herself wishing that amphibians had teeth. Before Whit could do anything about it, she leaped forward and knocked his hands apart. Liberated, the frog bounded into the reeds.

Whit's face turned puce. "What a yellow-bellied girlie thing to do, Jo Gilly!"

She narrowed her eyes. "Well, you're a mean, liver-sucking boy!"

She expected Whit to retaliate, not grab her hand. When she closed her fist, he put his fingers on her wrist, right where the pulse beat. "Shh," he said, "don't move." He opened her fingers.

She felt a prick in the center of her palm. "Ouch!"

Whit grinned at her. He was holding his open pocketknife over his own palm, she saw, and as she watched, he poked it into his own flesh, producing a smear of blood. "Give me your hand." He grabbed her wounded palm and pressed it fast to his. In between their skin, Jo could feel a warm, mingling slick. "Now we're even steven," he said after a moment, breaking his grip and snapping his pocketknife closed. "We're one and the same. No matter what happens, there's a little bit of you in me and some of me in you. I know how much you miss your brother. Now you'll never be alone again."

A rush of tears blurred her eyes. Whit

didn't understand at all. It wasn't that she wanted Henry back. She just never wanted him to be gone in the first place. But what would Whit, a privileged only son, the latest little Turner king, know about being half of a bigger whole? She wiped the back of her hand under her nose and sniffed.

"Thanks." She tried to sound like she meant it. Whit's chest puffed with pride. Jo watched him saunter down the lane, the cuffs of his pressed trousers rank with marsh mud, and then she bent to one of the evaporating basins and scooped a measure of the briny water into her palm, letting the liquid sting and purify. If she had to have a drop of Turner blood mixed into her, she figured, she might as well douse it, just to be on the safe side. She brushed the mud off her own clothes as best she could and then hurried back to the house before her mother began to miss her, feeling different but still the same. Probably she was just too plain for Whit's mumbo jumbo to have any effect, she thought, and that idea pleased her. It meant she was where she was supposed to be. Right before she opened the porch screen, somewhere in the distance, she thought she heard the bullfrog croak.

———o-o o-o———

For Whit, Jo believed she was like a cave—a dark place he could go to and be quiet. But for her, Whit was the opposite. He scooped her out of the hollow of the marsh and sped her up, making her take in the wider world, even if it was only Prospect.

"Did you know that Mr. Upton has a girlfriend in Hyannis?" he told her after he saw her in the market with her mother one afternoon. "A Chinese lady, supposedly. She works in a pharmacy there."

He knew that the postmistress sometimes read people's letters if she got bored, that the library had a book about sex hidden in the reference section, and that sometimes Fletcher's Tavern held secret gambling nights for the fishermen when they pulled back into port. Through Whit, Jo learned that even a town as sleepy as Prospect had some fascinating things happening behind the scenes.

Over time they developed a secret language to use in church. Five fingers spread apart wide was a warning: *I can't make it today. Can't say more.* Two balled fists signified a go for meeting up later, and one hand cupped meant, *Have I got a surprise for you.* It took Ida a few summers to catch on to their communications, but when she did, she started stacking the deck against them. She'd catch Jo on her way into Mass, grab her arm, and gloat, "Whit has a tennis date *all day* with a pretty girl from the mainland, so you'll be free to go back to your swamp after this. He'd tell you himself, but he'll already be gone."

Jo noticed that the older she and Whit got, the two of them hovering on and then crossing the threshold of adolescence, the more frequently Ida began to arrange female companionship for her son. She rounded up all the Annabels, Merediths, and every last Elizabeth on the Cape and paraded them in front of Whit at the country club and at parties at their house, but none of those girls knew how to whistle a hornpipe, and none of them ever laughed at Whit's knock-knock jokes. Ida started sitting between Whit and the center aisle during Mass, blocking his view of Jo, but it didn't matter how strict she got. By the time Jo was fifteen and Whit was thirteen, the thread between them had just pulled tauter.

Her own mother hated it as much as Ida did. "Don't you let that Whit Turner set his little toe on this land again," she warned after she caught Jo and Whit loitering in the marsh. "His mother probably just sends him out here to spy. You tell him to tell Ida that she can have this place when hell grows roses and blooms."

After that, Jo had to take Claire wherever she went. Eight-year-old Claire was worse than a parrot. She was her own walking secret police. If Jo snuck a piece of extra pie, if she skipped over scraping a single basin, Claire would broadcast her sins that night at dinner.

"Jo and Whit Eskimo-kissed," she reported not long after the marsh incident, tossing her hair. "I told Jo I was going to tell, and then she did this." She held up her arm, showing the place where Jo had given her a pinch. Jo sighed. Even Claire's skin was transparent.

"Whit Eskimo-kissed you, too," Jo said, and watched Claire turn a promising shade of red.

Their mother glowered and poured chipped-beef gravy over her peas. "If Ida finds out about that event, she's like as not to eat the pair of you alive, and then where will you be?"

The threat of Ida was a good one. No one ever knew what she was capable of, because there was so much of her that was uncharted territory. People in Prospect knew Ida's lowly background well enough, and of course no one was allowed to ignore her current social heights. Her life in between those two states was up for any- and everyone's speculation.

By the time Ida was seventeen, the story went, she'd scared off the boozy mistress who lolled in her father's shack, all the starched members of the Temperance League, the entire staff of teachers at Prospect High, and any girl in the town radius. The only two people she held any affection for were her sister and Father Patrick Flynn, who'd performed her First Communion, confirmed her, and confessed her every Saturday until Ida had developed the figure of Jezebel and then split from Prospect.

No one ever discovered where she went. Some folks whispered Boston or Concord, while others presumed that she somehow made it to Paris, where she learned to wear seamed stockings, gold jewelry, and lipstick the insulting color of coral. There were alternate theories, however, that swirled through the town: that Ida had taken refuge with a band of musical Gypsies, that she'd secretly married a wealthy older man and inherited his fortune when he died, that she'd found work in a dance hall or worse. And then there were those who said that Ida Dunn had gone no farther than the Temperance League's asylum for poor women and abandoned children, where she'd given birth to a child and learned the sorrowful arts of cross-stitching and lacework.

Ida never addressed the rumors, nor did she ever need to. A year and a half after she'd left town, she reappeared for her father's funeral. At the graveside she wore supple calfskin pumps with three-inch heels that wounded the ground under her feet and a noisy charm bracelet with a miniature anchor, a beaded cross, and a tiny dented heart. She also had on a black knit dress that covered her from neck to wrist to knee but somehow left very little to the imagination.

After the dismal service, she had her half-wit sister picked up and checked in to a state institution, and then she made her way to Fletcher's Tavern and bought herself a shot of the most expensive scotch available. She had just dipped the tip of her tongue into the glass when a masculine voice materialized in her left ear. "Ladies don't indulge in spirits unless they're out of them."

As Jo had always imagined it, Ida looked behind her to see Hamish Turner leaning on the bar, his imported silk necktie undone just enough to look suggestive. Hamish was the richest and the best-looking man in Prospect. He drove like a bandit going broke down Bank Street, skipped out on his checks at the diner, and never once got charged. Ida fluttered her eyelashes.

"I'm out of everything," she purred, stretching out her hand and thinking, *But not for long*. And just like that, for the price of a glass of whiskey on ice, Hamish Turner bought himself a wife.

As soon as the ink was dry on the marriage certificate and Ida had two pennies to rub together, she went on an acquisitions tear, growing paradoxically thinner and more pointed as she gained more land up and down the Cape. She added a wing to the already hulking Turner House and redecorated the interior with brocades so elaborate they gave the maids who cared for them migraines. Jo and her mother used to hear them complaining in Mr. Upton's grocery. Ida liked young, pretty Polish girls she brought up from Manhattan, or working-class girls with thick

Irish roots that she pulled from the alleys of South Boston.

"The side table has so much silver it's like King Solomon's mines," one housemaid would moan, reaching for a canister of silver polish. "Look how chapped my hands are."

"Don't get me started," the other would answer in a Slavic accent, flicking her braids. "Last week I spent two days beating the carpets from the library *by hand*, only to have Mrs. Turner find a spider. My arms are so sore I can almost not swing them."

Hearing these complaints, Jo's mother would snort and hustle her to the register, muttering to herself, until one day she said too much. "Ida Turner could burn her initials on every door in Prospect," Mama spit, slamming cans of evaporated milk onto Mr. Upton's counter, "but it wouldn't get her closer to Salt Creek Farm."

Before Jo could help herself, she chimed in, "But Whit said his mother wouldn't really do it—try to take the marsh."

Jo's mother paled and shot her a

quick look. Then her eyes softened as she handed Jo one of the grocery sacks. Jo gathered it into her arms and quickened her steps to match her mother's as she sped through the door back toward home. Mama did everything, Jo thought, with the fury of a woman chopping onions.

"Besides her trying to buy up all our land all the time, why do you and Ida hate each other so much?" Jo asked. She knew why she didn't like Ida. Ida was meaner than a fanged viper, she confiscated all the candy Jo shared with Whit, and she ratted out the kids who talked in church to Father Flynn. But those were complaints specific to childhood. The shifting hatred between Jo's mother and Ida was swift-running but also deeply submerged, Jo knew, like those currents under the ocean where creatures with tentacles swam. A place few souls ever saw. But her mother didn't take the bait.

"I don't hate Ida," she said, fixing her face into a smile Jo didn't for one minute believe. "I know far too many things about her for that. But the two of us agree on one thing: You and Whit need to stay away from each other. I'm telling you as one woman to another, Jo, that if I catch a single hint that Whit's put so much as a finger on you, I will make you so sorry you won't want to blink at him again."

Jo followed her mother's blaze of red hair up onto the porch, stomping hard on the soft wood. It was the first time her mother had acknowledged that Jo was becoming a woman, too, and a wave of pride swelled in her chest.

But pride steps highest before a fall—that went without saying—and that moment turned out to be the very first chink in the armor that Jo and Whit had thrown up against the rest of the world, a hole so small that Jo didn't even recognize it as a flaw. Instead she found herself gloating as she swung open the crooked screen door and floated past the ruined piano in the front hall, the paper grocery sack nestled on her hip, her head filled with the all-consuming business of becoming an adult. She wasn't particularly pretty. She knew that. She had hair the color of marsh scum and eyes as brown as the tip of a cattail, and she walked about as gracefully as one of the long-liner fishermen down at the dock, but nevertheless, it seemed, there was some speck in her after all that was Gilly to the core, and that was good enough for her.

———o-o o-o———

There was a heap Jo didn't know about womanhood, however—namely, that it's never the women you expect who cause you the most trouble in life, but rather the ones who lurk on the side-lines, quiet as pie. In Jo's case it was the Virgin.

At the end of the summer of 1959, life was a song—perfect breezes, easy temperatures, skies the color of a rob-in's egg. Bobby Fischer was a grand-master of chess, Elvis was in the army, and Jerry Lee Lewis was still in great balls of fire for marrying his thirteen-year-old cousin. On the last weekend of August, Whit didn't meet Jo on the beach as usual, which upset her, for that week was his last one in town. This year he'd be going off to boarding school in Connecticut, as befitted a Turner son, and Jo knew enough to suspect that when he came home, they might have trouble picking up where they'd left off.

She waited on the sand until the afternoon turned blistering and the winds died to a flicker, and then it was time to go scrape the day's crystals off the basins. Her family called them salt flowers, and in the hot shine of a late-summer afternoon the flakes really did look like a scattering of miniature petals, whiter than the grayish grains clumped underneath them, delicate as fairy wings. Jo took her flat wooden paddle and, holding her breath a little bit, extended it out over the surface of the basin, lowering it gently onto the other side of the crystals without disturbing them. People were willing to pay ten times as much for this salt. Her mother didn't even use it the same way as the ordinary gray stuff. She pinched it onto food only on special occasions and only right before serving, so as not to dull the sparkle in the flavor.

Keeping her salt rake steady, Jo gathered the fragile flakes into a cluster at her feet, then leaned down and scooped them into the shallow wooden bowl she'd brought with her. Only after she was sure she had collected all the crystals did she push the underlying gray sludge into a pile at the edge of the pond. She would let it dry overnight and then move it into yet a larger pile to sit for the rest of the season before she transported it all into the barn.

The barn reminded Jo of a kind of chapel. It was very old, original to the farm, in fact, and it was really more shed than barn. It didn't have the typical vaulted roof of a cheerful storybook structure, nor did it have a hayloft, but it did have room for animals (though the stalls were empty now) and wide double doors. Inside, it was gloomy, dusty, and dry. Over the years saline had stained the wooden walls and floor in patches and rings, giving the wood a diseased appearance that matched the beetles and potato bugs that crawled in the crannies. Jo emptied the flakes from her bowl into the season's pile and turned to hang her rake up in its place on the pegboard on the wall. Those actions were as familiar to her as brushing her teeth or polishing her boots and she performed them the same way every time. Even when Jo had nothing else, her mother had taught her, she could still have order.

That's why she didn't see Whit right away. He was standing in the shadows in the back of the barn. At first she thought he was a ghost. She jumped and dropped the rake before she could hang it. Then she recognized the familiar cock of his head, and her heart settled back in her chest. He whistled the three-beat trill they'd come up with as one of their private signals the summer he was ten and she was twelve.

"What on earth are you doing in here?" she said.

His voice shook a little, as if he were fighting back tears, but that couldn't be, Jo figured, because Whit Turner never cried. "I came to say good-bye to you. My mother just told me we're leaving early for boarding school."

Jo bit her lip, refusing to be sorry.

The people she loved always left: Henry, her father, and now Whit. The summer was ending, after all, and they were getting another year older. They never did see each other much in the winter anyway. As Jo was trying to gather her thoughts, Whit let go of her hands and fumbled in his pocket.

"I brought you something." He pulled out a small package wrapped in shiny paper and waited while Jo opened it. Underneath the wrapping was a small velvet box, and when she lifted the lid, Jo saw a heart-shaped locket threaded on a silver chain. Whit took the necklace from her hands and stepped behind her so he could fasten it around her neck.

"It reminds me of you," he said, tapping the locket with his fingernail. "Hard, but still pretty all the same." That kind of sweet talk was new between them, and Jo wasn't sure if she liked it. She reached up and grasped the necklace.

"What's this?" she asked, squinting.

Whit blushed. "I had it engraved. I put a *W* on it so you'll always remember me."

Jo caught her breath. Was Whit crazy? She couldn't walk around town with his initial strung around her throat. Ida would kill her if she ever saw, not to mention her own mother. It was the kind of thing a girlfriend would wear, and Jo wasn't Whit's girlfriend. She reached up and unhooked the neck-lace as fast as she could, dropping it back into Whit's palm. "I can't keep it."

Whit's fingers curled around hers like a question mark. "Why not?" His face was as open and soft as a baby's, but his eyes were as clear as she'd ever seen them. Suddenly, without warning, his lips found hers, and his tongue pressed against the seal of her mouth until she felt herself leaning into him and opening her jaw just a little. "Re-lax," Whit whispered. "It's what you're supposed to do when you're in love," and Jo wanted to, but something seemed terribly wrong. She had always assumed that kissing Whit would be as natural as running down the beach with him barefoot, but it didn't feel that way. It was a little like running barefoot, all right, but with sharp stones cutting her feet.

She jerked her head away. "Love is for fools, Whit Turner," she said, because she couldn't think of anything better. Then she took off.

"Jo, please!" Whit's voice rose up, but she was already running, obeying the urge to put as much distance between them as she could. She sprinted through the darkening marsh and brushed the back of her hand against her lips. The taste of Whit—a milky, wet flavor she couldn't name—still filled her. She spit into the mud.

She ended up at St. Agnes. Worried that Whit would come after her, she pushed open the sanctuary doors and slipped inside. Tonight only a single votive flickered at Our Lady's painted feet, and so Jo lit a second candle and knelt. The loose floorboards gave a little under her knees. The familiar smell of dry plaster and dust tickled her nose, but this evening the comfort of the familiar did little to ease her.

Up close, in the gathering dusk, the blank oval of the Virgin's missing face was even more pronounced, a puddle with no bottom. Maybe that's why the figure inspired confessions, Jo thought, but before she could follow that line of reasoning, Father Flynn's voice rang through the sanctuary, as if she'd conjured him. "Hello, child. This is quite a surprise." He stepped through the sacristy's open door and squinted at her. "Is everything fine?"

Jo blinked back her tears and bowed her head. "Not really."

Father Flynn took a seat in the pew behind her. He had a way of lurking that always made Jo want to spill her guts to him.

"I just made a mess of things with Whit Turner. He tried to give me something I couldn't take. And worse, he's going off to boarding school early. Did you know that?"

Father Flynn nodded. "What did he want to give you?" he finally asked.

"A locket with his initial on it."

She heard Father Flynn exhale sharply. "And why didn't you accept it?"

"I don't exactly know . . ." She trailed

off. It wasn't that she didn't like Whit, she realized. It was that she liked him far too deeply for a summer romance. "I don't guess Gillys and Turners are the best match," she said at last.

Father Flynn leaned back in the pew and looked at her gravely. "The thing about you and Whit is that you're a bit like mustard and vinegar. Good on your own, but a little overwhelming when paired up. And you're in the sweetest part of your life, my child. Try to re-member that." He hesitated, his eyes growing filmy. "You can come to me, you know, with anything that's in your heart. I know . . . well, I know you some-times must miss your father." Before Jo could respond, Father Flynn stood up and waved a hand at her. "You'd best be getting back to the marsh, my dear. It's almost dark."

Jo headed home, suddenly regret-ting returning the locket to Whit. It would have been a perfect token for Our Lady, she realized. As she picked her way along the edge of the marsh, she weighed the heft of the silver locket again in her mind, turning it one way and then another, like a stone dragging along a river bottom. What *would* Ida do if she caught Jo wearing something like that? Jo wondered. It was hard to know. Ida was a woman who had everything—jewels, furs, not to mention a husband she held on to like he was the outgoing tide and a son she'd do anything to protect.

But Ida had a few other things as well—namely, a past she'd never gotten rid of. And when a woman had too much, Jo mused, placing one careful foot in front of the other, what would she do? Why, she'd give some things away, that was what, whether they were last season's clothes, a set of dishes she no longer cared for, or—dared Jo even say—the illegitimate child no one could ever prove she'd borne, but half the town whispered that she had. Jo stepped onto the farmhouse's shambling front porch, glad for the single bulb's weak glow.

"Where the tarnation have you been?" her mother asked when Jo appeared in the kitchen. She nudged Jo's supper across the table. "Here. Soup's cold and the bread's hard, but you need something for your stomach."

"I went to St. Agnes," Jo said, sitting down. "Whit and I had an argument. I wondered if Father Flynn could help."

This elicited mere silence from her mother. She opened her mouth as if to tell Jo something, then changed her mind and clattered dishes into the sink. "And did he?" she finally asked, and Jo shook her head. Mama turned the tap on full force. "What does he know anyway?" she said eventually. "Father Flynn's just a priest. And worse than that, he's a man. He should keep his blasted nose out of women's business if he doesn't want it bitten clean off."

———∘–∘ ∘–∘———

In the morning Jo woke groggy and tired, and she saw that the weather had grown chilly and dark. When she came downstairs for breakfast, her mother handed her a loaf of brown bread and told her to deliver it to Father Flynn. "And after that," Mama said, "you can walk into town and stop at the post office for me. We're fresh out of stamps."

When Jo arrived at St. Agnes, the sanctuary was empty. It was so early that no one would have come out that way yet, Jo knew, and she appreciated the solitude. But as she edged down the center aisle, she saw that she was wrong. Someone had been here already, and that person had left something, too.

Despite the earliness of the hour, there was already a votive burning in front of the Virgin, and beneath it sat a cream-colored envelope with interlocked initials on the front. *IMT.* Ida May Turner. Jo stepped closer, puzzled. Out of all the women in Prospect, Ida was the only one who didn't openly adore Our Lady. "Pagan nonsense," she always barked whenever some poor fool asked her about it. "I didn't get where I am by groveling on my knees in front of some beat-up painting." In Jo's entire life, she'd never once seen Ida give the Virgin anything.

Lying next to the envelope was a necklace that looked vaguely familiar to Jo. It was the single pearl on a silver chain that Ida sometimes wore, in

marked contrast to her showier jewels.
Jo dropped the bread and salt in front
of the Virgin without even bothering to
genuflect, and then she committed a
sin so deep she never did confess it.

There was an unwritten law that
whatever was left out for the Virgin
would remain undisturbed until after
Mass on Sunday, when Father Flynn
would collect all the items. The slips of
prayers and written confessions he
burned without reading. Words to the
Virgin, whether scribbled or spoken,
were for her alone, and no one—not
even clergy—would have dared to vio-
late that covenant. But that day Jo did.
Looking around to see if anyone was
coming, she reached out and stuffed
first the letter and then the pearl into
her pocket.

"Child." She half choked on her own
breath and whipped her hand out of
her pocket. Father Flynn had the quietest feet in Christendom. She folded her
hands in her lap and looked at him out
of the sides of her eyes, but he didn't
seem to notice she'd done anything

wrong. "You're here awfully early," he said, kneeling next to her.

"Yes," Jo replied, her heart hammering. "I brought you some bread." She shoved the loaf at him.

"Thank you." He reached down and scooped it into his broad hands with no trace of suspicion. "You seem quiet this morning. Missing a certain young man, no doubt?"

Jo frowned. "No. We just have a lot of work to do yet in the marsh, and the weather's changing fast."

The father clapped a friendly palm on her shoulder. "Well, don't let me keep you." Jo waited until she was sure he was gone, and then she tiptoed out of the sanctuary, her hand anchored on the treasure in her pocket.

She wandered down the lane, constantly checking over her shoulder, though who she thought would have followed her, she didn't know. The bluff was about as deserted as a widow's house in February. Nevertheless, heart in her mouth, Jo kept walking, all the way to the bottom of Plover Hill. She stopped when she got to the pear tree.

It wasn't a place she ever had the occasion to frequent, it being a spot for lovers' trysts. The leaves had all turned brown and fallen off early, but Jo crunched through them anyway and sat under the canopy of bare branches, gazing up at the clapboard monstrosity that was Turner House. She put her hand on the letter again, thinking she had a good idea of what was inside it, but she had to be sure. Before she could change her mind, she ripped open the envelope, pulled out the pages, and read the words that would alter the rest of her life.

It was a simple story about a late-season storm and a pair of babies born—a tale Jo thought she knew, but never quite like this. She scanned the words three times to make sure she understood them, and when she was finished, she was certain of two things, the first being that she wished she hadn't stolen the letter, for she didn't desire the terrible knowledge about herself that it held, and second that even though they involved her, the words Jo held so loosely under that tree weren't hers to keep.

She should have done the proper thing and returned both the pearl and the letter to the Virgin, of course, or, barring that, she should have either buried or burned the evidence. But she was young, and secrets can be a weighty burden to carry when you're not used to them. She should have turned to Our Lady for solace, but the thought of her—faceless, faded, her skirts rubbed thin—made Jo's blood go cold. And more than anything, Jo wanted to know that another living heart was as nicked as hers, and she knew exactly whose heart she wanted it to be.

She slid the letter back into the envelope and added the necklace. And then, before she lost her nerve, she walked up Plover Hill to the iron gates of Turner House and the family's elaborate brass mailbox. Probably one of the maids collected the letters every day, Jo thought, but Ida would get this message. Jo had no doubt about that. She just wouldn't know who had sent it. Jo shut the little hinged door of the mail-box firmly and started her way back down the hill, glancing once over her shoulder to see if she could detect any movement in the house, but there was none. The family had all gone to take Whit to school.

Jo pictured Ida opening the envelope when she returned, the pearl falling into her cupped palm like a slap. It would be a gift she thought she'd never get back but wouldn't want to keep either, just like something else she'd once given away. Jo crunched home through the husks of the pear tree's leaves, pleased with herself. Now she and Ida were tit for tat. When it came down to it, in fact, they were just like each other. It turned out that Jo had a talent for getting rid of things, too.

Chapter Six

Sorrows tend to collect like dust throughout a person's life, but Claire had only one true sorrow to her name. She had not married the man she loved. The choice was never hers to make. She knew that truth, even as she resisted it. Some women were born to play the part of the good wife, while others were put on this earth to dabble with fire, and as soon as Claire was out of the womb, it became abundantly clear which path she'd been wound up and set on.

For starters there was the fact of her

hair: red as the day was long, wavy and thick. In Claire's childhood her mother had kept it in a bob, but when Claire was a teenager, she grew it out, much to Mama's dismay. "A waterfall of pure sin," Mama used to call it when she brushed it before Mass, scraping the boar bristles along Claire's scalp, making her head sting.

This always angered Claire. "It's just like yours," she'd point out, but Mama never answered to that. She only combed harder, tweaking Claire's ears and yanking in all the tender spots. "Best to keep it up," she'd mutter through a mouthful of hairpins, "away from the devil's temptation."

Claire couldn't argue with that logic. Even before she hit adolescence, she knew that the devil seemed to have one eye cocked for the Gilly ladies, who, the Good Lord help them, tended to love him right back. It was why everyone in town said matrimony never took with any of them. Because how could you wed a woman whose fingers were already ringed with brimstone?

"Marriage isn't for Gilly women,"

Mama always muttered whenever Claire asked about her father.

"That might be true for Jo, but it doesn't have to be true for me," Claire mused the day her mother got her ready for her Confirmation. She handed her mother a length of white ribbon to braid through her hair. She'd just started growing it, and it barely brushed the tops of her shoulders. Jo was seven years older than Claire, twenty to Claire's thirteen, but she was so square she might have been thirty or forty as far as Claire was concerned. She was Claire's own sister, but even Claire thought of her as an old maid.

But then Jo always had been prig-gish, even when *she'd* been a teenager. Claire remembered the summers when Jo and Whit had still been tight as two hoops on a barrel. They were almost even boyfriend and girlfriend, but never quite, maybe because they simply knew each other too well. The way Claire saw it, there were no mysteries left between them, and that was Jo's mistake, for a man needed to be curious in order to want to hold on to a woman. Even at thirteen Claire knew that much.

Mama snorted at her suggestion. "Gilly women and Turner men are the worst combination of all," she said, yanking a frail strand of hair down near Claire's neck. You can't trust a Turner," she added, patting her own hair. "They'd sell their own souls if they thought they could get two nickels for them."

Claire shook her mother's hands off her. "I don't believe those old stories."

Mama sighed. "Suit yourself," she said. Then she frowned and looked almost sorry. "Maybe it's better that way."

Claire turned on her heel and went to collect her sweater for church, but her mother's opinion stuck like glue. In fact, even though Claire didn't know it then, her mother was both right and wrong about the Turners. They *would* sell anything—even, perhaps, their own souls—but never for anything as paltry as a dime.

———o-o o-o———

Unlike Jo, Claire loathed everything about Mass—the fusty smoke from the incense pot, the smothered coughs and shuffling feet, the waxy press of the wafer against her tongue. Week after week she bowed her head and traced the Virgin's empty face with two fingers, whispering a running, more truthful catalog of her sins before she revised them for the ears of Father Flynn.

"You have anger twisted in your heart," he'd say with a sigh through the wooden partition of the confessional. "You must learn that God's will doesn't always coincide with your own. Say three Hail Marys."

"I feel like I'm in a time warp," Claire complained to Jo as they traveled down the lane to St. Agnes for weekly confession. "We do the same thing over and over. Dig salt and pray, and that's it."

But in this matter, as in most others, Jo was firmly rooted on her mother's side. She took Claire's arm. "Come on." The mosquitoes were feeding as they walked along the edge of the marsh and then down the lane to St. Agnes.

"I'm getting bitten alive," Claire

moaned, swatting at the whining insects but never getting any of them. Jo, in contrast, seemed oblivious to the pests. *Probably*, Claire thought, *they're swarming me because she's too dry to drink from.*

Inside the little church, they made their way to the Virgin and lit two votives. As usual, Claire's match flared too quickly, singeing her skin, and she cursed and dropped the candle, cracking the votive glass a little. "Shit," she muttered.

"Claire," Jo admonished. "You mustn't use that kind of language here. Have some manners, for heaven's sake."

Claire rolled her eyes and struck another match. This one behaved better. She stuck her charred fingers in her mouth. Jo shook her dark hair. Unlike Claire, she wore hers loose, straight down to her shoulders. She never did anything with it, but it was pretty all the same. "You better get over your clumsiness around fire," she sniffed. "Remember, it's your turn to step up to this year's December's Eve bonfire."

Claire's heart knotted. If there was anything she hated more than church, it was casting the salt on the town bonfire. It wasn't just the mean looks the townspeople gave her or the empty circle of frosted grass they left as she inched toward the flames, and neither was it the fact that she couldn't stay and celebrate—it was more basic than that. Claire simply hated holding all those people's fates in her hands. It should have made her feel powerful, she knew, like she could see something special about the world that no one else could, but it didn't. Instead, ever since the first time she'd sprinkled the fire and watched it spit out that horrifying plume of black smoke, all she felt was guilt. Even at age six, Claire could have told everyone standing around in the smoke that night that black futures were all they were ever going to get with her, but they wouldn't have believed her, she knew. Not until she grew up and made them.

She held her palm down over the votive, gathering the warmth of the flame to her skin, and looked at her sister.

Nothing bad ever happened when Jo threw the salt, but it didn't make anyone in town like her any better than they did Claire. A Gilly was a Gilly as far as Prospect was concerned. Claire sighed. "Why do we have to throw salt to the fire anyway?" she asked for the hundredth time.

Jo bit her lip and shrugged. "It's just what we've always done."

"Well, what if we didn't?"

Jo looked astonished. "What do you mean?"

"What if we didn't cast the salt for the town? What if there was no bonfire?"

Jo pushed herself up onto her feet. "I don't think that would be a good idea at all, Claire." And without saying anything more, she turned her back and ended the conversation. Claire flushed with impatience and leaned over to blow out her votive. The fire leaped and licked at her hair, but Jo leaned down and blew out the candle in the nick of time.

"Don't you dare tell Mama what you just said," she snapped. "And just for that"—she nodded at the extinguished votive—"you can take my shift scraping the ponds when we get back."

———◦–◦ ◦–◦———

For no other reason than to tempt fate, Claire started smoking. She picked it up from hanging around beach parties with the wealthy kids out on the Cape for the summer. They smoked only the harshest, most spartan cigarettes: unfiltered French brands, or ones mixed with cloves. Claire's asthmatic lungs belched and complained with every puff she took, but she loved cradling the delicate stick in between her fingers, listening to it crackle, and then grinding it out with the ball of her foot. And yes, she was always burning herself, trying to explain away the perfectly round holes in her clothes and the scar on her wrist where she'd bumped it with a live butt.

When tenth grade started, she refused to sit with the dirt-patch kids anymore, the ones who lived all the way across town, whose fathers worked as dishwashers in the tourist clam shacks, who hired themselves out on fishing trawlers or ran salvage yards. She learned to bring her hemlines up or let them down to the fashionable length, and she made sure that her hair was trimmed neatly, even if it was still bound in a braid, and that she picked exactly the right color binder out at Swenson's five-and-dime.

She tried out for the cheerleading squad and made it. She joined the homecoming committee and the yearbook staff and started eating lunch with Katy Diamond, Cecilia West, and Abigail Van Huben: the triumvirate of Prospect High. Because she was happy for the first time, her grades improved.

"You're going to be a college girl," Mama would whisper to her at night, smoothing Claire's hair with her rough fingers. "It's all taken care of. I borrowed the money just for you."

Jo had dropped out of school after her junior year, but it wasn't any secret that she was better with her hands than she was with books. Claire began to notice how one day slid into another with her mother and sister.

"I've just done the east ponds," Jo would inform Mama, coming in from the marsh.

"But the west ones will be needing a skim now," Mama would reply.

"One week is about the same as any other out here." Jo sniffed when Claire complained about this repetition. "The roof is leaking, there's snails in the garden, and we have mud up to our earlobes. It doesn't matter if I'm talking about today, tomorrow, or three days past."

"I guess you're right," Claire said, knotting the neck of another burlap sack of gray salt. "Time's not going anywhere fast out here."

But she was wrong. That year the shift from summer to fall would bring her something new, and when it did, the frame of her life would never be quite the same again.

———o-o o-o———

Before he became a priest, Ethan Stone was just a regular boy who lived at the edge of Prospect in a gray saltbox near the wharf, where his father and uncle kept a pair of diesel trawlers. It was ironic for men of the sea to be named Stone, but the name suited the Stone men, who were flinty, wordless, and rougher than granite. Every day for nine months of the year, no matter the weather, they set out on their boats and brought back what the Atlantic saw fit to throw at them. Mackerel. Scrod. The odd pilfered lobster or two. Cod in the autumn. The other three months of the year, when the waters heaved and roiled their discontent and the decks on his vessel froze, Chet occupied himself with the curious occupation of knitting, while Ethan's father, Merrett, slouched on a barstool in a tavern so seedy it had no name.

It must have been torture for a man like Merrett to have a child like Ethan, for if Merrett was an iceberg set adrift on the sea, then his son was more like the foam gathering on the crest of the waves. As a youth Ethan liked fishing well enough, but he also enjoyed watching his uncle knit. Worse, he liked poetry and the harmonic structures of classical music, and he absolutely loved nothing better than to serve as Father Flynn's altar boy. When Father Flynn discovered that Ethan could sing, he started having him perform the psalms, his airy voice purer than any girl's. Ethan's sickly mother, Ellen, would sit entranced, hands clasped beneath her chin, her lips quivering, while Merrett scowled.

"That boy has a voice like God's own lark," Claire's mother would say with a sigh, which produced in Claire a powerful urge to want to march straight up to Ethan Stone and shove her fist down his throat.

The summer they were fifteen, Ethan started skipping church and working on his father's boat, and St. Agnes rang empty without the dips and lilts of his voice. Even though it had changed over time, the timbre of it hadn't grown any less sweet, just richer, like a dessert that intensified in the oven. If Claire fidgeted and niggled her way through Mass and the other town boys sat sulking with their hands shoved in their pockets, Ethan had always been calm. He'd moved so smoothly as he lit the altar candles that the flames didn't even sputter, and Claire had always wondered how he did that, given her own calamitous relationship with church votives.

It took Ethan's absence to make her pay attention to him, and when she finally did, she wasn't the only one. Ethan reappeared in church after the fishing season ended on the first really cold day of autumn 1965, and every female in the congregation immediately sat up and noticed that the young man with the angel's voice had turned over a new leaf.

He'd grown as tall as Merrett, for starters, just as broad in the shoulders and neck. But whereas Merrett moved with steel-toed determination, knuckles held hard at his sides, Ethan walked with the courteous grace of a gentleman. His eyes were the color of the deep part of the Atlantic, where the biggest schools of fish ran, and his hair had gone straw blond from being out in the weather.

"That boy went and stole the looks off a Greek god," Claire heard Mrs.

Butler whisper too loud to her friend, and even Jo smiled at that.

All through Mass, Claire couldn't take her eyes off Ethan. When she stepped up to receive Communion, she was careful to smooth her skirt tight over her hips. She peeked over her shoulder at Ethan while she waited in line, but he was standing with his eyes fixed on the altar up front, oblivious to anything around him. Claire pouted and turned back around. Clearly, she would have to work on his priorities.

After services, while the adults drank coffee and mingled in the sanctuary, Claire bolted to the far side of the rectory so she could sneak a smoke. She thought she was out of the wind, but the first match didn't take, the second one blew out as soon as it caught, and the third one scorched her thumb.

"Damn it!" she cried, puffing and waving her hand in the icy breeze.

"Let me," a melodic voice said. She looked up just as Ethan Stone took the still-unlit cigarette from her lips, put it between his own, and scratched a new match off the book. He drew in a deep drag, telling Claire this wasn't his first, and handed the cigarette back to her. "These things will kill you," he said, eyes twinkling. "You should think about quitting."

"Uh . . . hey," she said, tongue-tied. "I haven't seen you at school." It was true, but only now did she care. The old Ethan was the kind of boy who could have eaten lunch hip to hip with her, stealing food from her bag, and she wouldn't have remembered him two seconds later, but this new Ethan was someone Claire couldn't forget if she tried. Ethan took the cigarette away from her again, and she watched his lips curl around the end. He blew out a steady plume.

"I've been working with my dad. But the season is wrapping up, and so I'm starting school again a little late." He frowned. "He didn't want me to go back to high school at all, but I want to finish, even if I am going to spend my life on the sea."

Claire inched a little closer and surprised herself by saying something true. "I guess it's good you like what your family does. I don't think I belong in salt at all, even though my mother and sister practically pray to it."

Ethan smiled and passed the half-smoked cigarette back to her. "So where *do* you belong, then?"

She thought about it. "Maybe on an island. Someplace really shaded and wet, where I couldn't make salt if I tried."

Ethan's face grew pensive. "I bet they'd still have fish there."

Claire nodded. "Probably." They both startled as people began shuffling out of the church. Ethan smiled at her, and she noticed again how much she liked his eyes.

"I'll see you around, Claire Gilly." She watched him go, shaky in the backs of her knees.

"Claire! Claire, where are you?" she heard her mother calling, and she tried to answer, but it was as if she were shouting down the tunnel of her own past from a great distance.

"Coming!" she finally cried, stubbing out the cigarette. "I'll be right there." She turned the corner of the building, wondering how quickly she could trade an existence of never-ending salt for a life of endless fish.

———o-o o-o———

Claire kept seeing Ethan at church and passing him in the halls at school, and he was always friendly, sometimes carrying her books for her, sometimes swapping half his sandwich for half of hers, but he didn't ask her out, and the longer the time stretched, the crabbier she grew.

What made it worse was that she wasn't the only girl who'd noticed that Ethan had undergone a transformation at sea. Cecilia West practically threw herself under his feet every time he stepped past her locker, and Abigail Van Huben wouldn't shut up about his eyes at lunch.

"I've just got to get him to kiss me at the December's Eve bonfire," she declared halfway through November. She kicked Claire in the ankle. "Oh, look, here he comes!"

Claire scowled and balled up her paper lunch sack, wishing she could sneak out of school for a smoke. Not only would it make her wheeze badly enough to get her excused from gym class, but it also helped her plot. More than anything, she knew, she didn't want Ethan going to the bonfire with Abigail. "He won't be there," she said before she even thought about it.

Abigail twisted up her face. "Why not?"

"Because he's spending the evening with me." As soon as she said it, she knew it was true. Ethan wouldn't want the hurly-burly of screaming girls, sparks, and boys trying to hide as many beers as they could under their coats. He was a boy who combed the town library's shelves for Wordsworth poems and Shakespeare plays about kings. Inside, he was the same as her, Claire was sure. He longed for the isolated calm of a rocky island, too.

Abigail's mouth fell open. "But what would he be doing with *you*? You can't even hang out at the fire. You're a Gilly."

Claire stood up and smiled. "Exactly." And then, before Abigail could stop her, or she could stop herself, she walked up to Ethan, wrapped her arms around him, and in full view of everyone gave him her very first kiss. Ethan's lips were cool against hers, but that was okay, she told herself. She had heat enough for both of them. She didn't need a bonfire to light any sparks in Ethan Stone's heart.

———o-o o-o———

On December's Eve, Claire's stomach was in knots as she made her way to the bonfire behind her mother and Jo. Would Ethan be waiting for her by the pear tree as he promised? she wondered. Her throat tightened with anticipation as she stepped onto the edge of Tappert's Green.

Just then a familiar voice rang out of the darkness. "Why, you've gone and changed, young Claire." Claire stopped and spun around. It was Whit Turner, recently back in town after graduating from Harvard. In the past eight years, Claire had barely seen him. First he'd gone off to boarding school when he was thirteen, and then his mother had died quite suddenly, Claire remembered. Whit had taken it hard. He'd stopped visiting Salt Creek Farm—and Jo—after that. For the past few years, his shadow had barely darkened Prospect. Claire had heard stories about his glamorous life around town. He was spending Christmas skiing with friends. He was in some secret club at Harvard. He even celebrated one Easter as a guest at a friend's ancestral pile in Scotland, where the golfing was out of this world.

But those days were done. He was home now to take over the family business. Hamish had grown doddering lately, and the Cape climate no longer suited him. He'd been spending winters in Palm Beach with his long-standing mistress, and now that Whit was home, the town freely speculated, there was no reason Hamish might not want to spend the rest of his time there, too.

Up close Whit was even handsomer than Claire remembered, his dark eyes twinkling with his old boyish charm, his mouth ready to twist into a grin at a moment's notice, pulling her into laughter with him. He was wearing a cashmere overcoat and soft, expensive shoes. His hair was neatly trimmed, and it cupped his skull in silky curls. He was very clearly a person who had everything he wanted, Claire thought with some envy. He had education. He had money. He had much of the land any of them in town could see—and probably even more that they couldn't. What he didn't have was a wife. There was a time in her early childhood when Claire might have put money on Jo's stepping into that role, but after the summer that Ida died, nothing between Whit and Jo was ever the same. Whit had absented himself from their lives, and Jo would never speak about it.

Whit took in the new womanly outline of Claire now. "You've changed," he said again, dragging his eyes back up to her head. "But your hair hasn't." Claire patted the nest of pins and curls her mother had made along her neckline, pleased with his assessment of her. He took a step closer. "You look like a dangerous woman now," he whispered, and she blushed.

Jo glanced over her shoulder to see

what was holding Claire up, and when she saw it was Whit, she stopped dead in her tracks and folded her arms. Claire sighed. "I have to go," she finally said, her mind already wandering off to the impending bonfire and the rustle of the pear tree's leaves. "Great to see you," she called into the darkness, trying to ignore the press of Whit's gaze along her backside. It was nice to have her own opinion of her looks confirmed, but she would much rather it be done by Ethan.

"What ails you?" Jo asked as Claire drew even with her and she gave Claire's elbow a pinch through her bulky coat. She lowered her voice so their mother couldn't hear. "What did he want anyway?"

"Nothing," Claire answered. "He just said hi."

Jo scowled. "Well, stay away from him. Just because he's come home to take charge of his family's real estate, that doesn't mean I'm suddenly going to melt at his feet. And you shouldn't either."

"I wasn't planning on it," Claire said,

but Jo didn't hear her. She'd charged ahead to the fire, which had just been lit and was sparking to life. Claire hurried along with her bag of salt. Maybe Jo was right, she reflected. The Turners were robber barons. Everyone knew that. And maybe Whit was the worst of them, for he hid that greed under dimples and winks, like one of those old-time villains from a black-and-white movie, dashing in a cape and a thin mustache but full of dastardly plans. Claire straightened her shoulders and followed Jo toward the crackling fire without a word. Anyway, what did she care about the silly Turners? She had bigger plans for the evening—for her whole life, as a matter of fact. For the first and only time, she couldn't wait to step forward and throw the salt.

———o-o o-o———

That spring Claire dug and shoveled the drainage ditches in the marsh and didn't even complain when her hands blistered so badly they started bleeding. Ethan would kiss them better when she saw him, and then she would take over from there. Love, she was discovering, could make even the salt sweet.

Ethan would go only so far with her, though. She'd worm her hands under his shirt, and he'd allow that. She'd lick the side of his neck, and he'd let her do that, too. But when she started tugging at his belt, he would grab her wrists. "If you don't stop," he'd say, lowering his arms, "I won't be able to either, and that's not what I want for us."

"What do you want?" she finally asked him, smiling. It was the end of March. They'd been a couple for four months, but Claire felt like a whole new girl. The first thing Ethan had gotten her to do was quit smoking.

"It makes your hair smell," he complained, unbraiding her red curls, "turns your fingers yellow, and how many times have you accidentally burned yourself?"

Claire bit her lip. "But you smoke."

He leaned down and kissed her. "I only do it in fishing season, for my father. It's one of his qualifications for official manhood. Promise me you'll stop."

She thought she would miss the sizzle of tobacco, but delayed gratification was even more delicious than indulgence, she was learning. She would run the pad of her thumb over her empty bottom lip and summon up the fullness of Ethan's mouth on hers, and her urge to smoke would vanish, replaced by a far more carnal craving.

Ethan loved to read poetry—the Romantics, especially: Keats, Wordsworth, Coleridge. He had an amazing memory and could quote entire passages to her as easily as if he were reciting the names of his family. When Ethan was busy down at the docks, Claire would wander the shelves of the library in Prospect, reading those poems for herself, bundling the words on her tongue and stowing them safe in her heart. She learned that to look at an object—a daffodil, a Greek urn—to really *look* at it through beautiful words could make the rest of her life seem beautiful, too.

Because of Ethan, Claire learned to sit still in Mass. He'd quit singing, but he still paid such rapt attention throughout the service that Claire started wondering if she was missing something

with all her fidgeting. She sat motion-
less on the pew, her hands folded on
her knees, her eyes drawn forward, and
she even started telling more of the
whole truth to Father Flynn during confession. On the surface, she knew, she
looked angelic—hair smoothed, lips
gently curved—but in her soul she was
still as choppy as the whitecaps breaking off Drake's Beach on a windy day.
She just no longer wanted everyone to
know it.

"What's with you these days anyway?" Jo ribbed her. "You've turned
into a regular Pollyanna. To be honest,
I think I liked the old Claire better. At
least we all knew what we were getting."

Claire shrugged. She couldn't explain
it either. It just made her happier to
please Ethan than it did to please herself.

Only one thing terrified her, however,
and it was something she kept to herself. Much as she scoffed about the
bad luck the women in their family had
with marriage, Claire secretly worried it
might be true. After all, no Gilly woman

that she knew of had ever managed to leave the salt, and no boys had ever managed to grow up in it. What if she and Ethan had a child together one day? Would her family's blight find them, adding another stone to the graveyard of dead boys by the barn? The idea made her shudder.

"Please keep Ethan safe," she prayed during Mass, trying not to catalog the accidents and disasters that could befall a man of the sea. "Keep watch over him. Keep him close. Keep him like your own."

Little did she know how powerful prayers could be. Even littler did she suspect how very well hers would be answered.

——o-o o-o——

By the end of high school, Claire was so in love with Ethan that it was old news in Prospect.

"Hey, it's the mister and missus," Mr. Hopper teased them one Saturday night when they came into the diner for burgers after a movie. They were seniors, and their futures were looming.

"When are you kids going to get hitched?"

Ethan blushed. "I think we're a little young."

Mr. Hopper waved a hand. "Best time for it! Before you know any better." And with a wink, he slid them free milk shakes.

Her own cheeks burning, Claire glanced at Ethan through lowered eyelashes. "Do you ever think about it?"

Ethan took a careful sip of his milk shake. "The future?"

"*Our* future." Her nerves thrilled just saying it. She tickled his wrist with her fingertips. "If we were married, you know what we could finally do . . ." Ethan edged his hand away. They'd experimented fairly creatively over the past three years, but Ethan always drew the line when things started getting too serious physically. There were some things Claire couldn't negotiate.

"Of course," he said, avoiding her eyes. "But we *are* young. I can't do something partway, Claire. You know that. I need to be sure first." It was true. It was one of the things she loved best about him. When he was away fishing in the summers, for instance, he was gone heart, soul, and body. When he studied, he concentrated so hard he couldn't hear anything around him, and when he prayed, angels could have trumpeted over his shoulder and he wouldn't have heard them. This year in particular, he'd been spending a lot of time with Father Flynn, but Claire couldn't fault him for that. If she had a father like Merrett, she thought, she'd look for a substitute, too, but maybe she'd choose someone closer to home, like Ethan's uncle, Chet.

As their senior year went on, Claire wondered if Ethan would propose. When Christmas came, she unwrapped the book of poems he'd bought her and thumbed through the pages without seeing any of the words. On Valentine's Day she buried her nose in the folds of the red rose he'd presented, hoping to feel the hard glint of a ring in the petals. By the time the prom arrived, she was floating in a fevered cloud of silk, perfume, and hair spray. But Ethan just swayed with his hands anchored on her hips like usual and whispered "I love you" in her ear, but he didn't get down on one knee.

By graduation Claire had gnawed her fingernails to ragged crescents. Ethan accepted his diploma with a firm handshake and threw his mortarboard in the air with everyone else, but he didn't pull her into the dusty shadows and reach into the pocket of his robe for a small velvet box. Claire entered salt season as bitter as a crabapple that year and straightaway reverted to squabbling with Jo.

"Do you ever think you're just going to dry up in all this stuff?" she asked. They were in the barn, making up little burlap sacks. Claire flicked her braid over her shoulder and watched as Jo wrenched another bag's neck closed with twine. It reminded her of the way Mama wrung chicken necks whenever they decided it was time to eat from the coop.

"Just be glad you don't have to sell it, too," Jo said. That was *her* job—sitting in the makeshift stall they'd decided to set up in town, shilling Cape salt to tourists. Claire hated the commerce as much as she loathed the marsh. It was another embarrassment. She didn't bother to answer Jo now. Instead she lit a cigarette. Ethan had been gone for three weeks already on his father's boat, and her nerves were ringing like firehouse bells.

She looked up to see Jo wildly flapping her arms. "Put that out! You know this place is a pile of timber sticks!" It was true. Smoking in the barn was about as dumb as puffing away next to a gasoline pump. The dust alone was so arid it was already halfway to fire, never mind the worm-infested siding, the warped flooring, and the splintery roof.

Claire didn't care. She tilted her head and blew a stream of smoke straight up. "Don't be such an old biddy," she said. "You never have any fun."

Jo ground her teeth. She looked about an inch away from killing Claire. Claire could tell how mad Jo was by how quiet her voice came out. "Of course I don't have any fun! Take a good look around, Claire. Daddy never left a forwarding address, Mama and I work seven days a week, yet the sea doesn't stop flowing, the salt doesn't stop forming, and things around here don't stop breaking." She narrowed her eyes and stepped closer to Claire. "Gilly women weren't put on the earth to have fun."

Claire took a final drag off her cigarette and rolled her eyes before she stubbed it out. No one had to tell her that twice, which was exactly why she wasn't planning on staying a Gilly for long.

"Suit yourself," she said. "Die an old maid. See if I care." And without another glance, she left Jo to finish all the work.

Chapter Seven

The first summer that Whit returned from boarding school, he and Jo agreed through their usual signals to meet on Drake's Beach a full hour after Mass was over. It was later than their normal time, but Whit let Jo know with a waggle of his eyebrows that he had a surprise in store for her. She blushed in her pew, glancing over to make sure her mother hadn't noticed, and hid her face. On the one hand, the old thrill of Whit's impish charm pulled at her, tempting her to match his acts of derring-do with some of her own, but things had changed between them. At least they had for her. Since that awkward kiss he'd given her in the barn and after his months away, Jo had had time to figure some things out, and she knew without a doubt that no matter what happened, she and Whit could never be a couple.

In the course of the past year, Whit had grown much taller, and his shoulders were filling out while his hair had gotten even darker, flopping over one eye in a manner that Jo was sure the girls in his set found irresistible. In fact, he seemed almost a different person, stretched to unfamiliar proportions, an impostor who somehow knew all the tics and signs of their secret language. Jo watched as he helped Ida out of her pew and then shook Father Flynn's hand with both of his own, as if they were playing a game of fists that Whit was determined to win.

An hour later, against all her better judgment, Jo was on Drake's Beach, the wind whipping through her dark hair, her toes curled like anxious snails in the sand. The beach was so weather-beaten and stony that going barefoot on it was a trial of faith, but Jo did it anyway, figuring if she could bear the pain, she could handle almost anything. Again and again she glanced up through the dunes, to where the lane ran, but no one arrived. Relieved, she turned to go back to the marsh, but just then she heard a whistle coming from the sea. Two beats, then a pause, then the same two beats again.

She turned to the water and saw that Whit had chosen to inaugurate their season of beachcombing by sailing a brand-new dinghy around the point. He navigated the surf easily, arriving in a flurry of sailcloth and breeze, and threw his legs over the side, jumping down to steady the little craft.

At the sight of the boat, Jo's mouth filled with saliva and her hands started sweating. In spite of living among the puddles of the marsh, she was distrustful of the sea. It had to do with Henry's death. She pictured the bloated corpse of her brother as her parents hauled him from the inundation pond, his arms spread wide like a person throwing out a warning, and she took a step back toward the dunes. She did not want to go sailing.

Whit was oblivious to her discomfort. He jumped into the surf and held the boat steady. "What do you think?" he crowed. "She's brand new! I joined the sailing team at school. My mother just bought me this for getting decent grades, but she doesn't know that it's only because I pay my nerdy dormmate Peter Peckman to do my homework for me."

The old Whit would have understood her hesitation, Jo thought, about sailing and about their meeting like this at all. The boy who'd cut his palm and held it to hers, the boy who'd rubbed salt on her lips—that person would have sensed her fear and pulled the craft up onto the sand right then and there. But Whit had changed, she realized, in more than just looks.

"Hop in!" he said. Now that he was out of his church clothes, Jo noticed even more how lean and taut his legs had stretched and how broadly his shoulders were starting to spread. He resembled his father—Brahmin jaw, thick hair, Roman nose—but his eyes were as smoky and heavy-lidded as Ida's. They made it hard for Jo to tell what he was really thinking. *Ida's right*, Jo thought. *We don't belong, even if we are the same inside.* "Come on, chicken legs," he taunted. "Don't make me stand here all day. I won't, you know."

Jo moved through the surf.

"That's better," Whit said, throwing himself in after her, gathering up the lines in one hand and the tiller in the other. "Watch out for the boom!" he cried, swinging the sail in front of them, pulling on the line clutched in his hand and setting back out toward the open sea. Jo gripped the rail of the boat and tried not to let her teeth chatter.

"You're a maniac," she said, struggling to keep her voice light, and Whit cackled.

"And you're still short and boring," he answered, grinning at her.

Jo blushed. She'd quit growing, it was true, but she wasn't really that short. It was just that Whit had gotten so tall so quickly. The boring part she hadn't expected to hear out of his mouth, though. That comment stung. It was something Ida would have said. Jo shifted a hair away from Whit, and the dinghy suddenly dipped in a wave. Her stomach lurched. Whit shoved the tiller over, and the boat's far rail rolled up toward them.

"Up and over," Whit said, scrambling across to the other side, keeping his head tucked.

Jo followed him, banging her shin in the process, trying not to whimper. The sail rippled, and the boat settled back into a more reasonable angle.

"Are you okay?" Whit asked, peering at her.

She glanced back at the beach. They'd turned, but they were still headed out to the horizon. The swells under the boat were getting more regular, but bigger. Suddenly Jo wasn't comfortable at all, bobbing like a lost cork out there with someone who looked and sounded a lot like Whit but who didn't feel like him. She clenched her fists. "Go back."

Whit swept his arm out at the point. "But we need to be out this far to clear the rocks at Drake's Point."

Jo resisted the urge to stamp her foot like Claire. "Just go back!" Sweat beaded along her temples. She didn't want to tell Whit, but it was the first time she'd ever been in a boat, and she was worried that if they did manage to cross the bay, it just might decide to cross them back.

Whit scowled. "Fine, if you're going to be that way about it." He shoved the tiller over once again, making the boat tip and roll while they switched sides one more time. If Whit kept up with the tacking, Jo knew, she really would be at sea, unable to tell anymore if she was coming or going. "Here," he said, "you steer. Best cure for seasickness." He put her hand on the tiller and then covered it with his own.

They'd touched each other before, of course, too many times to count. On the hottest days, they'd wrestle each other in the waves, tangling their legs underwater, trying to knock each other off balance, and Whit had a habit of grabbing her hand when he wanted her attention, but this was different. His fingers insinuated themselves in between hers now, and his leg pressed firmly against hers. She could hear his breath coming hard and fast, and she knew she had to pull her hand out from under his, but he was holding on too tightly.

"Jo," he murmured, and leaned close to her, his lips parting. The sail rippled above them, and she stiffened, her nerves electric with alarm. Whatever happened, she knew, she mustn't allow him any nearer. Those times between them were over.

"Watch out," she said, and pulled on the tiller, making the boat careen. Whit grabbed her hand then, squeezing too tight, his fist crushing her fingers. "Ow!" she squealed, trying to snatch her hand away from his, but he wouldn't let go. His face had a mean cast to it that she'd never seen before.

"Don't go thinking you're too good for me," he snarled, giving her wrist a painful wrench. Jo was tempted to smack him, but she was too afraid the boat would tip over, so she said nothing, and Whit inched away from her and turned his focus to the sail. They didn't say anything else the rest of the way back.

"Oh, thank goodness!" Jo cried when Whit pulled the boat near the sand. She didn't wait for him to steady it. She just slid her legs over the side and fell into the surf up to her hips, freeing her hand from his in the process.

Claire was waiting for them on the beach with a pair of fishing poles, squealing in all her eleven-year-old glory. Whit pulled up the centerboard and tugged the dinghy onto the sand while Claire unfolded a ratty blanket she'd brought with her. Jo watched Whit stretch himself out across the plaid and cross his ankles. It was clear he already knew he was someone who would succeed in life without very much effort, and for a moment she envied him that.

Claire started telling him something about her school gymnastics team. "It's not fair that Cecilia West gets to be captain just because she can do a back handspring when she can't even do the splits all the way," she said with a pout. Jo threaded bait onto the first pole's hook, cast the line out into the surf, then anchored the pole in the sand and went to work on the second barb.

"Poor Claire." Whit made a face at her.

She sniffed. "It's harder than it looks. I bet you can't do the splits."

Whit dusted sand off his palm. "You're right, but then I don't want to."

He had Claire there. She flopped back down next to him on the blanket—too close, Jo thought, her stomach still lurching from the boat ride.

"I don't really want to do them either," she said, waving her feet in the air, "but the girls on the gymnastics team are popular, and it's easier to be popular."

Just then Jo caught a fish. She let out a yell and began tugging on the line, reeling it in as fast as she could. Whit sprang off the blanket and rushed over to help, but she waved him away. She already had the fish off the hook, writhing in her palms. Whit stayed at the edge of the surf, his hands in his pockets, his eyes narrowed.

"Claire," Jo called. "Come help me for a minute." She dumped the fish into a bucket. Claire sighed and stretched off the blanket, and for a moment Jo could read on her little sister's face how much she hated all the elements of her life: salt, fish, rust, and sand.

"Check the other line," Jo told her. "I think there's another bite on it." Another fish would be good. Their mother would mull the flaky flesh with potatoes, bay leaves, and broth, and the three of them would bow their heads that evening and thank the Lord for his gift.

Jo saw Claire pull the rod out of the sand and rest it against her hip. A wave rushed in and almost knocked her off balance, but Whit was suddenly there, his sturdy arms looped around her waist, righting her. "Hang on, baby doll," he said, and put his hands on top of Claire's on the reel. "Take it steady and slow." Together they reeled in a mackerel. "Want me to gut it for you?" Whit asked. The fish bucked, then stilled.

Claire considered. "No. We should throw it back."

Whit shrugged. "Whatever you want, kiddo." He handed her the rod, rooted in the tackle box for pliers, pinched the end of the barb, and pried the fish from it. Then he lowered the creature back under the incoming water. It perked up and began thrashing again. "And away you go," Whit said, opening his hands.

Jo splashed closer, watching as the fish flicked its tail, righting itself in the current before swimming away from shore. "What'd you go and do that for, Claire?" she reprimanded. "I swear, you're such a ninny."

Claire turned away, tears building in her eyes, and it was then that Jo saw she had somehow gotten the barb from the mackerel hooked into the center of her palm. A spot of blood shimmered.

"Oh, for goodness' sakes," Jo said, snatching at Claire's wrist. She snipped the hook off the end of the line so she could push it all the way through Claire's hand. It was just like Claire to have to suffer along with a stupid fish, Jo thought. She always did have to be the center of attention. Jo gave the hook a final wrench, and it came free. "You're a worse ninny than I thought," she said, putting the maimed hook in the tackle box. "It doesn't pay to be tender when you work in salt."

Whit gave Claire's shoulder a squeeze. "Aw, leave her alone, Jo. She's sensitive, that's all."

Jo scowled. What did a boy like Whit Turner know about their lives anyway? she thought. Sensitive didn't put dinner on the table. It didn't pay their electricity bill, and it didn't buy Claire the fancy clothes she was always wanting. Jo's own hard work did that, and if Claire was delicate . . . well, that was her problem. Jo threaded a new hook back onto the end of the line and then flicked the rod over her shoulder and cast back out into the surf.

"Come on, Jo." Whit leaned close to her, his breath tickling her neck. "Don't be like that. You know I'd be a catch for you." He put his hand on her back and leaned closer, as if he would try again to kiss her, but she jerked away at the last minute, her heart pounding, her mouth dry, all the little hairs on her arms raised.

"Not in front of Claire," she murmured, though that was far from the real reason she wouldn't kiss him.

He groaned in frustration and stepped away from her. "I've got to return the boat," he said. "I'm supposed to play a tennis match. My mother will be looking for me to go to the club. God, I'd do *anything* to get out of this boring town for the summer. Half my friends are in Europe."

Claire waved wildly with one arm, still sucking on her wounded palm, but Whit ignored her. He ignored Jo, too, refusing to say anything as he pushed the little craft back out through the breakers and filled the sails with wind, disappearing around the point. Jo didn't worry, though. They'd fought before and always made up.

But he didn't come the next week, or the week after that. When she saw him in church, he seemed distracted, keeping his face pointed toward Father Flynn. When he stood up to leave, he still helped his mother out of the pew, nodding to the elderly ladies of the little congregation, but he declined to glance at Jo. After Mass she'd wander the beach alone, morose, dipping her toes in the water. *It's the way it has to be*, she told herself. They were growing up and apart. Everyone had always said that it would happen, and now it finally was. Whit's life was fanning open while hers was closing shut as a clamshell.

———○-○ ○-○———

The salt was running thin that year, so of course Ida soon came sniffing around, cash in hand. Mama would never sell, though, even if it meant they lived on bread and pickles for the entire winter.

"You're a fool, Sarah Gilly," Ida declared through the sagging screen of the porch door as Claire and Jo stood fast behind Mama. "You're never going to have better, but what about your girls? Don't they want out of this place? Maybe not her"—she aimed a bejeweled finger at Jo—"but that one seems like she has potential." She moved her hand toward Claire, who started to puff with pride at this. Jo pinched her. "Think what you could do for her with my money."

At this point Claire shocked them. She was just eleven, but already starting to bloom her way out of childhood. She was pouty, daydreamy, and so averse to the salt that her fair skin sometimes broke out in hives after a day of skimming it, even when she was gloved and covered. "Maybe Ida's right," Claire piped up. "Think about it. I could go to college one day. And Jo . . ." She paused. "Well, Jo could do something," she finally said. "Why don't we take Ida's money?"

At that moment Jo wanted nothing more than to reach across and slap her sister silly, but Mama was always more forgiving when it came to Claire. She reached under Claire's chin with one finger and stared into her green eyes. "That's the problem," Mama said. "It will always be Ida's money. Don't you worry. If college is what you want, I got ways and means. Ida's not the only bank in town." And then, without further explanation, she told Ida to get off her porch and stay the hell away from her land.

"Where is Whit anyway?" Claire demanded after Ida left. "He hasn't been around at all this summer." She pouted. "He said he'd teach me chess."

Jo picked at the broken piano's keys, filling the hall with discordant notes. "You wouldn't like chess none," she said.

Claire stuck her arms akimbo. "I'd like it better than all this." For a moment Jo felt bad for her little sister. She was still just a kid, but nothing in her life indulged the whims of youth. Jo peered through the screen at the marsh's pools. They looked rather like a chessboard, but the rules out here were very different from anything Whit Turner would know about, with his fancy boarding school and fancier new friends, and the sooner Claire got that through her thick head, the better. Jo closed the front door, ignoring the heat.

"This is all we have," she said, and turned on her heel.

Still, it hurt when Jo stepped into the diner the next day to deliver salt and saw Whit sitting with a blond girl at the counter. She wasn't anyone Jo recognized from town, but a summer girl, high above Jo's station in life. She was wearing a madras skirt, a grosgrain ribbon in her hair, and shoes so white they made Jo's heart speed up. Whit blushed a furious red when he spotted Jo, and then he put his arm around the girl and swiveled his stool so his back was to her.

"Can we get some more fries here for my friend, old man?" he drawled, lazy as anything, winking at Mr. Hopper.

Jo dropped the bag of salt on the counter, her breath a hot animal in her chest. "You can pay me next time," she told Mr. Hopper. "I have to go." Keeping her eyes down, she hustled out of the diner before Whit decided to say anything. She wanted to rip the ribbon out of the girl's hair, muss up her skirt, and stomp on her silly white shoes. *Someone*, Jo thought, *should straighten that girl out*. Someone should tell her that love didn't waltz up to you while you were sitting at a diner counter swinging your feet, that it was in fact more like pulling a twelve-hour day in the marsh—something you had to work up to slowly before you could really stand it on a regular basis.

But that wasn't something easily said. Jo hadn't ever told it to Claire, after all, who could have used it the most, and given that general failing, what business did she have informing anyone else? No business, that's what. No one wanted to hear her story anyway, she thought as she straightened her spine and started back toward the farm. Considering her history with Whit, maybe that was for the best.

———○-○ ○-○———

Although Jo kept catching glimpses of Whit around town—at church, of course, and in the narrow aisles of Mr. Upton's store, or as he cruised down Bank Street at the helm of his family's convertible—the encounters felt harried and uncomfortable to her. Whit always clearly saw her, but he never acknowledged her, or if he did, it was invariably in a snide manner that Jo found bewildering. "Hey, Gilly girl," he'd call, "how's the salt treating you?" And then, just when Jo thought things couldn't get any worse, they did. On the second-to-last weekend of the summer, right before Whit was due to return to boarding school, Ida Turner had the poor grace to up and die, and life for everyone in Prospect ground to a spectacular halt.

The Turners never said what the actual cause of death was, but rumors flew along Bank Street, whipping through queues in the post office and the pharmacy, turning heads at the diner, and lingering in the aisles of Mr. Upton's grocery.

"I heard it was a heart attack," Timothy Weatherly said at the hardware counter, plunking down a quarter sack of nails and a length of rubber hosing. Dotty Friend, the proprietor's buxom wife, snorted and rolled her eyes.

"That's not possible. That woman had no heart. I bet you it was some kind of cancer and that she had it awhile. That would explain why she was so skinny."

Timothy Weatherly worked the plug of tobacco in his mouth and thought about that. Whatever had gotten Ida must have been something terrible indeed. At least more terrible than *she* had been.

Per Ida's instructions all the town flags were flown at half-staff for three days following her death, and the windows of the municipal buildings were draped in black crepe. Jo's mother shrieked with victory when she heard the news and then insisted on presenting herself at Ida's funeral swathed in a giant red shawl. The three of them squeezed into a pew at the back of the packed church.

"Besides her being a Turner and trying to grab up all our land, why did you hate her so much?" Claire whispered to Mama. Frankly, she said, she personally admired Ida. At least she'd traveled off the Cape and seen a little of the world, which was more than Claire could claim for her own sorry self. "Is it possible she wasn't really so awful?" she asked as Jo eyed the brass-and-mahogany coffin covered with wreaths of expensive and fragrant roses. Flowers like that were fit for a queen, Jo thought. It seemed a shame to waste them on the dead.

"Shh," Mama admonished. "Listen, Claire. Ida Turner came straight up from dirt, and now she's about to go back in it. Along the way she snatched everything she could and cast off anything she thought would weigh her down. You don't want to be like that."

After the service they waited in line to shake hands with Whit and his father, Hamish. By the time their turn came, the church was empty.

"I'm sorry for your loss," Claire's mother said primly, her red shawl giving away her real sentiments. "Ida was . . . someone we won't soon forget."

"Condolences," was all Jo said. Whit held her hand longer than she was comfortable with, however, longer than convention dictated.

"Jo . . ." he began, but she stepped away from him before he could get anything else out. Whit always did like to have the last word. This time she'd let him.

———o-o o-o———

After Ida's passing, the sky lowered and turned a shade darker, the pear tree's anemic leaves began skittering off the branches, and banks of clouds threatened but did not bring rain. The summer people began packing up and leaving, and the afternoon winds cooled. Jo started counting the days until Whit left town again. She didn't hold out hope for any sort of formal good-bye, certainly not given his family's current circumstances, so she was surprised to catch him lurking at the edge of the marsh on his final morning in town. He was making notes, she saw, in a tiny leather notebook.

"Solving for x?" she asked, dropping her wooden paddle on the narrow dike between two collecting basins.

He looked up but didn't smile. "Something like that." But Jo knew Whit too well for small talk. He didn't look right. He had dark semicircles smeared under his eyes and the sickly cast of someone who hadn't seen the sun for days. His hands shook when he jotted in his book. Jo stepped closer and peered at what he was writing. It looked like some kind of accounting. Dollar signs and scribbles filled the pages, along with too many minus signs.

"Looks like you're short a bob or two," Jo joked, and then she recoiled as Whit kicked at the dirt. He was in no mood for joking.

"That's what my father told me," he said, wiping a tear away from his cheek. "We've overextended ourselves. We own a lot, but none of it is going up. No more new sailboats for me, he said. There's enough for my education and a few extras, and that's about it. When I'm done with college, I get to come back here"—he squinted spitefully around the marsh—"and fill my father's shoes. 'I hope you'll do a better job of it, son,' he told me. 'And I hope you leave off your mother's foolishness.'"

Jo cocked her head. "Fool" was one word she'd never have applied to Ida. "What do you mean?"

Whit sniffed. "Mother was always

banging on about this place. I guess she had the idea that if she could get her hands on it, if she only had the salt to her name and could harness its power, the family coffers would fill right back up. But she left one curious thing in her will. It said I was forbidden ever to marry you. That if I did, I would be immediately disinherited."

Jo paled. "That's ridiculous," she said. "And if the salt could be controlled, do you think we'd be as close to the bone as we are?" Whit was clearly grief-addled, but she understood that instead of mourning like a normal human being he had taken on his mother's cause of trying to snatch up the farm, as if he could cancel out his recent loss by gaining something Ida had always wanted so badly. But things didn't work that way on Salt Creek Farm. In the marsh, loss was permanent and irrevocable. "Give it up," Jo said. "The salt's not going to bring back what your family lost, and this land will *never* sit in Turner hands. Your mother needn't have worried about you marrying me for that."

Whit flipped his notebook closed, stuffed it in his pocket, then rocked back on his heels, his composure regained. He looked down his nose at Jo like he'd just dealt her a crooked hand of cards. When they were younger, Jo reflected, his impish cheating had been charming and funny, but now it had an edge to it that was unsettling. She saw that she was never going to crack the beetle shell he'd grown around him while he was away—not today, not tomorrow, probably never.

"I don't exactly get how the salt works, Jo," he said. "But my mother was no fool, and if she thought it would save our family's legacy . . . well, I'm not going to drop this." And without saying anything else, he turned and sauntered back down the lane, whistling as if he were happy, when Jo knew better.

"It'll be a cold day in hell before you have any say over the salt, Whit Turner!" she shouted after him, but he pretended that he didn't hear. Secretly Jo worried a little that Whit had more up his sleeve than she knew.

Mama shrugged off those concerns when Jo came into the kitchen and related what had happened. She turned back to her bread dough, kneading the knot of it in smooth, even turns. "Don't be stupid," she said. "Plots like Whit's don't just pop out at you like a jack-in-the-box toy. The future gets laid brick by plain old brick, so slow you don't even know it's happening."

"I guess you're right," Jo mumbled.

Mama smacked her palms together and flipped the bread over on the counter. She paused, the mass of deflated dough spread in front of her, possibility risen and punched back down by her own two hands. "Of course I am," she said, but her fingers stayed stuck in the dough, and Jo knew she was thinking about the day that Henry had drowned, how Mama had been standing in the kitchen then, too, and how it must have been a kind of explosion, that moment, when all her worries about the future collided with all the bad luck from her past, and how Jo was the spark of that combustion, another brick in the wall of her mother's daily misery.

"Let me," Jo said, nudging Mama over at the counter and placing her own hands in the bread.

"Thank you," Mama said, her voice husky, her back stiff.

"Next time I see Whit," Jo said, beginning to roll and push the dough with the same even strokes as her mother, "I'll remind him again that we're stuck to this land like barnacles."

"Make that man-eating barnacles," Mama said, and Jo laughed, rolling the dough in an easy swoop, passing it from one hand to the other, paying as little attention to it as she did to the act of combing her straight brown hair or buttoning her work shirt in the morning.

It was the last time she'd ever do anything so easy again.

Chapter Eight

The leaves were just beginning to kindle into russet the afternoon Ethan returned from his final fishing trip the summer after he and Claire graduated, in 1967. As always, they'd agreed to meet under the town's pear tree at sunset. Claire was wearing a new skirt she'd sewn, and her bare legs were starting to get cold as the sun went down. She was casting an eye around her, making sure no other amorous couples were headed for the shrubbery, when she heard a disembodied voice rise out of the thickening dusk.

"Whoever it is, he's not the one for you." She turned to see Whit Turner ducking into the shadow of the tree. She seemed to run into him when she least wanted to. He'd stayed in town after graduating college, just as everyone predicted, but he'd kept a careful distance from Claire's family. Whenever he and Jo saw each other in town, they pointedly ignored one another, but whenever he saw Claire, he usually winked, unless he was close enough for him to give her hair a twitch the way he used to when she was a child. Before she could stop him, he edged close to her and did that now, and she shivered. His fingers lingered along her blouse collar. "Definitely not the one for you," he said again.

"How would you know?" She stretched her back along the tree, wishing Whit would leave, but he just grinned and stepped even closer.

"Because I know all about you Gilly girls. Remember when"—he slid his thumb lower on her neck, down to the spot where her pulse beat—"you caught that fish and made me throw it back, and then you hooked your hand? I bet you're not so tender-handed now."

"I am, actually," Claire said, wrenching her neck away from his fingers, though he was more right than she wanted to let on. The fish had been a beautiful creature, Claire recalled, its belly a milky white, its scales the mottled greens and blues of a mermaid. Its gills had puffed in the palms of her hands, and its eye had been a fixed dial of panic as it opened and closed its mouth, loathing its fate but unable to do anything about it either, a dilemma Claire understood perfectly well. Whit had helped her to free the fish, and when he did, the hook had snagged in the center of her palm. Jo was the one who'd had to come over and push the barb all the way through Claire's skin.

It had stung something awful, but Jo hadn't cared. She'd called Claire a ninny for letting the fish go. She often called Claire names when she did something silly, but Claire knew that her sister was wrong about her, one hundred percent. She wasn't a ninny, and she wasn't sensitive. She just knew what to release and what to bother fighting for in life, and she was certain it didn't involve salt. She lifted her chin. "Jo's the one who hasn't changed, if you want to know."

Whit put his hands back into his pockets. When he answered, his voice could have chilled winter. "She knows why I've kept my distance from her." This was news to Claire. She had always thought it was the other way around between them. But before she could follow that thread of thought, she saw Ethan stepping through the evening shadows, and her heart set up a clattering so hard she was surprised that Whit couldn't hear it, too.

"I have to go," she said, tearing herself away from the tree trunk and rushing out from under its leafy canopy. She could still feel Whit there, though, lurking under the restless red leaves, his gaze sticking the way a ball of sap would in her hair, snarling so hard the only way to get it out would be with a pair of scissors and a good clean cut. No longer caring if Whit was watching, she ran to Ethan and threw her arms around his broad shoulders, pressing her face close to his chest and breathing him in. He still smelled like the sea, of places Claire would never go and things she would never witness. She pressed her nose against the side of his neck and blew against his skin, hoping to infuse him with homier smells of grass and mud and ripening pears.

"I missed you so much," she said as he kissed her and they made their way back under the tree, where she was relieved to see that Whit was gone. She spread her hands flat against the bare skin of Ethan's back, warm and hard from long days in the sun. She inched her fingers into the waistband of his jeans and felt him hesitate for a split second before he drew her closer.

Kissing Ethan always felt like a marvelous experiment that Claire was conducting. She unbuttoned his shirt while he slid her T-shirt higher, his other hand busy under her skirt. "Wait," she breathed, not quite believing that she was the one breaking things off. "We should stop." But he surprised her. Without a word he laid her down in the hollow amid the shrubbery, and when she struggled to sit up, he pulled her down against him.

"Are you sure?" she said. It wasn't the way she had planned this moment—under the pear tree and in the open like this—but it was thrilling, too.

Ethan grazed his lips across her breasts. "I need you, Claire. I know that now."

She ran her fingers through his thick blond hair and wondered what had happened to him out in the Atlantic, but the wind picked up and he moved over her, and then she stopped thinking at all. She leaned back onto the damp grass and the sandy earth, her hand grazing the trunk of the tree, its bark nicked and carved in a riot of communal desire, and, being young and in love, she assumed she had history trumped.

———o-o o-o———

"I'm getting married," she whispered to herself when she woke up the next morning. She threw the covers back and walked over to her dresser mirror, wondering if she looked different to anyone else but herself. She put her hands to her cheeks, feeling how hot they were, and tried to quit smiling.

Ethan hadn't exactly proposed the night before, but what else could their lovemaking have meant? He always said he didn't want to go all the way until they were engaged. Actually, when Claire thought about it, he hadn't said much of anything, but that didn't bother her. Ethan rarely talked as much as she did. Afterward he had walked her all the way back to the edge of the marsh, his fingers squeezing hers until they passed St. Agnes. He suddenly dropped her hand, but she'd taken it back in her own. She could do that now, she reasoned.

"I won't tell Father Flynn if you don't," she'd whispered, but he didn't laugh. He never did when it came to anything religious. Claire couldn't even tell priest jokes in front of him. She wondered if Ethan's devotions would loosen in married life or if hers would tighten to match his. They'd rounded the corner, and the marsh had appeared before them, some of the basins shimmering, some just empty holes. In the moonlight the place looked worse than haunted. It just appeared worn out, too plain even for ghosts. Claire had turned to kiss Ethan good night but found he was already beating her to it.

"Claire, let's talk tomorrow," he'd murmured, his thumb tracing the outline of her jaw.

She'd tried to hide her smile. She wanted a long wedding dress, she knew, but now she supposed it would have to be ivory. "Okay," she'd said, too happy to add anything else. He'd walked away without kissing her one last time like she wanted, but she forgave him. After all, they were going to have a lifetime of embraces ahead of them.

She was waiting for him early in the dunes the next afternoon. She bit her lips, trying to force some color into them so they would look rosy when Ethan bent to kiss her. She hoped she would like her ring.

But something was wrong. Ethan only brushed his lips against her cheek, and he didn't linger as long as usual.

He didn't lean over and thread his fingers along the base of her skull or pull her in tight to him. In fact, he kissed her more like a brother might a sister. Claire settled down next to him in the sand, confused.

"Before I say anything, you should know that last night was amazing," he began. "It was everything I thought it would be. More, even. If I was looking for a sign, Claire, I swear, I would have said that last night was it."

She blushed and stared down at her tennis shoes. In the daylight she couldn't believe some of the places she'd let him put his mouth and where she'd put hers. She reached up now and brushed his hair, wondering when they could be together again. "I love you," she said.

He pulled her hand away. "Let me finish. I have something very difficult to tell you."

Her heart quit pounding. It quit doing anything at all. It was a frightening sensation, really, like dying on the spot without going anywhere. Above her she watched clouds rearrange themselves.

Ethan bent forward and leaned his

head against his knees. "You know how important church has always been to me, but what you don't know is that for months now I've been debating joining the priesthood. The only thing stopping me was the thought of having to give you up. I even applied to a seminary, but I never heard from them, and then this whole season when I was at sea, all I could think about was you, and I figured it was a sign. Last night I thought I knew exactly what I was going to do: propose today. But after I dropped you off here, I stopped into St. Agnes to see Father Flynn, and he gave me this."

He pulled out a folded letter embossed with seals and a crest. Claire took it from him and then realized she was trying to read it upside down. Ethan turned it around for her. It was an acceptance letter from a seminary. Ethan had applied in February, right around Valentine's Day.

"I don't understand," she mumbled through numb lips, ignoring the print in front of her.

Ethan sighed. "Claire, being with you was as wonderful as I always thought it would be. It was even close to prayer, but when Father Flynn gave me this letter, I realized that it *wasn't* prayer, and I really think I'm called to that path."

She buried one hand in the sand. "You think or you know?"

"I know. Believe me, Claire, this is just as hard for me as it is for you."

She choked back a sob. "I doubt it."

He hung his head. "If I go, I have to leave next week." His finger underlined a phrase in the letter. "They're willing to give me a full scholarship. It's the opportunity of a lifetime."

There was nothing to lean on in the dunes. No boulder propped in the sand, no split logs. Just sand and spiky grass. Claire bent over her own legs. "Where?"

Ethan took a breath. "California." It was so far that it sounded final. His voice softened. "Be honest. You wouldn't be happy if I stayed and went out on the boats every year with my uncle and my dad. You're about as suited to a life of fish, Claire, as you are to one of salt."

She squeezed her hands into fists, trying to get her blood to circulate, but it didn't help. Her fingers were freezing. *All this time*, she thought, *I was never really first with him*. That was the thing that hurt the most. She'd spent her whole life trailing in someone else's muddy footsteps, she realized: her mother's, her dead brother's, Jo's. Not to mention the entire scraggly line of Gilly women before her. Even the poems that Ethan loved so much were just someone else's words. She stood up and dusted off the seat of her overalls.

"I have to go." She wished she could have said it the way she felt it. She wished she could have poisoned the phrase. But it came out as a lament. She wanted to hate Ethan, but she couldn't, and that made her want to hate him more.

He folded up the letter, shoved it back into his pocket, and then stood up, too. "I could come back later."

"For what?"

Ethan's eyes swam. "Come on, Claire. We should talk about this more. Just because I'm choosing this path doesn't mean we shouldn't stay friends."

She ground her teeth. "That's exactly what it means, Ethan Stone." Her blood was flowing high again—a reassuring tide that was spilling up and out of her. "You've no idea what you've just done." Tears were already leaking down her cheeks. Before more could fall, she turned and ran.

By the time she reached the salt barn, every element on earth was clashing inside her—stone and wood, water and ash. And the only one of them she wanted to entertain was fire. She kicked the barn doors open, making dust devils, and entered the dark of the place, rummaging in the broken barrow for a packet of cigarettes she'd hidden.

Jo's voice materialized out of the gloom. "Goddamn it, Claire. Where have you been? The ponds need scraping."

The first match didn't take. Her hands were shaking too badly. Same for the second one, but the third one was the charm. Perhaps too much so. The air in front of Claire flared with sulfur and nicotine, and then there was another flash, a bigger one down where she'd thrown the charred match. The dust in the barn began dancing.

"What is that?" she tried to say, wondering if her grief was making her see things, and then realized it was smoke. She turned and saw a rush of flames clawing across the floor, blocking the door, trapping her in the back corner of the barn. She tried to breathe, but her lungs felt like they were on fire, too. Suddenly she focused. She still had the lit cigarette in her hand. Stupidly, she threw it down, and it started a new line of tiny flames.

She tried to call to Jo, but her lungs were closing up and she couldn't get the sound out. Then she thought she heard Jo yelling something. What was it? Her vision started blurring. It probably included the words "I told you so," Claire thought. It would be just like Jo, who spent her days patrolling the squared-off hollows of Salt Creek Farm, to want to maintain boundaries at a time like this. Claire's knees started to buckle. Clearly, Jo's rules were a line Claire was never going to toe, just as she was never going to do a lot of things—leave this stupid marsh, marry Ethan, make her way out of this burning barn.

"Claire!" She heard her name again just as the first flames roared back toward her. Her legs gave out entirely, but for the first time in her life she found that she wasn't stuck in Jo's footsteps. Instead she was cradled in her sister's arms, and then she was pitched through the air, free.

"Jo . . ." she tried to choke out, but there was a huge crash, a fountain of spitting embers, and she ran out of oxygen. In the distance she heard a siren, and then she turned her head as the barn came down, throwing her hands up over her eyes, unwilling to watch any more of what her broken heart had wrought.

Chapter Nine

At first Jo thought Claire might have been trying to kill her when she set the barn on fire, but later, after she found out that Ethan had run off to join the damn priesthood, she decided that maybe Claire had simply been trying to kill herself and Jo had just gotten in her way. That would be more typical of Claire, Jo thought, who tended to conduct her affairs like a mad dog on the hunt. She went where instinct told her and never stopped to consider the poor creatures she might flush out into the open.

Claire had been a pain in the ass all that summer, mooning over Ethan and not doing much else. Mama hadn't been well, and even more of the burden of the marsh was teetering on Jo's shoulders, which were sturdy enough, but even she had her limits.

The fire Claire had started that day did more than tear Jo's body in half. It split her memory, too, for whenever she tried to compose a whole picture from that evening, all she ever wound up with were a handful of molten fragments, and she couldn't ever do much with those except scoop them together and return them to the flames. The thing she most recalled was how fast Claire had disappeared behind the shifting blaze. One minute Jo was telling her not to light her stupid cigarette, and the next Claire was just the outline of a girl consumed by sparks and a wall of smoke. It was like a magician's trick gone wrong, and Jo's only thought had been that if she didn't get Claire out of that barn, she would disappear for good, and Jo had had enough of people disappearing out of her life.

Jo ended up burned on almost 40 percent of her body, all of it on her right side. For weeks she lay cocooned in the special burn unit in Boston, moist bandages covering her seared skin and eyes, drifting in and out of consciousness. Even though she couldn't remember actually saving Claire, she had an impression of her sister's bird-thin wrist gripped in her palm and of the weight of Claire's bones. But the details—whether she'd carried or dragged Claire, whether they'd escaped out a window or the flaming doors—were fuzzy. According to Mama, Jo had thrown Claire from the barn doorway and then gotten trapped when the beams came down, but the person she wanted to ask about that was Claire herself. Whenever she fought her way up through the haze of drugs and pain, however, Claire was never there. And then one afternoon she suddenly was, her voice trilling and rising like a bird in pain.

"No," she was pleading. "Please don't make me. I know what she did for me, but Jo's so strong, and I'm not like her. Please."

"But your sister's already endured so much trauma," another voice responded, a female's, lower in register, weary with a hint of impatience laced behind it. It was Dr. Meyer, the only female doctor Jo had ever known. "It's still an experimental procedure, but we've had wonderful success with the ones we've performed. We would take the skin from your buttock area," she was explaining, "and graft it onto your sister. Normally we like to use skin from the patient herself, but in this case we think you'd be the best match to prevent donor rejection."

No one spoke. To Jo it felt as if the sanitized hospital air had turned back into a cloud of oily smoke. *How bad is it?* she wondered. She hadn't yet been able to open her eyes or see herself, but everything about her hurt.

Dr. Meyer spoke again. "You don't have to decide today, but we need to know soon. This could make an enormous difference to your sister."

There was another silence in the room, but this one was a thick sort of silence, like a pillow being pressed over a sleeping person's face. Then Jo heard her mother pull the doctor to the far corner of the room and start whispering. Lying blinded for so many days had made Jo weirdly attuned to the quietest of noises. Through the fog of drugs, she tried to pick out her mother's hushed speech. *Nor'easter. Two, not one. Our Lady.* She quit listening. It was a story she already knew.

"I see," Jo heard the doctor say. Now Dr. Meyer knew it, too. Jo rolled her swollen tongue in her mouth and tried to squeeze the walls of her throat together to make a sound, but she only managed to moan.

"Joanna?" Dr. Meyer's clothing rustled as she approached and bent over the bed, checking equipment, flipping open her chart. Jo moaned again and tried to move her head, but the bees in her brain escaped to her skin, stinging with such venom that she gasped.

"Lie still," the doctor commanded, and she rang for a nurse.

Jo heard Claire step to the other side of her, the long red ends of her hair brushing the sheets. Even without sight

Jo could picture Claire's face, as milky and smooth as a piece of sea glass. The fire had not touched even an inch of her, Jo was guessing. She'd made sure of that. But, of course, Claire was nursing her own wounds.

"She hasn't spoken to Ethan once," Mama had told Jo in one of the long hours she'd spent sitting vigil by Jo's bedside. "She won't see him, and he's due to leave in just a few days. She won't hardly speak to no one."

Claire was talking now, though. "I called Whit for you," she breathed in Jo's ear, her breath even then tinged with a trace of tobacco. "I thought you'd want me to. He says—" She hesitated, and in her voice Jo detected a small channel of envy she'd never noticed before. "He says he sends his best regards. He asked me to give them to you for him. So here." Claire leaned down closer, careful not to touch any part of Jo except her left side, and pecked her with cherry-scented lips. Jo wondered if Claire was being cautious or calculating, for she had picked her good side, the part of her that could still get hurt. She listened to Claire's light footsteps retreat down the hall like rain slipping off a roof, and in spite of herself she began to ponder all the things Claire hadn't said. *Forgive me*, for instance, or *Thank you*, or *I love you*. Her steps disappeared, and Jo lay there trapped in a charred cocoon of skin, wondering what to call someone who was kin, yes, but also the better half of her flesh, the ambulatory part, walking all the paths Jo now knew she was never going to get to.

———o-o o-o———

At first the hospital staff seemed concerned about Jo's mental faculties. They kept asking her if she knew what year it was and who the president was, which she did. "Lyndon B. Johnson," she croaked, wanting to add that he had a face like a dried-apple doll and a personality to match, but lacking the energy to do so. Her vocal cords hurt just from breathing.

Above all, the doctors and nurses liked to warn her about her future. "Your life won't be like it was before," Dr.

Meyer told her in her deadpan fashion, flipping through charts and scribbling notes all at once. "Not right away. But after some time, you will begin to feel like your old self inside."

"New skin for a new soul," Bea, her favorite nurse, clucked. "Now's your chance to become whoever you wanted, honey. Just go for it."

"Take it day by day." That was Raymond, the night orderly. "Real slow. It's better that way." Jo thought maybe that's why he'd chosen to work nights, because he liked to stay in the dark.

Three months later, when the nurses finally peeled back her bandages and masks and she got her hands on a mirror, Jo figured out why she'd become a lightning rod for other people's concern. Her face had melted into a contradiction in flesh, tattered and seared on the right side and perfectly preserved on the left, as if her whole self had been forever stopped in one burning moment. People never knew which side to look at when they were talking to her, she discovered, and she couldn't help them out any, for she didn't know herself yet which half she desired to inflict on the world.

She was fitted with a new glass eye that she could pop out of her socket and roll in the palm of her hand like an egg if she wanted. "You'll have to develop strategies to compensate for the loss of vision," Dr. Wynn, her portly ophthalmologist, chirped in the British accent that Jo sometimes found annoying and sometimes soothing. "Driving will be challenging. You will need to exercise caution when it comes to stairs and uneven terrain, but on the whole you'll make out fine, I should think. What do you do for a profession?"

Jo settled her forehead into the metal band of the complicated machine in front of her, resting her chin on the foam pad. She fought off the image of cows lining up in an abattoir. "Salt," she murmured, running her tongue over her teeth, missing the crunch of gray salt between them. The hospital food was so bland. "My family scrapes salt and sells it." Dr. Wynn adjusted a dial, and a miniature sun seemed to ignite in Jo's remaining eye. She struggled not to blink.

"Do you really? Now, that's absolutely fascinating. Have you ever baked a salt-crusted fish?" When Jo didn't answer, he continued on, adjusting knobs and dials on his side of the examining contraption. "You take a whole fish," he chortled, "bury it under a mound of salt mixed with egg whites, and then pop it in the oven for a few hours." He switched off the light shining in her eye. "Sounds dreadful, but it's absolutely scrumptious. Try it."

She blinked, still shocked by the way her eyelid curved over the glass like a tongue skimming a tooth. It was the only smooth thing on that side of her body. Jo felt her real eye grow heavy and wondered if she would only cry half as much now, or if her body would just send all its grief scooting over to her remaining eye. It didn't seem like a fair arrangement to have twice as much sorrow jamming up a single outlet, but Jo wouldn't have been surprised to find out that that was how things were going to work from now on.

"Here." Dr. Wynn spun around on his metal stool and handed her a prescription for eyedrops. He wasn't nearly as old as his speech made him sound, Jo realized. From certain angles he was almost even handsome, if also balding and a little paunchy. But he made up for it with his kind gaze.

"How's your family handling all this?" he asked, and Jo didn't answer. Mama had been a rock, but Claire had only come to see Jo three times—once when she'd refused to donate the skin graft, once when Jo had the first surgery on her face, and once when Jo had a fever so high that devils could have danced on the ceiling and she would have called them blessed.

"Claire doesn't like the hospital," Mama had tried to explain. "You know that. She's still so young. And you know how teenagers are—wrapped up in their own lives."

No, Jo had wanted to snap. *I have no idea how teenagers are. I never got to be one.*

Dr. Wynn's voice broke into her

thoughts. "You'll need to use these for the first few weeks until everything is fully healed. The dosage is written at the top." His plump forefinger under-lined a row of chicken scratch on the page, which Jo pretended to decipher.

She reached out and accepted the paper. "Thank you."

It was time for her to stand up, which still occurred in stages: first the dulled soles of her feet applied to the ground, then a rickety heaving of knees, hip bones, shoulders, and finally her head. None of her seemed to go together the same way it used to.

Dr. Wynn cleared his throat. "Take care of that eye, then," he said, and Jo wondered if he meant her real eye or the fake one. "Call if there are any prob-lems, and remember that a blind leap of faith is more than just an expres-sion."

He closed his office door, leaving her to shuffle and grope her way to the or-derly, pondering whether it still counted as a leap if her feet never left the ground.

———o-o o-o———

The next morning Mama drove her home, stopping as they neared the long, sandy lane to wind down the car windows. It was the tail end of the cold season, and the frosted air stirred up the ends of what was left of Jo's cropped hair. She had missed the fall and most of the winter. Two seasons gone.

"That's better," Mama said. She'd grown so thin over the past few months, Jo noted. The worry over Jo's health and the crushing burden of the medical bills was taking its toll, but Mama still sat straight as a sergeant, her hands at two and ten o'clock on the wheel. "Good salt air," she said. "Makes a solid change from that hospital. A solid change."

Even with a single eye, Jo could see that nothing on Salt Creek Farm was any different—only the season. Then they rounded the last corner and she spied the black scar where the barn had stood. It had been skeletal before the accident, but now there was only a suggestion of a structure. One charred beam remained, stuck up into the sky like a bony middle finger. "What about the salt?" she asked.

Mama set her lips and pushed her foot down a little on the gas. "Gone good. But there's more where it came from."

Jo couldn't argue as she touched the new geography of her face. The nerves that hadn't died were in full revolt. They screamed at the contact with her fingers, but she clenched her teeth and took deep, even breaths. Mama was trying so hard, she knew, and she didn't want to ruin this moment for anything, but she couldn't help asking the one question that was sure to make the pain worse. "Where's Claire?" she asked.

Mama's voice gave nothing away. "Claire's at a stenographers' course in Hyannis. She'll be home later."

Jo turned her face back to the landscape she knew so well. Here she was, finally home, and her sister was still looking for ways to leave. Nothing had changed after all.

———o-o o-o———

As usual, Jo heard Claire coming before she saw her. Claire had a tendency
to bang into the house like a burst of
chilly wind, all fury and impatience. Jo
heard her dump her books onto the old
piano in the hall, one of the volumes
knocking against the warped keys, and
listened to the thunk of her shoes hitting the bare floor as Claire kicked them
off. Jo peeked around the corner of the
kitchen door with her good eye and
watched as Claire paused to scrape
her hair back into a messy ponytail.
With her feet planted and her arms upraised like that, she looked like a half-
assembled scarecrow. She glanced up,
spotted Jo, and froze. Jo's instinct was
to duck behind the door again, but she
fought the urge and emerged into the
hallway, still dragging her right leg a little, watching as Claire took her first real
look at her since the hospital.

Jo still had bandages covering much
of her torso, but the loose clothing her
mother had fished out of her closet dis-
guised those. Her hair was growing
back in, but not well. She had only a
few tufts on the right side of her scalp,

wispy and undecided as baby hair. The doctors said that would fill in and expand over time, but for now Jo knew that it looked problematic. And of course there was the flat glare of her new glass eye.

Claire let out a squeak and stumbled back against the door. "I didn't know you'd be here already," she said with one hand on her chest. "I thought you and Mama were due home tomorrow."

Jo shrugged. "They let me go a day early."

Claire took a faltering breath. "That's good, right?"

"Does it look that way to you?"

"No, I guess not." Claire bowed her head and tapped her fingers against the door. Jo could tell how much she wanted to fling it open and run through it.

Just to make her miserable, Jo stepped closer to her. "You never came to visit."

Claire blinked. "That's not true. I did."

"Not often."

Claire looked down at her fingers, white and delicate as lily petals. Even before the fire, Jo's hands had never looked like that. "I've been taking a course," she said, half sheepish, half proud. Jo felt a twinge of her own guilt. Any chance that Claire would have to attend college had gone up in smoke with the barn. Burn therapy didn't come cheap.

She lifted her gaze from Claire's alabaster hands. "Mama told me. Stenography, right?"

Claire nodded, and it was then that Jo saw the semicircles of grief ringed underneath her sister's eyes. Her skin looked pale, her cheekbones had grown sharper, and for the first time since high school she hadn't bothered with her clothes. She was wearing a moth-eaten sweater that used to be Jo's, jeans with the bottoms rolled, and no makeup. She put her hands over her face, and Jo knew she was going to try to apologize. "Oh, my God, Jo, I'm so sorry," she said. "You always told me not to smoke in the barn, and I didn't listen. I'm so stupid."

Jo was willing to grant her that. Claire looked up, her face tear-streaked and miserable. "Will you ever be able to forgive me?"

Jo hesitated. She knew what the right answer should be, and she thought she was prepared to give it, but her heart couldn't force her mouth to utter the words. Not charred the way it was. Not just then. "I don't know," she admitted, and immediately regretted it.

Claire nodded slowly and folded her arms back around herself. "Okay," she whispered. She turned on her heel and crept upstairs without saying one word more while Jo stood alone in the hall, her new eye hanging heavy in its socket, a bunch of unused words taking up all the extra space in her mouth, squashing her tongue to a loose pulp.

The next morning Mama suggested that the two of them take a walk out to St. Agnes. "You need the exercise after being cooped up so long," she said to Jo. "And it will be good for you to see a familiar face." Jo scowled, not sure she wanted to see anyone outside the family yet, but resisting Mama was about as useless as swimming against a tide.

For Jo, unaccustomed to the exercise, the stroll was a painful stretch of skin and will, but complaining wouldn't have done any good. Mama just would have shushed her. The only other creatures out that morning were the gulls, and they cared only about the worries of their own kind.

Jo was relieved when they arrived at St. Agnes. She took a deep breath of the familiar air, rich with beeswax and lemon polish, and knelt next to her mother at Our Lady's feet, but her mind wouldn't quiet. What was there left to pray for? she wondered. The only real thing she longed for was to swing back time, but not even the Virgin could grant her that.

She lit a candle for Henry, and then Father Flynn entered the sanctuary. Mama dug in her handbag and drew out a small bag of salt.

"Give this to the father," she said, handing it to Jo, who took it with a scowl. She knew what her mother was doing. Right from day one in the hospital, Mama had always told Jo she wouldn't let her hide behind her scars, and now she was making good on her word. "Go on," she said, giving Jo a nudge. "You're still going to have to look folks straight in the eye. Now's your first chance."

Father Flynn took the bag of salt from her carefully and then ran his hands lightly in front of her face, as if he wanted to touch her but thought better of it. "God acts with peculiar reason, child," he finally said. "His methods are not always known to us—" He paused. Jo studied his face, which was turned toward the portrait of Our Lady. "I won't say it's for the best," he said at last, flicking his eyes back to her. "I certainly won't ever say that. But you may, over the course of your life, come to see this pain as a blessing in disguise."

Jo had her doubts about the truth of that, but instead of offending Father Flynn with her bad attitude, she regarded the Virgin. "I guess I'm just like her now," she said. "A lady that's gone and lost her looks."

Father Flynn hesitated again. He had never been fond of the painting, Jo knew, so his reply surprised her. "Why, there's a little of the Virgin in every woman, child. Your own mother knows that better than most."

Jo glanced toward Mama, who was still kneeling in front of the candles, hands clasped, lips fluttering in silent prayer. "Don't go bringing up tales you're not prepared to tell, Father," Jo snapped, and the old priest paled.

"Jo, what do you mean?" The hurt in his eyes made him look like a boy who'd just lost his favorite ball.

"Magna est veritas, et praevalibet," Jo said, steadily regarding him with her one good eye. "What does that mean?"

Father Flynn stammered. "Why, it's from the Vulgate, the old Latin version of the Bible. It means 'Truth is great and it will prevail.' What a curious thing to ask. Why do you bring it up, child?"

Jo shrugged. It was a line she remembered from Ida's letter. She wanted to see Father Flynn's reaction when she uttered it. She had never been so vile to Father Flynn before—she realized that—but she was a new person, was she not? Now she had layers to herself that even she couldn't identify. For the first time in her life, she could see why people were tempted by cruelty. There was an electrifying fizz to it.

"No reason," she said, and then turned her back on Father Flynn and marched out of St. Agnes, leaving her mother behind. Right before the doors slammed, however, she observed something curious. In spite of his total aversion to Our Lady and the adoration around her, Jo could have sworn she saw Father Flynn place the bag of salt her mother had brought at the Virgin's pockmarked feet and bow his head in prayer or sorrow—Jo couldn't tell which and wasn't sure she cared, for one was much like the other, she was starting to believe, and she wanted nothing to do with either.

—◦◦ ◦◦—

Salt was not a substance forgiving of absence, and while the hospital in Boston had advocated its particular methods of healing, Jo created her own rules of recuperation once she got home. She took her time and went slowly, choosing to return herself to the salt by degrees: first by sight, then by taste, then, hardest of all, by touch.

She soaked strips of rags in a solution of lavender oil and chamomile and layered them across the bubbled patches of her skin. At first the contact stung, but gradually her nerves learned to tolerate the antiseptic blast. Next she poured a stream of salt under the tap in the bath, watching as the last dead pieces of tissue detached themselves from her wounds and floated away. Finally she made a paste of salt and water and applied it straight to her skin, letting the brine chap her scars into armor.

She and Claire worked out a system of avoiding each other, except for necessary interaction at mealtimes or the awkward seconds when they stepped around each other in the hall, both of them wanting to use the bathroom first. Ever since Jo's return, Claire had stayed more or less silent—hunkered over her stenography books by the hour, her hair bound so tight it tipped up the corners of her eyes, or disappearing for mysterious stretches of time. Once Jo caught her sneaking in at midnight, and when she saw Jo, Claire jumped and put her hand on her neck, the way she used to when she was hiding love bites from Ethan. Her old girlfriends from high school—the cheerleaders and yearbook girls—were always ringing up, but Claire never returned their calls, opting to let her friends slip away until the phone sat silent. And she flat out refused to go to church.

"If God gets to have Ethan," she spit when Mama suggested she get her tail into Mass, "then Satan can have me."

Mama slapped her for that, right across her mouth, but Claire just wiped the back of her hand across her lips and set them into a hard little smirk. That Sunday she didn't come downstairs until noon, two hours after Mass was done. Father Flynn didn't bother to ask where she was that day, and Mama didn't offer an explanation.

But Claire's disobedience didn't stop with Mass. Just as she was quitting the Lord, it seemed, she was also refusing anything to do with the salt. She wouldn't put it on her food, she declined to scoop the winter store of it into bags, she turned up her nose at the idea of helping Jo repair the sluices, and she plain balked at going anywhere near the ruin of the barn.

In contrast, Jo spent hours back on the land, relishing the humid odors and the riot of insects coming out after a long winter. One evening she came upon Whit lingering at the edge of the marsh. Behind him the outline of the barn was taking shape, its unpainted boards and planks so fresh they still leaked little pinpoints of sap. The ponds were newly flooded, and so far all the omens were fine for that year. The seawater was frothing at the right temperature. The clouds were lining themselves up in even bolls, and Henry's pond was deepening into pink.

Whit looked up when he heard her approach, and if he was shocked by the ruin of Jo's face, he didn't show it. Instead he was all business. "Looks like you're busy," he said, sweeping an arm out at the half-built barn.

Jo dug a toe into the mud. "I wouldn't

say that. Salt's still forming. We just don't have a place to put it."

Whit reached into his jacket pocket and withdrew a checkbook. "I could change that. I could make you an offer right now. You and your family let me own the marsh, and I'll let you stay. You could pay for that new barn in the blink of an eye and maybe even cover your medical bills." His eyes roved over her scars, calculating.

Jo held her breath, thinking. Ida had never given them an option to stay on the farm, but Jo knew that it would be a cold day in hell before she signed her life over to a Turner, no matter how skint she was. "Go away, Whit," she finally said, tired all of a sudden. She turned and started walking back toward the house, skirting the horseshoe of graves. What was it about her family's land, she wondered, that made the past so burdensome, and why didn't the Turners, with all the acres they owned, have the same problem?

That spring, while Jo's scars finished healing and the new salt barn rose from the ashes of the old, Jo started to think that maybe she'd finally exorcised her family ghosts. The worst had happened, but she and Mama and Claire had survived, and the salt was still theirs. Maybe, Jo thought as she scraped the crumbling sides of yet another ditch, it was better that Ethan had left Claire. Claire had paid a terrible price for that loss, but Jo still had her sister. They would grow old together in the marsh, she and Claire, with her sister maybe bringing in a little extra cash from secretarial work, maiden spinsters to the end, the last of the Gilly line. Now that Ethan was gone, Claire would surely turn back to Jo, and as they stepped into the future together, they'd also travel back to a time when they'd both loved Our Lady, and Claire still consented to work the salt, and Jo wasn't reminded every instance she looked in a mirror that she had a pretty big ugly side.

Chapter Ten

Dee had kept her eyes peeled for legitimate signs of autumn—crispy red leaves, the glories of an Indian summer, hard apples sold in bushels by the roadside—but she guessed she must have been looking for the wrong kinds of things, because the weather just turned nasty and wet, the sky overhead about as attractive as a leaky nose.

As if in compensation, the diner's business increased when the town's last few fishing boats docked and the area's surrounding bars closed shop for the season. Suddenly the Lighthouse turned bustling and friendly. All day the cloudy lanterns that Cutt had reclaimed cast a mellow glow on the checkered linoleum, and the deep crimson of the booths was warm against the rain outside. Cutt started adding an extra dollop of butter to his simmered vegetables and stews, and even they started looking pretty good.

For the first time since her mother had died, the tight bands in between Dee's ribs loosened a nudge and she started to feel like she could breathe deeply again—that she wasn't taking anything away from the memory of her mother by doing so. Her father felt the same way, too, she could see. He started whistling as he mopped the kitchen floor at the end of the day, and every now and then he even cracked jokes over the grill, although they were the kinds of things a person would tell a five-year-old and not funny—knock-knock jokes and riddles about animals. Dee's mother had been the one with the better sense of humor. Neither Cutt nor Dee had gotten any of that from her, and they both knew it. Still, Dee would laugh, just to show her father she noticed the effort he was making, and in return he'd hold off on shouting at her for forgetting to replenish the napkin dispensers or refill the mustard pots.

Dee would have thought the constant rain would have deterred Claire from her morning rides, but Claire's huge white horse didn't appear to mind a jaunt through slush, and neither did Claire. The only difference that Dee could see was that Claire didn't tie the beast up outside anymore, for fear he'd get a chill. Instead she now arrived after her ride in her red sports car, the convertible roof thrown back to the elements, spray flying as she squealed into any old parking spot she liked. No one, it seemed, was going to ticket Claire Turner.

Mr. Weatherly noticed how antsy Dee grew every time Claire swished into the diner for her single egg and mug of coffee. "Aye," he muttered, nodding as he took a sip from his own mug, his eyes following Dee's across the diner to where Claire was bent over her newspaper. "You're wise to stay skittish around that one. Pretty as a morning glory she is, but with poison lacing her veins."

Dee put down her coffeepot and leaned forward across the counter on her elbows, lowering her voice. "She doesn't want us to serve Jo's salt, you know. That's why we don't have it out on the tables. I just bring it to the few customers who want it. Do Jo and Claire really hate each other that much?"

Mr. Weatherly fixed her with his cloudy eyes. It amazed Dee that someone as papery and frail-looking as Timothy Weatherly could still swing a hammer, but he did, hitting the nail perfectly every time before he took his handkerchief out and wiped his forehead. He worked his mouth in a circle, swallowing his coffee. "How old are you?" he asked, dabbing at his chin with a napkin.

"Seventeen," Dee answered. "I'll be eighteen in January."

A little smile danced around the edges of Mr. Weatherly's thin lips, and Dee suddenly wondered what he'd been like when he was her age. Her father had told her how he'd heard that back in the day Mr. Weatherly used to be quite the town hunk. He and his brother used to juice up cars. They'd been famous for it up and down the Cape. Dee tried to imagine the man stooped across from her now with shiny muscles and black hair combed into a ducktail, but she failed. That was nothing new. She never did have a very good imagination beyond the here and now.

"You're still so young," Mr. Weatherly said, putting some change down on the counter. He was a dime short, but Dee didn't bother to point that out. He fixed her with his eyes like a chicken homing in on feed. "Young and foolish, but young most of all. And that's the point. Claire ain't young."

Dee snuck a look over at Claire. "Well, she's not exactly old."

Mr. Weatherly worked his gums. "Not exactly old ain't the same as young. The fact that you don't know that yet proves my point." He took a knotted piece of string out of his pocket and set it down on the counter next to his change. "Here," he said. "That's for you."

Dee frowned. The string was yellow and dirty. She didn't really want to touch it. "What is it?"

"A knot charm. Go on. Take it. I can make another one."

Dee took the snarled length of string off the counter and slipped it into her pocket. "Thank you. What does it do?"

Mr. Weatherly's face grew serious. "Tangles up trouble before it finds you. The fishermen around here use them."

Dee tried to hide her smile. "I really don't think there's much to worry about in a tiny town like Prospect," she said, lifting the coffeepot again. "Especially not in the dead of winter." Any day now, she thought looking out the window, the freezing rain would switch to snow and everything would grow hushed until spring.

Mr. Weatherly shook his head as if he were shaking away flies. "That's when you'll need it most," he insisted, unfolding his long limbs off the stool.

"That's when trouble always begins in this town."

"What are you talking about?" Dee asked, and Mr. Weatherly looked at her like she was stupid.

"Why, the December's Eve bonfire, girl. Can't invite more trouble than that." And without further explanation, he hobbled out the door, tipping his hat to Claire.

Dee whisked his dishes into the kitchen and dumped them in the sink. Maybe Mr. Weatherly was totally right about her, she mused. She was dumb and young. Here she was trying to play both sides of the salt when the Gilly sisters themselves hadn't even been able to do that. She touched the twisted charm in her pocket and smiled. It was such a small, silly object. Still, it had been sweet of Mr. Weatherly to worry about trouble finding her, Dee thought, especially since in her experience it usually happened the other way around.

———o-o o-o———

That Sunday, Dee knelt next to her father in St. Agnes, as usual. The tiny

church was almost empty, except for
Mr. Weatherly, the postmistress, and a
few other souls Dee didn't recognize.
And, of course, Whit and Claire. They
arrived last as they always did, waiting
to make an entrance even though everyone was so used to them that they
were no longer impressed.

Over the past month, Whit had gotten bolder with her. His flirty orders had
turned into outright insinuations. "The
coffee's not the only thing that's hot today," he'd say, taking the steaming mug
from her tray. Or he'd ask with a wink,
"What else can I get here on the side?"
Normally such over-the-top suggestions would have come out creepy, Dee
thought, but there was something about
the way Whit said them, laughing at
himself even as he leered, that made
her want to play along with the joke.
And besides, he was a great tipper.

Her father, of course, loved him. They
were both Red Sox fans, it turned out,
and every time he came in to the Lighthouse, Whit made it a point to talk
some ball with Cutt before he sat down
and ordered.

"He's not the first man in this town for nothing," Cutt would say, watching Whit climb into his car after a quick meal. "Mr. Friend over at the hardware said Whit even organizes a little pool for the town every year during the World Series. Now, that's the kind of civic duty I like to see. He's got brains and money, sure, but he's not afraid to shoot the shit like a regular guy either."

Dee wondered what her father would say if he knew what else Whit wasn't afraid to do, but she kept the flirtation between herself and Whit quiet. For one thing, Cutt would just blame her for it and, for another, she actually liked the attention.

She shook herself and blinked. Mass was ending, so she crossed herself one last time, touching her thumb to her head and her heart, her left shoulder and then her right, realizing that her feet were freezing in their thin loafers. She was just about to stand up when Father Flynn surprised her by spreading his arms out and asking all the worshippers to stay seated for an extra moment.

"I have an announcement," he said, his voice warbling. Dee sighed and settled herself back into the pew. "As you know," the old priest said, his eyes growing rheumy, "I have served this parish faithfully for the past several decades—for most of my adult life, as a matter of fact." He looked around at the faces in the pews, as if remembering better days, then sighed and continued. "Well, to paraphrase Ecclesiastes, there is a time for everything under the sun, and I'm afraid mine has come. I regret to inform you that in February I will be handing over the reins of this parish."

There was an intake of breath, and Father Flynn held his arms a little higher. "Fear not," he said. "You will be in good hands. In familiar hands, as a matter of fact. My replacement is someone you all know very well. It's young Ethan Stone—now Father Stone."

The chilly air in the church grew so still that Dee wouldn't have been surprised if it actually cracked down the middle like a block of ice. No one moved, not even Father Flynn. Eventually he put his arms down, bowed his head, and made his way to the rear of the church, where he took up his customary place by the door, waiting to send his parishioners off into the miserable weather with blessings and a plea to return next week.

Cutt leaned down to Dee, his brow furrowed. "Isn't Ethan Stone that fella Whit's wife used to date when she was young?" Dee nodded, watching as Claire moved stiffly down the aisle on Whit's arm, her green eyes hard as hammers.

"Well," Cutt said, his mouth curving with amusement. "This ought to get people's tongues moving. Guess we know what the topic of conversation will be at the counter for the next few weeks."

———o-o o-o———

The day was frigid outside St. Agnes, and the sky was as damp as an old sponge, but Dee was so restless she decided to take her usual walk anyway. She knew that the beach would be empty, but for good reason. It was so windy over there that she'd get sand-blasted for sure. She stood for a moment, weighing her options, and finally wrapped her scarf tight around her neck, tucked her chin close to her chest, and started ambling down the lane into the tight breeze, letting the cold pinch at the corners of her mouth and eyes.

A huge gust of wind swooped across the dunes and almost knocked her sideways as the sky began spitting a heavy mist. She stumbled a bit, buttoning the highest button on her coat collar, her bare fingers tingling in the cold. As she neared the marsh, she stopped in the middle of the empty path, the wind urging her to keep traveling, to step through the grasses and down to Salt Creek Farm, even while her better sense screamed at her to stop and mind her own business. She took another pace forward. Joanna wouldn't be out in weather like this, she calculated. Dee would have the place all to herself. Maybe she could even poke around in that barn.

But she was wrong. She wasn't as

alone as she thought. A dark, glossy car pulled up next to her, spraying sand over her loafers, its engine purring. Dee squinted through the wind, wiping rain from her forehead, but she didn't need to look twice to know who it was. Only one man in Prospect drove an auto that shiny. She glanced into the interior of the car, but the seat beside him was free and empty. Whit was alone. He leaned over and opened the passenger door for Dee, letting out a pulse of heat. "Get in," he said. "You look like a drowned rat. What are you doing out here?"

She hesitated for a fraction longer, but the lure of warm leather and the low rumble of the engine tempted her too much. She slid into the front seat as a burst of legitimate rain splattered over the windshield. "Taking a walk," she answered, shaking water out of her hair. "What are *you* doing out here?"

Whit put the car back into gear and continued idling down the rutted lane. "I dropped Claire off at home and am on my way to see Jo."

Dee lurched forward in her seat as

they rattled over a pothole and she bit the corner of her mouth by accident. "Jo?" she echoed, dabbing at the corner of her lip. "What on earth for?" Whit glanced sideways at her, and Dee's pulse sped up. She took a deep breath and smoothed her skirt over her knees. After Claire and her father, Dee thought that Whit might be next on her list of people she wanted to hide her visits to the marsh from. "I mean, do you call on Jo often?" she asked, folding her hands demurely in her lap.

Whit didn't look fooled. "Only when there's unfinished business," he said through clenched teeth, pulling the car up to the barn and turning to Dee. He raked her with his eyes, dragging his gaze over her breasts and back again, until Dee couldn't take it anymore and she looked away, blushing. He raised his hand, and for a moment she thought he was about to stroke her cheek, but he put the car keys into her palm instead. "This won't take long," he said, closing her fingers over the metal. "I'd like very much to give you a ride back to town. If you get cold, start the engine."

And then he was jogging across the muddy marsh with his jacket held half over his head, squinting against the slashing rain. Dee watched him and then leaned back in her seat, spreading her hands on the fine leather. The car was so luxurious she wanted to sleep in it. She guessed Whit must have come to visit Joanna with some sort of business proposition, and she wondered how that would go. Jo didn't seem like she'd be too agreeable when it came to that kind of thing. Jo wasn't really agreeable when it came to much.

Dee closed her eyes and listened to the rain falling on the roof of the car. The sound cocooned her, making everything feel dreamlike. Well, it kind of was. After all, here she was waiting in Whit Turner's car—on a Sunday, no less—parked at what might as well have been the edge of the world. She closed her fist tightly around the keys, liking the way the metal felt as it bit into her skin, both cold and hot at once. It matched what was going on inside her.

Whit startled her, reappearing without her seeing him, throwing the door open so suddenly that Dee grew chilled all over again. He was soaking wet, his hair dripping onto his collar, his cheeks running with rain, and he was pissed, Dee could tell. He took the keys from her without a word and threw the car into reverse so hard her head snapped.

"So . . . um, it didn't go well?" she finally said, peeking at Whit from beneath her eyelashes and wishing she had a towel to give him. He didn't answer, just clenched his teeth and bounced the car hard over the lane's potholes.

They passed St. Agnes and reached the last turn before town. Dee straightened up in her seat, arranging her coat, which had fallen open. She was feeling foolish all of a sudden. *He thinks I'm just a kid*, she told herself. *He's just being nice.* She reached into her pocket and felt the knot charm that Mr. Weatherly had given her. Maybe it was working after all, when she least wanted it to.

They were on the wrong side of Tappert's Green. Another stretch and a bend and they'd be on Bank Street. Back at the diner. Back to her room with the dormer ceiling and the creaky bed and her father muttering to himself through the walls. Dee sighed, and Whit glanced across at her, and then, without warning, he pulled the car over to the side of the road and turned off the engine.

"I'm sorry," he said, his eyes crinkling at the edges again, his lip curving in a most pleasing manner. "Here I have a lovely companion sitting next to me, and what do I do but go and ignore her?" Dee blushed, but before she could say anything, Whit leaned across the console and put one hand up to her cheek. "What wouldn't I do," he murmured, stretching even closer.

Dee held her breath for a moment and half closed her eyes. This was her last chance, she knew, to push him away, to tell him he had the wrong idea after all. Instead she leaned into him as he touched his lips to her neck and then opened her lips to his mouth, letting the hot point of his tongue shock hers. He pulled away a little and took a breath.

"Damn," he breathed, "you're tastier than anything in your father's diner. I've wanted to do that since the moment I first saw you."

Dee hid her smile. She knew she should probably be scrambling out of the car right about now, but there was something thrilling about this moment. She brought her palms up to Whit's cheeks, feeling as if she were taming a large cat, and started kissing him again, letting all the pain and boredom of the last few months melt away as Whit undid her coat and worked his hands up under her sweater.

"You like that, don't you?" he said, his fingers tracing light circles over her breasts.

And she did. Whit was nothing like any of the doltish boys she'd been with before, with all their panting and jerky impatience. He knew exactly what he was doing and why. In fact, Dee thought, he probably knew her better than she knew her own self.

They twined around each other further, navigating the clumsy console between them, Dee's skirt riding higher as Whit's hands went exploring, and just when she was ready to lean back and let him have his way with her, he cleared his throat and sat up.

"The rain's stopped," he said, lifting his head from her neck. "It's clearing up." He rearranged his wet shirt and combed a hand through his hair. "You *are* young," he said, cocking an eyebrow at Dee, "but not so innocent, I think." She blushed and tried to look wicked, then stopped, worried that she just looked pinched instead.

Whit circled her wrist with his fingers, pressing hard on the tendons. "We can't be seen like this," he said. "You'd better get out of here." Dee pouted, and he chuckled. "Don't worry. I'll tell you when and where we can meet." He watched her slide out of the car into the freezing wet. "I'll come into the diner tomorrow—after my wife, of course. You can give it to me hot."

And with a delicious grin, he slammed the door and rounded the final bend into town, leaving Dee to stumble back to Bank Street alone, thoughts of Claire's red hair and white skin mingling with the press of Whit's lips on her throat until everything was a twist of confusion for her. Was she hungry for Claire's husband or just Claire? she wondered. Which Turner would she really be serving tomorrow at the Lighthouse anyway—man or wife—and where was the dividing line between them?

She reached the diner and glanced into one of the front windows, darkened in the late afternoon, and her reflection caught her off guard. She stared at her face—leaner in the window than in real life, dotted with water droplets—and it occurred to her that maybe she was the line. Before she could think too hard about that, however, she moved, breaking the image into pieces and scattering the doubtful part of her back into the rain, leaving behind only a solitary pane of glass, unreflective in the autumn gloom.

Chapter Eleven

Shovel fast on a Sunday, Jo's mother used to say when Jo was growing up and the year got cold enough for the salt to be hauled from the ponds to the barn. *Lucifer's got time on his hands, but we don't.* This would be just when the first threat of the season's rain was shimmering on the horizon, when neat V's of geese were streaking the sky with their plaintive honking and frantic wings.

This particular year Jo had ended up with salt heaped only to her hip. It would barely be enough to keep her in good with the fishermen through the winter, and certainly not enough to keep the bank at bay. Come spring, she knew, Harbor Bank was going to want to skim more fat off the land than she had to give.

She'd cleaned out her life's savings and been dismayed to discover that it amounted to only the three months of back mortgage payments plus two extra months. She tried to do the math on all of it and failed. Somehow the bank had won the round. She presented them with a lifetime of work, and they reciprocated with five meager months in return. *Oh, well*, Jo thought, trying to push the worry out of her head the way she was shoving around the piles of salt. *I got one more season to make it all last.* Winter. The longest months with the shortest days. A time when the marsh froze and everything hung suspended. From down the lane, she could hear the tarnished bell of St. Agnes clanging out a dented version of a song. In a few more weeks, she knew, even that would freeze, plunging the marsh into an icy and profound silence.

She tugged open the barn doors and shoved the barrow across the threshold just as the first fat drops of rain started to plop, noisy as gulls on the wing. She huddled inside the doorway, watching the changing sky, and then she went on with her business: upending the barrow, unloading the salt into an empty wooden box, sweeping up the scattered grains that had fallen to the wayside.

She pulled the cover into place over the storage box and brushed her hands together, wrinkled palm to smooth one. Usually she wore gloves, but she'd forgotten about them today, and now it was too late. If she wasn't careful, she knew, dust and dirt would settle into the whorls of her scars and stain her hands mocha. A scuffling noise outside the barn interrupted her thoughts, and then, cutting through the noise of the rain and the wind, Whit Turner's voice flew up to the rafters, where it hovered and hung in judgment.

"I know you're in there, Joanna," he called through the crack of the barn door, scraping his shoes on the wet clay. "Open up."

What could he want? She hesitated, her heart pounding for six, and then she took the biggest breath she could and flung open the door, squinting in the rain. "Don't you take a single step closer," she said. She'd grabbed an old scythe left behind by one of her doomed male ancestors, but the blade was rusted and unreliable-looking, and Whit just flicked his eyes over it. She lowered the tool and leaned against the splintered threshold, hoping the backs of her knees would harden from the jelly they'd turned to. "To what do I owe the honor?" she asked.

Every time she got close to Whit these days, she was always surprised to see how the years were crimping the skin around his eyes and jaw and how his hair was starting to silver at the temples. He must have just come from Mass, Jo realized, for he was wearing a fine woolen blazer and pressed trousers—clothes her sister had no doubt chosen for him with care. She looked for any sign of the boy who'd taught her to whistle a hornpipe, who could palm the ace of hearts and make it re-appear from her sleeve, but failed to find even a glimmer of him. Instead she saw Ida taking on a second life in the features of her only son, and for a quick heartbeat Jo was almost grateful for the scar tissue dimpled across her cheek, forehead, and chin. No one would ever be able to invade her face, she realized. She would always simply be herself, whether she liked it or not.

"Are you the one behind the non-sense I'm hearing about Ethan Stone's return?" Whit asked, his lips white with rage.

She let out a careful breath, trying not to show her surprise. To be honest, she wasn't sure how to answer that question. It was true that two weeks ago Father Flynn had sat in her front parlor and told her that his soul was heavy. She'd poured him a cup of tea. "Then you should lighten it," she'd re-plied, and handed him the drink.

Father Flynn had sipped and then sipped again, his face growing ever more thoughtful. "What's the only way to fix a hole, my dear?" he'd asked.

Jo had taken her own taste of tea. "Why, fill it in, I guess." Her answer had seemed to please the father.

"Exactly," he'd replied, nodding. "That's just what I was thinking." He leaned over and gave her a quick peck on her smooth cheek. "Thank you. You always say the right thing."

At the time Jo had just chalked his behavior up to the ramblings of a lonely old man, but the penny was falling through the slot for her now, and she was starting to see that maybe Father Flynn was cagier than she gave him credit for. He must have been plotting how to bring Ethan Stone home, Jo realized. Not that it would do to let Whit know that. She worked her tongue along the roof of her mouth. "I wish I could take credit," she said, staring into his eyes, "but the Lord's work is beyond me."

Whit didn't blink, and Jo remembered that about him, how he'd always won every staring contest they'd ever had, every card game, and always, without fail, all the best marbles. "But you knew."

She looked down at her boots. "Yes," she admitted. "I guess I did."

Whit extracted a pair of gloves from the inner pocket of his jacket and began pulling them on, and Jo saw how the skin on the backs of his hands was still flecked with faint freckles, the way hers used to be. She wondered what Ethan Stone was going to look like after all this time. He'd come back to Prospect only once for his mother's funeral, but that was ten years ago, and he'd been so swamped with grief he hadn't been quite himself. When his father died, he'd stayed away, and no one blamed him for that, given the man's foul temperament. Merrett always seemed to have had one foot planted in the great beyond anyway.

Whit's lips curled into a sneer. He leaned forward, and Jo caught a whiff of his cologne—a curious aroma that reminded her of wet ink. He glanced around the dusty barn at her pitiful heaps of salt. "Doesn't look like you're doing too well," he said.

Jo didn't reply, just tipped her chin higher.

"You know," Whit continued, folding his fingers, his gloves sodden now, "nothing's changed. Let me take this place off your hands. You're just fighting a losing battle out here, Jo."

This was true. Claire's insinuations and rumors about the salt had shriveled almost all of Jo's customary accounts over the years. To make a sale, she was having to drive farther and farther away—not always a certain endeavor in her truck. In fact, if it weren't for the likes of Chet Stone and the rest of the fishermen's steady business, she thought, she might have had no choice but to take Whit's money.

In the beginning the drop in business had been bearable, but then Claire had gone and done the worst thing imaginable. She'd banned the salt from the December's Eve bonfire. Something about violating a municipal order of burning chemicals in public, the constable told Jo, but she knew it was all just a bunch of puffed-up nonsense. Claire had always hated the whole ritual, and now that she was Mrs. Whittington Turner, she'd decided she was free to live without it, the rest of Prospect be damned.

"But what will you tell the townspeople?" Jo had asked the constable as he'd stood shuffling his shiny black boots on her porch, cradling his hat in his beefy hands. "How are you going to break the news that this year the town won't have a future?"

He'd just shaken his head. "Guess you'll just have to keep what you know to yourself this year," he said, and he didn't look all the way sorry about it either.

Whit was standing in the doorway of the barn much as the constable had taken possession of her porch, Jo thought—ready to spit bad news in her direction. The thing was, she wasn't ready to let him. She took a step into the open air, braving the weather.

"What are you still fighting your mother's battles for?" she said, oddly tempted to reach out and stroke Whit on the cheek even as she scolded him. "When are you finally going to be your

own man, Whit? This place isn't going
to help you build up your business
again." She gestured at the ruins of the
autumn ponds. "Look at it. It's a cursed
bog. And my sister doesn't want it either. You should have buried whatever
beef your mother had with this land
along with her." *Besides*, she wanted to
add, *you've already won, and you know
it. You took Claire.*

Whit slowly buttoned his jacket. Even
in the rain, he managed to stay perfectly groomed, and Jo remembered
how when they'd split from a day of
playing as children, all the muck and
mud would have stuck fast to her and
he'd be spotless as a dish of baking
soda. It had never bothered Jo, though.
In fact, she'd been happy to have some
visible proof of their friendship worked
into the knees and elbows of her
clothes. She didn't know then that some
stains don't wash out.

"Claire wants what I want," he said.
"She's a Turner. And what we want is
to finish the work my mother started.
My only regret is that she won't see it
come to light." He leaned down closer

to Jo, and for the first time that day she felt the air's chill. "But you will," he said. "I'll make sure of that." He dropped his voice almost to a croon. "I know people at Harbor Bank, Jo. You haven't got too long left out here. I'm coming here friendly. Sell it to me now for a decent price and we'll both be happy. If you want to go belly-up, that's your business. I'll just wait and buy from the bank. One way or another, this place will be mine."

Jo watched him walk out into the wet, wandering off to the same spot where he always parked on the lane—the place where he'd waited for Claire before speeding her off into her new future as a Turner. Back then Whit had been all about the future. Jo wondered when he'd gotten so caught up in the past.

It didn't matter. Claire wasn't coming back—and Ethan Stone was, and Whit couldn't do a damn thing about it. Nor would he get his hands on her land. But what if he did? Her stomach clenched. Where would she go?

————o-o o-o————

It irked Jo that Whit set foot in the marsh only when he wanted to steal something—the title to the land, the secret of the salt, her sister. Jo never knew what until it was too late. Take the day he'd come to get Claire, for instance.

It had been an early-June evening and lovely, if Jo remembered right, except for the sight of Whit lurking out by the barn. As Jo stumped across the marsh to see what he wanted, a miniature blue butterfly had risen up from the mud and fluttered against her arm. She batted it away. Most people would have said they were pretty, but Jo saw them as a plague. Mama always said they were bad luck, but then Mama thought lots of things were bad luck. Jo neared the barn, but she stopped when she realized that Whit wasn't standing alone. She caught her breath, trying to understand what she was seeing.

It was Claire, her russet hair pulled back, her bones so delicate they looked like they would buckle in a hard wind, except Jo knew that they were really lined with iron for marrow. Claire seemed to be wrapped in Whit's canvas jacket. There was a movement between them, a rearrangement of arms and limbs, and Jo's blood ran cold. Claire and Whit had twined their arms together, she saw, and had tilted their heads to touching—a breathless posture they couldn't sustain for long, but they didn't have to, because before Jo could let herself think twice, she charged toward them to save Claire from making a terrible mistake. Just as she arrived, Whit dislodged one of his hands and put it up to Claire's flushed cheeks, staring into her eyes. He opened his lips as if to say something, and that's when Claire spotted her and made an ugly little noise of surprise.

Whit half turned, as if he'd suspected all along that Jo was there, but couldn't be bothered to face her. He folded Claire into him, tucking her under his arm like a bird to the wing, and then he said the worst thing Jo could imagine: "Meet my future wife."

Jo waited for Claire to do something—anything. Slap Whit, maybe, or run away, or fall to her knees. But she didn't. Instead she smiled. Not a large smile, just the corners of her mouth readjusting a little, getting used to her new position in the world, seeing what it was going to feel like to be a Turner. A butterfly landed on the crown of Claire's head, and though Jo had the urge to brush it away, she didn't. She'd saved Claire enough, she decided. She took a step backward. Whit's eyes combed the ruin of her face, a barely concealed expression of disgust on his.

"Claire," he said, his eyes riveted on Jo. "Go get your things." Without looking at Jo, Claire scurried off, and Jo waited until she was a little ways across the marsh before she spoke. Even in a whirl of fury, she still had the urge to protect Claire.

"It won't work," she said. "You won't get your hands on our land like this. Gilly women don't thrive out of the salt."

Whit took a step toward her. With implacable logic he replied, "Then I suppose it's lucky for all of us that

Claire's decided to become a Turner."
He smirked. "My mother's will only stip-
ulated that I couldn't marry you, Jo. It
never said anything about Claire."

"How are you going to support her?"
Jo asked. "Claire thinks you're richer
than Midas, but I know better. What are
you going to do when she discovers
that the Turner coffers aren't quite as
full as she thought?"

Whit looked bored. "Claire will think
she's in Shangri-la," he replied, running
his eyes across the marsh. "Especially
compared to this place. A girl like her
deserves better, and I can give it to her.
I can at least do that."

What could Jo say to that? One way
or another, Claire had always meant to
leave. If she couldn't do it with Ethan,
then she would take Whit, the only man
in town brazen enough to have a Gilly
woman. Jo wondered if Claire's future
would be a happy one or if, after a few
years of living in Ida's house and sleeping in her bed, she, too, would start
wearing too much makeup, too many
jewels, and thinking only of the things
she didn't have.

She tried to imagine Claire rambling around in that big house up on Plover Hill, locked away behind the iron gates, the taste of salt a memory on her lips, but she couldn't make the picture fit. She sighed. "Claire doesn't love you," she said. "And I doubt she ever will."

Whit's face slammed shut at that, like a door pushed by the wind. Still, he didn't like anyone to have the last word. He regarded her with sorrow, and for a moment Jo saw the boy trapped in the glass tank of Whit's body. "I guess love comes and goes," he finally said. "Tell Claire I'm waiting for her with the car down the lane. Tell her I won't wait forever." And with that he sauntered away, the mud from the marsh darkening the fine soles of his shoes, making the going rough.

—∘-∘ ∘-∘—

Claire and Whit didn't waste time on a long engagement. A few weeks after her departure, Claire sent a gold-engraved invitation to the marsh, and Jo peeled back the tissue and linen layers of it, opening cards and envelopes, trying—and failing—to find one scrap of Claire in all of it.

"Look, Mama." Jo brandished the invitation. Since Claire's quick departure, Mama's health had worsened, and she was often in bed. "They're getting married in St. Agnes. I'd have thought they would have picked something fancier." But Mama just turned her head and said nothing, so Jo sent the return envelope back empty of words and filled with salt. Just because she wasn't planning on attending Claire's nuptials, that didn't mean she was going to ignore them. Not hardly. She had a special gift planned for Claire.

The morning of the wedding, Jo snuck out of the marsh and over to the church early, long before the sun was up and long before even Father Flynn would have risen for prayer. She carried, hidden in a burlap sack, a jar of ashes, a pot of paint, and a paintbrush.

It wasn't hard to pick the lock on the church's weathered double doors—it was old and just for show, mostly to keep the wind from blowing them apart during storms. A twist with a hairpin, a wrench of the wrist, and the antique lock yielded, clicking open. Jo pulled out the hairpin, stuck it back in her pocket, and stepped into the dark sanctuary.

Even though she knew the dips and hollows of that old floor as well as she knew the mud of the marsh, even though she could have moved down the tiny center aisle with her eyes closed, she walked slowly, first so as not to wake Father Flynn, asleep in the little attached rectory, and second because the white plane of Our Lady's bare face seemed to float in the dark.

"Hello," Jo whispered to her, opening the jar of ashes and fishing the paintbrush out of her bag. It pleased Jo that Claire would have to enter St. Agnes again to be married, when Jo knew she hated the place. She hoped the memory of Ethan pained Claire every Sunday from there on out as she knelt next to Whit, but in case it didn't, Jo had a plan to make it so.

She pried the lid off the can of paint. She'd found it left behind in the new barn by the Weatherly brothers during their renovations. It was grayish and thick, used to seal the trim around the doors, but it would work just fine for her purposes. She dipped the bristles of the brush in the paint, let the excess color drip for a moment, and then brought her hand to the wall.

She worked quickly, without letting herself think, flicking her wrist as lightly as she could, making six hook shapes on the hem of the Virgin's gown, the lines as sharp and clear as any words Jo could have written. Breathing fast, she stepped away from the wall and studied her handiwork. Would it be enough to make Claire remember? Would she see the barbs and recall the day on the beach when she'd gotten the fishhook stuck in her hand and Jo had pulled it out? *It doesn't pay to be tender when you work in salt*, Jo had barked at her, but Claire hadn't wanted to listen. This time Jo would make her.

She bit her lip and dipped her brush again. She outlined an eye on Our Lady's open palm, in the same spot where the barb had gone into Claire's skin. *An eye for an eye*, Jo thought, tracing the iris, then the lashes. It didn't matter that Claire was leaving the marsh, Jo wanted her to know. No matter what she did or where she went, Jo's eyes would always be on her—both of them, the one burned to jelly in the barn and the one still left in her head.

Finally she opened the jar of ashes and scattered them all around the front of the Virgin. When Claire knelt before Our Lady to light her bridal candle, the satin train of her gown would spread around her like lily petals and she would rise with dirty knees, tainted by the marks of fire.

For the remainder of that morning, Jo rattled through the house, sorting through piles of old junk, jangly as an antique telephone. At last Mama had had enough. "Go on," she snapped, taking a dented oilcan out of Jo's hands. "Go and see your sister married."

Jo squeezed her mother's thin shoulders. "I'll tell you what she's wearing," she said, and Mama nodded.

"I'd like that."

The wedding had already started by the time Jo snuck up to the blurry arched windows and peeped through one of them. Claire was standing at the altar shrouded in satin and lace, her head bowed. Ever since her engagement to Whit, who was devout, she'd started attending church again, but it was still a shock to see her standing in front of St. Agnes's little altar, a bride to someone besides Ethan, her mouth forming the words of prayers Jo knew that her sister reviled.

Her school friends Cecilia West and Katy Diamond stood up next to her, beaming in hideous satin dresses, and in the pews were the faces of everyone Jo had ever known: Mr. Upton, Mr. Hopper from the diner, even horrible Agnes Greene, who used to tease Claire about her clothes at school. She was simpering now, impressed by the size of the diamonds on the band sliding onto Claire's finger. Claire didn't look exactly radiant. Instead she moved with stiff slowness, as if just standing in St. Agnes was making her blood freeze— and Jo hoped it really was.

Claire didn't look at Whit when he slipped the jeweled ring on her finger, or when Father Flynn pronounced them man and wife. And when Whit threw back her veil and kissed her, she kept her eyes closed. Jo knew it must have been Ethan's mouth she was imagining. She saw Claire glance at the newly improved Our Lady once, an expression of worry flashing across her face.

When everything was over, Claire stepped out of the church, pale as when she'd arrived. No one threw rice. None of the guests cheered, and there was no music, just the hard rustle of an Atlantic wind. Before anyone could see her, Jo ducked behind the church and down to Drake's Beach, where she paced along the water's edge, remembering the day Whit had found her digging for clams and asked where they came from. Where had all the time gone? Soon she heard footsteps gaining behind her. "Ashes to ashes," Father Flynn said, falling into a rhythm beside her.

She frowned at him. She didn't want company. "What?"

"I noticed that your sister ruined her

gown," he said, unruffled as a rogue wave doused the hems of his trousers.

Jo moved out of the way and kicked at the sand. "My sister ruined a lot of things."

Father Flynn joined her on higher ground. A question hung in his eyes, but he didn't dare ask it. Instead he folded his hands and sighed. "Just as someone ruined Our Lady this morning." Jo didn't say anything, and Father Flynn surprised her by letting the matter drop. *He must like Our Lady even less than I do*, Jo thought, which was saying a lot. He cleared his throat and slowed his pace to match hers. "Not speaking to your sister won't change anything—not about the fire and not about her marriage to Whit. Won't you consider forgiving her?"

Jo squinted out at the waves. Her vision was getting better, but she still had only her left eye to depend on. She shook her head. "I don't think so. Not this time. No."

Father Flynn's shoulders sagged a little more. He rattled a pair of stones in his pocket, as if they were words he was weighing. "You have been dealt some heavy blows of late," he said eventually. "I realize that. But try to re-member that the arms of God are lon-ger and stronger than you will ever know, even if you can't always feel them around you." He reached out and cupped Jo's chin. So far, of all the peo-ple in Prospect, he was the only one who seemed to have no reaction to her scars. Now he looked at her probingly. "I always have you in my heart, Jo. Know that. Don't be wrathful."

She bowed her head, feeling a rush of guilt for what she'd done to the Vir-gin. "Wrath is the *only* thing I feel any-more," she confessed.

Father Flynn gave her a gentle pat. "Nevertheless, try not to lose touch with the Lord, however that may be." He left her to pick her way through the dunes alone, wondering who had the better hold on her—God or the devil—because it felt like one of them was crushing what was left of her in his al-mighty fist.

—o-o o-o—

After Claire married Whit, Jo's mother grew thinner and weaker by the day, and Jo knew that the time they had left together was short. After she finished her morning chores in the marsh, she would climb into her mother's bed and just hold her while she slept, trying to memorize her particular arrangement of muscle and bone.

"It's not a real ending," Mama whispered as she grew frailer. "It's only a readjustment of the soul. Don't waste your time in grief." She took a breath and motioned Jo closer. "Promise me you'll stay in the salt," she said. "Promise you'll look after Claire."

At the mention of Claire, Jo set her jaw. "Whit's already doing that, Mama," she said. "You don't have to worry."

Her mother stared at her with watery eyes. "Don't I?" Then she exhaled and fell into a restless sleep.

She died one month later and was buried in the Gillys' weedy plot at the edge of the town cemetery. No women were ever laid to rest in the marsh— only the unlucky men. Jo tried to honor her mother's wishes not to grieve, but it was a difficult undertaking. She was alone for the first time in her life, and her mother's absence was made all the worse by the fact that her salt apron still hung in the barn, her clothes still hung in her closet, and the mismatch of cups and plates she'd collected over the years still sat in the kitchen cupboard. Every morning when Jo woke up, the silence of the house was almost alive, as if insects had crawled in between the spaces in the walls and were vibrating their thousands of wings. She tended to think about Claire in those moments. Was she feeling the same unease living behind Ida's walls?

Jo sat down and tried to write a note to Claire, but she couldn't think of what to say, so in the end she shut the pencil and paper back in the parlor desk. Prospect was small enough, she figured. Claire would hear the news in her own way and make a decision about what to do, though Jo had her suspicions it wouldn't be much. Once Claire turned her back on something, it was usually final.

When the morning of her mother's

funeral arrived, Jo walked alone out to St. Agnes, presentable enough in a black shirtwaist dress, combed as nice as she could get. She set off for the funeral with a bag of salt in her hand and a sense of resolve in her chest. Claire would be there, she knew, but Jo thought she could face her. Our Lady would back her up with her arsenal of hooks.

Jo had just stepped up the three bowed steps of the church and was about to enter when she saw her sister. She and Whit were kneeling together in his family pew, the red twist of Claire's hair as bright as a firecracker. On top of Mama's plain coffin, there was a showy spray of orange lilies, the one flower Jo knew that her mother had always hated but Claire had always loved. Besides Whit and Claire, there were a handful of other mourners: Mr. Upton from the grocery, Mr. Hopper from the diner, and the Friends from the hardware. The Stone brothers and their respective wives. Most of the people Jo sold salt to. Father Flynn spied her hovering in the doorway.

"Jo," he said, relief on his face, "we've been waiting." At that, Claire and Whit turned as one, her hand cupped in his. It was the first time Jo had seen her sister since before the wedding, and months of marriage seemed to have aged Claire years. She was wearing a crimson lipstick that was too heavy for her thin lips and, Jo was shocked to see, Ida's pearl, the one Jo had stolen and returned all those years ago.

The air around her thinned, and her vision narrowed to the single pale point of the pearl. How wrong, she thought, that Claire should be the one sitting in that place, next to their mother's body, next to Whit, while she hung in the doorway like a banished ghost. She glanced again at Our Lady, a phantom herself with her missing face and bald patches rubbed in her skirts, a lady with a heart of stone.

"Aren't you coming in, child?" Father Flynn asked, his expression patient as ever. Without saying a word to him, and without taking her eyes off Our Lady, Jo slowly marched up the church's small aisle to the feet of the Virgin and gently laid down her bag of salt. Then she took a place at the end of a pew, across the church from Whit and Claire, and bent her head. All through the short service, Jo could feel Whit's eyes on her. He was fidgety, tapping the toe of one of his expensive loafers, smoothing his silk tie over and over. And Jo knew why.

He waited until all the mourners had left before he approached her, catching her just as she was bundling up to leave. "When is the will being read?" he asked, skipping any niceties. Jo glanced over to Claire, who was waiting up near the altar, two bright spots of color staining her cheeks. *He's greedier than even I knew*, Jo thought. *Mama's not yet in the ground, and here he is busting to take what's not his.*

Jo ran her tongue around her mouth, savoring what she was about to say. She sucked in her stomach. "I wouldn't get your trousers in a bunch, Whit. Claire got nothing."

Across the church Claire let out a little gasp, and Whit grabbed Jo by the arm. "What do you mean, nothing?

How is that possible? Salt Creek Farm is half hers, damn it!"

Jo regarded him coolly. "It *was* half hers. But she left. It was her choice. Anyway, it seems like she's well enough provided for." Jo took in the gleam of Claire's new shoes, the twinkle of her diamond wedding rings.

Whit's face had turned a chalky white. "You Gillys ruin everything," he spit.

Before he could say anything else, Jo turned and fled, flinging open the church's doors and hurtling down the lane. Her skin was still stiff and uncomfortable, and it made it difficult to move. She thought of everything she was running from—Claire, Whit, the accusing face of Our Lady and her attendant sorrows—and she knew that if she didn't get back to the salt, she would dissolve forever, like a spoonful of soda lowered into a kettle of lye.

Whether Jo liked it or not, her future was finally sealed. She'd been given to the marsh, one of a pair, she knew, and it was too late to leave it now, for she owed Salt Creek Farm far more than her living. She owed it her very life.

Chapter Twelve

With Father Flynn's announcement that Ethan Stone was returning to Prospect and St. Agnes, everything for Claire changed in an instant: the weather, the way she and Whit spoke to each other over the dinner table—or more often didn't—even her aversion to the salt.

As the December's Eve bonfire began to approach, the wind combed the town, brittle and hard. It was the kind of weather designed to make people resent all the things they were missing, and Claire was no exception. The cold settled into the unused rooms of Turner

House, lurked in the shadowy hallways, and waited to snap at her toes when she poked them out of the covers in the morning. Whit was worried about the heating bill and didn't like her to turn up the thermostat. Claire started staying in bed longer and longer, watching frost lace the outsides of the windows of her bedroom while she picked through the icy carcass of her past, trying to determine its freezing point, even though she knew it surely had to be the day after the fire in the barn, when Whit Turner found her crying under the pear tree and thought to offer her his handkerchief.

Her mother had been in the hospital with Jo, and Claire had been trusted to be alone. Left to her own devices, she was aimless, disoriented. Wanting company, she drifted into town, then realized she couldn't be around people after all and so found herself loitering under the pear tree, mourning the loss of Ethan and cursing her bad luck.

She never saw Whit coming. "You look like you need this," he said, pulling a clean square of white cotton out of his blazer and handing it to her. She knew he must have heard about the fire, because instead of tweaking her hair and calling her silly, he helped her stand up, carefully brushed the dirt off her skirt for her, and then took her for a cup of coffee.

She broached the subject first. "I guess you know what I did," she said, sniffling, but she discovered that Whit was a man of few words when it came to the vortex of town gossip, maybe because his mother was usually at the core of it.

"I heard," was all he said, his tone telling her he didn't wish to discuss it, and that was a comfort to Claire, for neither did she.

It felt strange to sit at the diner counter—a place she'd gone hundreds of times with Ethan—and sip coffee next to Whit. She drank slowly, careful not to drip anything on her blouse, and wondered if rich people had different rules for holding their cups. She glanced out of the corner of her eye at Whit, but he held his mug just the same as she did hers. He smiled, running his eyes over her hair, and then dropped them down to her chest and waist. She blushed and twisted on her stool, but it didn't deter Whit. He kept staring at her. Then he leaned over and motioned for her to do so, too. When he spoke, his breath tickled her ear. "That Ethan Stone is going to wake up one day and be very sorry he left you," he said.

Claire put down her cup and sniffled. Just the sound of Ethan's name still made her want to cry all over again, but something told her that if Whit was not a man for gossip, neither was he one for tears. She forced herself to sit up straight and look him in the eye. "How do you know that?"

Whit smiled and covered her hand with his own. "Because I'm going to *make* him sorry," he said.

Claire blushed and looked down at their hands joined on the counter, watching Whit watch her. "I have to go," she whispered. "Thank you very much for the coffee." And she slid her fingers out from under his, telling herself this was just a onetime date, that he felt sorry for her, that in his eyes she was still a knock-kneed, freckled girl with two loose teeth. She also remembered that he'd once been as sweet on Jo as she'd been on Ethan. She'd just burned her sister's heart. She didn't want to break it, too.

And yet when Whit found her the next week while she was picking up groceries, she didn't say no to the suggestion of a walk. "Come on," he insisted, taking the basket off her arm. "The sunset is going to be gorgeous." So she let him lead her out the door of Mr. Upton's and down Bank Street, and when he slipped an arm around her waist, pulling her close to his side, she didn't resist. He wasn't the same as Ethan, but that was good, too. It was nice to be held by someone who wanted her more than she wanted him.

After that they quietly began courting every few days. Whit was the one who suggested that Claire take the stenography course—he even signed her up for it—saying she needed something to focus her attention on while her mother and sister were gone, and he was the one who pointed out that she should wear plainer clothes to better accent her hair and eyes, and who taught her how to nestle a knife and fork together across her plate at a restaurant to signal when she was finished eating.

But he never tried to kiss her, not even once, and for that Claire was half glad and half irritated out of her mind. She wondered if Whit's restraint was due to his history with Jo but knew she couldn't ask. Did he care too much or too little about Jo? Claire wondered. She couldn't tell. Finally she parked those thoughts in a dark corner of her mind. She didn't like to dwell on what might remain between Whit and Jo. She didn't like to think about anything to do with Jo at all, as a matter of fact.

But Whit made her confront that, too. "You have to visit her," he eventually insisted, about a month after they'd started seeing each other. They were sitting together in the dunes. "The only way to be free of something is to face it."

Claire wanted to point out that her sister, lying burned in a hospital because of her, wasn't an *it*, but she didn't.

Besides, Whit was right. "What if I don't want to be free?" she said, pulling her hair in front of her face.

Whit drew it aside. "I think you do," he said, making her remember her dream of running away with Ethan to a shady place where salt never formed but fish swam.

She averted her face. "Well, that's not going to happen now."

Whit leaned even closer to her, and she caught her breath, thinking he finally meant to kiss her, but he simply traced a finger around her cheeks and chin, the way the townswomen circled Our Lady's face before they made confession. "Don't be too sure," he said. "You may not have gotten what you want"—Claire blushed, knowing he was referring to Ethan—"but I always do."

He slipped his gaze down to her thigh, exposed where her dress had ridden up over it, and she gave a half-hearted yank to the hem. It concealed her leg but didn't accomplish much otherwise. She could still see the outline of her flesh underneath the dress's thin material, and she sighed, brushing sand off her lap, not knowing if she'd helped matters or just made them worse by covering up what was bound to burst out sooner or later.

———o-o o-o———

Whenever Claire looked back on the afternoon that she traded Salt Creek Farm for Plover Hill, she could never help but wonder if maybe the whole thing had been some kind of blunder or misunderstanding on her part. After all, Whit didn't come bearing a ring the day he proposed. He didn't drop to one knee the way Claire had always dreamed of Ethan doing. He didn't stammer with nerves when he asked her to be his wife, or take deep shaky breaths, and he certainly never put the matter of matrimony to her in the form of a question. Instead he did what he did best— made an executive decision—and Claire, good stenography student that she was, took him at his word.

She was sludging mud out of one of the empty evaporating pools that day. Whit had never set foot on the farm to see her before, but there he was, handsome as ever, stepping along the edge of the marsh as if he owned it. Flustered, Claire immediately smoothed her hair and tried to wipe some of the dirt off her hands, but it didn't do any good. She still felt like a hobo greeting a king. "What on earth are you doing here?" she said when he got close. "I don't think it's a great idea for us to meet in the marsh. You know, given everything."

But Whit just put his hands on her shoulders. "My thoughts exactly."

Her heart beat faster, and she cast an eye around for signs of Jo. "What do you want?" she asked, her voice low and cautious.

His dark eyes watched her as if he were keeping track of a clock. "You."

Claire snorted. "Don't be ridiculous."

Whit spread his arms. "What can a place like this offer a girl like you?"

Claire paused. It was the same question she'd been asking her whole life, but walking out on your existence was easier said than done. *I need a sign*, Claire thought, *just something little*, and at that moment one of those pesky blue butterflies, the ones her mother always said were bad luck, landed on her shoulder, followed by two more. Claire shuddered and tried to flick them off, but before she could, Whit threw his jacket around her. It only made the situation worse. She imagined the crushed bodies of the insects creeping down the coat's lining and fought off an urge to toss his jacket down into the mud.

Whit had fallen silent, and Claire realized he must have asked her a question. She looked up and found him standing almost nose to nose with her, staring into her eyes. That close, he smelled delicious, like spices and fine leather, and his skin was so polished that Claire was tempted to rub him to see if he squeaked or, better yet, granted her a wish. As if in a trance, she leaned toward him, preparing to kiss him right then and there, but that's when she saw Jo. She made a funny kind of noise, thinking even as she did that she had nothing to be guilty of, and then, before she could stop him, Whit was crushing her to his side and pronouncing her his future wife.

Everything in the world seemed to

hold its breath for a moment—the clouds, the water slipping over the weir, the salt leaching under Claire's feet. *Wife.* It was a word she had so long wanted to embody and thought she never would. If she couldn't be Ethan's wife, she debated with herself, would it be so bad to be wed to Whit? He was rich, after all, and handsome, and there was that undercurrent that bubbled between them, like the riptide at Drake's Beach, dragging along just beneath the surface of the water. Claire let her shoulder and then her hip relax into Whit, feeling the determined length of him, and thought it might be nice to live with a man who was dedicated solely to matters of the here and now rather than to the stupid spirit.

"Yes," she whispered, so low she wasn't even sure she was saying it, and he gave her a squeeze.

"Go get your things. I'll wait down the lane, engine running."

When she got into the house, she was confronted with the sorry truth that there was nothing she wanted to take. Certainly she wouldn't bring anything pertaining to Ethan—no yearbooks, or prom photos, or any of the poems he'd copied out to her. Besides those few mementos, her room might have been a nun's cell. In the end she shoved two pairs of jeans, three blouses, and a week's worth of underwear into a canvas bag, recognizing even then that it was a formality. Whit had told her to collect her things, so collect some of them she would, but she knew that nothing of her old self would survive the crossing out of Salt Creek Farm, and for Claire that was the whole point. Nothing would hurt anymore either.

Before she left, she paused for a moment by her window, which looked out over the marsh. Her mother had driven to Hyannis—there was no point looking for her—but in the distance Claire could see Jo's stooped back as she leaned down over one of the levees. She still hadn't gotten used to the crooked hang of Jo's body and wasn't sure she ever would. For Claire, having to look at what she'd done to Jo was like staring into a mirror that showed her all the awful parts of herself. She half raised her hand to the pane, as if waving farewell, but Jo couldn't see her and wouldn't have waved back even if she could. Claire lowered her arm. The two of them had shared about six words since Jo's accident. Clearly, "good-bye" wouldn't be one of them.

Claire backed away from the glass and picked up her little bag. Whit would wait only so long on the lane with his convertible's engine idling, she knew. If she just sat on her bed until the sun turned down a notch in the sky, he would be gone when she arrived. She thought about that for a moment, then closed the curtains on Jo and the marsh, and shut off the lamp, and then she took off running, first down the steps, then across the porch, the marsh, and finally the lane, going as fast as she could, then faster still, a burning arrow shot to uncertain flight.

———o-o o-o———

Jo had tried to roughen Claire's new life with her additions to the Virgin— those awful hooks snared along Our Lady's hem and that eye staring out with accusation. They were the first things Claire saw when she stepped inside St. Agnes for her wedding, her veil thick across her eyes, her hands shaking in their lace gloves. Without any words she knew exactly the message her sister meant to send. Jo was placing the weight of the eye she'd lost in the fire in Claire's open hand, where it did indeed sting and prick like those painted barbs. Underneath her veil Claire had blanched.

And yet. Even mourning her mother's death (sudden but not totally unforeseen) couldn't dampen Claire's new sense of contentment. Okay, maybe Turner House was a little shabbier inside than she'd expected, many of the items so used they had dents or holes, but the furnishings had clearly once been fine, and to Claire they were more extravagant than anything she'd ever before possessed.

And the Turner name was still good as gold. Claire made friends with the kinds of people who'd have eaten mud before they would have bought her family's salt, not just girls like Agnes

Greene but ladies from Boston and big estates in Connecticut. Whit showed her the country club, where he still had a social membership. She sped through town in his family's old red convertible, parking it wherever she liked and knowing she'd never get a ticket, and when she told Mr. Upton that he had to start carrying caviar in his grocery, he couldn't fill out the order form quickly enough. The good parts of her new life were scrumptious.

At first, using the silver cutlery and bone china, or sitting at Ida's Baroque lady's desk, Claire had felt a little like an impostor, but soon she found her fingers learning to curve around fountain pens and fish forks. She became adept with finger bowls and figured out how to knot a tuxedo tie for Whit. Every morning she marched down the house's main staircase and passed Ida's portrait on the landing, and she automatically smoothed her hair as if the painting could see her. It was silly, but she thought she could feel Ida's spirit lingering in the eaves of the house, waiting to see who would be banished from it first: the ghost of the mother-in-law or the wicked bones of the usurping daughter-in-law. The sheets even still smelled like Ida's sachets of lavender and attar of roses. Claire had new sheets sent from Boston, but when she opened the package, the same floral odor seemed to rise from the fabric and she ran to the nearest sink and vomited.

When the same thing happened the next two days in a row, Claire started to think that maybe the problem wasn't the sheets. Instead it was more organic. She was pregnant.

"I hope it's a boy," Whit said, sweeping her off her feet and gently placing her in the middle of the sheets she so hated. "A Turner boy with black eyes like me, red hair like you, and a temper to beat the wind." She caught her breath. *A boy*, she thought. Not blond, not with Ethan's blue eyes, but not born in the salt marsh either, where the weir had teeth and the graves had long memories.

Still. What if the bad Gilly luck found Claire anyway, high on Plover Hill? Better to be safe than sorry, she thought. Better to take matters into her own hands than to let the past she'd set free come back to dance on her future son's grave. What if the rumors she'd been spreading about the salt were true? Maybe the stuff *was* poison. Maybe that's why all the boys always died on their land.

She redoubled her efforts around town, reminding Mr. Upton that the salt wasn't regulated in any proper way and slipping hints to Mr. Hopper that an epidemic of food poisoning would be tragic for the diner. It was enough to remind her lady friends that too much sodium put weight on the hips. The only people she didn't get anywhere with were the fishermen down at the harbor, and that was largely because Claire couldn't bear to approach Ethan's uncle, Chet, who had Ethan's same eyes and voice, and an unflattering opinion about Claire's advantageous marriage that he wasn't afraid to share.

For a while she believed that her scheme was working. She thought she'd eluded fate, that she was safe, but it wasn't to be. Four months into her pregnancy, she began to bleed, first a little and then in a hot rush, until everything was gone and she was just her old self again, but emptier. To compensate for purging the salt from Prospect, she took an offering of honey to the Virgin. Normally it was something only new mothers would do, but Claire was trying to sweeten Our Lady into giving her another chance at motherhood. She pictured the gravestones—both old and recent—tilted in the marsh. If she had a son, she didn't want him to join her unholy brethren. She dipped her finger in honey and left a smear on the Virgin's patchy skirts, then touched her forehead to them.

"If I ever have a boy," she whispered to the painting, "I'll give you back your face." She waited, but there was no sign that the image had heard her. Claire was just alone, talking to a wall.

———o-o o-o———

A month after she lost the baby, Whit told her he had a gift for her and tied a shockingly expensive silk scarf around her eyes. She originally thought that was the gift, but when she said this to Whit, he laughed and led her through the vast Turner kitchen, across the back porch, and out to the small pasture behind the house.

"Put your hands here," he said, wrapping her fingers firmly around the split rails of the fence. "No peeking." Claire licked her lips and sniffed the air. She'd been spending almost all her time indoors, and it was nice to be outside again. She could smell grass and another musty odor she couldn't identify. There was a rustling, and then Whit was untying the scarf, letting his hands linger on her braid. Claire opened her eyes and saw that he had bought her a white horse.

"He's an albino," Whit said. "Not perfect, but good enough. Sired by an Arabian. Someone owed me a favor, so I let him pay me in kind." He stroked the horse's neck, impressed with his own command, which could summon a horse just because he wanted it. "I named him Icicle."

Claire regarded the animal, and as

she did, it stretched its neck forward and sank its downy muzzle into her open hands. Her heart immediately melted. Was love really so easy, she wondered, like the flood tide washing into the salt channels? Was that what Ethan had found in God, what she would have felt for a child? She scowled and pushed Icicle's nose away. "I don't ride."

Whit chuckled. "Don't worry, my love, we'll see to that." He was tying the blue scarf at her throat now—a little too tightly. He stepped back and surveyed the knot. "Don't you know?" he said. "There's not a thing about you that we can't change." And even though they were outside, well away from the damp mortar and plaster of Turner House, Claire thought she could hear a faint spectral laughing.

———o-o o-o———

The night she and Whit returned from their honeymoon, Claire was combing her hair before bed when Whit snuck up behind her and whispered against the side of her neck, "Don't ever cut it."

She laid down the silver brush, not sure whether to smile or sigh. Men were so easily led, pulled by threads as thin as a strand of red hair, and Whit was no exception. The only man whose heart she hadn't been able to hold was Ethan. She tilted her chin, watching her reflection in the mirror, seeing the new hollows and angles that had already formed since she'd undertaken the mysteries of matrimony. "What would you do if I did cut it off?" she asked.

Behind her, Whit's face darkened. "I hope you never go against me, Claire." His words slunk down her spine and into her belly. She looked at her hands and the chunky diamond ring that had once been Ida's. When she looked up again, she saw that Whit was holding out a necklace for her, not a pendant with sapphires or a jeweled cross, as Claire would have expected, but a dinky pearl on a silver chain.

Solemnly, he fastened it around her neck, and then his fingers strayed to her shoulders, digging into her flesh like a hoe breaking spring ground. Claire reached up and fondled the pearl, think-

ing it was more like something Ethan
would have bought for her and then
wishing she could crush her time with
him into a ball that was as shiny and
smooth and wear that instead. *No*, she
told herself. Better to leave the past
unadorned. Unbidden, a line from one
of Ethan's favorite poems leaped into
her mind: *Asleep! O sleep a little while,
white pearl! / And let me kneel, and let
me pray to thee.* Claire brought a fist to
her mouth. Ethan's prayers were to a
different God now.

"This used to be my mother's," Whit
said, adjusting the chain around her
neck, and the way he did it, with his
wrists heavy on her clavicles, made it
clear that he was sealing a pact between them. He had that tendency,
Claire was learning, to want to remind
her that she was his, but in sneaky
ways—with trinkets and unexpectedly
passionate kisses at inappropriate
times. None of the women on the society circuit recognized this side of Whit.

"He's Rhett to your Scarlett," the girls
at the country club would say when he
dipped Claire too low on the dance

floor. "Heathcliff to your Cathy." Claire never pointed out to them that neither of those couples had a happy outcome. The girls in her new set weren't big readers.

"She would want you to have it," Whit said, and Claire had to suppress a snort. The wedding ring, Icicle's fine profile, the pearl—they were the *last* things Ida would want to see a Gilly woman possess. Claire shivered as an early-autumn chill slipped through the drawn curtains and the windows rattled, but she accepted the gift. That was one advantage the living had over the dead, she thought. They could still say yes to such things.

"Thank you." Something hard—a stray twig, maybe—thumped against the window. Whit scowled and twitched the curtains tighter, then returned to her, winding his hands around her waist.

"Come to bed," he said, and it was half a command and half a dare. Claire let him draw her by the wrist down onto the mattress. He pinned her arms with his knees and leaned over her, letting his breath stroke her neck. "If you ever try to break the strings between us, you'll fail," he said, biting her gently at first and then harder. "You know that, right?" Sex with Whit could be rough, sometimes even almost painful, but it was exciting in a way Claire had never imagined possible. Each time she let him have her, she felt like she'd survived something dangerous, which only made her want to do it again, and she succumbed now, letting her arms relax under the weight of his knees and her head fall back in pleasure.

After Whit fell asleep, she crept out of bed and eased over to Ida's vanity. Claire ran her fingers lightly over the table's ornate drawer pulls. Up until now she'd avoided peeking into them, as if Ida might resurrect herself, leap through the wall, and sever her hands for the crime. Claire did her own makeup in the bathroom, keeping her small stash of cosmetics in one of the drawers there. She glanced over to Whit, but he was out cold, sprawled on his back and snoring. Taking a deep breath, she reached down to pull the middle drawer open.

She had to jiggle it back and forth to make it slide. Something was caught in the back. She tugged harder, and the drawer flew open, knocking her hand into her belly. Holding her breath, she leaned down. Inside, she found a pair of silver nail scissors, a cracked tortoiseshell compact, a string of cloisonné beads, and, oddly, a tiny linen bag of salt crystals, torn a little from where the drawer edge had pinched it. Perhaps that's what had made the drawer stick. Claire frowned and reached for it. The fabric was brittle and faded. She slid it out, not wanting to break the fibers of the sack further. Some of the crystals spilled into her palm nevertheless, where they winked in the moonlight, the source of all her troubles. She licked her finger and brought it to her lips, grimacing at the familiar bite—the taste of home that she'd tried so hard to forget.

Why would Ida, of all people, have kept a sack of salt in her drawer? Claire wondered. She knew that Ida loathed everything about the marsh even as she kept trying to buy it from Claire's

mother. Maybe for Ida, Claire rumi-
nated, the salt had been like the grit in
an oyster shell. It was what spurred her
on to produce something unexpected
and marvelous. The air in the room had
grown so still that Claire worried she
might shatter it by breathing. She listened for a rattle at the window, a rustling in the walls, but there was nothing,
and that was more frightening to her
than any ghoulish noise the house could
produce, for Ida wasn't gone, Claire
knew. She would never be gone. She
was simply waiting to see what Claire
would do in her place. Sitting here in
Ida's seat, wearing her diamond wedding band and her old necklace, Claire
was just taking up where Ida had left
off, and she wasn't sure she wanted to
do that. She unclipped the pearl from
around her neck, dropped it on the corner of the vanity, and turned to go lie
with her husband in the bed she'd made
for herself.

———o-o o-o———

The fourth time Claire lost a child was
the quickest and the last—a swirl of

blood laced down her thighs, a dizzy spell, and then it was over, like Genesis in reverse. Instead of starting out covered with a vast blanket of nothing, Claire ended up that way, tucked knees to chest in bed, empty as a begging bowl in a famine. She took off all her jewelry—Ida's pearl that she always wore, earrings, even her wedding ring—and stowed everything in the vanity. From now on, she vowed, she would be as plain as she could get. She would meet the world on its own terms alone, no adornments.

Whit took her to a specialist in Boston and then to another doctor for a second opinion, but the verdict was always the same. Nothing seemed to be wrong, and yet everything was.

"What about adoption?" she croaked at Whit after five days, the first words she'd spoken.

He sat down next to her on the bed, an anvil of judgment. "Absolutely out of the question. I need a proper son and heir, a Turner child by blood, not some lowlife that no one else wants." He leaned down and gave her a little pep

talk. "Claire, you can't let these inci-
dents defeat you. We'll just keep trying.
The Turner name can't die." He reached
out and gripped her thigh under the
blanket, then inched his hand up her
body. She locked whatever joint he
chose to touch—shoulder, elbow,
wrist—but Whit didn't seem to notice
or care. "Anyway, you have lots of other
responsibilities. What about your committee work? Also, Icicle needs a good
run."

That was true. Now that Claire had
learned to ride him, Icicle was a solace,
a miracle of muscle and intuition. But
he grew agitated when he didn't get his
daily exercise, Claire knew. She sat up
and sighed. She wasn't sure what it
said about her marriage that a horse
could get her out of bed when her husband couldn't, but she didn't think it
was anything good.

So she rose, slipped her jeweled
wedding band back on, then a pair of
earrings, a brooch, and the pearl necklace, and accomplished a great deal. In
a single week, she reorganized the library by subject and letter, taking the

collection of antique books with damaged spines to the bookbinder for repair. She sorted out the china cabinet in the dining room, discarding the chipped gravy boat and two cracked dinner plates. She rolled up the threadbare Persian runner in the downstairs hall and replaced it with a new carpet of sea grass and leather.

"Have you lost weight?" Cecilia West asked her over lunch in Wellfleet. "You look thinner, and you've been so quiet lately!"

Katy Diamond, their third, eyed her critically. "Yes," she agreed, "quite thin."

"I've had a stomach bug," Claire replied, unfolding her napkin across her lap and moving the salt shaker across the table. She wanted to pick it up and smash it.

"Lady problems?" Cecilia asked, and before Claire could even deny it, Katy laid her hand on Claire's arm and squeezed out her sympathy.

"I heard that in Europe women drink barley water for those things," Katy said.

Claire eyed her coldly and shrugged

the other woman's fingers off her forearm. Katy had a fat toddler at home
and a second baby on the way. She
could drink any kind of water she
wanted, apparently.

Claire stuck out her chin and accepted the menu from the waiter. "Well,
at least I'll be able to fit into my new
bathing suit come this summer," she
said, eyeing Katy's bulk and flipping
open the menu. "Unless, of course, I
lose any more weight and it ends up
being too big. Maybe you'll want it if
that happens?"

Katy blushed furiously and stared
down at her plate.

"Where have you been?" Agnes
Greene screeched when Claire returned
to the library committee. "We've been
lost without your suggestions regarding cocktails for the August benefit.
What do you think? Should we serve
sidecars or not?"

Claire wanted to tell Agnes that she
could drown herself in stupid Katy Diamond's barley water for all she cared,
but the woman's chatter was unrelent-
ing, and soon she found herself pulled

under a wave of chintz tablecloth samples, plans for shopping trips to Boston, and debates over whether married women should dare try to wear miniskirts. Claire closed her eyes. Elsewhere in the country, protests over the conflict in Vietnam were raging, and men were walking on the moon, but here in Prospect, it seemed, earthbound life would never change.

That year, as Claire watched the annual bonfire pyre rise on Tappert's Green, she felt as brittle as the sticks being heaped on top of one another. Every morning, as she cantered past the structure on Icicle, she measured its progress: First it rose to her hips, then to her waist, then to her shoulders and beyond. Icicle spooked at the building racket and almost threw her, and she yanked hard on his bit to get him under control. She rode home in a snit.

Nothing in her life was working out the way she'd thought it would. She'd left the marsh fully prepared to be dazzled by the wealth of Turner House, only to find out that it wasn't as ritzy inside as she'd believed. Lately she'd noticed curious things going missing. First it was the portrait of Armistead Turner, the family founder, which had hung at the end of the upstairs hallway. Claire had woken one morning to a dark and empty square where the painting once was. Then it was a set of china she used every Christmas, and next it was a diamond choker of Ida's that Claire had never been allowed to wear. Initially she speculated that perhaps the items had been sent out for repair or restoration, but when months went by without their returning, she started to think otherwise.

It was true that Whit had his moments of generosity—with Icicle, for instance—but mostly he kept the household finances on a tight lead, begrudging Claire's requests for tennis lessons or trips to Europe, things her richer friends enjoyed. His temper could flare then. "Lord, Claire. What do you think? That I'm made of money?" Actually, that *was* what Claire thought. He was born from Ida, wasn't he, flesh of her flesh, all his genes Turner ones? Money had made Whit. It seemed logical that he would make money in turn. Claire couldn't understand why on earth he stewed over Salt Creek Farm. He'd grown up alongside her and Jo, after all. He'd seen firsthand what life in the marsh was like. There was no way she was going back there.

As Claire watched the final touches being put on the bonfire pyre, an idea came to her. Maybe if Whit saw how nonsensical people's belief in the salt really was, he'd give up pursuing ownership of the marsh. Clearly, telling people that the stuff was toxic hadn't broken the pull of the salt over the town. Chet Stone and his buddies completely ignored all Claire's warnings and insinuations, and she knew perfectly well that people like Mr. Upton kept stashes handy. It was time for more drastic measures. "I don't want people burning salt at this year's bonfire," she told Whit that evening over dinner.

He looked at her blandly. If Claire had changed during their years of marriage—her bones thinning out, her hair dulling to a more manageable crimson—he'd changed, too. Threads of gray flecked his temples, and his eyes were growing deeper-set. Looking at him, Claire realized she couldn't remember the last time they'd made love. Well before her most recent miscarriage, she knew, but when? She felt a rush of heat spread across her belly and thighs and a flush steal over her chest, but Whit was impervious to her arousal. He sawed at his steak, one eye on the clock set on the mantel.

"Good point," he said. "The less anyone else has to do with the salt, the better. I'll talk to the constable. Salt's a chemical, right? There must be some law on record that bans burning chemicals in public areas." He folded his napkin in perfect thirds and laid it next to his plate, the half-finished steak a pulpy mess in the middle of the white porcelain. Claire averted her eyes. Whit hadn't attended a December's Eve festival since they'd gotten married six years ago, Claire knew, though, unlike her, the town would have welcomed his presence with open arms. But Whit wasn't a man who required adoration—not even, she realized as he strode from the room without even a peck on her cheek or a single backward glance, from his own wife.

The night of the bonfire, Claire left the bedroom window cracked open to the wintry air as she combed her hair before bed and waited for Whit to come upstairs—one hundred cruel strokes with a coarse boar-bristle brush, a penance for beauty. Through the gap in the window, she could smell the quivering excitement of smoke building and then the headier notes of pitch and wood turning to ash.

She sat very still in front of Ida's vanity, shivering in her sleeveless nightgown, her electrified hair spread down her back, and she waited, but there came none of the familiar sounds of flute trills, or the happy squeals of teenagers, or the usual bursts of delighted laughter when Jo threw the salt packet to the flames and a bright flash of peaceful blue erupted. Instead Claire heard indistinct murmurings and the crunching of feet on iced-up grass as small groups formed, broke apart, and came together again without any center to hold them. As children on this night, she and Jo used to huddle together in bed, a hot-water bottle between them, their arms wrapped around each other's waist for comfort.

Claire waited for the familiar sounds of the bonfire celebration to begin, but the night air hung dead and thick like the poisoned atmosphere inside a bell jar. Without the salt, the fire had lost its appeal for people. She listened as, one by one, the citizens of Prospect began to depart, fracturing off from one another in disconsolate pairs or trios, dragging their feet in the frost-laden grass of Tappert's Green, fishing in their pockets for noisy rings of house keys, resigned to going home without a glimpse of what the year would bring them.

Claire closed the window and climbed into bed, waiting for Whit to come and join her, and when he did, she rolled toward him, her nightdress bunched around her waist, her lips parted, but he simply turned off the light, folded the covers over himself, and patted her arm absently. "Not tonight," he said. "I have an early meeting tomorrow about a property near Hyannis." Claire's belly clenched, but Whit was her husband, the choice she'd made, and so she snapped off her own light and stretched out like a dead woman next to him.

She rose before the sun was up, ripped from sleep by a choking sensation—her old asthma. Her mother used to bring her a steaming bowl of salt water and cover her head with a towel when she got like that, Claire remembered, forcing her to breathe the salt, but now she fumbled for her inhaler, trying not to wake Whit.

When she could suck air in again, she slipped out of bed, dressed quickly, and tiptoed out to the stable behind the house to saddle up Icicle. The sky brightened to a half-lit moment between night and dawn, and before she could stop herself, Claire cantered through town, down the lane, and out to the marsh. She slowed Icicle to a walk and then dismounted at the boundary of rushes between the lane and Salt Creek Farm, pulled back to a place she didn't want to be.

Wheezing a little, she stepped through the rushes, passing in front of the new barn. She looked down at the ground near the barn's foundation, but the marsh's earth had healed itself faster than its inhabitants had. Any traces of the fire—any signs of scorching or left-over ash—were long gone, absorbed into the ground's fecund mud.

She turned to the graves. Stone was the only material that lasted out here. Everything else—wood, earth, cinders, and even human bones—was indifferent fodder for the salt. Out of old habit, Claire walked to the weir where her brother had drowned so long ago, and saw that Jo had flooded the basins for the winter. Nothing remained of them but murky surface water.

Claire returned to the graves and sank down by them, regretting that she had nothing to offer any of her kin, living or dead. For a brief moment, she thought about leaving some kind of token for Jo, but she'd come to Salt Creek Farm bearing nothing, not even a tarnished penny, and besides, what would she have offered her sister? Nothing seemed adequate. A flower or a leaf? The autumn had taken them all. A message scratched in the mud? But expressing what? The more Claire longed to say, the less she was able.

In the end the sun started to peek over the horizon, breaking the morning's spell, and Claire ran out of time. Jo would rise soon, too, and if Claire wasn't careful, she knew that her sister would spy her through the kitchen window. Before it grew any lighter, she stepped back onto the lane and swung herself up onto Icicle again and retreated the same way she'd come: empty-handed, heavy-hearted, leaving only a trail of curved hoof prints hooked in the sand behind her, never guessing that one day they would lead her back home.

Chapter Thirteen

——o-o ◖◗ o-o——

Right from the start, Whit Turner seemed to like to give Dee things, which was tremendous, because she enjoyed taking them. She didn't feel a lick bad about the arrangement either. In fact, the opposite was true. The more she got from Whit, the more she wanted, and as a result their affair moved quicker than it otherwise might have, which suited Dee just fine. It wasn't like she'd found anything else to occupy her during her first month in town.

Dee learned about Whit's quirks and preferences on the down low. They met a few times a week in hidden kinds of spots—on the beach, cradled in the sand dunes, or at a picnic table behind a clam shack closed for the season. Always at night and always in secret, but that just made it more exciting whenever Whit sauntered into the diner, ordered up some coffee and eggs, and winked at her when her father wasn't looking.

By the middle of November, Dee had started looking forward to Whit's gifts with an open greed she didn't know she had. It was all she could do not to snatch the things he presented to her out of his hands with her teeth and then turn her bite on him. In short order he bestowed upon her a bottle of fancy skin lotion, a lipstick in a silver case, and a box of chocolates too pretty to eat.

The night of the first snow, he nibbled the side of her neck and asked her, "Which do you like better, satin or silk?" Before she could answer, he pulled out a pair of black French panties. Dee didn't bother to point out that she couldn't tell the first difference between either kind of fabric. All the textures of her life were exactly the same: rough.

"They're so soft," she breathed, rubbing a little of the lace between her thumb and forefinger. She couldn't wait to slip them on or, better yet, have Whit do it for her. She leaned back in the passenger seat of his car and pulled off the cotton underpants she was wearing, letting her head fall onto the top of the seat to see if Whit was watching. He was.

"Don't bother," he growled, reaching across the seat to pin her to the leather.

The next time they were together, he gave her a tiny sample bottle of perfume. It didn't smell too good to Dee, to be honest, but she'd smell any way Whit wanted her to if it meant they could keep riding around in his car, parking in places where they could see the stars.

"It's very expensive," he said. "Here, try it." He dabbed a dot behind one of Dee's ears, and she inhaled and grew almost dizzy. She'd never worn real perfume before. She put the lid back on the bottle and turned to face Whit.

"Does Claire wear this?" she asked. She pictured bending over to serve Claire breakfast the next morning and watching her pert nose wrinkle.

What's that smell? Claire would say, not quite believing what her nostrils were telling her. *It's familiar.* And Dee would just waltz off without a word.

At the mention of his wife's name, Whit's face grew hard and still. He dropped his fingers from Dee's hair. "She doesn't like perfume, and she'd be furious if she found out about our meetings, so you better not say anything."

Dee closed her fingers tightly around the bottle. Whit didn't need to bring up Claire's temper. Dee had experienced it for herself in the diner the single time she didn't get Claire's order right. If Claire never raised her voice, Dee thought, it was because she didn't have to. Her silence was far more terrifying.

"I won't say anything," Dee promised, and Whit leaned over and buried his nose at the base of her throat.

"It's nice to have a woman smell the way I want her to for a change," he said.

Dee put her hand on his cheek, flattered that he'd called her a woman and not a chubby kid, which was all she ever saw when she looked in the mirror, silk French panties or no. She remembered Mr. Weatherly telling her that Claire had been near to her age when she'd gotten married, and Dee wondered if that's when Claire had made the transition from awkward girl to a pair of arched eyebrows and a stare that could stop a speeding truck. Now more than ever, Dee wondered what the link between her and Claire might be. The only common factor they seemed to have between them was the absence of one. Whit probably liked her, Dee thought, not because she reminded him of Claire but because she was so fundamentally Claire's opposite. She dabbed more perfume on her wrist and took another sniff before she turned to Whit. "What does Claire smell like, then?" she asked.

Whit considered that for a moment.

"Saddle soap and plain soap," he finally answered. "Sometimes hay. And she sprinkles on baby powder before bed."

No wonder he's parked out here in the bushes off the lane, necking with the likes of me, Dee thought. She wasn't even to her twenties yet, but she had enough experience with males of all ages to know that they were fickle as a pack of crows. Unless you had something shiny and dangly, they just flew right past you.

"That's enough talking," Whit said, pulling her on top of him and opening her blouse. "We have to hurry and get you home before your father starts to worry. What have you told him anyway?"

"That I met a nice boy," Dee lied. In fact, she'd told Cutt nothing. His curiosity stopped at the rim of his evening bottle. Once he passed out, nothing on earth could wake him, not even the noisy fumbling of a girl drunk on love. Whit placed his thumbs over the tips of Dee's breasts, and an electric current passed from her chest to her groin. She moved her hips against his.

"A nice boy," he said, and chuckled, pushing her bra down and replacing it with his mouth. "How little you know. I never was that."

"I don't believe you," Dee whispered, and then they didn't speak any longer.

———o-o o-o———

Mr. Weatherly had the oddest way of answering questions, Dee thought. She was asking him about the upcoming December's Eve bonfire, and at first she was confused by his rambling response, but as she listened, she realized he was telling her two things at once. Mr. Weatherly was sneaky like that, Dee decided. He never lectured or gave his personal opinion, but sometimes after she was done talking with him, after she watched him hitch up his pants and shuffle away, she would realize that she'd been given a moral lesson of sorts, even if she could never figure out exactly what it was.

Now that the end of November was near, the bonfire had started going up on Tappert's Green tidier than Dee expected—the base planks crossed over the top of one another and then the bigger pieces of wood leaning up against those in stark rows. Apparently the town elders had decided on a new design for the pyre, square instead of round. The unexpected order of the structure didn't reassure Dee. It just made the sight of the pyre even creepier to her. Fires didn't always spring up unbidden. She had never thought much about that simple fact before.

"Aye, every year it gets a little bigger," Mr. Weatherly mumbled over his plate of turkey and mash at the counter, staring at Dee darkly. "And every year it burns a little faster. Used to be we'd all linger over the coals late as anything, thinking about the future, but Claire put an end to that business with her string of unborns."

At the mention of Claire's name, Dee felt a familiar buzz start up at the back of her neck, but now a tiny chill of worry joined that excitement. Lately she'd stopped pestering Mr. Weatherly with questions about the Gilly sisters, especially Claire, but she still woke in the gray smear of dawn and waited for horse's hooves to sound beneath her window. She still studied Claire during church, memorizing the exact color of her sweater set, trying to decide what shade her lipstick would be called, even though Dee definitely didn't dare bring up Claire's name anywhere outside the diner. No more conversations with the postmistress about Claire's past loves. No more questions to Mr. Upton in his claustrophobic little store about Claire's favorite foods. Dee didn't want tongues to start wagging.

Cutt had instructed Dee to ask Mr. Weatherly if they should bother staying open the night of the bonfire in hopes of collecting some extra business. Maybe people would want something hot to drink, he thought, and a little something sweet on their tongues. But Mr. Weatherly just shook his head. "Not likely," he said, his face as hangdog as Dee had ever seen a man's. "Not after what Claire did on account of all her unborn babies."

Nervously, she peeked around the diner, but they were in between lunch and dinner services, and the only other customer was ancient Mrs. Butler huddled in a back booth with her old lady friend, and neither of them could hear a thing. Dee picked up a rag and started polishing the counter, trying not to let her interest show.

"What do you mean, Claire's unborns?" she said, moving the cloth in tight and calculated circles, hoping that Mr. Weatherly would be distracted by the motion and keep talking. The trick worked. He leaned over his plate and squinted at her.

"You're sorta young to be telling this kind of thing to," he proclaimed. "Still got the puppy fat hanging thick around your middle, don't you? My girl Doreen had that at your age, but she's as thin as a birch branch now."

Dee flushed, but then she had to hide her smile behind her hand. If Mr. Weatherly knew the positions she could get that puppy fat into, he might not be so quick to call attention to it. She started circling her rag on the counter again. "What do you mean by *unborns*?" she asked again.

Mr. Weatherly helped himself to a full

bite of mashed potato. "I took a crib delivery up to their house one time, and then, six weeks later, got called to take it back again. Then I noticed people kind of going off the salt around town. Herman Upton was still selling it under the counter, but he got skittish about it. Harlan Friend in the hardware said his wife had switched to boxed. Said it tasted better, too." He took another bite of potato. "Every time Claire got her dander up and started spouting off about her family's salt being poison, I figured she must have lost another babe. And then, finally"—he pushed his plate toward Dee, and she quickly dumped it into the plastic bin beneath the counter—"there weren't no more salt to get rid of but the stuff the fishermen used—and even Claire knew that was a lost cause—and the bonfire salt."

Dee wrinkled her forehead. "What do you mean?"

Mr. Weatherly fixed her with his stare. "Why do you think we have the blasted thing in the first place?" he said. "It's not just for our entertainment. Ever since there's been Gillys in this town, they've tossed salt to the fire to see what the future has in store for us. If the smoke flashes blue, that's good. Red means someone will be falling in love, yellow's a warning, and black . . . well, black is . . . not good. . . ." His voice trailed off, and his eyes looked wet around their rims. Then he fished his wallet out of his pocket. "Claire made us stop, though. She had the constable tell everybody we were in violation of some code or another. He threatened to arrest anyone throwing chemicals into the fire. Kind of took the festivity out of the evening. Claire's never said nothing about it, but we all know it was her doing. I can only imagine how much it cost her in donations to local law enforcement to pull it off."

"So why keep having the fire at all?" Dee asked.

Mr. Weatherly jammed his cap on his head. "Sometimes it's not what we do that matters so much as why we gather to do it in the first place. Besides, I guess it's too late to change our ways now. We just go on the best we can." Dee watched him let himself out into the icy clutches of the afternoon, snow flurries whipping around him like devils intent on making mischief, and she wondered if, more than just the bonfire, he maybe was referring to the whole damn town—leached now of its salt, frozen down to its foundations, heavy with the weight of Claire's unborn babies. She picked up the rag again and wrung it out, trying to lighten at least one little thing around the place the best her hands could do.

———o-o o-o———

In the end Dee was relieved to find that the bonfire was just as Mr. Weatherly had promised it would be. The night was pure and almost clinically cold. The stars buzzed like small insects, and as if in protest, the wood of the newly square pyre groaned and crackled as it caught fire. Dee watched people's faces twist and dance in the orange light of the flames. The citizens of Prospect clustered into firm little groups, their hands shoved in their pockets. A few souls took deep pulls from flasks and discussed their plans for the upcoming summer, even though to Dee it seemed impossible that the world would ever thaw and that she would gaze on bright green grass again.

She stood alone. Her father had chosen to keep the diner open after all, and though folks recognized her, they didn't know her well enough to invite her into their huddles. She watched a group of high-school girls about her age giggling over a boy they liked, but when they saw her looking at them, their faces hardened into blank masks, and Dee quickly moved farther around the other side of the fire, thinking how just a few months ago she could have had a part in their plots and girlish plans. She stepped a little closer to the heat of the blaze and let herself, for a brief moment, regret her mother's death and wonder what she would have made of this celebration, but before Dee could wallow too much in her own loss, she felt a hand grab her shoulder, and she knew that Whit had found her, as they'd planned.

"Let's get out of here," he said, "before people realize I'm here." Dee almost didn't recognize him herself. He was wearing a watch cap like many of the other men, a dark parka, and jeans. He looked so uncomfortable that she almost burst out laughing, but then her stomach twisted at the thought of the effort he'd made to join her. She wondered where the clothes had come from but decided not to ask. With Whit it was better not to know the little details of the bigger situation.

He let her slip her arm around his waist once they were far enough away from the fire and hidden by shadows. If anyone was looking, Dee thought, they could have been any couple. All anyone would have seen was their posture of togetherness and none of the things that actually kept them separated: their different stations in life, his marriage, their ages. They skirted the edge of the green without speaking and then sauntered to the bottom of Plover Hill and the pear tree, safe in the darkness. Every now and then, a stray spark floated above them, flaring brightly at first and then fading into a white fleck of useless ash. Without preamble Whit leaned Dee

up against the trunk and starting un-
buttoning her pants.

"Open your legs a little more." His
voice was a hot buzz in her ear, and for
a minute it sounded to her like he was
asking her to open her heart, so she
inched up on her toes and let him lift
her thigh.

"Wait." She tried to shift his hand out
from under her leg, but things were too
far gone between them, and he took
her movement as an invitation to close
the deal. It wasn't unpleasant either,
even if the pear tree's bark did rub her
ass an unholy pink, a fact Whit couldn't
see in the dark but one he probably
would have appreciated. He liked tangible results, Dee was learning, whether
it was a love rash down her neck or a
toothy bruise tattooing her soft stomach. She could imagine him wanting to
notch his initials into her skin the way
people carved the bark of the old pear
tree, nicking a crude heart around the
letters and sticking them through with
an arrow. The sick thing is, she probably would have let him.

She was starting to wonder if maybe

she was in a bit over her head. She leaned back against the pear tree's trunk while Whit did up his trousers, and she closed her eyes, picturing herself driving Claire's little sports car, hands all buckled up in expensive leather gloves, hair tied inside a giant silk scarf, just like some old-time movie actress. Claire never wore a scarf that way, but if Dee had a flaming head of hair like Claire's, she wouldn't either.

"You still haven't told anyone, have you?" Whit's voice smacked her like a splintery paddle breaking up still water. Dee opened her eyes and pulled her shirt closed. In the moonlight the line of Whit's jaw was as hard as the wood behind her back, maybe harder.

"No." *Really*, she wanted to ask, *who would I tell?* Whit Turner might have been richer, older, and a heap and a half more educated than she was, but he was still a man, and like all men, in Dee's opinion, he still thought with his prick.

"Good." He leaned in close and pressed his full lips against the bottom of her throat. "I have something special for you," he said.

They didn't have much more time, Dee knew. She was supposed to rush back and help her father at the diner. Whit opened her hand and put something into it, and when Dee looked down, she saw a tarnished silver locket in the shape of a heart. She turned it over. On the back, in florid script, was a single *W*.

"So you don't forget me." Whit grinned.

Dee frowned. Compared to the other things he'd dangled in front of her over the past few weeks, this trinket looked shabby, like something one of those high-school boys back in Vermont would have presented to her, convinced it was as precious as all the tea in China. On the other hand, none of them had actually given her jewelry before. She should take what she could get, Dee thought. She let Whit fasten the chain around her neck.

"Don't make that face," he said, putting a finger under her chin. "This locket has been around longer than you have, and I just happened to find it again the other day. It means something to me. If I catch you without it"—his expression turned naughty—"I'm going to have to spank you. Although"—he turned serious again—"maybe you should tuck it under your uniform during the day. I wouldn't want Claire seeing this." That made Dee giggle, but Whit didn't laugh with her. He pressed the locket into her chest, hard. "I'm not kidding," he said. "Don't lose this. It's old."

Dee shrugged. Honestly, she wasn't interested in the old with Whit. She wanted the new. "I thought this night was supposed to be about the future," she said with a pout. Immediately she realized she'd said something wrong.

Whit's face closed up like a fist. "Who told you that?"

She swallowed and pushed a stray piece of hair away from her face. She was starting to shiver. "I heard about it from Mr. Weatherly," she said vaguely. "About how the Gillys used to burn salt to predict everyone's futures . . ." She trailed off into silence, the secret of the babies Claire hadn't been able to carry a clumsy burden on her tongue. Whit waited for her to finish. "And now they don't," she said lamely.

Whit stepped away from her so she couldn't see his face. When he spoke, his voice cracked. "You know nothing about my past, Dee."

And then he was gone, melted right into the night. Except not exactly. Turns out he wasn't as tricky as all that. There was the rustle of his footsteps through the snow for one thing, heading back up the hill to Claire, and the faint glow of his bare hands under the moon. And his scent, peeling away from Dee in long, slow strips like the pieces of paper she'd unwrap off a present she good and sure wanted to make last.

She brushed off her jeans and set to walking the long way back to Bank Street, unwilling to give up the serenity of the night for the harsh lights of the diner. She took slower and slower steps, but in spite of herself she was there before she knew it, facing the slanty windows, the crooked door, and, worst of all, the silhouette of her father, hovering behind the counter like a battle flag hoisted for a fight Dee knew she didn't have a prayer of winning.

———o-o o-o———

Weeks after the bonfire, she started craving cashews. She began carrying bags of them with her everywhere she went, her pockets bulging like the cheeks of a squirrel.

"What's with all the nuts?" Cutt asked as she crunched yet another one of the curved kernels between her teeth at the diner's counter. She'd eaten so many cashews in the past week that her tongue was coated with a strange white scum she couldn't brush off in the mornings.

She shrugged. "Nothing. I just like them."

"Since when? I thought your favorite thing was a burger and fries."

"I'm still eating the burger and fries," she pointed out. "It's just that now I'm also eating cashews."

Cutt squinted at her. "You have circles under your eyes."

Dee tucked her arms around her

chest. Her breasts ached, and she was crabby. "I haven't been sleeping well."

"And what's with the ratty clothes? Did you lose an argument with a mower?"

She stared down at her faded gray corduroy pants and the navy blue sweater with a hole in one elbow. "They're clean."

Cutt snorted. "They look like they've been *used* to clean. Go put on your uniform. It's hanging in the utility closet." While she was fetching her work clothes Dee closed her eyes, and Whit's serious, square jaw swam into view, followed by the memory of the fleshy pockets of his palms, the hollow at the bottom of his neck, and the broad ripple of muscle that was his back. There was a spot in between his ribs where, if Dee held her palm, she could feel his heart beating. Since the bonfire they'd still been meeting, but he'd talked even less than usual, and he hadn't given her anything since the locket. The floor seemed to lurch slightly under her, and she let out a little burp, remembering she was supposed to go change clothes. Her father was waiting for her with the mop when she came back.

"You don't have a boyfriend, do you?" he asked, peering at her with suspicion. Beads of sweat broke out on Dee's forehead. Whit had warned her about a thousand and one times that she'd better not let a soul know what they were up to—especially not her father, he'd said, pressing the hard tips of his fingers into the soft upper chunks of her arms. When he'd pulled his hands away, he'd left little dents. At the time Dee had liked it, but now she wished she could get rid of the feeling. She was starting to suspect that once bestowed, Whit's gifts weren't so easily disposed of, and she hadn't thought to worry about that. It had never occurred to her that he might give her something he wouldn't be willing to take back.

"Nope," she said, grabbing the mop and avoiding her father's eyes. "No boys. I'm over boys for good." That was true. Whit was all man.

"Fine, then," Cutt said, turning away from her. "I don't know what guys would want with you anyway. You're not really the kind of girl they'd marry, Dee."

She reached for another cashew and crunched it. Given the fact that she was pregnant with Whit's child, wedlock was turning out to be more problematic for her than Cutt would even begin to guess.

Chapter Fourteen

Claire first heard about Jo's money problems through Whit, and although the thought of the marsh falling into ruin didn't bother her in the least, her concern for Jo caught her off guard.

"But where will she go?" she asked when Whit informed her that Jo had three months left on the farm—four at the most. Jo wasn't young anymore. Not old, certainly—only in her late thirties—but not exactly young either. Who would ever hire her? Especially since all she knew was salt.

"That's not my problem," Whit said.

"She should have taken me up on my earlier offers. I said she could stay if she would only sell me the land, but she practically spit in my face."

Claire narrowed her eyes. "When was this?" She knew that Ida had tried to buy the farm, of course, and she knew that Whit had had his eye on the place for years, but she'd been unaware that he'd had any contact with Jo since Mama's funeral.

Whit waved a hand. "It doesn't matter."

Claire pouted. "I don't want anything to do with that place. I married you to get away from it!" As soon as the words were out, she regretted them.

Whit's gaze solidified, and he bit down on *his* words. "And I married *you* to get my hands on it."

Claire paled. "What are you talking about?"

"Oh, come on," Whit snarled. "Don't be so naïve. You don't really think I married into your family out of love, do you? No. I admit, I thought you were pretty and we've had some fun, but I married you for your half of the marsh.

Only your fool mother put the brakes on that when she rewrote her will."

Claire put a hand up to her throat. "What do you mean?" she croaked.

"Jo's not the only one with money worries, Claire. Ever since I came home after college, I've been trying to turn the family holdings around, but the property business has been hard going these past few years."

Claire thought about the empty space on the wall where Armistead Turner's portrait used to be, and the missing set of plates, and Ida's vanished diamond necklace. She swallowed and listened as Whit continued.

"Mother always said that if she could only own the salt, it would cancel out her debts." His eyes glittered.

"But that's ridiculous," Claire said. "Look at Jo. The salt hasn't done a damn thing for her. What makes you think you'd do any better with the place?"

Whit puffed up his chest. "Because I'm a Turner, that's why. Jo and your mother and the women before them have always had the salt backing them up. Everyone knows it. That's why the Gillys have always been feared. Nobody wanted to marry them when they had nature on their side. But I wasn't afraid. I married you, didn't I? Once the salt is in my hands, everything will turn around." He took a step closer and gripped Claire's shoulders too tightly. "You better not stand in my way. I mean it."

Claire tossed her head, trying to squirm free of Whit's painful grasp. "If you're so broke, what are you going to use to buy the place? A set of dishes isn't going to get you far, even if the land *is* cheap." She thought about the portrait of Ida she hated so much hanging over the stairs. If she was lucky, Whit would sell that, but she somehow doubted it. Ida was to blame for this mess in the first place.

Whit pushed his face close to Claire's. "If I have to dump this place to get my hands on Salt Creek Farm, I will. It'd be worth it."

Claire finally worked one of her shoulders free from his grip and flicked her braid, staring straight into his eyes. So

Whit had never loved her. That was fine. She'd never really loved him either. They were even. "The only way you're going to buy the marsh is over my dead body," she said, trying to keep her voice from quivering and her temper calm.

Whit smiled then, but not all the way. Not with his eyes. He took his other hand off Claire's shoulder, leaving that spot of her skin chilled. "Don't tempt me," he said.

———o-o o-o———

With great sorrow and much deliberation, Claire poured a second scoop of sugar into her coffee and stirred. It was very early spring, the first week of Lent, and when dawn did break, Claire suspected, the sky would hold all the appeal of a dented tin canteen.

She was sitting in a back booth at the Lighthouse, and, as usual, she was the diner's first customer of the day. She gazed through the front windows but was confronted by nothing but her own reflection: a hard ghost flattened onto a lifeless surface. She flicked her eyes down to the table, but then, her stomach cramping, she glanced up again, squinting to make sure that neither her eyes nor her heart was playing tricks. They weren't. Outside on Bank Street, she saw Ethan Stone marching toward the diner.

Her heart started thumping so loudly she thought it might crack the glass as she shrank back into the booth. She watched Ethan shiver and wrap his coat tighter, as if trying to stave off the intrepid spring wind. He appeared older than Claire expected, his hair cut very short, his lips more defined. He also looked numb, damp, and hungry, and she saw immediately that his image in the window was still dear to her. She sat up a little higher and watched as he considered the Lighthouse, still unaware of her presence. She hoped he wouldn't come in—she wasn't ready to face him yet, never mind in public—but the cold won out, and he pushed his way inside, setting off the bell over the door.

Ethan loosened his overcoat and stamped the mist from his boots. He looked around for the row of brass hooks to the left of the door and then spied Claire hunched down over her cup of coffee in the booth. He froze, as startled as she was, and then he smiled, and Claire saw with deep regret that the light in his eyes was the same as ever.

"May I?" He gestured to the bench opposite her, and she hesitated.

"Hello, Ethan," she finally managed to say. She watched him flush and adjust the band around his neck. She wondered if his skin felt too exposed and raw when he removed it at night. Maybe it was a relief to put it back on again in the morning. Then she scolded herself for having any kinds of thoughts of Ethan at night.

"Claire," he croaked, and offered his hand. When he laid his palm against her skin, she almost gasped, for at his touch the years between them dissolved. If Claire had closed her eyes at that moment, she would have sworn they were once again eighteen and about to embrace under the carved-up pear tree.

She looked up and saw Cutt watching from behind the diner counter. He spent an inordinate amount of time, Claire noticed, loitering at the cash register when he wasn't cooking—all the better to collect the local news, she supposed, much of which she knew involved her. She took her fingers away from Ethan's and laid them back on the table, innocent and alone. Her diamond wedding band caught the light, a glaring circle, bright as any lighthouse beam.

She put her hands in her lap. "I'm sorry about your father passing," she said, even though it was a lie. No one in town had been sorry, not even Ethan's uncle Chet, who had taken over Merrett's boat and doubled his seasonal haul.

Ethan sighed. "Thank you. Maybe the ocean misses him, but I doubt anyone else around here does. My uncle's doing well, though. He keeps offering me my old job back." Claire blushed, and just then Cutt appeared with a menu and hung over the table while Ethan contemplated his choices.

"I'll have the pancakes," he finally

said, and Cutt took the order with the temper of a man who bathed in vinegar and washed his feet in lye.

"I'll send Dee over with the coffee," he barked. Ethan nodded thank you, and Claire noticed a few beads of sweat clinging to his hairline. In manhood he looked more like his father than he used to, but his mannerisms were the opposite of Merrett's. Ethan's gestures were circumspect, almost stilted. Even the way he blinked seemed deliberate, as if in every movement he was reminding himself that he wasn't his own master.

He gazed around the diner, taking in all the changes, and then his brow wrinkled. "What happened to all the salt?" he said.

Claire flushed, but before she could answer, Cutt's oxen-boned daughter arrived with a half-empty coffeepot atilt in one of her hands and a plate of pancakes in the other, her mouth hanging open in an unattractive stupor. Claire wanted to slide out from behind the table and press the child's lips together, but it wouldn't have done any good, she suspected. Everything on the girl was so loose it rattled, including her brains. Dee leaned over to refill Claire's cup and accidentally dribbled coffee on her sleeve, the girl's mouth falling open even wider as she watched the stain bloom.

"Don't worry about it," Claire said, dabbing at it with her napkin. "This shirt's old." She looked up at Dee's plain features. She wasn't exactly pretty—her face was too bland for that—but Claire could see how there was something about Dee that might make a man want to strip her bare and see all of her at once. She put her hand on Dee's wrist. "I know you wouldn't be dumb enough to deliberately ruin my clothing, would you, dear?"

Dee blushed an impressive scarlet but didn't say anything, and Ethan looked shocked at Claire's rudeness, but Claire didn't care, she decided. Twelve years was a long time. Ethan had no idea that there were times, moments like this, for instance, when she felt more like Ida Turner than the heartbroken girl he'd left sitting in the sand. Claire waited until Dee clomped off, her chubby hips swinging, and then she leaned forward, lowering her voice.

"What made you really come back here?" she asked. He opened his eyes and blinked again in his new and annoyingly assured way, and Claire was suddenly glad she'd deprived him of the familiar taste of her family's salt. Maybe missing it would remind him of all the other things he could no longer have.

He put down his fork and shook his head. "I don't half know, to be perfectly honest. It wasn't my idea. Father Flynn called me home, and my superiors approved it."

Her stomach relaxed a little. His return had nothing to do with God or her, then, and everything to do with the fickle tempers of men. Claire put her coffee cup on the table and smeared her palms flat on the booth's sticky leather. When she moved them, they left sweaty prints. Ethan glanced up at her and smiled, and his eyes seemed to get bluer. "Do you still go to church, Claire?" he asked.

She inched back in the booth, her

heart pounding slightly, overly aware of how dark the wood trim was around the door, how thick the air, and how Dee was also now holding her head cocked in their direction over at the cash register. "Whit and I attend." She raised her voice a little so Cutt and his bovine daughter would hear. "You'll see us there on Sunday." She knew that Ethan was waiting to see if she'd bring up Jo, but it had been twelve years since her sister's name had dropped out of Claire's mouth, and she was damned if Ethan Stone was going to be the first person to hear it.

There was so much you didn't know at any given moment, Claire thought— namely, not to discount the weight of the past on your future. At that instant, sitting across from Ethan again, she began to suspect that the tidy rows of her life were little more secure than dominoes lined up on a warped floor. She shoved her mug to the center of the table and stood. Outside the window she could see Icicle stamping his feet and exhaling great clouds. Her chest felt like it had bricks sitting on it, and her voice came out higher than usual. "I have to go."

"Wait." Ethan tried to put his hand on top of hers, but she moved it just in time. She didn't turn to look as he followed her outside. "Saints and sinners," he muttered under his breath, and watched as Claire mounted Icicle, tucking her braid down the back of her blouse. Before she could step to the side of the road, Icicle whinnied and reared, kicking his forelegs out, narrowly missing Ethan's chest.

"Icicle! No." She lurched in the saddle, then tugged the reins and brought him back down to all four feet. Another brief struggle, a subtle squeeze of her thighs, and he soon stood quiet, snorting and shivering beneath her.

"I'm so sorry," she said to Ethan. "He's not usually like this. Are you all right?" Her tongue felt swollen behind the cage of her teeth. He nodded, but before he could answer, her eyes flashed. "You should be more careful. Prospect isn't quite as sleepy as it used to be. Cars will pop out of nowhere now, especially in the summer."

She could tell that there was much more Ethan wanted to say, but she didn't feel like giving him the chance. She slapped Icicle's reins and took off back to Plover Hill, back to her husband and his stern habits, back to hushed rooms and the tick of the clock in the upstairs hall, back, in short, to the flesh-bound life of a marriage she never expected to make but couldn't turn away from now.

—∘∘ ∘∘—

Whit and Claire were on their way to Ethan's first Mass at St. Agnes when Claire discovered an earring that wasn't hers in the car. They were running late, and Whit was speeding, driving with hard jerks and turns, something she hated. "Can you just slow down?" she begged, but Whit ignored her, so she reached her hand out to the dashboard to turn on music but then hesitated, her eye caught by something shiny stuck between her seat and the center console.

Glancing over to see if Whit was watching, she pulled out a plain hoop earring, not too large, not very expensive, and certainly not hers. She let it wink in her palm for a moment and then slipped it into her pocket before Whit took his eyes off the road, all the while keeping her face relaxed in spite of the murderous thoughts reeling through her mind. Learning of your husband's infidelity wasn't a sin, Claire knew very well, but the desire to kill him probably was.

She leaned her head back against the car's leather seat and wished she were at home, wearing the softest breeches she had and a thick barn jacket topped with a ratty scarf. She would shake her hair down from its complicated updo and fix it back into a braid. She'd grab a beat-up riding helmet with one hand and a pair of gloves with the other, and then she'd fling open the kitchen door and let the spring air sting her cheeks. Instead she let Whit hold the door of the car for her as they reached St. Agnes. She climbed out and smoothed her skirt, then followed him up the church steps the way she'd done hundreds of times before. She knelt down next to him, folded her hands with deceptive peace, and bowed her head, the picture of deportment.

The service went on around her like a dream, and Claire watched it all from the center of a terrible calm. Faces always revealed so much when they were sunk in worship, she thought, especially when the new priest was young and handsome and everyone was aware that he used to be in love with the town's richest woman. *Used to be*, Claire thought. No one loved her now, apparently not even her husband, and they weren't nearly as rich as everyone thought. She lifted her head and forced herself to gaze upon Ethan in prayer.

His expression was detached, as if communion with God blotted out all his earthly concerns. In contrast, across from Claire, Cutt Pitman prayed like the ex–navy man he was, hands clenched in tight formation, his neck bent the requisite forty-five degrees, with Dee kneeling to his left. A beam of light happened to pass over Dee's face, turning her features from ordinary to blessed and just as quickly back again. She looked up and noticed Claire staring at her, then dropped her eyes, flushing to one of her unattractive and uneven blotches.

Next to Claire, Whit was worshipping with his usual arrogant determination. Instead of folding or interlacing his fingers, he held his palms open and out to his sides, as if he were tempting fate to come and get him. So far it hadn't. Today he was dressed in the cashmere blazer that Claire had given him last Christmas, and fine woolen trousers. A tiny smile played at the corners of his mouth, as if he and he alone were hearing the good news of Jesus and finding it more than satisfactory. Claire squeezed her fingers around the strange silver hoop in her pocket and fought off the urge to punch him.

"Please be seated," Ethan said, and with a rumble the members of the congregation rearranged themselves. Up at the altar, Ethan looked solemn in his vestments. He caught Claire's eye, half smiled, and she shifted on the pew. To her right, the mural of Our Lady of Perpetual Salt seemed to shimmer in the thin spring sunshine, and Claire frowned and looked away from her.

After the service was over, Ethan stood at the door in Father Flynn's old place, greeting each of his new flock. When it came time to shake Claire's hand, he gripped it a little tighter than he should have. The nest of his palm was warm and dense, and Claire fought an urge to leave her fingers in the security of it. Too soon, Ethan broke their grasp and turned to Whit.

"Good sermon, Father," Whit said, and then put his hand on Claire's elbow. After Ethan's fingers they felt as sharp as January ice. Claire noticed Cutt stealing a sidelong glance at her, and she held her breath, hoping he wouldn't say anything about her previous meeting with Ethan in the diner. She was relieved when he drifted to the side of the church with Dee, chattering with old Mrs. Butler, who was eager to hear his latest gossip but too deaf to get it right.

"Hello, Ethan," Claire said. She'd taken extra care with her clothes that day, choosing a cashmere sweater she knew matched her eyes and a tweed skirt that flared along her hips. Instead of heels she wore her usual polished boots, and she'd twisted her hair into a chignon, which she adjusted now. All through Mass she'd been aware of Ethan watching her. He'd stared as Claire had closed her eyes to recite the Lord's Prayer and as she sipped the Communion wine. When she finally met his gaze, it was so clear and penetrating as to be almost surgical. He could still see straight into her, Claire realized, and she wondered if she could do the same to him. She waited until Whit joined Cutt across the church, and then she turned to Ethan.

"You were watching me during Mass." She kept her voice so low that only he could hear it. He blushed along the side of his neck, and Claire struggled with an impulse to stroke him there, the way she used to.

"It's just that you seem so different from when I met you at the Lighthouse." He paused, and Claire knew he meant to say she seemed different in the presence of Whit, and she bit the inside of her cheek, hoping he wouldn't bring up Whit's name. He didn't. Instead he asked about Jo. "How's your sister?" he said. "I was thinking of paying her a visit. I understand she doesn't come to services anymore. Uncle Chet said things have been pretty rough for her lately."

Claire's heart kicked in her chest as it always did at the mention of Jo's name. She sniffed. "I'm sure you've heard by now that we don't speak," she said, glaring at Ethan. "If you want to get along here again, Ethan Stone," she added, her lips cold, "you'd best remember how to navigate between the Gillys and the Turners, and you'd best do it quick."

Ethan leaned so close to her that she could smell the faint wintergreen of his breath. "Which one are you these days?" he asked, and Claire hesitated.

"Turner, I suppose. At least according to my marriage license." An awkward pause fell between them. It was maddening to have Ethan standing in front of her in robes, so near and yet marked so fully by his vocation that just thinking of him in carnal terms was a sin, she was sure. She wondered if his faith was really his own or something he simply pulled on when it suited him, like his cassock. She licked her lips, turned her back, and walked away, winding a stray piece of hair in between her fingers. *Was all of this really worth leaving me for?* she wanted to ask.

———∞ ∞———

All that week Claire attended her committee meetings with fury—even ones to which she didn't belong.

"But you're not on the Garden Auxiliary," Agnes Greene pointed out when she showed up for the annual tea.

"I am now," Claire said, stealing the chair she guessed Agnes normally sat in and fixing her with her best lady-who-lunches smile.

Agnes took a seat beside Claire and ground her teeth. "Of course, we're just *thrilled* to have you," she simpered, and then turned to the woman on her left for the rest of the time.

When civic duties didn't calm Claire's nerves, she rode poor Icicle harder than she ever had, driving him through a punishing series of gallops and jumping him in the ring. He did everything she asked without complaint, which made her feel even worse. To compensate she spent extra time rubbing him down and gave him extra feed. She thought about going to confession but skipped it. Nevertheless, Sunday—and her excited dread of facing Ethan again—loomed ahead of her, not to mention all the questions she had about that earring she'd found in Whit's car. Should she confront him? she wondered. Should she wait to unearth further evidence? She was more than sure there would be some.

Before she could decide, a hard wind woke her. It was Friday night, and she and Whit had been to a function at the club, where Claire had had too much wine. She startled up in bed, the covers puddling around her hips, and instinctively reached out for Whit, but her hand found nothing. He was gone. For a moment she was afraid, and then she was pedal-to-the-metal furious. No doubt he'd snuck out to meet the strumpet he was seeing. She pictured a busty woman with long, supple legs, or maybe a woman who was always a little dirty-looking, like she needed to wash her hair. Certainly someone who rolled her ass when she walked, though, and smiled too slowly on purpose.

Claire leaned back on the pillows and tried to fall asleep again, but it was useless. A full moon was spilling iodized light across the floor, and the wind was making a symphony out of all the loose ends in the world. An owl wailed in the distance and then once again, and Claire listened harder. *No, not an owl*, she surmised, but definitely something animal and in pain. *Icicle*, she thought, her heart quickening.

She got up and felt her way down the stairs, not bothering with the lights. After twelve years she knew her way around Turner House as well as she knew any place, and anyway, the moon was so bright. She threw on a duffel coat, stuffed her feet into a pair of rubber boots, and then flung open the mudroom door, straining to hear the noise again, and there it was—an off-key wailing like a wounded fox.

"Whit?" she called into the darkness, but there was no answer. She cursed him as she shuffled toward the paddock to check on Icicle. What kind of man left his sleeping wife for another woman? Was he roaming because of the babies Claire had lost? When she found Whit, she planned on asking him all that and more, and then she would tell him some things of her own.

She neared the stable and was about to step out of the shadows when she noticed two things. First, the floodlights outside were on. And second, the top of the split stable door was hinged back like a penny tossed without a care. She scanned the dark paddock for Icicle but didn't see anything, and so she started forward to close up the door. Before she reached it, a pair of rising voices stopped her. One of them was Whit's.

"You have to!" he urged. "You're in no position—" A panicked female voice answered him, breathy with alarm.

"We could leave! We could go somewhere else and start all over. Please, I didn't plan this. I have nowhere else to go. My father just threw me out."

"Shut up," Whit said, his voice a furious rasp. "I'm not going anywhere with you. And I'm not about to let a little slut like you tarnish my good name. It's the only thing of value I have left. If you ruin that, you ruin everything. I'm not giving you the chance, do you hear me?"

"I thought you wanted . . ." the girl tried to say, but he didn't let her finish.

"Not like this. Not with someone like you . . ." Whit replied, and then his words trailed off, and Claire didn't hear anything, just scuffling and a terrible heavy silence.

She tiptoed closer to the open threshold and peered into the darkness, squinting, and then she saw Whit embracing a young woman. Only something was wrong. The girl wasn't moving. Claire crept closer and saw one of the girl's feet sliding out from under her. Claire realized she was choking. And it was Whit who was choking her.

Claire couldn't explain what happened to her next except to say that she finally felt what Jo must have when she pulled Claire from the fire. It was like she was burning all over, her skin so hot she was shivering, and there was nothing in her ears but a smoky roar. She flexed her arms, and her muscles quivered. From somewhere deep inside herself, the real Claire crouched and watched to see what this new version would do.

She did it without thinking—grabbed the shovel in the corner and wheeled straight at Whit, her arms upraised, a scream she didn't recognize tearing her lips. At that moment she was pure Gilly again: red-haired, with fury for blood, perfect aim, and nothing left to lose.

Startled, Whit let go of the girl, who fell in a heap at his feet. He spun around to face Claire, dodging left just as she brought the edge of the shovel down on his skull. There was a sickening crack of metal on bone and then a second thump as Whit collapsed, a trickle of blood oozing along his ear. Claire stood over him, debating whether or not to keep going, but the girl suddenly gasped and flailed her legs, and only then did Claire see that it was Dee Pitman from the Lighthouse Diner. Cutt's daughter. Barely eighteen if she was a day.

"Thank God," the girl said, hitching herself onto one elbow, and then she closed her eyes and sank back down again on the boards.

Icicle nickered and shifted in his stall, agitated by the commotion. At the sound, Claire returned to herself, becoming Claire Turner again, as cool-headed as she'd been on the morning of her wedding when she'd written the Turner name front and center in her heart and soul. And from that moment until this one, she'd checked everything against it. Now, however, she was glad for it. It made it so much easier to stand over the slumped bodies of her husband and his mistress, one of whom she wanted to murder and the other of whom she thought she already might have.

She squatted down and pressed her fingers to Whit's neck, relieved to feel his pulse beating, and then she turned her attention to Dee, who was still unmoving. Her eyes looked bruised, and her lip was a swollen plum. Claire stepped over Whit and knelt down in front of Dee.

Dee looked up at Claire, her nose filmed with snot, her eyes confused as a child's. "I'm sorry," she said. "I don't even know what to do." Well, she was a child, Claire thought. "I can't go home," Dee blubbered. "Not now."

Claire sighed. She knew everything one person could about not going home, and frankly, it was a story she was sick of. In the darkness Icicle stamped a foot and whinnied, as if to get her attention.

"Stay here," she whispered, settling Dee against the stable wall. "Don't move," she added. She led Icicle out of his stall. She gathered a blanket, his bridle, and a saddle, and then she fed the bit into his mouth and cinched the saddle tight.

"Put your foot in here," she told Dee, guiding her toes into the stirrup. "Lean against me and throw your leg up. Now sit tight." Dee did, wide-eyed but obedient as Claire also swung onto Icicle's back.

"Hang on," Claire said, nudging Icicle out of the barn. They started down Plover Hill, picking up speed once they got to the bottom. It was much later than Claire had realized. Very soon the sun would come up. Already the sky had the hazy, undecided look it always got right before it burst into full morning.

She dug her heels into Icicle's flanks, and he broke into a canter. She felt Dee tighten her legs so she wouldn't fall. The girl didn't ask where they were going, and Claire didn't tell her, but the salt ponds would be waiting, Claire knew, glowing in the dawn like the thick lace veil she'd worn pulled across her face on her wedding day and which she'd been tangled up in ever since, for richer or poorer, for better or worse, Whit's chattel until death did one of them part, and please God, she prayed as she streaked through the last of the darkness, let it not be her.

Chapter Fifteen

It was the strangled call of one of those damn marsh cats that woke Jo, but it was the added noise of horse's hooves on clay that got her out of bed. It was barely dawn, but already the spring gulls were out fierce and fast. The wind had shifted direction overnight, and whenever it did that, Jo knew, the birds were always the first to say anything about it.

She couldn't claim she was surprised when she spied the spare shape of a white horse drifting into the marsh. She was used to seeing Claire ride out here at daybreak. About six years back, Claire had started coming by the graves. Jo knew all about her sister's visits and the little piles of salt she sometimes left on Henry's grave, just the way their mother had taught them. Jo didn't like it, but she also didn't think she could stop Claire. There were some things that were beyond human contention.

But Claire didn't rein in her horse at the edge of the marsh that morning the way she normally did, and there wasn't just one silhouette on the beast's back—there were two. The light was misty and weak, true, and the farmhouse glass was old and blurred, but Jo didn't think she was wrong to believe what she was seeing. She watched as the horse slowed and neared the house and two women got off, one followed by the other, arms looped around each other's waist, beloved from the looks of it, but Jo knew that couldn't be, because Claire was a woman who loved only herself.

Jo pulled back from the window and held her breath, hoping that the vision of Claire would fade away, but she kept coming. Jo could hear feet dragging out of kilter up the porch steps, and she sighed. If trouble came in the shape of a stranger, as Mama had always said, then the appearance of long-absent loved ones was even worse. True calamity was always stuck to them like the stripe on a skunk.

Claire's fist sounded on the door, and Jo weighed the option of hiding. She glanced at the closet in the far corner of the room and then considered the nook between the grandfather clock and the sofa downstairs, but Claire was like the damn weather. You couldn't outrun her, you couldn't change her, and it would be just plain stupid to try to avoid her. With Claire a body was always better off battening down the hatches and waiting to see what would happen. Jo heard a heavy stumbling inside the house and then a heavier thump.

"Goddamn it, Joanna!" Claire called. After twelve years her voice was sharper than Jo remembered. "I know you're standing on the stairs," she said. "I can see you. Get down here and help me!"

Jo took a deep breath, filling herself like a sail, and descended, thinking she had the situation more or less under control. But when she got downstairs, she wasn't the least bit prepared for what she found. In the front hallway, she saw Claire crouched in a ball over the unconscious blob of Dee Pitman.

Jo cocked her head. The stairs were dark, and her vision was one-sided, but Claire didn't look like someone who had chosen to lop herself off at the roots and blow away free. She was wearing a duffel coat over a white cotton nightgown and rubber boots, and with her braid sprung loose down her back she appeared to be all of eighteen again.

"Help me," she demanded, and Jo crept closer, already regretting getting involved, but what else could she do? When life dumped a mess on your doorstep, you had to get out the mop and start wiping it up.

"Let me," she said, kneeling to scoop her good arm under Dee's neck, loosening the girl's scarf a little. She blew on Dee's cheeks until her eyelids fluttered, and then she laid Dee's head back down and stepped away before the girl regained full consciousness. Jo didn't know what Dee was doing here in her house, but that wasn't her concern. Let Claire deal with her.

"Fuck," Dee moaned. "Holy fuck." *Charming*, Jo thought. Dee hitched herself onto an elbow and looked at her without comprehension. "Where am I?"

Claire stepped forward, her nightdress billowing under her coat. "My sister will get you some water if you want."

Perfect, Jo thought. Here was Claire back for all of five minutes, and already she was giving orders.

Dee sucked in a breath, and her eyes went wide with terror. "You brought me to Salt Creek Farm?"

Claire sighed. "I didn't know what else to do with you. You said you couldn't go home. You said your father had thrown you out, remember?"

Dee rolled onto her side for a moment, then flipped herself onto her hands and knees like a cat. She sat back on her knees and blinked. "So you brought me *here*?"

Claire sniffed. "Here's as good a place as any. And besides, beggars can't be choosers."

Jo interceded. "But what are *you* doing here, Claire?" If they were going to play twenty questions, Jo didn't think it was fair that Dee should be the only one in the hot seat. Claire just chewed on a piece of her hair and said nothing, so Jo turned to Dee. She had a stubborn stare, Jo saw, and the way her mouth pinched at the corners told Jo that Dee knew more about hard times than her age suggested. "How old are you anyway?" she asked. She thought she remembered Dee's father telling her she was quite young.

Dee's lip trembled. "Eighteen last week."

A babe, Jo thought. "Why can't you go home?" She pictured Cutt's tattooed forearms and military-shorn hair. He seemed to move only in straight lines. Jo couldn't think of one soft thing about him. She didn't know what Dee's trouble was, but Jo wouldn't want to go home to him either, she decided.

Dee rubbed the side of her neck, pulling her scarf open, and Jo saw that a row of purple ghost prints was starting to bloom on her skin. She was a girl who stumbled over her words, flattening one down more than the last like she was closing a fan in her throat, but it didn't matter. Her tongue could have been oiled with the honey of heaven and there wouldn't have been any good way for her to say what she did next. She rolled her hands together in a little ball, the only tidy thing about her. "I'm pregnant. It's Whit's. Only"—she wiped away a tear—"he doesn't want me, and he doesn't want the baby like I thought he would. He wants to get rid of us both."

Jo supposed she shouldn't have been surprised, but Claire let out a shriek. At first Jo thought it was surprise at the news, but then she followed Claire's eyes and spied the necklace around Dee's throat. It was a heart-shaped locket hung on a silver chain and embossed with a large and florid

W—a bauble Jo knew very well. Before Jo could stop her, Claire reached out and snatched it clean off Dee's neck, shoving it in the pocket of her coat. *Whoever said that memory carried no weight was wrong*, Jo thought. Clearly it did, especially when it was nestled in the palm of your hand.

Claire settled her face inches away from Dee's. She shook her head so furiously that Jo wouldn't have been surprised to see sparks fly off her hair. "This is Whit's initial! He monograms everything with this exact script. You're a little thief! You have no right—to any of it!" She sat back on her heels, covered her eyes with the white stems of her fingers, and began to cry.

Jo wrapped Dee in one of the scratchy blankets she found in the hall closet and left her to shiver on the sofa in the parlor. "Not like this," she told Claire. "Come with me." She led her to the kitchen. "This isn't the time or the place. It's just a cheap old necklace, after all." She thought it prudent to stay silent on the fact that before any of the mess now unfolding in her hall, the locket on that chain was supposed to be hers.

———o-o o-o———

"What happened?" Jo poured out two cups of peppermint tea and sat Claire at the table in the center of the kitchen.

Claire rubbed her eyes. "I woke up and heard a noise, and Whit was gone. He wasn't in bed, and he wasn't anywhere in the house. That's been happening a lot lately, him coming home late or leaving before dawn. I figured something was going on, but I didn't know with whom.

"The noise was coming from the stable. The moon was so bright I decided to check on Icicle. I thought it was him. But, when I got there, I saw Whit and Dee, having an argument. She was saying they could go away, and he was saying he wouldn't let her tarnish his name, and then, without any warning, Whit started choking her." Claire shuddered and tipped the teacup to her mouth, then wiped her fingers across her lips. "I stopped him."

Jo's heart skipped a beat. "Claire," she said carefully. "What did you do?"

"He's fine." Claire put down the cup. "I just hit him with a shovel, is all. He'll most definitely have a headache in the morning, but he still had a pulse. I checked before I saddled up Icicle." She shifted in her chair and lowered her voice. "I don't care if Dee's father does skin her alive and place her in a vat of boiling blood. She has to go." She took the necklace from her pocket and laid it out on the table. "What the hell is this? Clearly it's from him, but it's not his style."

A gust of wind clattered over the roof, and Jo shivered. The morning was turning out to be nasty in all senses of the word, she thought. At any moment rain would start thumping down, churning up the salt marsh, watering the mud she was trying to scoop. "Come on, Claire," Jo said. "You're the big church-goer now. What about making room at the inn?"

Claire banged her fist on the table. "This isn't the Christmas story! We're not talking about an innocent virgin, here. That tramp was fucking my husband."

Jo shrugged. "She only did what you once did."

Claire's rosebud lips fell open. "Is that what this is about for you? Settling scores?" She spread her hands on the table, her diamond wedding band winking at Jo like a fox's crafty eye. "Look, all my old wounds are open for business. Are you happy?"

Jo slid her eyes away from her sister. "I don't reckon it matters how I feel about things anymore, Claire. There's something you should know before you decide if you want to stay here. We've both got scores to settle that are out of our hands."

Claire chewed her lip. "What do you mean?"

Jo bowed her head. "Remember your dreams of college?" she said. "Well, I'm paying for those now, thanks to Mama." Jo told her then about the second loan on the farm and how Mama had taken it out to use for Claire before all their plans went up in smoke. She finished by admitting how if she didn't come up with some cold hard cash in the very near future, the bank would be taking the marsh.

Claire sighed and pursed her lips—an old habit that signaled she was about to admit something. What she said next shocked Jo. "I already know. Whit's been talking about it. It's almost *all* he talks about now. He has this crazy idea that if he can buy this place, everything will turn around for him."

Jo snorted. "That doesn't mean I'll sell." She grew sober. "But he does have the dollars in his pocket to do it."

Claire hesitated. "Not really," she said, and Jo leaned forward. "Things aren't quite as on the up-and-up with Whit's business as you might think," Claire said. "Over the years he's been selling off paintings and family silver, even his mother's old fur coat. I don't know how much he has left, but it can't be much."

Jo sat back hard in her chair. A waft of peppermint tea stung her good eye. Claire always did have the ability to reach under a person's ribs and get to the heart of a matter, she reflected. It used to drive their mother crazy, and Jo could see how it might be unpleasant in a marriage, especially if you were married to a man like Whit, who preferred his secrets boxed on a shelf and covered with dust.

Jo sized up her sister. "Tell me, Claire, if it hadn't been for finding Dee and Whit together in your stable, would you ever have come back here?"

Claire blinked, and Jo could see the network of tiny wrinkles that had burrowed into the outer corners of her eyes, perhaps a sign that things hadn't been going well with Whit—and not just lately either. Lines like that took time to groove into skin, like water wearing down rock, and if anyone knew the slow ways grief could carve flesh, Jo did.

Claire bowed her head. "I don't know. Maybe. Eventually."

That did it for Jo. She pushed her chair back from the table and stood. "She stays."

Claire looked around as if waking from a long, unpleasant dream. She gnawed her thumbnail for a moment, considering, then went ahead and tossed her fate in with Jo, raising the stakes between them. She picked up her teacup. "Then I guess I'm not going anywhere either."

And just like that, they became three.

Chapter Sixteen

There was no etiquette guide in the universe that told you how to handle waking up in a house you'd fled from as a teenager with your estranged sister in one room across the hall and your husband's pregnant teenage mistress in the other. If there were, Claire thought, the prevailing wisdom would surely just be, *Don't.* Don't wake up. Don't rise to the occasion. Don't go back in the first place.

Her first day home had been full of logistics—which room Dee would take, which of Claire's old clothes still fit, what to do with Icicle—and her first night had been an agony of bad dreams compounded by a lumpy mattress. She rolled onto her side in her childhood bed, tangling her legs in the faded sheets, and considered scratching a tick on the wall the way prisoners did in movies, but the prisoners only did that because they hoped they might be free one day, Claire knew, whereas she had nowhere else to go.

She sat up and yawned. It was still early, only around six, she guessed, from the color of the sky, but she remembered this bluish hour on Salt Creek Farm all too well. She never admitted it to anyone, but this was also the hour when she occasionally prayed, and so that's what she did now, slipping her legs over the narrow edge of her bed and sinking to her knees, asking for the backbone to get through the next few hours ahead of her.

Our Father, who art in heaven, she began reciting in her head, but her mind soon wandered. She gave up and stared out the window at the bleak acres of mud below her. Scraped empty before the spring flood, the basins were nothing to her. In fact, it was hard to believe they were the source of so much trouble in her mind. She'd spent the past decade blaming the salt for everything acrid in her life: her miscarriages, her increasing struggles with Whit, their money problems. But now, viewing the marsh like this, she saw how wrong she'd been about everything from the ground up.

She scrambled to her feet and rummaged in the wardrobe until she found a set of old clothes: faded denim trousers worn thin and a pale linen shirt. How odd that her old things, her former skin, had been waiting all this time for her to slip back into them, but then nothing ever went away on Salt Creek Farm. The junk around the place was testimony to that. Claire wound her hair back and pinned it into place, then took a hard look in the mirror. She was only thirty-one, but over the past year she'd begun to notice rogue strands of gray colonizing her temples and crown. It didn't really bother her, though. She figured that since everything else in her life with Whit had faded and muted, why should she be any different?

Claire scowled and yanked the curtains closed. How long would she get alone up here? she wondered. An hour? An entire day? Soon enough Jo would come knocking, and Claire would have no choice but to slide on a pair of boots, pick up a shovel, and step back out into the salt as if she'd never left it. There was only one rule for women on Salt Creek Farm, but it had lasted the ages: If you were standing on the land, you worked it, strong or weak, sick or well, like it or not. It was digging season, Claire's least favorite time. No matter what chore she ever did in the spring—repairing sluices, scraping mud from the shallow collection basins— she always ended up with dirt packed under her torn fingernails, bloody blisters on her palms, and sore muscles. Jo never got so much as a splinter.

Claire spread her fingers apart on the windowsill, her eye catching on the hefty diamonds in her wedding band, and without stopping to think she slipped the ring off and tucked it into the top drawer of the bureau. There. That was easy. The first step of separation: Remove the visible vestiges of marriage. Each day, Claire vowed, she would shed another piece of Whit until she was as slick and raw as one of the salt basins, no better than the low land spread out around her. She touched the pearl around her throat and hesitated. That she would keep. She had earned it.

She shivered and buttoned the top button on her shirt placket, and then she flung open her door, blinking against the spring wind. She eased down the steps, skipping the fifth one that always squeaked, and found some boots by the door, and then, without a noise, she slipped out of the house and, for the first time in twelve years, turned herself free.

———o-o o-o———

She needed to check on Icicle. Jo had sequestered him in the back of the salt barn the day before, and he seemed fine there, but Claire would have to get some feed in for him, she knew, and straw for underfoot, and he was due for new shoes in two weeks' time. She tried not to think about the beautiful old tack she'd left behind in the stable on Plover Hill: the hand-stitched saddle, the engraved steel bit, and the stirrups to go with it. The reins she'd worn to buttery softness. Three sets of riding boots, all of her breeches, her dressage coat, plus velvet-covered helmets and kidskin gloves.

She wrapped her arms around herself. These clothes were far lighter than she was used to, and they were currently all that stood between her goose-pimpled skin and the larger world. She wasn't wearing her coat. She wasn't wearing socks with her boots. She wasn't even wearing a bra.

And it was fine. It was better than fine. Laughing a little, she opened the barn and greeted Icicle, then fed him the bit and eased him outside, where she swung up and over his broad back—no saddle, no stirrups, no blanket, even. Just the familiar heat of Icicle moving through the air, threading through the dunes and then flying down the wet sand onto Drake's Beach.

She might have run forever—or at least as long as the beach—but a figure stopped her. She squinted, wanting and not wanting it to be who she thought it was. She slowed Icicle to a walk and picked her way closer, and there, wavering like a vision in a dream, was Ethan Stone, gathering sea glass by the water's edge, his black trousers rolled neatly above his delicate ankles, sandy hair whipping across his eyes, not looking a thing as he had the last time they'd met in church. He hastily stood up when he saw Claire coming.

"Claire. Out again, I see," he said, reaching up and helping her dismount, his hands resting on her hips as he drew her level with him. His voice was husky in the morning air, deeper than when he was conducting services, and the one word of her name was a whole song when he said it.

She took a quick step away from him. She hadn't slept, she was disoriented, and what she wanted to do was fold herself against his chest. She wanted to lift the edge of his shirt just a little and test his skin to see if it was cool and slippery, like swimming-pool tiles, or warm like the belly of a sleeping cat. Instead she curled the reins around her hand and wished she'd worn a pair of gloves, not to mention a bra.

"What are you doing all the way out here?" Ethan asked as she relaxed one of her fists and smoothed a stray piece of hair off her face.

Claire knew what he was really asking. What was she doing so close to the marsh? She looked down at her feet. "I come here sometimes."

Ethan gazed out at the water. "Do you know how long it's been since I've stood at the edge of the Atlantic? I've forgotten how green it can look. I wonder if I still have my old sea legs."

"I thought you purposefully gave up a life of fish."

Ethan laughed. "I did. But not all of the old tar got removed." He turned his gaze on her. "What about you? Do you ever regret the life of salt you left?"

Claire avoided his eyes. How would

she even begin a catalog of her life's laments? At the start or the end? *Maybe the middle*, she decided, for if she wanted to name the beginning, it would have to be Ethan. "No," she said.

Of course, he didn't know she'd just come full circle, back to the place where she started. She wondered if his gaze would change when he finally started hearing all the things that were whispered about her in Prospect, if he hadn't already. If so, she figured she might as well be the source. She took a deep breath and bowed her head.

"Okay, sometimes I do wonder if I made the right choice," she admitted, and then a confession slipped out of her that she had no intention of revealing. "I had a miscarriage sometime ago," she heard herself say. "My fourth one." She hadn't meant to tell Ethan that part of her story—not so abruptly— but the words tumbled from her lips accidentally, like a plate falling from a high shelf.

Ethan took a step closer to her and reached out as if to take her hand, then thought better of it. "I'm so sorry, Claire."

He meant it, Claire could tell, but was he grieved as a priest or as someone who'd once loved her? She knew it shouldn't matter, but it did. She rested her chin against her chest. How many times had they stood in this same spot just like this? How long had it been since Claire had felt so safe?

If she was confessing, she thought, she might as well tell it all, whether the context was human or divine. There were things she had wanted to say to him for years, and who knew if she would ever get another chance as good as this one? She lowered her voice out of habit. The walls in Turner House had been porous. It was not a house that facilitated the keeping of secrets. She stared up at Ethan. "I'm sorry I never let you say good-bye. I should have. After the fire I just—"

He stepped closer. "We were so young, Claire. I didn't handle things the right way with you." All these years she'd been waiting to hear words like these, but now that she just had, she found they weren't enough. She wanted him to say he'd been wrong.

He brushed a toe in the sand. "I feel partly responsible for the fire, too, you know. If you hadn't been so upset, you might not have lit the match."

Claire fell silent at that, remembering the awful crush of panic she'd felt in the barn as the temperature had risen and ashes swirled around her head.

Ethan cleared his throat. "So how is Jo?"

Claire shrugged. Her sister seemed a stranger to her now, even with a thin wall between them. She bit her thumb. She could feel the heat radiating from the fronts of Ethan's thighs. And then, without thinking twice about it, she reached up and shook her hair loose, remembering how Ethan used to inch his fingers across her scalp and hold the back of her head steady when he bent down and kissed her—his lips as tender as the sole of a newborn's foot. Claire leaned closer, but Ethan cleared his throat and took a step away from her, as if he'd been reading her thoughts.

A rush of shame came over her, and she tucked her hair back behind her collar again. She shuffled her feet on the damp sand, trying to think of what to say, but longing had made her dumb. She reached up and began winding her hair back into its braid, pulling as tightly as she could until every last piece was in place. She would put herself back together, she thought. It could be done. Choices could be made and unmade, truths blotted out like the Virgin's face.

He's a priest, she told herself as she turned back to Icicle. *He's taken vows to keep people's secrets.* Yet her soul still rested uneasy. She closed her eyes, but all she could conjure were the grayish series of salt piles heaped along the edges of the marsh at the end of a long, hot summer. What would they say if they could speak, Claire wondered, and would it even matter?

An engine sputtered in the distance, and she tensed. Across the dunes she spied the glare of a red car, the one she used to drive, speeding toward Salt Creek Farm. Without hesitating she threw her leg over Icicle, who snorted and took an uneasy step sideways.

"Claire!" She could hear Ethan calling her name, a question buffeted by the wind, but there was no time to answer it. For the second time since Ethan had returned, Claire spun her back on him and fled. At that moment all she cared about was beating Whit back to Salt Creek Farm.

Chapter Seventeen

During Dee's first morning on Salt Creek Farm, she began to suspect she might have been better off on the street, where her father had threatened to throw her headfirst. At least there she might have gotten more sleep.

"Get up." She was already awake, but Jo marched into the room anyway and yanked the covers down. Apparently, awake wasn't good enough for Jo. A body had to be upright and busy as well. Dee groaned and flexed her calves.

"Leg cramps?" Jo asked, folding her

arms across her square chest. "I've heard that pregnant girls can get those. You should eat a little extra salt."

Dee scowled and sat up. *A little extra salt?* Was Jo kidding? Had she looked around her lately? Dee snickered. "I guess that's not really a problem, is it?" she said with teenage sarcasm. "All I have to do is walk outside and lick the ground."

For a cripple, Dee thought, Jo moved pretty fast. One minute she was looming over the mattress like some warden in a prison movie, and the next she was way too close and personal, snorting the odors of bacon and coffee into Dee's face. "If you knew how to look a little harder at the world, maybe you wouldn't have landed in this predicament, girl. Lesson number one: Salt is never just salt. It's my livelihood, and I take it serious. And if you're going to get along with me, you better learn to take it serious, too." She flicked a plaid shirt at Dee. "Get up. Get dressed, and meet me downstairs in five minutes. And just so you know, I have a clock down there. Don't think I won't be watching it."

She left the door open as she departed. *Thump, thump, thump.* If her steps were any more regular, Dee thought, shoving her head through the neck of the shirt, Jo would turn into a damned clock herself.

When Dee entered the kitchen with one minute to spare, she saw that Jo had set several small bowls of salt out on the table. The first bowl was chipped, with shamrocks painted around its rim, and it held a mound of familiar gray salt. The heavy grains looked almost wet, all clumped together. The second bowl was a scoop of polished wood, and those granules were an alarming bloodred. They must have come from that funny pond in the marsh, Dee thought. There was a plastic mixing bowl sitting half filled with ordinary table salt, and then, placed in the middle of everything, Dee saw a crystal bowl filled with a kind of salt so flaky and lush that it reminded her of the coconut shavings on a wedding cake. She licked her lips at the sight of it. She was very hungry.

Jo gestured at the table. "Which one do you like? Which bowl makes your mouth start watering?"

"I don't know. What's the difference" Dee slid her gaze sideways, but Jo stepped a little to the right, back into her field of vision, forcing her to confront Jo's scars head-on. Dee tried to swivel her head, but Jo stopped her.

"You don't get to do that," she said. "Not out here."

Dee bit her thumbnail and eyed Jo balefully. "Do what?"

"Look away. Pretend you're bored and not answer my questions. I saw you staring at the table. I know something snagged your attention. I saw you lick your lips." Dee glanced at the crystal bowl in the middle of the table again. The etched glass looked like ice and the salt like the last of the season's snow—but the pure storybook kind. Flakes that never touched the ground, just hung around in the air, thumbing their noses at gravity. This wasn't the same salt Jo delivered for the tables at the Lighthouse. It was *wealthy* salt, Dee thought. It was the kind of salt Claire would eat if she so chose.

"That one." Dee turned her cheek and pointed at the crappy plastic bowl of ordinary salt. Everyone knew about that kind of salt. It was loose. It poured in all kinds of weather. You could get it anywhere, and, of course, it was dirt cheap.

Jo raised her eyebrow. "Really? That one?"

Dee just shrugged. She was legitimately starving now. Like, Africa starving. What was up with the twenty questions? She put her hands on her hips. If Jo was going to dish it out, Dee could go her one better. "What's the deal anyway?" she demanded. "I don't get it. What makes your salt so special?"

Jo appeared taken aback for a moment, and then a canny look crept into her eye. "I don't really know," she said. "It's been here long before any of us, and it will be here long after we're gone. It feels the weather, and it knows both the land and sea, and that's good enough for me."

"And the future," Dee piped up. *And maybe the past, too*, she mused, thinking of Claire's unborn babies. She really wanted to ask Jo about them, but she didn't dare.

Jo shook her head. "No, child. That's just what people like to think." She bent down close to Dee. "Listen, this is important. The salt just heightens what's already in people's lives, the same way it does with food. It brings out the sweet and the sour, and when they ignore what it tells them, when they ignore the truth of their own selves, that's when trouble starts." Jo straightened herself and slammed the cupboard door, then leaned against the counter. "To really know the salt, you have to wait until summer."

Summer, Dee thought. Where would she be by then? The baby and her, that was. She looked at the salt on the table. Jo followed her gaze.

"This." Jo drew a tight circle in the air over the white flakes. "This is the real magic, wouldn't you agree?"

Dee's mouth watered again, and she yearned to take just a single morsel onto her tongue. *That's it*, she thought. *That's exactly what I want.* She opened her lips to ask for a taste, but old habits died hard, and she found herself insulting Jo instead. "Magic is for little kids and old women," she said, tossing her hair. "Now, can I please get something real to eat?"

Jo regarded her for a moment, then stuck a dented spoon in the plastic bowl of cheap salt and handed it to her. "You said you liked this one. You can have all you want. When something nicer comes out of your mouth, you can have something tastier to put in it. Until then, enjoy." She turned on her heel, leaving Dee holding the bowl in her confused hands, doomed to hunger by her own stupid words, another test failed. It was going to be a long morning.

———o-o o-o———

If Dee was wondering how and when Whit would come to find her, it turned out she didn't have long to wait. She had just finished a plate of scrambled eggs when he squealed his car up to the front of the house, whirling mad and hell-bent on causing the maximum amount of damage. She and Claire might have tumbled onto Salt Creek Farm like a bursting squall, she thought, but Whit blew into the place with the fury of a tornado.

Jo and Dee stared at each other, and then Jo clamped her lips tight and began clearing the table while Dee backed up to the far counter, holding its edge for balance. She remembered the way Whit had pinched his hands around her throat in the barn and how Claire's fingers had wound tightly around the shovel handle. She remembered clinging to Claire's narrow waist for dear life as they galloped down Plover Hill in the half-light of dawn. If it had been any lighter, Dee wondered, would Claire have scooped her up like that and saved her? Or would she have taken a better look at the situation and then aimed the shovel a little differently?

Dee scanned the room again, searching for angles of escape. The window above the sink? No. The door behind her? The broom closet? No way. She shivered. No escape, then. Just the full morning light, her enraged lover, his wife, and too much salt for anybody's taste.

Whit began his onslaught with the rushes at the edge of the porch. He kicked those to kingdom come, then stomped his way up the porch's warped steps. Hearing the wood crack under his heavy steps, Jo just shook her head. He burst through the front door in the hall without asking, marched past the broken piano, banging the few keys that worked just to set the mood, and arrived in the kitchen doorway out of breath, the side of his face bruised from where Claire had whacked him with the shovel, in absolutely no mood to wait. "Where is my murderous wife?" he said.

Dee cowered at the counter and began rattling the spoons in the silverware drawer until Jo reached out and gave her a little pinch to make her stop. Dee began stirring a cup of tea instead, dragging her spoon along the bottom of the mug, and that was even worse. Jo cleared her throat, and Dee set the tea down. She'd accidentally scooped salt into the cup instead of sugar anyway.

If a bear on the attack ever came for her, Dee's father had always told her in Vermont, one of the actions she was supposed to take was to make herself look bigger, and she thought that maybe Jo had heard that same thing, because that's what she did now, planting her feet on the speckled linoleum, jamming her fists on her hips, and taking the deepest breath she could. She kicked a chair away from the table and motioned to it.

Whit stood stock-still for a moment, letting his gaze rove Jo's face like someone searching for the X on a treasure map. He must not have found what he was looking for, though, because he gave up, sneered, and took a seat. That's how Dee knew they were ready to get down to business.

He glared at Dee next, but it was the way a person would eye a ghost he didn't believe in. Dee angled her shoulders away from him, even though she was used to his stares. *Still*, she thought. It would have been kind of thrilling if

Whit had made the trip out here for her. She snuck another glimpse at him, but he didn't register her. What were they to each other, she wondered? Was there even a word for it? Not true lovers. Not companions. Something between intimates and strangers. Dee knew she didn't have Whit's same appetites running wild in her blood, but she had sure liked satisfying his. Maybe that counted for something.

The three of them started when the hall door crashed open, letting in a howl of wind, and then Claire appeared, as hasty as Whit and twice as mad. Without meaning to, Dee started up her infernal stirring again, the teaspoon chattering against the side of the mug like a set of windup teeth.

"You son of a bitch asshole bastard!" Claire came roaring into the kitchen, and Dee gaped. Claire had the hair of a scarlet woman, but until now Dee hadn't thought she possessed the mouth to match. She had to admit that the transformation seemed to suit Claire. Her cheeks were blazing, giving her face a liveliness it probably hadn't possessed for the past twelve years, and her eyes snapped and bit like those nasty turtles that had swum at the bottom of the pond back in Vermont. Claire grabbed two plates and sent them winging straight toward Whit's naked throat, missing by a fraction.

"Amen, the Gilly fury has risen!" Jo crowed, smacking her hands together, and just like that, as if she'd somehow summoned him, Father Stone stepped into the fray, moving up behind Claire so quickly she didn't even know he was there. He wrapped his arms around her, took out of her hand the extra plate she'd reloaded, and held her a moment, tighter than Dee thought he needed to.

"Not like this," he said, moving her across the kitchen and then releasing her. "I think," Ethan said, eyeing Whit's bruised head and the marks ringing Dee's throat, "that some explanations are in order here."

Whit smashed his fist into his palm and took a step toward Claire. "Really? It seems to me that you're the intruder, Father. This business doesn't concern you."

Ethan paled, and Dee felt a twinge of pity for him. Here he probably thought he'd be the hero and rescue Claire, only to realize too late that he'd stepped into a viper's nest. His voice shook a little as he faced Whit. "I'm not leaving unless the Gilly sisters ask me to. What is it you want?"

Looking at Claire, Dee could have answered that question in a flash, but Whit beat her to it. He glowered at Claire. "I don't want my wife running off into the night, for starters. I don't want an illegitimate child from a tramp, and most of all I would like Jo to come to her senses and work with me a little." He turned his attention to her. "You haven't got much time left, Jo. I know people at Harbor Bank. Wouldn't you rather strike a deal with me? I might even let you stay awhile."

Ethan looked blank, his eyes bouncing between Whit and Dee, Whit and Claire, Whit and Jo, trying to add them all up. "Illegitimate child?" he said.

Jo shoved Dee's shoulder. "Dee here is pregnant."

Ethan raised his eyebrows and looked

to Claire, then to Whit, who was hunkering as cold as an iced-over stone. Then he said the least helpful thing Dee thought possible, given the situation. "You realize that it would be a mortal sin for Dee not to have the baby, don't you?"

That gave Whit pause. In spite of all his sinning, he was still a churchgoing man, dogmatic to the core. He stood up and paced toward the kitchen door, throwing down his last words like a punch, but getting to have the last word wasn't the same as winning a case. Even Dee knew that much.

He looked hard at Father Stone, then turned his fury on Dee. "Know this," he said, his voice low. "The first thing I'm going to do is go tell your father where he can find his whore of a daughter." She paled and bit her lips. "I don't know if he'll try to kill me or you," Whit said, "but I'm willing to take my chances. And the second thing I'm going to do, Jo"—he turned toward her—"is tell my friends at Harbor Bank that you just refused to accept an offer that would save you and the farm. We'll see what

they think about that." And then, without another word, he let himself out the
same way he'd come in, alone and
snarling.

"How I ever thought I loved that son
of a bitch is beyond me." Claire sighed,
her lips white, at which point Dee burst
into tears, one of her arms cradling her
belly. Dee couldn't really imagine a
whole baby sprouting in such an unfor-
tunate environment, but if a weed could
flourish in a sidewalk crack, she guessed
a kid could survive this abuse.

"Dee's pregnant?" Father Stone said
as if he'd missed the whole scene they'd
all just been through, and he sank into
Whit's empty chair.

Jo looked over at Claire, who was
still a little pale around the chops, but
Claire avoided her eyes and took up
banging a spoon around a cup of her
own. "You know this isn't the end of it,"
Jo said to Claire's back. "You know he
won't stop with empty threats. And
you're not cut out for the salt. We both
know that. You could still go back if you
wanted. It's not too late." Dee was surprised to find herself hoping Claire

wouldn't. "You could be Claire Turner again, lady on the hill, and everything would go back to normal," Jo said. "She could go away"—she jerked her chin at Dee—"and no one would be the wiser."

Claire turned around, and though her skin was white, her eyes were full of flash. "That's the whole problem. *I* haven't been very wise, have I?"

If Dee had wanted to, she could have done the wrong thing yet again and taken advantage of Claire at that moment. She'd never seen her look so bad. Claire had circles smudged under her eyes, her hair was a mess, and her shirt hung off her shoulders. Dee could have asked her if the farmhouse seemed smaller after years of rattling under the Turners' vast roof. Dee could have remarked how odd it must be to have to put rags back on after getting used to cashmere and silk. Or, she thought, she could just pick up a shovel the next time Claire did and find out for herself what salt did to a woman. She stepped over to Claire and stood before her with her head down. "I'm sorry for the trouble," she said. "Please don't make me leave."

To her surprise, Claire reached out and gave the girl's arm a quick squeeze, and a little thread of tension between them snapped. Claire pulled away and swiped the skin underneath her eyes. "How pregnant *are* you anyway?" she asked, putting a hand on Dee's belly. Before Dee could answer, Claire tucked back the stray pieces of her hair and cast a glance to the chair where Ethan was still sitting.

"Oh, goodness!" she cried. "Get a load of us. Weeping and trembling like Whit is the big bad wolf or something. Forgive us, Ethan." He looked up at Claire so keenly that right then Dee knew he was hooked tight as a trout, man of God or no. *Well*, she thought. She guessed the world saw fit to deliver love when people needed it most, just maybe not in the manner they were expecting.

Right then the baby jabbed her in the bladder with some sharp part of its anatomy, as if to prod her back to the moment, and it dawned on her that all

Jo had been trying to do with the dishes
and the salt that morning was get her
to pay attention to what was happening under her nose. Hearts were going
to break or turn upside down out here—
Dee wasn't sure which, and she wasn't
sure whose—but she had a feeling that
when everything was said and done,
none of them would be sure anymore
which piece belonged to whom.

Chapter Eighteen

With the arrival of Dee and Claire, Jo's life had jumped from being a peaceful and plain stretch of road to being so full of cracks and dips that she barely knew anymore how to navigate it. On the one hand, she couldn't say she was unhappy about having extra bodies around the place—maybe the help would be just the thing to get the farm back in shape—but she never knew what to do in the mornings when she stepped across the hall and spied Claire sitting sideways on her bed, crying. Claire would look up when she heard

Jo's footsteps, wipe the tears off her cheeks, and scowl something terrible, and that at least made Jo feel a little better. At least some kernel of Claire had stayed the same.

Jo gave her sister a week to sulk, and in the space of that time they received three different letters from Whit threatening everything from divorce (Claire just shrugged and shoved the document in the top drawer of her bureau) to Salt Creek Farm's imminent bankruptcy (Jo threw that note in the trash, then dumped coffee grounds on it) to an outrageous lawsuit stemming from the pain Claire had inflicted on him with the shovel (Claire and Jo buried that one together in the wilds of the kitchen's junk drawer).

It occurred to Jo that now might be the time to swallow her pride and ask Claire for some help. Surely, in spite of what Claire said were Whit's money problems, she'd have a little something socked away. She owed Jo at least that much. Every morning Jo poured herself a stiff cup of coffee, steeled her spine and tried to find a way to mouth the words.

But before she could utter a single syllable, Claire got another letter from Whit, and this time the man went and crossed the line. Jo knew that it was bad, because Claire opened the envelope and didn't say a word. Jo waited, expecting Claire's usual flurry of huffs and spiked comments, but she just smoothed a hand down the length of her braid and pressed her lips together the way she did when she was really mad.

"What's it say?" Jo asked. They were in the kitchen, and Dee was sitting at the table with them. Claire glanced at her, shook her head the tiniest fraction, and handed Jo the letter. Jo scanned it. Whit had jotted this particular note in his own hand, and he'd gone and brought up the marsh's string of cursed sons. *"Get your sister to sell the land, and you can end this now,"* he'd written to Claire, *"unless you're prepared for another dead child on your hands."*

"No fucking way," said Claire, and

Dee looked up from her bowl of cereal. Jo shook her head at Claire to tell her to keep quiet. She didn't want the expectant Dee infected by such nonsense, even if Gilly history did bear it out as truth.

On the other hand, if Whit was going to bring up the past, Jo thought, then she had more than enough ammunition to fight him. She wadded up the letter and added it to the other correspondence in the trash, bank letters among them. "Don't worry," she reassured Claire. "When it comes down to this, I've got Whit Turner right where I want him."

Claire eyed her steadily. "And he's got us in the same spot."

Jo wondered if the rumors she'd heard about Claire's being barren were really true, but even she had the delicacy not to ask. Not now at least. She put her hands on her hips. "Well, okay, then," she said. "At least we know none of us are going anywhere. Not if I have anything to say about it."

———o-o o-o———

After they disposed of the letter from Whit, Jo marched Claire straight out to a row of evaporating pools, deposited an assemblage of rusted tools next to her, and then thought better of it and climbed in the ditch, too, indicating with her chin which half of the territory was Claire's.

Jo could see that Claire's body had forgotten how to do hard labor in spite of all her riding. Every time Claire bit into the ground with the edge of her hoe, she winced. The pain seemed to loosen her tongue. With every strike at the soil, she unearthed a few more unsavory details about her marriage.

"I should have known it," she said, slapping her hoe into the earth. "I should have known when he was out all those times." She switched to a shovel and began scooping out mud.

"Do you know that one time he compared me to a Roman courtesan at a dinner party?" she added. "I was so dumb I thought it was a compliment. Or the time"—she stabbed the dirt— "he stripped the room I had set up as a nursery. He had Timothy Weatherly come in, take all the furniture, and put it in storage because he said I was barren." Jo didn't say anything to that. The idea of Claire grieving the loss of a child was still startling to her.

"Hey," she finally said, pulling Claire out of her thoughts, "this basin isn't going to clean itself." She stepped closer to Claire's side of the ditch.

Claire dug her blade back into the clay. "Sorry."

No, I'm sorry, Jo wanted to say but didn't. She started a rhythm again with her rake, and Claire joined it. They worked in silence for a moment, and then Jo asked, "Anyone in particular?"

"Huh?" Claire winced and inspected a blister that was rising on her thumb. But Jo knew why her tongue was stuck in her mouth like a broken bell clapper. The more you wanted something you knew was forbidden, the less you wanted to say about it.

"The person you're thinking about. Does he maybe wear black and conduct Mass?"

Claire's cheeks flamed, and she caught her breath. She opened her lips

to explain, but when it came to Father
Ethan Stone, Jo knew very well, Claire
couldn't half articulate her feelings to
herself, let alone to anyone else. Once
upon a time, the same thing had happened to Jo with Whit, who'd been just
as taboo, but for different reasons.

*Let your speech . . . be seasoned
with salt*, the Bible said, meaning speak
with grace. Before Claire returned to
Salt Creek Farm, Jo would have inter-
preted that as a prescription for telling
people what they wanted to hear. Now
that Claire was home, however, Jo had
changed her mind. The word of God
wasn't a plumb line dropped straight
into the heart, Jo decided. It was more
like a tangled web, spread to catch
whatever it could.

"Are you going to services tomorrow?" she asked. "You'll see Ethan
there."

Claire shook her head and then
sneezed. She was still allergic to pol-
len. "I want to stay out here and cook."

Claire was making a big Sunday meal
for the three of them, Jo knew, as a
kind of peace offering to her and Dee:

ham, scalloped potatoes, and the first of the season's pickleweed, pickled just days ago. Jo preserved jars of it on the kitchen counter, and she liked to gaze through the glass to see the plant's tender shoots floating like strands of memory. She frowned at her sister. Some recollections were maybe best left bottled up.

Jo put down her shovel. Her side of the evaporating basin was scraped as clean as she could get it. Earlier in the day, she'd primed the sluices, suspecting that it might be time to let the water back into the marsh. It wasn't a decision she took lightly, and though it was still only early April, she was sensing that the moment had arrived to let the floodgates open and bring what they would. She nodded to herself. "I'm going to do the spring flood," she announced.

Claire looked up. She never had understood how Jo and her mother had decided on a time to deluge the marsh and begin the season of salt production. "Now? So soon?"

Jo shrugged. "Why not?"

"How do you know?"

"There isn't a trick to it, Claire, just practice." And repetition, Jo knew, the patience to witness the season's change and do what it told her, even if she didn't always like what that was. She looked at her sister. Her hair was as red as Henry's salt, but Claire had never made that connection. The day she did, Jo thought, was the moment she'd understand she already possessed all the knowledge she needed to ken the weather of this place.

In reality there really *was* a trick to predicting the time to start a season. Before any flood, Jo simply consulted Henry's salt. The best time to open the gates was when the crystals were just beginning to glimmer pink in the mud. Any sooner and the wind would still be too cold. Any later and the ground would be too thirsty. If Jo waited until the salt became a real red, the clay and silt walls of the channels and ponds would start crumbling, threatening to collapse completely. If she flooded the marsh then, she'd just end up with a muddy mess on her hands. Today, however, the color was right—the faint blush of a rose before it opened. She walked down the main channel, avoiding the weir, as she usually did, even though she was grown now and her twin was long in the ground. She'd timed it perfectly, she saw. The tide was at its highest, throwing waves onto the beach. She twisted the iron clamps holding the main channel's sluice, lifted the gate, and stepped aside as frigid seawater chugged past her boots.

Always the omens that would forecast how the rest of the season would go were hidden somewhere in this moment. It was never just one thing, and it was never the same from year to year. Jo thought back to the white moths they had suffered the spring after Henry had died and the tiny blue butterflies that had swarmed the day Claire had left with Whit. Both of those salt seasons had been cloudy and wet and had produced mostly gray, silt-laden brine. But Jo had a better feeling about this spring. The wild irises had stuck their noses up early, and flocks of geese were already returning, flying overhead in their military V's. The ground was drying up nicely. All in all, Jo thought, they could be in for a banner year.

Satisfied that the levees were holding, she turned to go check on the other, smaller gates—she was worried about the latch holding on the last one—when she saw Dee wavering at the edge of the pools, so pale in the late-afternoon light that she looked only half real. Of course, that was an easy mistake to make, especially out in the marsh, where sky and water did strange things to one's vision and worse to a person's reason.

Jo watched the girl drift past the cluster of gravestones. Dee paused to read the inscriptions, lingering. A weedy single-file path led from the gravestones along the far side of the ponds, and as Dee neared her, Jo realized that she must look equally ghostly. She was wearing gauzy layers: a man's pale linen shirt over lightweight trousers that were tucked into rubber boots. On her head she had a straw hat tied down by a gossamer-thin scarf to keep out what little sun there was. Dee finally arrived, slightly breathless.

"Wow," she said, her eyes wide. "I never knew how big this place really was." She snuffled a bit in the cold, and Jo felt an unexpected stab of pity for her. She was out of her depth in this place. And to get involved with a man like Whit, she must really have been adrift. It must be terrible to have to steal someone's affection like a crow snitching silver, Jo thought, but to whom did Whit really belong anyway? Once she had believed it was to her, and then Claire, but now she would say it was only to himself. Trying to claim Whit had always been like trying to clench her fist around water. The liquid shimmied away, and her fingers snapped together on nothing. Jo moved closer to Dee. Maybe it was better if they both shut up and did some work before she started saying too much. She grabbed Dee's arm.

"Come on. You can make yourself useful. I still have some salt hanging around from last summer, and I hear there are some new restaurants opening up in Wellfleet. Maybe they'll be interested. Salt sales have been awful in Prospect, and I really ought to be making more of an effort to sell the stuff elsewhere. You can help me scoop and tie sample bags."

Dee scrambled after Jo, puffing a little. She spoke in quick bursts that reminded Jo of a lapdog nipping at someone's heels. "I'm real sorry about Whit sending all those mean letters, and I'm sorry he's making trouble for Father Stone."

Jo snorted. So Dee had seen the letter she and Claire had tried to hide. What had the child done, dug through the trash? She eyed Dee, wondering if she'd underestimated her. "I generally consider Whit to be in the same category as those brown slugs I pull out of the mud," she said. "He's been trying to get his mitts on this land for years, you know, but so far nothing's worked. Marrying my sister hasn't got him any closer, and neither has any of his legal hoodoo. Whit Turner can have Salt Creek Farm after he does his time in hell, and that's that." Jo was talking to herself as much as she was to Dee. She turned to see the girl still planted in the mud like a stubborn beetle. "Are you coming?" she barked. Behind her she heard Dee scurrying to catch up in all senses of the phrase.

Chapter Nineteen

On Easter morning Claire rose before anyone else in the house, tied an apron around her hips, and set about creating her own personal resurrection.

In her life with Whit, the act of cooking had been as structured as everything else. Claire had made lists of complicated ingredients—pickled asparagus, sesame oil, salmon roe—done the shopping, and then she would come home and follow the recipe as if it were a set of instructions for nuclear fusion. Her food came out technically perfect but tasteless all the same. She never noticed Whit taking pleasure in it, and by the time dinner rolled around, she was often too exhausted to eat. She'd box the leftovers, and the housekeeper (now long gone, thanks to Whit's increasingly draconian budget) would eat them for lunch the next day, no more enthused than Whit had been the night before.

The thing was, elaborate wasn't an option on Salt Creek Farm. For one thing, Claire was miles from the store, and for another, there were no cookbooks. So Claire simply used what was at hand. Salt, of course, for she no longer had anything to fear from it. And eggs, butter, a dollop of farmer's cheese. Sugar, flour, and a cluster of spring herbs pulled from the cold morning ground outside the kitchen door.

She whipped the egg whites to foamy peaks and combined them with the cheese, the chives, and the golden yolks, then set the dish in the oven to rise. She made basic dough and twisted out rounds of floury biscuits, anointing them with a splash of vanilla, then shoved them into the oven with the eggy pudding. She found a paper bag of tiny new strawberries in the back of the refrigerator and combined them with sugar and mint, letting them soak into a syrup.

The sun rose and spread like a smear of fat melting across a pan, and the kitchen began to fill with the aromas of dough, melting cheese, and steaming vanilla. Satisfied, Claire leaned against the counter, sipping a cup of bitter coffee and fingering the heart locket she'd reclaimed from Dee and now wore along with Ida's pearl at the hollow of her throat. If her past had its own size and weight, she thought, that pearl might be its physical manifestation: a ball of calcium and mineral meant to smother the single grain that didn't belong. The timer on the oven buzzed, and Claire got up to check on the biscuits, opening the oven too suddenly and scalding her eyes in the process. She stepped back and fanned her face. *Really*, she thought, *all these years, and here I am still rushing into things, sticking my nose where it doesn't belong, and, of course, getting burned for it.*

Except all her scars were on the inside. What, exactly, would the reverse of a scar be anyway? Claire wondered. She pulled the tray from the oven and stared down at the round moons of pastry puffed in neat rows. They reminded her of Our Lady's empty face. *That's it*, she thought, closing the oven again. The opposite of a scar was simply the gaping hole left when the heart was ripped out of something.

She broke open one of the biscuits, releasing curls of steam, and then ate the whole thing in four bites. She sipped more coffee and waited for the cheese pudding to finish baking and the biscuits to cool. It occurred to her that she should make a list of anything she had of value. There was Icicle, but selling him would break her heart. There were the few dollars she'd managed to sock away in her own bank account without Whit's knowing, but the amount was laughable. Her eyes drifted down to her naked hands. Of course! There were Ida's rings sitting in the drawer upstairs. Maybe she could sell them, if she dared. Nothing would give her more pleasure.

And anyway, Ida had never been one to turn up her nose at a hard profit, even if it came at her own personal expense.

Claire reached for another biscuit, amazed at how little there was of her in her own life, but it was her own fault. She had filled her days with the idle chatter of friends she didn't care about, tasks she performed just to keep busy, and a husband she never really loved. She shivered in the warm kitchen and finished her second biscuit. Out here she slept so soundly she didn't even dream, but nevertheless she still woke with stiff cheeks and a sore neck, as if she'd been clenching back tears all night. In the mornings Jo was usually gone by the time Claire came downstairs, and on the rare occasion when they did eat together, they were so mute that monks could have meditated on the table between them.

"Claire?" Jo stepped into the kitchen, and Claire blinked. "Is everything okay?"

Jo poured a cup of coffee and blew on it. Claire scowled, swimming back to the present moment. The oven buzzed again, and she slipped on a pair of padded mitts.

"I made a pudding," she said, and opened the oven, this time remembering to avert her face from the heat.

Jo cleared space on the counter for the hot dish. "You never used to cook."

Claire took the mitts off her hands. Her finger still looked naked to her without the yoke of her ring. "I don't know what's got into me. Maybe it's all the physical work, but my appetite's gone crazy." She scooped two mounds of the pudding into bowls and handed one to Jo. "Everything I make here just turns out *good*. Taste it." Claire chewed for a moment, then hesitated, her eyebrows drawn. Normally she ate her food plain no matter how bland it was, but now she reached for the cellar of gray salt, scooping into the bowl with her fingers. She sprinkled a measure over her pudding and then another and another, ignoring Jo's puzzled look.

"Claire, what are you doing?" Claire barely heard her as she lifted the fork to her mouth. Mama had always told her that if she had a question, a pinch of salt would provide the answer, but Claire had never understood that, maybe because she'd never really salted her food. Now, however, she saw what her mother had meant. It was impossible to lie to yourself when you had a mouthful of salt, for it amplified all the flavors in your life—sour and spicy, tasty and sweet, bitter and rotten—making them too loud to ignore.

Claire thought she'd done such a clever job marrying Whit and trading in the damp earth of Salt Creek Farm for hard Turner wood. She recalled the paneled dining room in Turner House, but everything in this kitchen was different. Here there were no razor corners, no polished surfaces, only wear and tear, scratches and bangs, milky opacity. Claire took another bite of pudding and chewed five times, then five times again, mashing everything together in her mouth before swallowing, trying to ignore the cluster of worries hanging over her like overripe vine fruit—that Whit was going to try to pull Salt Creek Farm out from under their feet, that Dee was going to have the child Claire should be bearing, that one day she'd glance in the mirror and appear as faceless as the Virgin, because Jo would finally have claimed her skin. And what could Claire say to that, when Jo deserved it? After all, Jo had saved her—or tried to.

Jo's voice broke through the running brook of her worries. "Were you by any chance out with Icicle this morning?"

Claire blinked. "No. But I need to go check on him. I might give him a run." Jo turned her lips down, and a stab of panic flashed into Claire's heart. *You can't ever leave me,* Whit's voice echoed in her ears. *Not now. Not ever.* She tried to keep her voice light. "Why, what's wrong?"

"Nothing. Did you forget to latch the barn door last night? When I went out this morning to check the basins, Icicle was pacing around outside, that's all." Jo hesitated. "Do you think you forgot to latch the barn?"

Claire clattered the dishes together in the sink, splashing suds across her shirt and watching the stains spread, their edges seeping out like ragged moth wings. She knew exactly what her sister was asking but not saying.

"I probably did. You know what I'm like." Claire held her hands out to her sides, showing off the batter stains and flour smudges on her blouse. "I mean, look at me. I'm a mess. In fact, I need to go change. Then I'll go out to Icicle."

Upstairs, she pulled on an old T-shirt with a hole in it and a clean cable-knit sweater. She *had* latched the barn door. She was a hundred percent certain about that, just as she was positive she knew who'd opened it. She looked in the mirror and licked her lips. No makeup, hair uncombed, her cheeks windburned and plumped. These days she hardly recognized herself. Not that it mattered. She could put on a thousand disguises, she knew, but as long as Whit Turner was out there, the only thing she was ever going to be was a marked woman.

———o-o o-o———

As Claire unlatched the barn, she saw a scatter of footprints so deliberate they could only belong to one person. Whit had most certainly been lurking around the edges of Salt Creek Farm. Claire could still feel him.

The sun had wholly risen and the day was turning mild. It was the first time Claire had skipped an Easter Mass since she'd been married, and it seemed vaguely criminal. Her sins were starting to fill her up, pressing against her ribs like a flock of caged birds desperate to get free. The only cure for that, she knew, was work. It was something Jo would have said, and Claire laughed a little, recognizing that perhaps she was a daughter of the salt after all. She fetched Icicle's currycomb and a mane brush and started grooming him.

She'd just finished his tail when the barn doors opened and Dee appeared silhouetted on the threshold. She had on one of Jo's old linen blouses, a ratty cardigan, a pair of long wool socks, and sweatpants. Up until now Claire had refused to be alone with Dee. If she opened her bedroom door and saw the girl in the hall, she slammed it. She stomped out of the salt ponds if Dee set foot in them and pushed her chair away from the table as soon as Dee bellied up to it. Claire wanted an apology, but she wasn't sure in what guise. Did she want Dee to hoist her sleeve and display a lattice of fresh cuts, or lop off all her hair, or quit eating until she and her baby wasted conveniently away? Or, worse, did she just want the girl to disappear and leave the child with her? It felt to Claire as if Dee had stolen something she'd been meant to have.

"Please don't meddle with my horse," she finally said, debating whether or not to add *in addition to my husband*, though she wasn't sure she could call Whit that any longer.

Dee frowned and thrust out her jaw, and that action maddened Claire. Here she had readied herself for an apology only to be startled instead by a surge of adolescent rudeness.

"Seems like all that riding's left you up on a high horse," Dee said.

Claire raised her eyebrows, and when Dee didn't respond, she wondered if the girl really was lackadaisical or just plain stupid. She fiddled with Icicle's mane.

"Do you ever wonder how I knew about you and Whit?" Claire asked suddenly, but Dee didn't rush to answer the question. Maybe this was how the child planned on apologizing, Claire considered—with simple silence. Maybe she was trying to convey negative sorrow. But wouldn't that end up being joy? And Dee was about as far away from a state of delight as Salt Creek Farm was from heaven. "I found your earring in our car," Claire continued. "Some trashy silver hoop. I threw it out and didn't say anything to Whit, but that's how I knew."

Dee reached up and fondled her own earlobe. It pleased Claire to see that she didn't have any jewelry to her name out here—not since Claire had ripped the locket off her throat and put it around her own. Of course, Dee should have known better than to accept it from Whit in the first place. Claire could just imagine him pulling it out of his pocket and dangling it off his forefinger and thumb as if daring Dee to take some kind of gateway drug.

Dee blushed. "I didn't go after him, you know," she whispered. "I wasn't the one who started it. You have to believe that." She eased toward the barn doors, eager to leave, but Claire wasn't done. She stretched out her hands, her fingers spread like tentacles.

"What were you thinking? He's twice your age and married. Did that even matter to you? He was way too much for you to handle. Why, I caught him trying to choke you to death!"

Dee pursed her lips and picked at the skin around her fingernails. "He didn't really mean it. He was just surprised. About the baby and everything."

Claire narrowed her eyes. "Are you serious? Are you really that naïve? Because if there's one thing I can tell you about Whit, my dear, it's that he *always* means it."

Dee shook her head. "I know what you're trying to do, and it's not going to work. When Whit lays eyes on his child, he'll want me back. I know it. And he wasn't trying to kill me. He was just scared, is all." She stood up and pulled her cardigan closed tighter. "In the meantime stay away from me, and I won't go near you."

She tried to pass Claire, but Claire reached out and seized one of Dee's fleshy upper arms, digging her fingers in hard. "I wouldn't be throwing ultimatums around if I were in your shoes, Dee. There isn't a Temperance League you can go running to for charity anymore, and I doubt anyone else in town is going to risk your father's or Whit's wrath just to give you a bed and a hot plate of food every night. It's us or no one." Dee wrenched her arm free and glared at Claire. "How far along are you anyway?" Claire asked, nodding at Dee's stomach.

Dee wrapped her arms around her middle like she was trying to hold in a secret, but it was a little late for that in Claire's opinion. "Six months," she whispered.

Claire gasped. "Are you *serious*?" She turned away from Dee, doing some quick math in her head and not liking the sum she came up with. "What are you planning on doing?"

Dee's lip wobbled. "I don't know anymore."

Claire gazed out the open doors of the barn to the newly flooded evaporating pools and thought about the babies she'd lost. She'd never gotten a chance to hold any of them. Dee's child might be the closest she ever came, but if Dee left the marsh, it would mean another child Claire never embraced.

However, Salt Creek Farm was a dangerous place for an infant in more ways than one. Claire thought of the stopped hearts of the boys in the graves across the salt flats, her own brother among them.

"What should I do?" Dee asked.

Don't let her go, a voice inside Claire urged. But if she was going to get Dee to stay, she was going to need help. She was the last woman on earth Dee would want to listen to, although that could be fixed. Claire knew how salt could corrode a person's better judgment and wear down second thoughts. She took Dee by the hand, gripping harder when she tried to pull away.

"No, I want to help," she said, smil-

ing, making sure to show all her teeth
the way she did when she wanted to
coerce her coterie of country-club ladies. "You need a friend now, a soul
you can confide in. Luckily, I know just
the right someone."

Still clutching Dee by the wrist, Claire
led her out of the barn and closed the
doors, moving with the slow deliberate-
ness she'd use around a horse she
didn't want to spook.

"Come on," she said, and set off
down the lane. It was Easter, Claire
thought, her heart swelling with a rush
of extra blood, the time for offerings,
and at long last she had a gift for Our
Lady that couldn't possibly be refused.

Chapter Twenty

Dee might never have been an ace student or anything, but she wasn't a total dimwit either. When Claire accused her of letting Icicle out of the barn, she knew it was Claire's way of telling her to keep her hands off her horse, her man, and everything else in her life.

But that proved easier said than done. Now that Dee was living in close quarters with Claire, her curiosity was stronger than it ever had been. When Claire was out working or riding Icicle, Dee would sometimes sneak into Claire's room and have a little look around. She started off just standing there, inhaling the air, but after a while she began prying more boldly, cracking open the wardrobe and rifling through Claire's old salt clothes, fiddling with the hairbrush on top of the dresser, examining what kind of skin cream Claire liked. When Dee found Claire's diamond wedding band in the bureau's top drawer, she tried to slip it on her finger, but it only went to the knuckle. She sighed in frustration and put it back. There were other things she would have liked to explore—a faded diary with a broken lock, a packet of photographs of Claire in high school, a series of birthday cards—but she was always too scared she'd get caught.

Sharing space with Claire allowed Dee to see that Claire wasn't exactly the fire-wielding vixen she'd painted in her imagination. Around Jo, Dee was surprised to find that Claire was polite and almost meek. And Jo, who never uttered more than three words in a row to anyone in town, was turning out to be so bossy that Dee sometimes wished she could tape up Jo's mouth for a little peace and quiet. And then there were all the crazy things going on with Dee's body. Her breasts felt like a pair of party balloons. There were days she swore she was retaining half the world's water. Even her face was changing shape.

Her father had called her a slut and said she deserved what she was getting, and Whit had gone one step further and called up the devil against her, but if salt could change how she saw Claire, Dee thought, maybe there was hope for her, too. Maybe by the time the baby came, all the bad parts would have leached out of her, leaving her as pure and shining as a flake of Joanna's good stuff.

She pushed the drawer closed, her knees aching as she crossed the room. It was Easter, but she couldn't tell it from the quiet out on the farm. Claire had baked something that smelled cheesy and promising, but that was the only sign of any kind of celebration. Dee listened, but the house was truly empty. She'd go out and see Icicle, she decided. At least he was good company.

"I'm taking a walk," she called loudly, just in case anyone cared. "I'll be out in the barn." But no one answered. Not even the clock ticked.

———o-o o-o———

The place Dee felt best in was the salt barn. The dry aroma cleared her mind and relaxed her aching back. She swung open the door and inhaled, wishing she could knit something for herself out of that smell and live co-cooned in it. It was better than the hip-pie sticks of incense that kids used to burn at high-school parties back in Ver-mont—probably better than the pot they scored. Even Icicle, tucked away in the corner with his hay, and in spite of his manure, made the whole atmo-sphere kind of cozy.

He always nickered when he heard Dee enter, but she'd come prepared, pulling a carrot out of her coat pocket. She let him nuzzle her neck with his hot nose, then fed him the carrot, flat-palmed, taking pleasure in the chomp-ing noises he made and laughing when he bumped her, knocking her a little sideways.

Her center of gravity was shifting. That was for sure. When she climbed stairs these days, her hips felt disjointed and her knees rubberized, but there was more than just a physical adjustment going on inside her. Right before she'd dropped out of school, they'd studied rivers in geography, the only class Dee had ever liked, maybe because she knew that it was the closest she was going to come to traveling. Rivers, the teacher had told them, sometimes reversed their courses under amazing circumstances, say, giant earthquakes. Dee pondered that now. The more pregnant she got, the more she felt like one of those waterways. She might be confused and churned up at the moment, but she was starting to suspect that giving birth was going to upend her completely. For the hundredth time, she wished she didn't have to do it.

Life is hard, her father had always droned whenever she complained about the littlest thing. Back then she'd assumed he was trying to get her to shut up, but what if he'd been telling her the absolute truth? Day-to-day existence wasn't hard, Dee was starting to see; all of *life* was. As far as she could tell, it began with bone-grinding pain and ended even worse, and what a person was supposed to do with the parts in between seemed to her to be about as clear as a dream.

She remembered the time after her mother had died, when the air in the house seemed to have stilled forever. The clocks were stopped. The phone was left unanswered. Even the refrigerator hummed more quietly. Dee wasn't sure she hadn't died, too. Cutt barely looked at her. Her relatives arrived and vanished. Dee returned to school, where no one mentioned she'd been gone, and came home to an empty house. The details of Dee's mother—the smoky color of her eyes, her funny laugh, the shape of her feet—faded a little bit more each day.

Dee wondered if Cutt missed her like that now, if the rooms above the diner seemed empty to him when he came up after his shifts, and she decided probably not. For one thing, she wasn't really gone, not all the way. The day after she arrived on Salt Creek Farm, she'd even called Cutt and told him where she was.

"I don't have a daughter," he'd said, and then hung up the phone, loud and hard. Her father knew where to find her. He just didn't want to.

Still, it was funny. Out on Salt Creek Farm, where there wasn't much of anything, Dee felt more alive than she had in months. Maybe, she thought, nestling one hand under her belly, it was the baby weight, filling up the parts of her she hadn't known were empty, or maybe what people in town said about Gilly salt really was true. It was playing tricks on her mind, making her think she was full when she wasn't, happy when she was sad, and worth more to somebody than a plate of eggs and ham.

———o-o o-o———

Claire just about scared the piss out of Dee when she jumped out of the shadows in the barn. Dee knew perfectly well that three women shut up to-gether—one of them pregnant and cranky, one nursing a broken heart and a grudge, and one who was half french fry—couldn't be a good combination, especially when they were all there be-cause of the same man.

But she was wrong again. Claire wasn't out to get her. She just wanted to help. *You need a friend*, she said, coming up close to Dee and slipping her white fingers around the girl's wrist, right over her pulse, the same way Whit had. She pulled Dee out of the barn and down the dusty lane. *And I know the right someone.*

For a blind moment, Dee worried that Claire was taking her into the dunes for a private beating, so she was relieved when the place they stopped at turned out only to be St. Agnes. The last of the handful of Easter worshippers had left, and Father Ethan Stone was just stepping out of the rectory. He blushed hard when he saw Claire, but he didn't take his eyes off her either, Dee no-ticed. Claire grew as fidgety as a grasshopper in Ethan's presence, and he wasn't much better. He blinked at Claire.

"Hello," he said, adjusting his collar like he wanted to remind her—or maybe just himself—of his vows. On her part, Claire was shameless. She stretched her neck and tugged on her braid, biting her bottom lip.

"Happy Easter," she said. Dee felt as if she were watching a girl her own age instead of a woman of thirty-one. In contrast, the Virgin shone behind Claire in a little patch of sun, keeping all her secrets to herself.

"Oh." Dee startled herself by speaking out loud, understanding blooming in her brain. "You brought me to see the Virgin."

Claire regarded her. "Who did you think I meant?" Dee didn't answer, but Father Stone smiled, and Claire raised her eyebrows at him.

He wasn't born a priest, Dee said to herself. *And if Claire keeps it up, he won't stay one for long.* Which, if you asked Dee, would be a general service to womankind. A man that fine shouldn't be locked away in a musty old church, she thought. Claire put her hands on Dee's shoulders and pushed her past Father Stone toward the sanctuary door. Dee raised her own eyebrows at him, the way Claire had.

"This is women's business, Ethan," Claire called over her shoulder. "We need to borrow the church for a little while, if you don't mind." And, the Lord bless him, the man scrambled out the door like he couldn't wait to get away. Dee didn't catch his reply, but if it matched the heat in his eyes as he stared at Claire, she thought that was probably for the best.

Inside, she halted, struck dumb by the light bathing the Virgin, her gaze getting stuck on all the strange things about the painting: the gray fishhooks scooped along the hemline, the open eye painted on the palm.

Dee followed Claire up the center of the church's tiny aisle. Dee was in trouble and needed someone on her side, she knew, and maybe Our Lady was really good for it. She kind of covered all the bases. She was holy, but human, too. Dee had never really thought about it before, but the Holy Family was a lot more like a regular family than she'd ever given them credit for. Their problems were pretty familiar—unexplained pregnancy, a rebellious son, his weird friends. She looked at her own situation in comparison and thanked her lucky stars that when she died and went to judgment, at least she'd get herself some resolution. Poor Jesus just got himself resurrected. His troubles never ended. One day he'd even have to return again, to judge the living and the dead, but hopefully that was still a long ways off.

Claire crossed herself and slid into a middle pew, and after a moment Dee did the same. They were silent for the longest time, both of them facing the altar, as if they were passengers on a perilous mountain road, unwilling to take their eyes off the twists and turns unfolding in front of them. It was worse than actual church. Finally Claire cleared her throat and got right down to the heart of things. *"Why?"* she cried.

For a moment Dee panicked. For

such a little word, "why" sounded pretty big. What was Claire asking about? Dee wondered, her brain racing lickety-split. The times Dee had snuck into her room lately and tried on Claire's wedding ring? Or the fact that she hadn't been completely forthcoming about how far along she really was in her pregnancy? As if to prove a point, the baby kicked her just then, and she shifted, not wanting to call attention to it. She bowed her head. No. She knew exactly what Claire was asking when she asked the question why. She wanted to know about Whit. Dee didn't have anything to offer her but the truth. She held it out, her voice wavering. "I thought maybe he really loved me."

"I suppose you thought you loved him, too," Claire said, her lips barely moving, her shoulders straight. For the first time, Dee realized that Claire always held herself as if she were on the back of a horse—upright, ready to yank the reins if she needed to. Dee wondered if that came naturally or if it was a by-product of life with Whit. She considered Claire's statement. Had she thought she loved Whit? That question was easy to answer. It was the easiest one, in fact. "Yes," she admitted. She shifted her bulk. If Claire was going to ask her questions, she figured, she was going to do the same. "And what about you? Did you love him when you got married?"

Claire's head snapped up. "What?" She didn't pronounce this word the way she'd said why. This was an accusation, a *How dare you?*

Dee eased an inch to the left on the pew. "It's just that . . . well, I heard all about how you once loved Father Stone, and I wondered if you loved Whit like that, too." She balled her hands back into fists and held her breath.

Claire seemed to weigh Dee's insinuation, but when she spoke again, it wasn't to address questions of her own past. She leaned forward, and her voice got so low it almost flickered. "I know you've been going through my things," she said. "Next time you snoop, you might want to close the curtains."

Dee rubbed the pew's fine wood, her fingertips searching for a crack or cranny in which to hide. She was damned if she'd cry in front of Claire. "What do you want from me?" she finally asked, but before Claire could respond, the answer came swelling up through Dee like the vibration of a huge bell, so powerful she wondered that half the town couldn't hear it, too. *Your baby.*

She sat back, breathless. Of course. It was so plain. Claire was exactly the kind of person who wanted all the things she didn't have—children, Whit when he'd belonged to her sister, Ethan when he belonged to God. And Dee bet that Claire didn't care how she got them. She folded her hands around her belly and stood up. "We can go now." The baby gurgled and twisted, and Dee laid a hand on top of it, as if to reassure it for the first time that everything was going to be fine, even if she wasn't sure that was true.

"Did you get the answer you needed?" Claire's voice jabbed behind her like a spade plunging into earth. Dee squared her shoulders and steeled herself. She wasn't going to let Claire—or anyone— dig into her. Not anymore.

"Sure," she said. "For now."

Chapter Twenty-one

By the end of June, summer had finally started unfurling itself in earnest, a bright flag that had been rolled too tight during winter. Eelgrass, pea blossoms, climbing roses, ticks, mice, and even moles poked their dim noses up out of the blessed black dirt and took a sniff of the new season. As if in celebration, the first crust of salt formed early on the eastern basins, turning the ponds from plain mud puddles to pools frosted with delicacy.

Jo couldn't enjoy the bounty, however. Her savings had run completely out, and once again, as the bank had predicted, she'd fallen behind on the payments. Whit had made good on his word, too. He *did* have friends at Harbor Bank, and as bad luck would have it, they agreed with Whit's view of the situation.

"You have a reasonable offer on the property, Miss Gilly," Mr. Monaghy had said through the telephone two days after her latest letter from them. "It is our honest advice that you take it. To tell you the truth, we don't really *want* the property, but we're beholden to follow the rules of the loan. We view this offer as a win-win situation for all parties involved."

"I wasn't aware that this was a game," Jo had snapped. "The answer is no." And she'd slammed down the phone.

Jo gazed out toward the horizon now, at a point that should have been mysterious and vast but which, down low in the belly of the marsh, was merely a dot of unrealized potential. She turned her face back to the salt ponds. If she was going to dig her way out of her hole of debt, she was going to have to pay attention to the resources at hand. This spot of earth could be fertile in the right circumstances, Jo knew. In fact, the outer banks of the Cape had once been famous for their salt. Now her farm was just the last ghost of that fecundity. Put like that, Jo thought, the marsh seemed less a historical relic than an undiscovered treasure. Funny how perspective worked, she mused, climbing over a crumbling levee and lowering herself even further into the bog. It wasn't until you were on the verge of losing something that you saw it for what it really was.

———o-o o-o———

"It looks like snow." Dee was balanced on a narrow levee, blinking against the late-afternoon sun, her belly fully swollen in the last stage of her pregnancy. Jo thought she'd never seen anyone so pregnant, and in fact she hadn't.

Claire had been furious when she'd found out how far along Dee was in her pregnancy, but Jo wasn't surprised a bit. A child built like Dee could probably keep a huge amount under her belt, Jo thought, before it would start to show. She wondered what else Dee hadn't told them about. With her it could be almost anything. Once Jo had caught Dee coming out of Claire's room.

"I was . . . I was just looking to see if I could borrow an old blouse," she'd stammered, but hadn't Jo just given her a pile of extra clothes the day before?

"Better take one of mine," Jo had said. "And if I were you, I'd give my sister a wide berth." Even though Claire was civil enough to Dee, greeting her with cold nods or single words, Jo still couldn't be sure she wasn't cooking up a plan for revenge along with all her sweeter confections. Jo sighed now and wiped her brow, regarding the basin in front of her.

"Are you sure I should be doing this?" Dee asked her. "It feels like I'm going to pop any second."

Jo continued to rake. "This is the best crust of the year so far." Her voice grew softer. "Once there were salt works all up and down this coast. Did you know that? When I was little, there were even some of the old vats left. They were empty and half rotten, of course, but still there."

Jo dipped her finger into the bowl of flakes she was accumulating and offered a pinch to Dee. She waited for Dee to put it in her mouth, and then she decided to give the girl a test. "Quick," she said, "without thinking, tell me your first memory."

Dee closed her eyes, and a smile crept over her round face. "My mother singing before I fell asleep."

"Who do you love?" Jo asked, praying that Dee wouldn't say Whit and sighing with relief when her hands simply circled her belly. So far Dee's heart seemed pure, but Jo had covered only the past and the present. The future was open to interpretation.

"What did you think you'd find here?" she asked, and with that, Dee's eyes flew open, hooded and suspicious.

"What do you mean?" she said, but the salt's spell was broken, Jo saw. Dee wasn't going to tell her more. Jo handed her a wide wooden bowl. If she couldn't get answers out of Dee, at least she could get some help. "Hold this steady," she said.

Dee couldn't possibly screw *that* up, she thought. Right after the spring flood, Jo had tried showing Dee how to work the sluices, but she and Claire had ended up hauling her out of one of the inundation pools by her armpits. When Dee had attempted the process again in early May, she'd come back to the barn bleeding from her thumb, one of her boots covered entirely in mud. Jo never did figure out what had happened that time. It was astonishing, really. She'd never met anyone so clumsy. When the baby was born, Jo thought, she and Claire might have to string up a safety net under its tiny little bones.

The bowl wobbled and tipped in Dee's arms, and Jo righted it. She couldn't afford to lose this load, her most expensive commodity, the one that the tourists hungry for any scrap of Cape Cod authenticity had started to snap up recently like greedy dogs. She imagined the women and men who bought it back at home in their designer kitchens, sprinkling the flakes on thick slabs of steak with the intensity of chemists. Did they even taste it, she wondered, the way the people of Prospect used to when they would add it to their cakes and pies, knowing that all the sweet in the world was useless without a little snap to set it off?

Dee trailed behind her across the patchwork spine of levees, cradling the bowl as Jo had shown her to, stumbling once or twice. "Should I carry the kid like this once it's born?" she joked, and Jo winced, for Dee had no idea, of course, that Jo's mother had done just that, lining a giant salt bowl and nestling Jo and her twin brother in its broad curve. Claire, too. Jo remembered rocking Claire to sleep in such a bowl and then carrying the whole thing over near the hearth to keep her sister warm while she slept.

I must get some soft blankets, she thought. *And linen squares. We're going to need diapers, and pacifiers, and bibs.* And what was that lullaby Mama used to sing? Jo stopped short, and Dee almost plowed into her.

What's happening to me? Jo scolded herself. She sounded like Mother Goose. She knew that the choice of bringing this child into the marsh wasn't hers to make, especially if it turned out to be a boy who might fall victim to the salt's bad luck. Only Dee could decide that. Sooner or later Jo was going to have to have a talk with her.

Dee puffed out her cheeks and put the bowl at her feet. It wasn't heavy, just bulky. Jo didn't think it would cause any harm for Dee to carry it, but still. She didn't really know.

Dee eyed her uneasily. "Did I say something wrong? I was only kidding about hauling the baby around in the bowl."

Jo traded her for the paddle, turned around, and started walking again. As they neared the house, a faint smell of something sweet in the oven tinged the air. Jo regarded the clapboard house she'd lived in all her life. It was a little weed-ridden, okay, but also weather-tight, breezy in the summer, and stuffed with an interesting history. Maybe it wasn't the best place to raise a baby, but it wasn't the worst either.

They reached the porch steps, and Jo turned to Dee. *She's a child having a child*, she thought. *She's going to need some guidance.* Jo wasn't a mother, but hadn't she grown up looking after Claire? Her advice had to be better than nothing, and besides, it was currently all Dee had.

The longer Dee stayed on Salt Creek Farm, the more Jo was starting to feel as if the child really belonged there. Even now Jo could tell that Dee knew where to step on the porch to avoid the soft spots. Dee remembered that the screen door could be left to slam because Jo had added the spring to catch it at the last second. Jo watched her step out of her canvas tennis shoes and throw them into the corner of the hall with Claire's same impatience. Dee knew that they kept the truck keys in a bowl on top of the tuneless hall piano; she knew which cupboard had rice and which one held cereal, and how long the water had to run before it turned hot, then scalding, then cooled again.

She was learning the nuts and bolts of Salt Creek Farm—she was even learning to distinguish the types of salt—but when it came to the secret of the marsh's history, its pulsing heart, Jo worried that Dee was still blind. But maybe that was the best thing for now, Jo decided. Some things were better left alone.

———○○ ○○———

Claire had gone into town, but there was a note from her on the kitchen table: *"Cinnamon cake in the oven. Timer is on. Let cool before slicing. Back by five. C."*

Jo emptied the pile of salt she'd collected into a glass jar and set it aside for Claire. Lately Claire had taken to adding all kinds of crazy things to the salt: vanilla pods, sprigs of lavender, rose petals. And the things she then went and put the salt into were even more unusual: puddings, ice cream, every sort of bread. Jo wasn't sure she'd be able to sell any of the doctored salt, but Claire had streamlined the labels for the bags Jo used and reassured her she could charge double. "Now it's not just a handmade local product—it's a *gourmet* handmade local product," she'd said, swiping a hank of red hair out of her eyes. "Trust me, the tourists will go bananas over it. I've already phoned three stores in Hyannis, and they can't wait to stock this."

Jo had just shrugged. Claire floated in the wider world more lightly than she did, what with her former membership to the country club in Wellfleet, and her dressage competitions, and living all those years in big, fancy Turner House. Out by Salt Creek Farm, the coast was still wild and plain. Still, much as Jo knew she couldn't *really* count on Claire, a little kernel of hope began to glow deep down in her. Maybe, with the extra hands and some new ideas, the farm could be saved after all. Jo lit the stove and put on the kettle for tea.

Dee rubbed a palm over her belly and gazed out the kitchen windows. "The marsh has changed so much just since I've been here. And who knows what will happen after this guy comes out?"

Jo sat forward, terribly alert. "You think it's a boy?"

Dee pressed her lips tight, but she couldn't contain her smile. Jo's heart started pounding.

"Oh, I don't know. I just have a feeling."

Jo crossed her legs, trying not to show any anxiety. "How much have you told Whit about this baby?"

"Nothing. Only that it's coming. Why?"

Jo surveyed Dee. The girl's eyes were widened, a sign of innocence, but the corners of her mouth were tense, like she was awaiting bad news, and the innocent were never expecting bad news, Jo knew. It was what made them innocent.

"Dee," Jo said slowly and a little too loudly, as if speaking to a slow-witted foreigner, "you must promise, I mean *promise*, that you won't contact Whit, that you won't tell him anything about this child. You don't know what he's capable of."

"You sound just like Claire."

Jo's nose twitched. She remembered

seeing Dee and Claire on Easter, walking step in step across the marsh, as if they were stamping down a secret together. "Why? What did my sister say?" And there it was again, the curtain lowering on Dee's face—the clenched jaw, the eyes maybe now a little too wide. *What does she know that she's not telling me?* Jo wondered, stirring her tea. This was the disadvantage to letting other people—even family—onto Salt Creek Farm. More and more things would start unraveling at the edges, Jo suspected, where she had no hope of seeing them, until something terrible finally shook loose. And what would everyone do then? Ask Jo for help, was what.

She sighed and ran a hand over her face. "You know, Whit and I used to be very good friends."

Dee nodded, and Jo kept speaking, the words burning her throat like too-hot coffee. Half of Jo hoped Dee would run and repeat them to Claire, just as the other half of her knew that the girl wouldn't dare. "I can't believe it myself, but it's true. This is an odd story—I don't even know why I'm telling you, really—but the summer I was fifteen, Whit tried to give me something as a keepsake. Same thing he gave you, as a matter of fact. That locket carved with a *W*. I didn't dare keep it, though. I was too scared Ida Turner might find out about it and choke the life out of me. There's no love lost between the Turners and the Gillys, you know."

Dee nodded, so Jo kept talking, her voice straining with unaccustomed use. "Anyway, I think Ida did find out about it, because later, when I was delivering a loaf of bread to Father Flynn at St. Agnes, I stumbled on a letter laid out in front of the Virgin."

Dee leaned forward. "From whom?"

Jo paused. "Ida."

"Did you read it?"

Jo nodded. She'd never told anyone this before.

"What did it say?" Dee asked.

Jo's voice came out distant. "The last line's what stuck with me most. *'Magna est veritas, et praevalibet.'*"

Dee frowned. "What the heck does that mean?"

Jo translated. "*Truth is great and it will prevail.* It's from the Vulgate, the old Latin version of the Bible. I asked Father Flynn to tell me what it meant once. He always said he preferred the old Latin Mass." It was a sentiment Jo understood. There were times, she supposed, when a person might need to approach God not as a vessel brimming with human understanding but as a hollow one, ready to be filled. A stray gust of wind rattled the kitchen's window sashes. Evening was gathering.

Jo stood up and clattered the cups together, then dangled her hands by her sides, letting all her regrets bear down on her as sure and unstoppable as a millstone about to crush bone. The afternoon was wrung out and limp. It seemed as good a time as any for confessions. Jo turned around again.

"There's something you have to know if you're going to stay here."

Dee sat forward, unusually somber.

"I'm sure you've heard all the stories in town. This land's not so kind to boys." Jo hesitated. "I'm not saying I believe it, but stone doesn't lie. The only bones buried out here are male."

Dee was silent at this, so Jo took a deep breath and made another small confession.

"I think my mother might have tried to change that when my brother and I were born. Before she died, she told me a story about Our Lady. She did something terrible, but I can't say what."

Dee's eyes were saucers. "And did it work?"

Jo paused, knowing she was lingering at a dangerous crossroad, but she couldn't think of any good way to frame the rest of her story. She considered Dee's question. Had her mother changed their luck? Unknowingly, Dee had stabbed right into the heart of the matter.

"Yes and no," Jo finally said. "She didn't save my brother, but she did find something else that night."

Dee narrowed her eyes. "What?"

Jo shook her head. "That secret's not mine alone to tell."

"Does Claire know it?" Dee asked, and Jo shook her head again. How could she when Claire had spent the past decade perched on Plover Hill like a hawk in a tree?

Jo glanced out the window. A pair of gulls were squabbling over something they'd dug up, flapping their wings and squawking. "Look at that," she said. "The two of them fighting over one rotten piece of fish when there's thousands more in the sea. I guess secrets are like that, too. If you have one, you have many."

"But Gilly secrets aren't so easy to come by, are they?" Dee asked, and Jo gazed at her. It was so strange for Jo to have a young woman around the house, eager to unearth old truths better left unsaid. Dee didn't understand yet that a story needed someone to fall in order for it to go forward, just as it required someone to do the casting-out.

Is it better to be fallen than evil? Jo wondered. She had always thought so. Now she wasn't so sure. Perhaps that was just the way she'd chosen to justify the past to herself. But what if sin were something one inherited? Who would the villain in her tale be then? She wiped the counter and set the rag back in the sink.

"I guess the thing about this family's secrets is that they're right out in the open," she said at last, "if only you know where to look."

Chapter Twenty-two

Summer on the Cape had never felt quite real to Claire. It was the same sensation she'd had in the heady early days of her marriage whenever she'd gone to a country-club gala with Whit, swathed in one of Ida's old satin gowns, a tiny jeweled purse clutched in one hand. She was a fictional version of herself at those events, a woman with the same hair, the same eyes and nose, but nothing else in common with the person who shoveled out Icicle's stall, licked ice cream from the bottom of the bowl before she put it in the sink, and daydreamed her way through Mass.

Likewise, summer wasn't Prospect's natural season. The town grew too full too quickly. Lines developed at Mr. Upton's market, the library ran out of all its current novels, and even the Lighthouse stools were all occupied. The locals, torn between contempt for the soft-bellied tourists and appreciation of their money, closed ranks around themselves while the tourists, frisky and eager as puppies, stuck their noses in places they didn't belong. Every now and then, a few of them even stumbled onto Salt Creek Farm, blinking in confusion at the heaps of salt and the muddy ditches before backing away slowly from the wooden rake Jo brandished in their direction.

"We should show them around," Claire urged. "We could charge them for tours, and you could teach them about the salt." This year there were more tourists than ever, and Claire knew that a large part of it had to do with Whit's new developments around town. He owned beach cottages and markets, hotels and inns, but still his balance sheet was a long way from even. If he had it his way, Claire suspected, Whit would make summer last all year long.

"*You* teach them," Jo sniffed. "I have too much else to do." But it wouldn't be the same, Claire knew. She didn't have a feel for the salt the way Jo did. She could scrape it and pile it just fine, but in her hands it might as well have been sand. It was only when Jo's rake twirled through the brine that the stuff drew life and became the famous Gilly salt. Only Jo could put a pinch on her tongue and know if there was too much silt in it, and only Jo knew the exact moment when the flakes were dry enough to collect. She even used to be able sometimes to predict which batches would flare red and which would smoke blue when they were burned on December's Eve.

But that summer Claire learned she could do something with the salt that Jo couldn't. She could transform it. If the salt gained its perfect expression in Jo's hands, it turned pranks in Claire's.

She added it to cakes, to teas, to jams, and created a whole new sensation halfway between sour and sweet.

If June was a key month for salt on Salt Creek Farm, it was also a month for ghosts. For starters, Whit had been quiet lately—eerily so. Claire was convinced he was lurking about, planning something dreadful, but she could never be sure. Jo was managing to hold off the bank, at least for now, but still, Claire's neck was always tense, the tiny hairs on her arms always tingling.

And there was the faint presence of her brother, whom she couldn't remember, like the kind of rain that falls so lightly on your face you're not sure it's really there. There were the babies she'd lost. They were more tenacious, nipping at her all day long with their tiny, unformed lips like so many hungry tadpoles. Irritating more than anything, really, except for the times when Claire would wake gasping in the night, the nerves in her belly tingling, a grief so huge pressing on her that it was as if all the world's lost children had decided to come to her to roost. The ghost of her mother was more of a constant memory than a phantom, the gravel-pit voice in Claire's head that urged her to stand up straight, tie back her hair, and tell Whit to go hang himself. And, finally, Ethan haunted her. Claire knew perfectly well that his life was also filled with a ghost, but that, unlike hers, it was singular and holy. Lucky him.

Except for her visit to St. Agnes on Easter with Dee, Claire had avoided Ethan entirely. It made her heart too sore to see him. If they met in town, they nodded to each other, spoke about the weather, and crossed to opposite sides of the street. If she encountered him on the beach on her morning gallop with Icicle, she didn't slow down, just blew by him in a cloud of hooves and sand. But as much as Claire could ignore him publicly, Ethan was so unwaveringly present in her soul that she sometimes saw his face instead of her own when she looked in the mirror.

Every time she drove past St. Agnes, she fought an urge to pull over the car, fling open the sanctuary doors, and tell Ethan her feelings, but Jo reminded her that the less she did to enrage Whit, the better, and she was right. If Whit had found out the extent of her emotions for Ethan, Claire knew, he might scorch St. Agnes black as a grave and burn Ethan up with it, and while it was one thing for Whit to threaten her, it was quite another to think of him hurting Ethan.

Icicle nickered, and she shushed him, then took his tub of water away to empty and refill, letting him drink the cool liquid before she threw a blanket and saddle over his back and fed him the bit. "Come on," she whispered, leading him outside. She looked around for signs of Whit, but at this hour, out here on the marsh's spit of scrubland, she was profoundly alone. She swung a foot into the stirrup and lifted herself into the saddle, finally taking the deep breaths she'd been craving all night.

She threaded her way through the dunes, turned Icicle onto the hard sand on the beach, and gave him free rein, leaning forward as he gathered speed, comforted by the rocking motion of his canter. What would all the women from the country club say about her if they could see her now? she wondered, her hair uncombed, holes in her shirt, stripped of makeup. Would they turn their cheeks and ignore her or, worse, taunt her again about wearing rags?

She slowed Icicle to a trot and exhaled. She'd arrived almost at the end of the beach, near Drake's Rocks, and she had to admit to herself that the tide wasn't the only thing pulling at her soul. Ahead of her sat St. Agnes and Ethan. She stared down at the hard sand by the water, and it was like a blank canvas for everything that should have been. She watched as a wave came up and wiped the sand clean, but life wasn't so tidy for Claire. She couldn't get rid of the thoughts she was having.

Before she could lose her nerve, she picked her way up through the dunes and tied Icicle to the railing outside the church, and then she pushed open the door to the sanctuary, entering quietly, telling herself she wasn't there to see Ethan specifically, but only to say a Hail

Mary, light a candle, and leave. No harm done. Maybe he wouldn't even be there.

But he was—kneeling in front of the altar, his hands swept out to his sides, his head not bowed as Claire would have expected, but tossed back, his neck exposed as if he were making an offering of himself. Claire hung in the doorway, transfixed. She'd never seen a man look so vulnerable before, and it struck her as nearly obscene. Or it would have if Ethan hadn't been so lovely. She almost turned away but didn't. Instead she cleared her throat, and he startled and spun around.

"Claire." His voice was still thick with prayer, honey clinging to the comb. It told her everything she needed to know. A man with a clear conscience didn't stumble over his words the way Ethan did. *Once a sinner, always a sinner*, she thought as she walked to him, already untwisting her hair along with the last scrap of restraint she still had shriveled up inside her.

———o-o o-o———

Later she would blame Our Lady, who was faceless and therefore shameless, a very poor chaperone for mortals made blind by love, but the truth was that what had happened between Ethan and Claire was all too human, and it was all Claire's own fault.

She certainly hadn't entered St. Agnes with the intention of seducing Ethan. At least that's what she told herself. But as she'd stood in front of him, she could no longer deny the pull she still felt to him, and before she knew it, she'd stepped so close that she could feel the warmth of his skin.

"Claire," Ethan had said again, this time as a low warning. He'd tried to back away from her, but his eyes held the same questions as hers, and before he could object, Claire reached out and embraced him.

"You feel it, too. I know you do," she'd said. "You must." Her heart thudded as she felt him stiffen, and then a buzz of joy lit up her nerves as he wrapped his arms around her in return. *Is this how it would have been every day?* she wondered, remembering the rough thrills she'd experienced with Whit when they'd made love. *Would life have been this gentle?* She stifled a sob. Maybe then she would have been able to carry the child she'd so desperately craved.

At first it was enough simply to be circled again by Ethan, but Claire had never been a woman satisfied with what the Good Lord gave her, and so she put her lips to the side of his neck. He flinched with surprise, but soon he slipped into the past as well and lost the will to move away, and so she traced her mouth along his jaw until her lips met his, and he began kissing her back, his hands dropping from her waist to her hips, then going places no priest's hands should travel.

"Not here," he whispered, pulling her through the sanctuary and into the dark sacristy. Together they were eighteen again, entangled under the pear tree, and Claire still smelled of salt and Ethan of the sea.

At the outset his mouth was light on hers, but soon his kisses grew deeper. She lifted the edge of his shirt and slid her palms flat against his stomach, remembering the first time she'd done that and how hot his skin had felt. In response he leaned her against a shelf and pressed her hips tight to his, tugging up her shirt.

"Not here either," he said eventually. "No, Claire." Before he could really change his mind, she led him outside, down into the dunes on Drake's Beach, where they were hidden among the reeds, returned to the primacy of the earth, free at last from the judging eyes of God.

Ethan laid her down in the sand and leaned over her, hesitant, his eyes flickering, and Claire could tell he was experiencing a moment of doubt, the way he might an instant of physical pain, but she reached between his thighs and a passionate glaze soon replaced the questioning expression in his eyes. She smiled, believing she had won, but in this matter she was too hasty. She got what she'd long desired, but it wasn't the same as what she wanted.

"Forgive me, Father, for I have sinned," she murmured against Ethan's bare chest after their lovemaking, but he said nothing. Claire waited a moment and then had to ask. "Is this . . . ? I mean, have you ever . . . ?"

"No." His voice was curt.

She curled her body tighter. It was the answer she was expecting, but receiving it felt worse than she'd anticipated. "I'm sorry," she whispered, immediately wishing she hadn't apologized—because, really, she wasn't sorry. God might have a claim on Ethan, she reasoned, but hadn't she staked out his heart long ago? She was the lost tribes, the call of idols in the wilderness, the scrap of a prayer flag flapping in the ruins of a temple. Didn't Ethan know that?

He rolled onto his back and stared straight up at the sky. "Claire, what have we done?"

She scowled. "You seemed to want this as much as me."

He put his hands over his face. "I didn't seek this."

"Does that make a difference?"

"I don't know. I've never committed a sin of this magnitude before." He paused. "My superiors aren't very pleased with me."

Claire frowned, confused. "But I thought you said you'd never—"

"Don't be ridiculous. Not because of this. How could they know about this latest of my failings? No, it's because I've been plagued with other doubts that have nothing to do with you. But, Claire, you're a married woman. You belong with Whit."

At the mention of Whit's name, Claire felt her lips freeze, stung into a state of perfect numbness.

"He came to see me yesterday," Ethan said out of the blue, and Claire sat up, alarmed.

"What?"

"Claire, he still calls you his wife."

She ground her teeth, silent.

"He warned me to stay away from you and your sister. I don't know what I should do," Ethan finally said.

Claire blinked back tears. The answer was obvious to her. She didn't think she should even have to say it. "You could leave the priesthood." She stroked his chest. "We could go somewhere neither of us knows, and nothing ahead of us but the future. A rocky island in the shade. Remember? We could be just like we are now." She held her breath.

Ethan's voice, when he spoke, was low. He refused to look at her. "God's eyes are everywhere, Claire, not just on sanctified ground. And besides, I made my choice, never mind my doubts. I'm a man who honors my decisions. You know that."

She swallowed a sob. "What was this, then? A little nibble of forbidden fruit? A jaunt down memory lane?"

Ethan covered his face again. "I don't know. Do you think I was planning this? Do you understand the enormity of this transgression?"

She scrambled for her clothes, shaking sand out of them as best she could. "I understand perfectly, *Father.*" She paused, her knees quivering. "I've sacrificed, too, you know. You have no idea. After Jo was burned, after you left." She wiped a tear from her cheek. "Why did you really come back here, Ethan? Was it just because of Father

Flynn, or did it have something to do with me?"

Ethan gathered his own clothes. When he spoke, he wouldn't look at her. "I didn't want to come back, Claire. I tried everything to get them to send me anywhere else."

She thought about this. "Maybe this is supposed to be our second chance. Maybe Father Flynn knew that. Maybe that's why he sent for you."

Ethan let out a huge sigh. "I don't know, Claire. I'm going to have to pray and see what my heart tells me to do. I need time to sort this out. I wish I could tell you what you want to hear, but I can't."

"Why can't we just stay like this?" She gestured at the sand around them, but he didn't have a response.

"Claire," he said eventually. His voice was as familiar to her as the thudding of her own heartbeat.

"Yes?"

He reached out and caught her wrist. "Before you go, I need to tell you that Whit said something else I didn't like when he was out here yesterday."

She pursed her lips and waited.

Ethan paused, as if wondering how to continue, then sighed. "He said if you wanted to go back to a life of salt, that was fine with him. You could even take Dee with you. But then he reminded me what happens when salt gets into old wounds."

In spite of the warmth of Ethan's skin, Claire felt a chill needle her spine. "What's that?"

His eyes bored into hers. "It burns. He said if you weren't careful, you were going to end up like Jo. Totally burned."

A gull screamed overhead, and Claire's heart started hammering. She broke free of Ethan and searched for her shoes. She tried to make her voice light. "Let me take care of it."

Ethan eyed her with suspicion, as if he were suddenly remembering the streak of temper that ran through the Gilly women. "Maybe I shouldn't have said anything." He paused. "You're not going to do anything reckless, are you?"

Is he worried for my sake or his? Claire thought. She tied her loose hair back again and faced him. "No, of course not. But this is between me and Whit." That was a lie, of course. When it came to the Gillys and Turners, nothing was ever that clear-cut, which was a good thing, Claire vowed, because if Whit wanted to see her burn, he was going to have to come and dance in the fire right alongside her.

———o-o o-o———

Underneath the pear tree, she glanced at her watch. It was only nine in the morning, and it was Thursday. Whit would be out at his weekly tennis match in Wellfleet and wouldn't be home for at least an hour. Above her, Turner House loomed with its confusing garble of porches and balconies. She took a breath, stepping out from the tree's leafy shadow into the sun, and began pacing slowly up Plover Hill, trying to shrug off the feeling that she was being watched. It wasn't a sensation peculiar to her. Everyone felt that way around Turner House. It was part of the total Turner experience.

The spare key was still hidden under a Chinese pot of hydrangeas by the kitchen door—not very original, but keys were a mere formality for Whit. All the doors in Prospect were open to him all the time.

She let herself into the kitchen, inhaling the familiar odors of freshly ground coffee, the lemon wax she'd used to polish the counters with, and another smell—something clean and almost like ozone—that she'd never been able to identify. Bleach, maybe, or laundry starch? It was almost the same odor as a dollar bill, except Turner money was plenty dirty.

She paused a moment to let her heart quit hammering. If Whit caught her here, there was no telling what he would do. Call the constable? Choke her the way he had Dee? On the other hand, if he thought she'd crumple under threats, he was dead wrong. Over the past three months, the mud of Salt Creek Farm had fused to Claire as tightly as the patchwork of scars that covered Jo's right side, giving her a new strength. Unlike Jo's, Claire's wounds festered on the inside of her heart, where no one could see them.

She took several deep breaths and moved from the kitchen through the dining room. The china cupboard in the corner was almost empty, save for a gravy pitcher and a lone dented candlestick. Claire shook her head and paced into the living room, where she saw more empty squares on the walls where paintings had hung and noticed the absence of the piano. She scooted up the main stairs past the pristine guest rooms, the upstairs den, and then pushed her way into the master suite.

Here, too, things were missing. The silver clock that used to sit on the mantel of the fireplace. A finely threaded tapestry that had decorated half a wall. The empty bed was still unmade. Whit had apparently migrated to the center of the mattress in his sleep now, banishing all but a solitary pillow to the window seat, as if he would spurn even that comfort. The covers were neatly folded back, the sheets barely mussed. The man slept like a vampire, Claire thought, shoving away the contrasting image of Ethan sprawled half dressed in the dunes, his eyes closed in passion as she ran her hands over his ribs, lower and lower. She swallowed and returned her focus to the room. She didn't have much time.

On her nightstand her alarm clock and a few books were still stacked. They looked so strange just sitting there. The filigreed hands of her antique clock read 9:25. Across the room a flicker of movement caught Claire's eye, and the sight drew her up short. Blood rushed to her ears and eyes, paralyzing her. Then she realized that she was simply confronting her own reflection in the vanity's mirror. She sighed and relaxed, then examined her image.

She was rosy from the sun for the first time in thirteen years, her nose freckled, her hair lightened to a strawberry crimson. She had a bruise at the bottom of her throat from Ethan's lips, and if she wasn't wrong, she was starting to get a slight double chin from all the baking she'd been doing. She crossed the room and leaned close to the mirror.

There was nothing like Turner glass

for showing you what you were and what you were not. This wasn't farmhouse glass, blurred by too many generations of women and too many years of use. Turner glass was harder stuff than that. It was made for show, glittering in the cases in the library, where rows of Whit's football and hockey trophies from high school squatted, or gleaming in the etched frame that held his diploma from Harvard.

As if to further underscore familial dominance, all the drinking vessels in the house were monogrammed—cut-glass tumblers for whiskey and taller, thinner glasses for juice in the morning, everything etched with either Ida's or Whit's spiky, vertical initials. Not a rounded letter between them.

The Turners had a mania for initialing their belongings, gouging either their letters or the family crest into objects as if the family were in danger of forgetting its own identity. Claire had never understood it and over the years had resisted having anything embroidered or engraved if she could help it. It seemed too permanent, as if by fixing her name in metal or weaving it into cotton or silk she were somehow un-threading part of her soul for a collective she wasn't sure she wanted to join.

It was fitting, she thought, picking up her old hairbrush and smoothing the stray tendrils at her temples, that a man who was so privately entrenched would be so eager to eradicate Prospect's history. Whit would love to keep only the stage-prop bits of Prospect, she knew—the weathered patina on the town's shingles, the graceful arched windows of the library, the picturesque sailboats, but not the half-rotten wharf or the fishing vessels belching in their slips, and certainly not Salt Creek Farm.

Claire put down the brush and tugged open the vanity's drawers. The first one still held Ida's old makeup and combs, and the middle one stuck, as always. Claire remembered when Whit had given her the pearl in this spot, and the memory made her tug on the drawer with a savage wrench. It flew open. She looked inside and saw the usual jumble of junk, and then, maybe because the light was different or maybe because *she* was different, she spied something she never had before. There was some kind of letter taped flat at the very back of the drawer cavity. A corner of the rich cream envelope had come unstuck, calling attention to itself. Claire snaked her hand inside the drawer and, with some difficulty, pulled the letter out.

It was Ida's stationery, monogrammed like everything else she owned, as if her own words put on paper weren't enough. Someone had opened it once, however, for the seal was broken. Claire slid it open and drew out the paper, scanning Ida's armored-looking hand-writing and taking shorter and shorter breaths.

When she was finished, she sat back stunned, grappling with the fallout that a revision of any history creates, but especially a personal history. All this time Claire had thought of herself as the one who didn't belong on Salt Creek Farm, but it turned out she was wrong, and Ida had known this about her. Whether she liked it or not, Claire really was a girl with roots deep in the salt.

Jo, on the other hand, was quite a different story.

Claire slipped the letter into her pocket and picked up the silver brush off the top of the vanity, eyeing herself in the mirror. Frankly, she was tired of being haunted by the past, she decided. She'd had enough of virgins, pearls, and letters written by dead women. The time had come, she decided, to break free and create a future of her own.

Once, when they were first married, Whit had out of the blue compared her to a hummingbird. Delicate, he called her, but deceptively strong. They'd been in bed, and he'd had his hands twined in her hair, his fingers cupping her scalp like the protective twigs of a nest. Claire hadn't known she'd still be feeling them over a decade later, tighter every day and not like twigs at all anymore, for she could snap those if she needed to.

She remembered when Whit had presented her with his mother's pearl necklace, how he'd clasped the chain around her neck. *If you ever try to break the strings between us, you'll fail*, he'd said to her as they'd made love that evening. *You know that, right?*

She would see about that. She went into the closet and found a canvas bag and shoved as much of her riding clothing into it as she could. Then she paused. In the very back of the wardrobe, entombed in plastic, her wedding gown hung. She shoved her clothes aside and unzipped the bag, inhaling the fragrance of powder mixed with something earthier. She ran a finger down the satin and then pulled out her veil. Age had brittled it and turned it yellow. Claire sighed and zipped the bag up again. On the other side of the wardrobe, the suit that Whit had worn was pressed neatly and hung with a matching tie. He must have had it on recently. What else had Whit donned that day? Claire mused. A boutonniere to match her bouquet and oh, yes, his father's watch. Where was that? She opened the mahogany box that Whit kept in his top drawer and found it. *A place for everything and everything in its place*, Ida had always insisted, and even now, more than a decade after her death, no one in Prospect had the courage to defy that edict.

Well, there's a first time for everything, Claire thought, slipping the watch into her pocket along with the cream-colored envelope engraved with Ida's spiky initials. She closed the closet door and then let herself out through the house's front door, whistling as she passed, leaving it wide open to whatever kind of ghouls Whit wanted to send her way.

Chapter Twenty-three

—∘-∘ ⟨⟩ ∘-∘—

Dee was making toast in the kitchen when Claire came into the house, and she was so quiet that Dee almost didn't hear her. Claire could be like a cat when she wanted, all velvet steps and slinky moves, but Dee had gotten good at tracking her. *She* was getting kind of catlike, too.

Normally Claire made so much noise that Dee could hear her coming three days off. She'd throw her shoes into the corner of the front hall and bang on the old piano's keys as she walked by, as if she wanted even the air of this place to know she was back. But today there was none of that. Just the suspicious creak of a floorboard and then a heavy silence.

Dee peeked around the kitchen door, but the hall was empty, so she tiptoed down the hall and peeked in around the parlor door, where Claire was standing over the desk in the corner, riffling through some papers. Before she was caught, Dee scurried back to the kitchen, and a second later Claire loped in, scowling so heavily that Dee half thought she might curdle the milk. Claire could be moodier than a three-year-old, but that wasn't the reason Dee was staring at her. For the first time since Dee had known her, Claire was wearing her hair hanging down her back.

"What did you do to your hair?" Dee said.

Claire reached up and stroked the long red waves, as if she'd already forgotten about them. "I made a change," she answered breezily.

"I'll say." With her hair free like that, Claire looked like a different person—a nicer one, perhaps. Dee examined her more closely. Now that she was looking, she could see that Claire's hands were trembling slightly—unusual given how steady she could hold Icicle on a lead. "What's in the bag?" Dee asked.

Claire sank into a chair and stared straight ahead of her—at what, Dee couldn't tell, but that was worrisome, too, because Claire usually focused on things as if she had sabers hidden behind her eyes. "Riding gear," she answered.

The back of Dee's neck began tingling, and she eased herself into a chair across from Claire at the table. "Wait, you went back to Turner House? Are you crazy? Was Whit there?"

Claire shook her head and took a sip of milk. "It's his tennis morning."

Dee bit her lip and tried to hide her disappointment. Dee had been as meek as a lamb about not contacting Whit, not even once. She knew a good thing when she had it. In spite of the creepy stories about all the little dead boys around this place, she didn't want to get thrown ass over heels off Salt Creek

Farm in her current condition. She needed Jo's and Claire's help—for now at least. In fact, aside from her appointments at the clinic, Dee hadn't even left the place at all, content enough to read the trashy magazines Jo bought her at the supermarket, helping with the salt as much as she could, and getting ready for the baby, not that there was much to do there either. Jo had found a secondhand crib and changing table in the paper and set them up in Dee's room, and Claire had brought home a pastel assortment of tiny pajama sets and about a month's worth of diapers, and she'd amassed a bewildering collection of bottles, brushes, pacifiers, bibs, and a rubber bulb.

"For when the baby has a cold," Claire said, laying it in the drawer of the changing table, as if that explained everything. After she'd left the room, Dee had opened the drawer and squeezed the bulb, wondering if she was supposed to suction the baby's ears, nose, or mouth, and for how long. Jo wouldn't have the foggiest idea, and Dee didn't want to ask Claire. Who was to say the baby would get sick anyhow, and why was Claire already appointing herself as nurse? She should stick to fussing over her horse, Dee thought. It was the one thing that seemed to love her.

Dee put a hand on the side of her belly while the baby writhed. It might happen anytime now, the midwives in Hyannis had told her. If she felt regular pains, they'd instructed, she should come in. She shouldn't wait—not when they had to drive from Prospect. Claire, who'd driven Dee to her last prenatal visit, had insisted on accompanying her into the examination room, and she'd immediately reassured the midwife. "Someone will be with her right up through the birth and after." She'd squeezed Dee's hand. "Right, Dee?"

Dee hadn't returned her smile. The midwife let her wriggle back into her maternity pants while the midwife and Claire had a discussion about pain medications during labor.

"Of course it's up to Dee," Claire had said, putting her hand on Dee's knee once she was dressed, "but obviously my sister and I want her to be as comfortable as can be."

My sister and I. It was like having a pair of overprotective fairy godmothers as bodyguards. They meant well, Dee knew, but she was still wary of pissing the two of them off. A life with Cutt had taught her that a person's mood could curdle like cream in vinegar, and now that she'd seen how nice Jo and Claire could be, Dee had no desire to discover what happened when they got mad. If they wanted to sit next to her while she sweated, moaned, and pushed this kid out, she would more than welcome the company. There'd be time to figure everything else out later—like how she was going to get in touch with Whit.

Surely he'd want to see the baby when she had it, and once he did, once he saw her holding his child, wouldn't what he'd liked about her in the first place come rushing back to him? She hoped so. Besides, the man was a professed Catholic. Wasn't he virtually programmed to revere mothers cradling their infants? On the other hand, the mothers exalted in the Bible weren't scorned hussies living with scorned former wives on land their lover wanted to own.

She drummed her fingers on the kitchen table and reassessed Claire. She still hadn't moved, but now she was staring into space with a soft gaze, rounded cheeks, and her lips parted. Was that actual *contentment* on her face? Dee wondered. Before she could decide, Claire wiped her expression clean and readjusted her features into her original scowl. Dee sighed. Claire made it impossible to get a grip on her mood, and Dee couldn't figure why she cared, but she did. She jutted her chin toward the bag of riding gear. "So . . . did you get what you were after?"

Claire chewed a cuticle. Her scowl deepened. "No."

"Oh, that's too bad." Dee wasn't sure why, but she was getting the impression that they were talking about two different things. "So it wasn't worth the visit?"

Claire blinked, the fog parting before her once again. "What? Oh, you mean my expedition to Turner House."

"Where else did you go?" But Claire stood up and paced over the counter, ruffling her already messy hair. She took out the electric mixer and a huge enamel bowl.

"I've got four hours before I have to go scrape the evening salt crust. What do you think? Lemon meringues? And maybe a baked chicken for dinner?" The morning was heating up something awful, and the idea of rich food nauseated Dee, but she forced herself to smile and nod.

She piled her own lank hair up on top of her head, wishing she had the nerve to hack it off, but that wasn't her style. She wasn't good when it came to cutting things out of her life. She let down her hair again and blew on the pulse points on her wrists. "It sure is salt weather, isn't it? Hot, sticky, and still."

Claire paused, an egg poised on the edge of the bowl, ready for cracking. "What did you just say?"

Dee put her arms down. Great. What had she done now? Sometimes being around Claire was like trying to drive a car with terrible alignment. Dee had no idea where she was going or what she might hit. Jo, on the other hand, while a terror to look at with all her scars, was full of solid, no-bullshit phrases. When Dee did a crappy job pulling in salt, Jo told her so, and then she immediately told Dee how to fix the problem. "I just meant it's real hot, is all." Dee was relieved when Claire broke the egg and separated the yolk from the white. That little evil smile that Dee didn't trust was filling out Claire's bottom lip again.

"Do you realize what you just did? You're marking the weather with salt now. You'll be a real Gilly before you know it." She discarded the last yolk and turned on the mixer, frothing the whites into foam and then stiff peaks, and then she whipped in lemon zest, cream of tartar, and sugar until the substance in the bowl transformed into something entirely new. Dee felt a bit like that herself, like she was turning into something else. Was it really a Gilly? She wasn't sure. But she wasn't her old self either. What with the baby and living out here, she was definitely becoming something she didn't recognize. Unlike the meringues, however, she wasn't sure that that something was making her any sweeter.

———o-o o-o———

If the summer days made Dee irritable and anxious, the nights were a sight better. She knew she wasn't the only one awake in the house (sometimes a line of light glowed underneath Jo's door), but between the three of them, Dee was the only one who did anything about it. She roamed.

It was a habit she'd developed in Vermont after her mother had died and she was trying to come to grips with being stuck with her father. She missed him less with each passing day. Once in a while, if she was eating a fried egg or something, she wondered how he was getting on without her at the diner, but that speculation was more from the point of view of a bitter former employee and less as a bereft daughter. Now that she was near the end of her pregnancy, in fact, she was tempted to belly up to the Lighthouse counter one morning and order every breakfast item off the menu, taking a single bite out of each one before sending it all back. It was just the kind of thing that would drive Cutt nuts. He loathed waste of any kind and had no room in his life for excess, and Dee guessed that included her.

Cutt's military heart had never adapted very well to the patter of her footsteps running riot through his life, Dee realized. He'd passed plates to her over the diner counter and she'd brought them back empty, and that had mostly been the sum of things between them. By the time she'd started hooking up with Whit, Cutt had long since quit trying to map the coordinates of her comings and goings, and Dee had learned that while mouthwash and a shower covered up certain sins, silence concealed them even better.

But if she was able to scoot under the radar at her father's place, it wasn't so easy to do so on Salt Creek Farm. Even when Claire and Jo weren't physically with her in the same room, the evidence of them was. Claire constantly left coffee cups unwashed in the sink, and Jo forgot to pull the shower curtain closed and clean out the drain when she was done in the bathroom. Someone's socks were always wadded up on the bottom step, along with muddy boots in the hall, and Claire set used tea bags to weep on the counter. For Dee, who was used to a house as blank as a slate, the clutter was like having to listen to around-the-clock chatter.

And then there was the junk. Everywhere she looked—in every closet, on every shelf—odd collections of books, maps, machine parts, dismembered toys, and bits and bobs she couldn't even begin to identify lurked. When the baby was born, she thought, she'd have to be careful or she'd put the kid down and lose him in a morass of scraps.

At least at night, the house quieted. Initially she stuck to the upstairs in her wanderings, plodding back and forth between the bathroom and her room, but then, as she grew more comfortable, she started heading downstairs,

first for a glass of milk and a cracker
and then for more informative purposes.

Tonight Dee uncovered Claire's senior yearbook tucked high up on a parlor shelf and flipped through the pages
until she found the one where Claire
and Ethan had been voted Most in
Love. And they really did look it—their
heads tilted together, a pair of matching grins plastered across their faces.
Ethan's cheeks were much rounder,
and Claire's eyes had a twinkle dancing
in them instead of murderous sparks,
but her face held all the same dangerous angles. Dee wondered what *she*
might have been voted if she'd stayed
in school. Sluttiest, probably, or Most
Likely to Drop Out, but then she'd gone
and done exactly that, so she guessed
that was prophecy fulfilled right there.
She slammed the yearbook closed and
put it back. Behind her the room's stone
hearth took up most of the wall. Then
came a pair of sagging sofas, a battered coffee table, and an ancient,
shiplike desk shoved into the corner.
Dee wandered over to it, opened its
vast lid, and aimlessly began scuffling

through the detritus within. There was a man's watch that looked expensive. Dee fingered it, tempted, then laid it aside. Bills lay snarled in nests of old tidal charts, almanacs with their covers torn were tossed pell-mell, and a single cream-colored envelope with gilt script on its flap languished innocently under everything.

Frankly, it didn't look that interesting, but Dee plucked it out anyway and squinted to read the fancy initials. It wasn't easy. The script was faded and too full of spikes and loops. But that was Salt Creek Farm for you. Dee never knew what she was going to find. Something junky and boring-looking on the outside might really be a treasure. She started to open the flap of the envelope, but a pain squeezed her belly and she gasped and rocked back on her heels. It was shocking sometimes, how fiercely the baby could punch. She hoped it would stop doing that once it got born, or otherwise she was going to end up with a pair of black eyes when she went to change diapers. The baby twisted and gouged at her with as many of its sharp little extremities as it could manage, sending shocks all the way down through her bladder. Dee sighed in misery and slid the letter into her dressing gown's pocket.

She'd just reached the bottom of the steps when the pains began—not rolling Tahitian waves like the midwife had described, full of ukulele music and sunsets, but really bad ones that stole Dee's breath and pinched something awful. She staggered sideways and grabbed onto the banister, but before she could catch her breath, another contraction slammed into her, knocking her to her knees.

This so better be worth it, she thought, letting her head fall onto the lowest step. It occurred to her that when this was over, she just might kill someone, but just as she was deciding on the appropriate victim, something warm and sticky began running down the insides of her legs, a violent squeezing started low in her belly, and everything in front of her went mercifully black.

———o-o o-o———

By the time Dee saw her son good and proper, he was nothing like the little blue ball that Claire claimed came out of her. "I was right there when they cut you open," Claire told Dee, fixing her blankets, plumping her pillow even though Dee hadn't asked. "Just like I said I would be. Right there the whole time."

Already it was clear that the baby had changed, and this distressed Dee. It made her feel as if Claire had stolen something that should have been her own. But he was healthy, and for that, Dee gave thanks. The nurses had wrapped him up tight in a clean flannel blanket and stuck a knit cap on his head, and he was working his tongue in and out of his mouth like a hungry kitten.

"Go ahead, try to feed him," the nurse told Dee, handing her a bottle. But Dee was still too weak and out of it, so Claire took over, cooing and smiling as though she were the one who was pumped full of drugs instead of Dee.

"Don't worry," Claire assured Dee after she was done. "We're going to get you out of here just as soon as possible."

But to Dee the hospital was as good as a resort. Whenever she wanted it, the nurses fetched her Jell-O and ice, they whisked the baby away just as soon as he started bawling, and Dee didn't even have to get up to shower. The nurses came to do that, too, sponging down her arms and legs the way she assumed she was supposed to learn to do for her child.

"It's natural to feel so tired after what you've just been through," the pretty blond nurse told her. Dee guessed she meant almost dying and everything, though, to be honest, she didn't remember very much of the whole experience.

She recalled snooping in the parlor and finding that old letter, but everything after that went garbled and snowy, like television reception getting all screwed up from a storm. The picture wasn't very good, and none of the voices matched the action. They still kind of didn't. Dee remembered Jo holding her in the truck, and the bright lights when she looked up and found herself on a hospital gurney, and Claire's high-pitched voice urging the emergency surgeons to hurry. Her legs had felt all wet, and when she'd looked down, Dee remembered seeing a lot of blood. Even she knew that wasn't good.

When she'd come to, her stomach had become an empty pouch again and there was a strange baby crying in Claire's arms. "Look, he's perfect," Claire had said, leaning over and tilting the bundle toward Dee. "It's a boy. What should we name him?"

Dee didn't know what to say. All the names she'd picked out—the ones she thought would be so cool—suddenly seemed stupid in this clean and orderly place. She looked at the baby squirming in Claire's arms. He was clean, too, in spite of having a mess of a girl like Dee for a mother, and that simple fact gave her a little shot of hope. This baby deserved a pristine kind of name, she thought. It was the least she could do for him. She reached out her arms for him, thinking hard. "Jordan," she finally said. "For the river. I want to name him that."

But Claire didn't hand over the baby as Dee wanted her to. "Jordan," she said, stroking his tiny nose. "That's lovely. We can call him Jordy for short."

Dee was so drowsy that she let Claire keep rocking him. It still scared her to hold him anyway. But right before she drifted off again, an image of the marsh floated into her mind—the weather-beaten angles of the barn, the blush of pink on the oleanders. It occurred to her that once you planted something in the earth, it grew roots so thick you could count the generations on them. And now Jordy was the newest bud on that branch, fused to the Gillys in ways Dee had never anticipated.

Chapter Twenty-four

—◦◦ ◁◁◇ ◦◦—

Even in the waiting room, the hospital air was pungent with disinfectant. It pinched Jo's nose. She'd been sitting here for over an hour, and she was starting to get a headache.

Dee was going to be fine. The doctors had assured Jo of that before they'd wheeled her away down the hall. It was a good thing she was as much of an insomniac as Dee, Jo thought, because otherwise she might not have heard that thump downstairs, might not have sat up in bed, her nerves buzzing, and called Dee's name only to hear nothing but an ominous silence.

She glanced around the waiting room now, pleased to find it totally abandoned. No one else was in labor, and Claire was sequestered with Dee, so Jo took the envelope she'd found in Dee's coat pocket when she'd picked her up and carried her to the truck and unfolded it flat against her thighs. Immediately Ida's aggressive penmanship assaulted her, full of spiny angles and flourishes. And while Ida's words might have faded, Jo saw, they had not changed in the least.

Jo read:

Dearest,

Perhaps you're surprised to see this pearl returned to you again after all these years. I kept it, even though it would have been wiser not to, and now I've come to rue it, for even this one token between us is dangerous.

I am writing not out of regret, however, but resolve. I have gone from the bottom of this town's pile to the top, and I don't intend to let past mistakes throw me down again. I made my decision on a snow-ridden day years ago, and I have absolutely no intention of breaking it now.

Know that my fortune has had its own price. The sight of you, for instance, and the sight of our daughter. I know I have not been kind to her—quite the opposite, in fact—but the mere picture of her pains me. Her existence reminds me of everything I want to forget, and how odd that it should be so, that the presence of one person can evoke what we strive most to cover and hide. If I have been cruel to her, it's been for her own good. Ironic, is it not, that the one gentleness I've been able to bestow is meanness?

What if I'd never let you kiss me that first time? What if I'd let the Temperance women place Joanna in a far county like you wanted? What if I'd been born a better woman? What if Sarah Gilly hadn't met me kneeling at the feet of the Virgin the night of that terrible storm, her own babe in her arms?

There are no answers to those questions. One thing I've learned while living up on Plover Hill is that such elevation allows for marvelous perspective, but it also keeps one perpetually distant. In the end maybe that's for the best.

I tell you all this now only to prevent future catastrophe. There are twenty-odd reasons why Joanna Gilly is not a suitable girl for my son, but only one of those facts truly haunts me—and should you as well.

I have never come forward until now, but I am asking for your discreet help in this matter. Once, I remember, you offered to give everything up for me, and I would not let you. I think I knew even then that such gestures only lead to ruin and misery, and I was determined to be happy. And, in spite of everything, I have been. Maybe it's contrary to reason, maybe it's wrong, but that's a judgment to be decided upon my immortal soul and not in this worldly realm, and certainly not by you. Magna est veritas, et praevalibet.

Know that even though time has moved on, a constant part of me remains,

Ever Yours

Jo folded the letter back up, fighting down an old feeling of rage. She'd always believed that Ida had hated her, but the truth was more complicated. Ida hadn't loved her, Jo saw now, but she hadn't despised her either. Maybe the best way to put it was that Ida had simply regretted her. And with that regret came a measure of shame. It wasn't that Jo wasn't good enough for Whit—she was *too* good. In fact, she was exactly the same, of his line, with identical blood. Had circumstances been different, Jo might have even ended up a Turner herself, bonded to Whit not by affection but by name. Stale anger boiled in her chest, along with all the questions she'd tamped down for years, but the people who could answer them were either dead, in the case of Mama and Ida, or gone, in the case of Jo's long-lost father.

Isn't that just the way? Jo thought, shoving the letter back into her coat pocket. The present swept the past along like a river clearing its banks. At least that's how it was supposed to work, but some relic or another always got stuck. Her scars were proof enough of that. New did eventually grow atop the old, but never smoothly.

But how on earth had Dee ended up with the letter? Jo wondered. She looked up as Claire burst into the room, bluish circles smeared under her eyes, her cheeks pale, as if she'd just witnessed a battle. "It's a boy. Seven pounds, six ounces. Healthy as can be, but Dee's in rough shape. They did a C-section, and she lost a lot of blood, but she's regaining consciousness now. Do you want to come see them?"

"I'll be there in a minute," Jo said, trying to pull herself back to the present drama.

"Okay, but hurry." Claire was so intent on returning to Dee's bedside that she hadn't even noticed Jo's distraction, and maybe that was for the best, Jo thought. When they returned home, she'd throw Ida's letter into the rubbish, where it belonged, but first things first. She had some pressing questions.

"Claire," she said, "are you wearing the pearl?"

Claire spun on her heel in the doorway, confused. "What?"

"The pearl necklace that used to be Ida's. Do you have it on?"

Claire frowned. "Why on earth are you asking?"

On a hunch Jo pulled the letter out of her pocket. "When I found Dee, she was holding this."

Claire blanched and slid her eyes away from Jo's.

"Do you know how she got it?" Jo asked.

Claire pursed her lips. "I found it. When I went to the house the other day." Her voice was tiny.

"Have you read it?"

She paled further and sucked in her breath. "Have you?"

"Yes," Jo said, without adding when. Before Jo could stop her, Claire reached out and grabbed the letter, folding the envelope in half and tucking it into her own sweater pocket.

"We don't need to talk about this now," she said. "Not here. Besides, don't you think it's time we started paying more attention to the future and less to the past?" She smiled brightly. "Why, we've got a new baby waiting right in the very next room and a sick mother to take care of."

"My point exactly," Jo replied. "You said the baby's a boy. What if the same thing happens to him that fell on Henry? You know all the bad things that happen to boys in our marsh." *And what if Whit is the bad thing?* Jo almost added but didn't. What if Whit, in trying to get them off the land, went so far as threatening to sacrifice his own son, a child he never wanted to carry his name anyway?

Claire snorted. "Those are just a bunch of old wives' tales. Now, are you coming? Let's go see the baby."

Jo followed her, trying to shake off

the feeling that Claire knew more about her own past than she did.

———o-o o-o———

By the time they got to Dee's room, the baby was swaddled, blinking his brown seal eyes and suckling at his mother's little finger.

"Oh, he's perfect," Claire cooed, peeling back a corner of the blanket. "May I hold him?" Dee relinquished possession of Jordy, but not with the alacrity Jo would have expected. Claire practically had to tug him out of Dee's arms. It was as if in expelling Jordy into the world, Dee had come alive, too, Jo thought. Her eyes gleamed in a feverish new way, and even though she was so fatigued she could barely move, her muscles seemed attuned to every one of Jordy's tiny fingers and toes. Did motherhood really set anchor that quickly, Jo wondered, watching Claire rock the baby, and was it like that for every woman?

Claire paced over to where Jo was sitting. "Here. Have a go." She eased the complicated bundle of blanket and baby into the crook of Jo's good arm. "Isn't he just delicious?" Dee looked alarmed at that description, as if Claire might really devour Jordy whole, but Claire didn't notice. She stroked the side of her finger down his cheek and laughed as his mouth puckered open. "He has Whit's eyes," she said. Silence fell over the room, and it was up to Claire to break it. "Oh, heck," she finally said, and then, without anything further, she plucked Jordy from Jo's arm, returned him to his bassinet, and left the room.

"Is she going to be all right?" Dee asked as the door clicked closed.

Jo stood up and awkwardly patted the covers next to Dee. "She'll be fine."

Dee reached out and grabbed Jo's wrist. "I know this is all weird," she said, her eyes glittering. "Maybe it's best if I just leave Salt Creek Farm."

"No!" Jo was surprised by how loudly she said it. She hadn't realized how accustomed she'd become to seeing Dee folding laundry on the kitchen table or to hearing her laugh at something on the radio. She smoothed Dee's hair.

"Get some rest. I'll see you in the morning."

But Dee didn't hear her. She was already half asleep, so Jo tiptoed out of the room, closing the door gently, looking up and down the corridor for Claire. She found her at the other end of the hallway, by the elevator bank, pacing. Her eyes were red-rimmed, and she was sniffling.

She swiped the back of her hand under her nose. "I knew she was carrying Whit's baby, but I'd kind of pushed it out of my mind. God. I feel so stupid. Jealous of an eighteen-year-old dropout with no money, no friends, and no family."

"She has us," Jo said quietly, but Claire didn't make it look like that was a good thing.

"I know," she said, and clamped her mouth tight. They stood for a moment, shoulder to shoulder, close but not touching. Jo thought about the babies Claire had lost. Did something like that leave scars, Jo wondered, each time it happened? Was Claire roughed up, too, and put back together all wrong?

She had never thought about it before, but it made perfect sense.

All these years she'd believed she was the one who'd rescued Claire that day in the barn, but what if she were wrong? What if Claire had been the one who'd saved Jo by marrying Whit? *How much does Claire really know about that letter?* Jo wondered. It was obvious that Ida had written it, but it wasn't clear to whom. Jo squinted at Claire, and Claire scowled in return.

"What?"

"Nothing," Jo said. "I have to go home and check on the salt. What do you want to do?"

Claire wiped her eyes. "I'll stay here with Dee."

"Are you sure?"

"Absolutely."

"Okay, I'll be back, then, later."

They embraced quickly, folding each other close—hands spread across the other's back, cheeks turned in opposite directions, willing to give sisterhood a try but handicapped by the fact that there was only so much intimacy in this world that either one of them could bear.

———o-o o-o———

After the antiseptic air of the hospital, the summer heat smacked Jo like a wet hand when she walked outside. She drove back toward Salt Creek Farm with the windows of the truck open, letting the breeze lick over her. She was thinking about Whit. Jordy *did* have his eyes, and that had been a jarring reminder. What other traits of his father did Jordy carry? Jo wondered. Once she had loved Whit better than anyone else in the world. Would she come to feel that way about his son?

As she drove past St. Agnes, she noticed that the light in the window was on, and she spied Father Stone kneeling by the altar in prayer. She pulled the truck over and turned off the engine, watching him, but he didn't move, and Jo thought that was strange. No man—not even a priest—would stay bowed down before the Lord for so long unless he was carrying some heavy sins, she thought. She put her hand on the truck's door handle but then hesitated. If she went in, she would be interrupting a moment she had no right to break into. *The heck with it*, she finally thought, yanking the keys out of the ignition, and then strode over to the battered sanctuary doors and flung them open. Inside, the early-morning light streamed over the figure of Our Lady like a rebuke.

"Can I help you?" Ethan startled up from his bent position in front of the altar, his face so twisted that Jo almost couldn't place him. He raised his eyebrows when he recognized her, looking almost relieved. "Oh, it's only you, Jo. What on earth are you doing here?"

"Do you have Father Flynn's address?" Jo wasn't in the mood for pleasantries either.

Ethan's frown deepened. "Somewhere. He left it in case I had any questions. Why?"

"*I* have some questions."

Ethan didn't move. He glanced out the window, as if he really had been waiting for someone else and was disappointed to see only the empty lane.

Slowly, he got to his feet. "Is it anything I can answer?"

Jo put her hands on her hips. What would Ethan Stone think, she wondered, if she told him the real reason she hadn't grown up to marry Whit Turner? Would he be so shocked? Would he regret leaving Claire then? Jo sighed. "Just so you know, Claire's at the hospital. Dee had the baby last night. A little boy. She named him Jordan."

At Claire's name Ethan's ears turned red and he coughed, making his eyes water. "I'll have to stop by later and give her my best."

"Claire? Or Dee?"

Ethan blushed. "Dee, of course. I'm afraid Claire and I have had . . . a sort of falling-out."

Good Lord in heaven, Claire, Jo thought, *what have you gone and done now?* "I'm sorry," she said.

Ethan put his hands in his pockets and said through tight lips, "I've made a request to be transferred. You should tell that to your sister."

"I see." Jo cleared her throat. "Why don't you tell her yourself?"

Ethan hung his head. "I don't think that would be a good idea."

Oh, Claire, Jo thought. *When will you learn?* Claire's heart was going to break all over again, but this time it would be a mess of her own making. Jo squared her shoulders. "Can you just get me Father Flynn's address?"

Ethan blinked several times, pulling his eyebrows together again. "Of course. One moment while I find it." He disappeared, leaving Jo alone with Our Lady.

Reluctantly, Jo turned to face her. The paint on her skirts had faded to faint pastel, Jo saw, as well as the pale of her flesh. Her hands were almost invisible, save for the eye that Jo had painted on her palm, and the row of fishhooks looked more sinister than Jo remembered, their curves hasty and crude. Hesitating, she touched the Virgin's empty face and found herself wishing she had some salt—or anything—to offer. But it wouldn't have done any good. History hadn't been changed at all, certainly not by her mother, and Jo knew how she'd tried.

Mama had told Jo the story before she died. She'd come to the sanctuary as soon as she could after giving birth during that terrible nor'easter, she said. The roads were frozen, the houses buried under feet of snow, and trees were tossed from their tips to their roots across the lane. The church had been empty, and Father Flynn was stuck in town, as was Jo's father. Jo's mother was exhausted after giving birth, but she thought, *Now or never.* She packed a sharp chisel in her coat pocket and set forth out of doors.

Jo imagined Mama's surprise when, stepping into the church, she saw not just Our Lady but a second, more earthly Madonna—Ida May Dunn—crumpled at the feet of the Virgin, a newborn babe in her own arms, her clothing stained and rumpled.

The two women recoiled at first and then struck their deal, united in a common desire for secrecy. Jo's mother had come to break a curse, and Ida had come to unload one. And so it was done. Mama hammered the face out of the Virgin, hoping to put a crack in the past and somehow save Henry, and Ida helped her, and when it was over, neither woman left empty-handed. Mama walked out of the church with two babies instead of one—a girl to cancel out her doomed boy—and Ida departed with the last glimpse anyone would have of Our Lady's face, never guessing how it would come to haunt her.

"Here you are."

Jo jumped. Ethan had returned with Father Flynn's address. He held on to her hand a moment before he released it. If he knew what she needed it for, he might not give it to her at all, she reflected. Didn't priests always protect their own? On the other hand, maybe it would give him some peace when it came to Claire. He wasn't the only man in Prospect to have sinned on a spectacular scale, and no doubt he wouldn't be the last.

"Thank you," Jo said, putting the address in her pocket. She stared into Ethan's troubled eyes and was tempted to tell him how much Claire still cared for him, but it wasn't her place. She wasn't her sister's keeper, much as she sometimes felt she was. Hard as it was, she was going to have to get used to that, and maybe, just maybe, Claire would start to do the same in return. Jo gave one more uneasy glance to Our Lady and headed back into the full daylight, knowing that the scrap of paper in her pocket could provide either a beginning or an ending to her story, or maybe neither. Fate wasn't always so clearly written, and even when it was, who was to say it always stayed that way?

Chapter Twenty-five

Dee came home to Salt Creek Farm with Jordy in the middle of July, and to welcome him—the marsh's little king, its boy treasure—Claire embarked on an unparalleled march of culinary offerings. Each morning she rose before the sun and turned out marbled rings of cake, raisin and anise scones, flaky sheets of phyllo dough drizzled and rolled with honey, salt, and a secret blend of herbs. She scented ramekins of crème anglaise with rose water and orange, and made a peanut brittle so simultaneously salty and sweet that it confused her tongue into rapture.

It was a joy having a baby in the house, and Claire's body seemed to reflect that. Her clothes grew snug in all the right places, emphasizing her hips and breasts, putting extra swing into her steps, and her newly released hair began to settle into pleasing ripples and waves. She spent so much time in front of the steaming oven and stove that her skin became infused with the oily scents of vanilla, caramel, and brown butter. She dipped her fingers in so much chocolate and cocoa powder that she stained the tips of them a smoky espresso color.

"Nature's finest manicure," she pronounced with a laugh, waving her nails at Dee, but Dee didn't seem to notice. She was limp as old lettuce these days. Maybe it was the strain of taking care of a newborn, or perhaps it was hormonal. The nurses had warned all of them about that. The "baby blues," they called it, but Dee's blues seemed to have darkened from standard periwinkle to a dangerous indigo of late. Claire frothed a bowl of eggs harder and started sprinkling flour into the bowl.

"What do you think?" she asked Dee, checking to make sure she was still in the room. Sometimes she crept away before Claire even noticed, sneaking up the stairs to her room, where she would sleep for hours on end, letting Claire and Jo fuss and cluck over Jordy, changing him, swaddling him, heating his bottles like a pair of competing hens. "Clove cake, or lemon-lime? I could do either."

Jordy was on the table, nestled into the ample curve of an enormous wooden salt bowl that Claire had lined with a quilt. Dee had been horrified with this arrangement at first, but she re-laxed as soon as she saw how well the bowl cupped the baby.

"All Gillys get cradled in this," Claire reassured her. "My mother used to say it's what hardened our spines."

Claire glanced at Jordy now, marvel-ing that in six short weeks his eyes had changed to hazel, his hair had thick-ened, and he'd learned to suckle his fist. As if he sensed he was being watched, he woke with a startle, but he didn't cry. Claire waited to see if Dee would pick him up, but she didn't, so Claire banged her wooden spoon on the side of her mixing bowl, trying to snap Dee out of her funk.

Lemon-lime, Claire decided, reaching for the zester. It suited her mood. She squeezed some drops of citrus juice into the batter and tossed away the crushed fruit halves. The problem with happiness was that it was such a brittle net, she thought. Lately she didn't dare test it, for she worried it would snap under the pressure and spill out whatever she'd snared, leaving her with nothing. Maybe that's what Jo had been trying to tell her on her wedding day, she mused now, with those horrid hooks painted on Our Lady's gown— that sometimes you had to be cruel to feed your own soul. Claire remembered the day she'd let that fish go on the beach with Whit standing behind her. Maybe she had made a mistake after all, letting it slip away. She could see that now.

Jordy let out a mew, and Claire

twitched, but Dee unfolded his receiving blanket and hoisted him to her shoulder. Claire loved the way Jordy felt in her arms. He shared the same comforting heft of a sack of flour. Whenever she got the chance, she sniffed him as she would one of her pastries, wishing she could smooth icing over his velvety tummy and lick it off. She was ashamed to admit there were times when she almost thought he might be—should have been—hers.

For a moment, at the start of the C-section, the doctors hadn't been sure Dee was going to live. She was bleeding, her blood pressure had dropped to an almost subhuman level, and a nurse began readying a crash cart. Altogether it had been a terrifying moment for Claire, but not because of the graphic drama unfolding in front of her. On the contrary, it had been so very terrible because Claire had been forced to make an uncomfortable moral choice: For whom was she going to root? The baby or Dee? Mother or infant? Old life or new?

She chose the child.

Later, after Dee was recovering and the machines had stopped their beeping and nurses had taken some of the tubes out of her nose and arms, Claire wondered why she simply hadn't prayed for *both* Jordy and Dee. Was that maybe the way the human brain worked in emergencies, she wondered—shutting down critical blood vessels and nerves, vanquishing distractions, so a person could make impossible decisions? Or was this defect of loving too narrowly unique to her own hardened heart?

"We're never going to eat all this, you know." The flatness in Dee's voice sometimes tipped her most banal statements toward profundity. It drove Claire crazy. In this instance, however, she had to concede that Dee had a point. They hadn't even started on the Bundt cake from yesterday, and here Claire was piling lime sponge on top of it. A plate of plastic-wrapped doughnuts sat festering in the far corner of the counter, by the jug of wooden spoons, and the refrigerator harbored a week-old coconut custard. Claire sighed and stared down at the pan in her hands.

"Well, I've already gone and mixed the batter. I might as well bake it."

Dee checked Jordy's diaper and then, satisfied with the results, rearranged his clothes and slung him back over her shoulder, patting his back a little harder than Claire would have. Claire bit the inside of her cheek not to say anything.

"Why don't you sell all that stuff?" Dee asked.

Claire looked up. "What?"

"At the farmers' market in Wellfleet on Saturday."

It was stunning, really. The girl was duller than a box of rocks, but she flashed the occasional sign of intelligence. It wasn't a bad idea at all, Claire thought. The flavored salts she'd introduced in Hyannis were taking off. Maybe her baking would, too. The paltry amount of money she had left in her bank account was almost gone and the farm still had a heavy cloud of debt squatting over it, but maybe Claire's confections could help start to dispel it.

Dee's voice pulled her back to the

kitchen. "I could come with you. Well, Jordan and me. You know, for an extra pair of hands. Actually, four extra hands." Jordy let out another mew.

Claire eyed her, considering. Dee had been a terrible waitress, she remembered. Polite enough, but sulky and tragically inaccurate with her orders. She could never remember how customers wanted their coffee, how they took their eggs, or whether they preferred honey or syrup when it came to their pancakes. Or never *seemed* to remember. Now that Claire thought about it, Dee had always known what *she* wanted with no trouble.

She snapped back to the problem at hand. It would be healthy for Dee to get out of the house and mix with a little society. It would be good for them both. "Why not?" she said.

Who knows? she thought. Maybe Dee would turn out to be something of a saleswoman after all. She'd obviously sold herself hook, line, and sinker to Whit. Maybe a flirtation with the outside world wouldn't be the worst thing in the world for Salt Creek Farm. Maybe it was just what they needed.

———o-o o-o———

On Saturday morning Dee changed her mind. "I'm not feeling so well," she complained, pressing a hand to her temple. "The baby was fussing half the night, and I've got a headache something awful. I'm going to stay here and sleep with him."

Claire tried to hide her relief. Clattering around the kitchen with Dee slumped at the table while she baked was one thing, but being boxed behind a table together for hours in the heat was hardly an appealing prospect. Claire leaned down and gave Jordy a kiss, cupping the warm bulb of his head.

"Be good," she whispered, and went off to find Jo, who had some salt deliveries to make to restaurants and some errands to run. "Do you want us to bring you anything?" Claire asked, but Dee just shook her head.

A couple of hours later, Claire was sold out of everything at her stand.

"If I could, I would eat one of these

every single day of my life," her last customer raved as she devoured Claire's final banana muffin. "What did you put in here?"

Claire shrugged. "Sea salt, vanilla, and a little something secret."

"It's heaven. You should open your own shop or something."

Claire began to protest but then stopped. It wasn't such a stupid idea. Why *couldn't* she open her own shop? When was the last time she'd had anything of her own? She was living in her sister's house with her husband's mistress and son, working her family's salt flats. Even Icicle, her very soul, had been a gift from Whit. Claire looked at the woman, who was licking the last crumbs off her fingers like a famished cat. She was wearing tasteful brown lipstick and an enormous pair of diamond studs. Her capri pants were starched, her blouse clean, and she had on French espadrilles. Once Claire had dressed just like her. "Maybe one day," she said.

"Well, take this." The woman dug in her purse for her card. "Let me know if

you do. These muffins are to die for."
Claire took the card and then glanced
at her watch. She still had forty minutes before Jo was due back. Across
the aisle one of the vendors was selling
peaches so ripe they were almost
weeping. *Cobbler,* she thought. *And
peach-and-pepper jam.* She was halfway to the fruit stall before she realized
that Ethan was standing under its aw-
ning. She hadn't recognized him in the
shadows, and she hadn't seen him
since she'd left him half naked in the
sand.

"Ethan," she said, coming up behind
him. The one person she was both desperate to encounter and ashamed to.
He was wearing his collar, she noted,
but with a short-sleeved shirt that
showed off the graceful bows of his
forearms. If she looked hard enough,
Claire bet, she could find his pulse. It
was the same spot where she'd kissed
him over and over. She stared down at
her shoes, tongue-tied.

"Claire." Why did her name always
come out of his mouth like music ringing from a bell? She felt the vibration in

her stomach and the backs of her knees. "Your hair," he said, "it's—"

"Down." She reached up and smoothed the frayed ends.

"I like it. It suits you."

"Thanks." Claire was finding it difficult to catch her breath. She sometimes felt that over the past thirteen years her veins and arteries had constricted themselves to their smallest functional sizes, allowing her body's blood to circulate, but nothing extra. Not laughter. Not affection, and certainly not passion. At least not until Ethan had come along again. She'd been so ravenous for him that morning in the dunes that she hadn't even felt remorse, but what was she supposed to do? Sometimes, it seemed, the only way to exorcise the past was to relive it.

She clasped her fingers behind her back now and bit her bottom lip. Her problem, she realized, was that she was a woman who always had everything she didn't want. And maybe now that included Ethan. For he wasn't the same as the boy who'd left. He was a man with twelve years on him that

Claire knew nothing about. She'd been foolish to try to make herself believe that history didn't matter.

"What are you even doing out here?" she finally asked. Too late, the answer came to her. *Avoiding you.* He blushed. "Same as everyone else. Shopping. What about you?"

Was this what they were going to be reduced to? Claire wondered. The kind of small talk they might have made at a cocktail party? She couldn't imagine a future filled with chitchat about the weather. "I'm selling some things I baked," she replied.

"Business going well?"

She tried to keep her voice light. "I sold out of everything in two hours. If you come next week, I'll save something for you."

Ethan looked pained. "Claire, about that. I don't know how to say this, but . . . I've requested to be transferred. Wait—" He took her hand when she tried to pull it away. "I saw your sister the other day, and it started me thinking. What if I'm making a mistake?"

Claire felt her throat pinch closed.

They were the words she'd longed to hear from him for so long, but years too late. They were ghost words. Even if he did break his vows for her, Claire realized, she'd never banish the specter of God hanging between them. She hung her head. When was she going to learn? Love wasn't a list to be kept in the heart. It was the duties you got up to fulfill every day and the sacrifices you made. Jordy had made her see that. She shook her head, unable to force words out, and Ethan let go of her hand, tears welling in his eyes. "I guess we're done here," he choked.

Claire turned away. She couldn't look him in the face anymore. "Yeah," she managed. "I guess we are."

She could feel his eyes on her back as she walked toward her stall. Next week, she decided, she'd make devil's food cake spiked with rum, and she'd charge her customers double for it or let them stand there salivating. From now on, nothing of hers was going to be free for the taking again—not when it came to cooking, not when it came to Whit, and especially not when it came to Ethan Stone and her poor mangled heart.

——∘–∘ ∘–∘——

She and Jo drove back to Salt Creek Farm with the windows in the truck cab cranked all the way down. It didn't help with the heat, but at least it moved the air around, even if the breeze made conversation difficult, which was actually fine with Claire, since she was feeling about as friendly as a scorpion. They rolled onto the lane leading down to the marsh. In the distance the marsh was its usual summer patchwork of violently odd colors—magenta, green, iron red, and brown. With the heat and sun came algae and microorganisms, and then the mud in the salt flats bloomed into a harlequin's coat.

They still hadn't talked about what was in Ida's letter, not since the hospital, but it was growing between them like the season's heat. *If she knew who he was to her all along*, Claire mused, *why was she so angry when I went and married Whit?* It wasn't as if Jo ever could have. In fact, the idea was distressing, really. Claire wondered if Jo and Whit ever kissed before Jo read Ida's letter, and if Whit ever suspected their real relationship. If so, he'd done a remarkable job hiding it.

I should burn that letter, Claire thought. It was upstairs in her bureau drawer now. She'd grabbed it out of Jo's hand in the hospital and never given it back, but Jo hadn't asked for it. Even so, it wasn't Claire's to keep, and she was tired, she realized, of carrying the load of her sister's burdens. The truth was out now, and besides, there was only so much atonement one could make in life.

The cicadas were screaming, and a row of pelicans dipped and rose like a squadron of bombers cruising the horizon. Evening was settling over the marsh like a square of silk. Icicle would want a gallop on the beach and a splash in the surf, and then Claire would give him his feed. She felt the knot that had twisted in her stomach at the farmers' market begin to unravel. By the end of her ride, she hoped, her muscles would have relaxed completely and she'd be able to breathe again. As she neared the barn, however, she saw that the doors were open, which was odd. She'd been extra careful about closing them. She frowned and swung one door wider, a wave of heat hitting her as she took a step inside, and then she froze.

Icicle was collapsed on the floor, his hooves stilled in the hay, his flanks rigid and his nostrils dry. Already the flies were gathering. In disbelief, Claire sank to her knees and put her hand on his loyal chest. There was no life in him, as she knew there wouldn't be. She sat gasping for a moment, as if she'd just taken a fist to the stomach, and then she bent her head over him and wailed.

Sniffling, she closed Icicle's great solemn eyes and rubbed her cheek against his, wishing she'd been with him for his final moments, wishing she could have saved him, for Icicle hadn't been just a horse to her. He was the nobler part of her soul. Without him Claire wasn't sure what would happen to her better instincts. She ran her hand over his ears and down his forelock, then up under his neck. She searched the straw around his body, and her eye caught on a tiny slip of paper. A wrapper for a brand of cinnamon gum Whit loved. Claire plucked it up and inspected it. There was no code hidden inside, no secret signal to her. But then such subterfuge wasn't Whit's style. His message was clear enough. The only thing left to save now, Claire knew, was her own self.

Chapter Twenty-six

Things died on Salt Creek Farm all the time, Jo was perfectly aware—stray birds, the annual clutch of cats she had to drown, insects by the score, little boys. Some of those creatures left the world by the power of her hands and some as the result of a higher law, but Jo grieved them all. Some days she got to thinking the marsh was nothing more than an open wound sunk in the flesh of the earth, a festering raw place where the here and now met the great beyond. She had lived in it so long that she was immune to its harsh ways, but she couldn't say the same for Claire, who never did love the land the way Jo did. Icicle's death reminded Jo all over again that her sister had come home to a place where she couldn't turn her back on the intricacies of the world.

Jo had found Claire wandering in the salt ponds in the prime of the evening, when the marsh's packs of flies disappeared and gave way to the first of the night's bats. Normally Claire was skittish of them, but that night she didn't notice. Her face was the color of sand, and her eyes were two blank buttons, the way they'd been right before she'd set the barn on fire all those years ago. When something really distressed Claire, she turned into a living doll. You couldn't do anything with her.

"What happened?" Jo cried. "Is Jordy okay?" At the thought of him—round-bellied, sweet as a duckling—her heart fluttered, but Claire simply shook her head, grabbed Jo's good hand, and pulled her toward the barn, the red strands of her hair loud as any alarm. Mercifully, Jo saw, the building was still intact.

"Open the doors," Claire told her, putting her hands over her face. "I can't do it."

Jo obeyed, blinking to adjust her sight to the dimness. At first she didn't understood what she was seeing. She thought Icicle had fallen from some kind of attack or was sick, but Claire started sobbing, the noise cracking out of her throat. "He's dead," she sobbed. "Oh, Jo, he's *dead*."

Jo stepped farther into the barn. Just that morning Icicle had been perfectly healthy, stamping his feet and nickering when he heard her arrive. She knelt down over his inert body, a bad feeling starting to grow in the pit of her stomach. "What happened?" she asked. Even she knew that horses in their prime didn't just fall over dead for no reason.

Claire took her hands from her face. Some of her color was starting to return, Jo saw. "Don't be thick, Jo. Whit did it, of course."

Jo crouched over Icicle. He was such a beautiful beast. It made her heart hurt to see him lying so still. She rubbed his flank.

Claire sniffed. "What do you think he used?" she asked, but Jo was just a salt farmer, not a detective. She shrugged, and Claire nodded. "I guess you're right. I guess it doesn't matter. Whatever it was, it worked—and fast. Jo," Claire looked up at her, that doll-like glaze beginning to smear across her eyes again. "We have to do something. He wants us all off this land worse than Ida ever did, and you and I both know he'll do anything to make that happen." Claire's face paled from the color of sand to the whispery gray of ashes. "Can't we get some kind of restraining order?" she whispered.

Jo chewed her thumbnail. "But we don't have any proof that he's the one doing any of this."

Claire nodded. "That's true. Besides, Whit's got every local politician up and down the Cape in his back pocket, and that includes law enforcement." She blushed, remembering how she'd taken advantage of that fact to stop the bonfire salt.

Jo snorted. "When did Whit ever care about following the letter of the law? If he thinks he can get away with something—and he usually can—he goes ahead and does it."

"So what should we do?"

Jo looked at Icicle's lifeless body and shuddered. "I don't know." There were any number of strange accidents that could befall three women and a child on a remote farm alone. She turned her face away from Claire, sweat gathering under her ribs. *Let it out*, a voice inside her urged. Enough was enough. She and Claire had blamed each other for too many things for too long. Jo took a shaky breath.

"I know this isn't a good time, but I have to tell you something awful. I got a call from our friend Mr. Monaghy at the bank today. We've got thirty-six hours, and then they're taking the place off our hands. They have an 'interested buyer,' they say, which you and I both know is code for Whit Turner."

Claire blew out a breath. "Well," she said, sounding exactly like Jo. Suddenly her face brightened, and a foxlike grin spread across her face. "Don't worry," she said. "That's not going to happen."

Jo shook her head. "Claire, you're not listening. They're coming the day after *tomorrow*. Whit's won. It's over."

Claire rubbed her fingers together. "Not quite."

Jo pinched the bridge of her nose. "Unless you've got a golden egg stashed under your mattress, I don't see what you're getting at."

Claire's grin got bigger. "I've got something better," she said. "I've got Ida's diamond wedding band."

A corner of Jo's mouth twitched as she let out a low whistle. She bet that ring was worth a bundle. Maybe not enough to get them all the way out of hock, but possibly enough to placate the bank. And business had been better lately. Those crazy salts of Claire's were flying off the shelves in Hyannis. If they could keep it up, Jo thought, they might just be able to turn things around. She sank down into the straw, and Claire sank next to her. "Ida will roll over in her grave. It's perfect," Jo conceded.

But Claire's face darkened. "What if the money's not enough?"

Jo shrugged. "Some is better than none." They were silent a moment, and then Jo said, "You know that locket you were so het up about the night you and Dee arrived here? Well, you should know that Whit tried to give it to me first."

Claire sucked in her breath, and Jo worried that her temper was about to start spilling over. She put up a palm to stop Claire's outburst.

"I never accepted it," she explained. "I gave it back. Then, the next day, I saw that Ida had left the pearl out in front of Our Lady, along with a letter. I don't know why, but I took them. I read the letter, then put it back in Ida's mailbox, along with the necklace. After that, things weren't ever the same for me with Whit. They just couldn't be, not after I knew that Ida was my mother."

Claire swallowed. When it came to confessions, she was about as rusty as Jo. "That day when I went back to the house," she forced herself to say, "I went looking in Ida's vanity. That's where she'd put it. I read it there, on the spot. I'm sorry."

The air of the barn was so heavy it was almost a comfort. That made it easier for Jo to say the things she knew she had to. "After the fire, when Whit didn't come see me in the hospital, I thought maybe he'd finally given up the idea of owning the marsh."

Claire blushed. "I should have known better. He only wanted to marry me because he thought I'd inherit half of Salt Creek Farm. I was too damn young, and besides, I was still so heartbroken over Ethan. I was a fool." She wiped a tear from her cheek.

"I don't know about that. Whit can be very charming when he wants." Jo remembered all the carefree afternoons she and Whit had spent chasing each other on Drake's Beach, the warmth in his voice the evening he tried to give her the locket. She liked to think that some things stayed true. On the other hand, Whit was his mother's son, just as she was her daughter.

Claire hesitated, her brow furrowed.

The Gilly Salt Sisters

"So if Ida was your mother, who was your father?"

Jo took another, deeper breath. *Let it out*, the voice told her again. She licked her lips. "Father Flynn."

Claire sat up. "What? What on earth gave you that idea? The letter just said 'dearest.' That could be anyone."

"Or someone in particular she didn't want to name. Someone she couldn't name. I think it was Father Flynn."

Claire grew thoughtful. "So that's why Ida really left the letter in church. It wasn't for Our Lady at all."

"Exactly."

They fell silent for a moment, and then Claire scuffed her boots in the dust of the barn. She'd saved the worst for last. "All this time," she said, "all I could think was how much you must have hated me for marrying Whit. I thought you blamed me for starting the fire and robbing you of the future you should have had with him. But that wasn't it at all. Maybe you've despised me because we aren't real sisters." She sniffed and wiped away another tear, and Jo surprised herself by reaching out and embracing Claire, feeling how sturdy her arms and shoulders had grown over the course of the summer. She smoothed Claire's river of red hair. While they'd been talking, the stars had come out, along with a dainty crescent moon complicated by wisps of clouds. *A woman's moon*, Mama had always called it, and now Jo realized why. It was a moon for conspiracy, a moon for spinning plots.

"You're as real a sister to me as could ever be, Claire. You have to know that. I've been stubborn and foolish, but I never hated you. Not really."

Claire blew her nose. "Not as foolish as me. There's three of us out here all snarled up with Whit, but I was the only one dumb enough to marry him. How smart does that make me?" She took a small breath, on the verge of saying something else, but she bit her lip instead, and Jo could tell she was thinking about Ethan. "Maybe good sense is overrated," she said. "Maybe Dee is wiser than the two of us put together for knowing that. After all, she's the one who has Whit's child."

Jo snorted. "That girl doesn't have a wise organ in her body."

Claire chuckled at that, but she looked so wan and bleary-eyed that Jo had an urge to sit her down in the kitchen and force her to eat a big slice of pound cake sprinkled with honey and salt, the way she used to after school. They hadn't done that together in years, but the salted and the sugared, the past and the present, no longer seemed quite that far apart. So what if they weren't real sisters? So what if Jo wasn't a Gilly by blood? Time and tenacity had made her one, and for the first time in her life, Jo was truly glad.

"How do you tell the difference between carelessness and passion?" Claire asked as they paced back along the edge of the marsh. "Is there one? I mean, really, is there any way to love a person without getting the hell beat out of you for it?" She rubbed at the skin under her eyes, where dark circles would bloom in the morning. *She's not talking about Whit*, Jo realized. *She's trying to let Ethan out of her veins.*

Jo shook her head. She wished she had an answer for Claire, but as far as she knew, love would leave its marks. Sometimes it even took the skin right off you. She looped her good arm around Claire's shoulders and matched her steps. "I'm afraid not," she said, squeezing Claire so hard she could feel her skinny ribs under her fingers, and she wished she had better tidings to give. "At least not if you're a Gilly."

Chapter Twenty-seven

Whenever Dee started thinking that maybe life on Salt Creek Farm didn't suck so much after all, something else freaky went down and changed her mind, and burying Claire's horse was in that category for sure. Dee had been sitting in the parlor, peaceful as pie, when Jo stumped in with the grimmest look Dee had ever seen and told her to fetch a pair of boots, a shovel, and a flashlight, and get her ass out into the marsh.

Wide-eyed, Dee followed Jo and Claire out to the cluster of graves. By now she recognized all the names on them, even in the dark. She frowned and cast a nervous eye over to Jordy, who was sleeping in his salt bowl a few steps away, not bothered by the fact that it was sitting in the dirt, but what else was Dee supposed to do with him? Minute to minute—that's how she was living life these days, and frankly, she was getting a little tired of it. She adjusted the lantern near him so the glow wouldn't wake him.

Now that Jordy was out of her and in the world and everything, Dee had started thinking about the future in a whole new way—namely, that it had an unsettling habit of turning into the present quicker than seemed reasonable. And while it was A-OK to plop Jordy down in the dirt here like a watermelon while she helped bury a horse that wasn't hers, Dee knew the meter on that reality was running down fast.

Jo and Claire had been nice to her. She wasn't denying that. But in the middle of the night, when she was feeding Jordy his bottle, her mind got to wondering what they were getting out of it. She might have cut her ties with her father, but she was still his daughter, and Cutt had taught her that life worked on a bait-and-reward system. If Dee wanted something, she'd better be prepared to pay for it, he'd instructed, even for the stuff she thought was free. Lately she was starting to get the feeling that Claire and Jo weren't keeping her on Salt Creek Farm just out of the goodness of their hearts. If she left, she realized, the two of them would be stuck with each other, yowling and snarling like those damn barn cats she now understood why Jo drowned.

She paused in her digging and leaned on her shovel, not so much wiping sweat off her forehead as just smearing it around more. If it were light out, the ponds would be all different colors. Jo had tried to explain why the basins were going bananas, but Dee never understood a thing Jo said. She never would have expected salt to be both so plain and so complicated at the same time.

"Dee? Dee!" Claire was leaning on her shovel handle, too, and scowling at her. "Are you sure you didn't see or hear anything? Think hard. It's important."

Dee shook her head. "No, nothing. And I already told you. I was upstairs, sleeping with Jordy, and then I was in the parlor watching TV." The TV was new. Dee had made them get it for her. Some salt and solitude she could deal with, but she needed some connection to the real world or she knew she was going to lose what little she had left of her mind. "I gave Jordy a bottle, then took him into the kitchen and gave him a bath in the sink, and then you came home."

But she was lying. She knew full well what had happened to Icicle, even if she hadn't actually witnessed anything go down in the barn. She didn't have to. She'd been pouring water over Jordy's tummy when she'd spied Whit through the kitchen window, high-stepping his way along the salt levees.

Suddenly he'd stopped dead in his tracks and looked straight across the marsh toward the window and Dee. Her heart had started thumping, and she'd almost drowned poor Jordy, but she couldn't look away either. Everything about Whit came rushing back to her in that moment—the way the back of his neck felt so smooth under her palm, the ridges of his collarbones, and yes, even the squeeze of his hands around her throat.

Jordy had squawked just then, and Dee had glanced down to rearrange him in the sink. When she looked up again, Whit was slipping into the barn. She took Jordy out of the water and wrapped him in a white towel, squinting out the window. Whit paused and then turned toward the kitchen again. Very slowly, he drew his finger across his throat and then put his hand to his lips. Dee gasped and stepped away from the window. When she'd peered out of it once more, Whit was gone.

Jordy woke now and began to fuss in his patch of dirt. Claire sighed and gave the blade of her shovel a kick. "Take him back to the house. It's too late for him to be out here. After Jo and I finish, we're going to haul Icicle from the barn with the truck. You don't need to see that."

For once in her life, Dee wasn't inclined to argue. Jo and Claire were going to be a good few hours yet, so she picked Jordy up in his bowl and began making her way back down the lane toward the house. To her left, the silhouette of the barn loomed out of the darkness like a bad memory, and next to it the lane stretched straight ahead, daring her to go on and make an escape.

She shivered as she let herself into the house, even though it was a humid night. Was Whit still out there, watching the three of them? Probably not, Dee thought. He was a man of action and not observation. She sighed. Maybe this was the sign she needed to tell her that she was never the one for Whit Turner. She had thought that by tangling herself up with Jo and Claire, by becoming one of them, who were so much of his past, she might find the way into his future. Instead here she was—one of three—and trouble, her father had always told her, came in triples. But sometimes so did luck. As she leaned down and lifted Jordy to her shoulder, kissing his sweet head, breathing in the grassy baby smell of him, she found herself wishing she were better at telling the difference.

———o-o o-o———

After Icicle was gone, Dee couldn't seem to make her bones easy around Salt Creek Farm anymore. It seemed like everywhere she looked, there was some kind of danger she hadn't been clued into. The barn lurked all empty and spooky, the main channel that led to the sea looked like nothing so much as a giant throat waiting to swallow her alive, and everywhere she stepped, it seemed like there were unlovely creatures seething in the grasses and shadows. She started finding spiders in her sheets, crushed snails smeared on the bottoms of her rubber boots, and once, after she'd skimmed a pond, she had to pick tens of tiny blue moth wings off her blouse collar.

"It's more important than ever that you don't even think about contacting

Whit," Claire warned her in the kitchen a few days after they'd put Icicle in the ground. "Not for Jordy's sake. Not for your own. Not for anything. You've seen for yourself what he can do." Claire had sold her wedding rings to save Salt Creek Farm from the bank, Dee knew, and Whit was sure to be hopping mad about that. She remembered how sternly he'd ordered her never to lose that junky locket he'd given her. She could only imagine what he would do at the loss of a diamond.

"Well?" Claire said, snapping Dee back to the present. Claire was baking for her new stand in the farmers' market, and she had flour dusted in her hair and sugar spread on her hands. She looked sweet, but Dee was starting to suspect that that was all on the surface, like one of the crusts on her pies.

"Fine," she said, getting a glass of milk. "You already told me this about a thousand times. I won't go near Whit."

"I just want to be sure you got that message," Claire said, eyeing Jordy in his wooden bowl. "Now that you're a

mother and all, we can't be too careful." She started to reach down to the
baby, but before she could get her
mucky hands on him, Dee scooped
him up and pressed him to her chest.
Claire pretended she'd been reaching
for something else near the bowl—a
whisk. She turned back to the distraction of her baking.

"Don't you worry," she said, more to
herself than to Dee. "Once Jo and I are
through with Whit, he'll never want to
set foot in this place again." Dee remembered the strange vision of Whit
stepping out of the salt barn and drawing his finger across his throat. The
loyal half of her wanted to throw her
hat in with Claire and Jo, whatever they
were cooking up, but the more de-
praved half still wanted to follow Whit
down the empty lane and take her
chances. "What are you planning on
doing?" she asked, taking a sip from
her glass.

Claire started whipping a bowl of
cream. Her arm moved in faster and
faster circles. "That's for us to know
and you not to find out." She stopped

and smiled sweetly. "I'm sure you understand." She pushed a wisp of loose hair out of her green eyes. "After all, when it comes to a man like Whit, you can't be too careful. And careful"—she regarded Dee—"isn't really your strong suit, is it?"

———o-o o-o———

As the last of the autumn heat settled back into the earth and cold air began crystallizing on the horizon, Dee began to feel as if she'd been given a set of sharper eyes. For the first time, she started worrying for real about the future. She was coming to realize that the salt worked differently for everybody. Jo seemed happiest when she was toiling away in the stuff, and it seemed to drive Claire to the kitchen, but as far as Dee could tell, she herself was having a negative reaction. To date, the taste of the salt hadn't provided her with anything tangible. In fact, it had done the opposite. It summoned up everything she was missing—namely, living among people. She missed going to the movies and the shops, and she even craved the threads of gossip float-ing around the booths in her father's diner. But most of all she still ached for Whit.

She started dreaming about the apartment she'd like to have for her and Jordy one day—something on a high floor, maybe even a converted attic with cozy sloping eaves and a view over water. She thought about going to beauty school and opening up a little salon somewhere plain on the coast like Gloucester—a place where the women weren't glam but wanted to be—and when Jordy was old enough, she'd buy him a little shaggy dog, and the three of them would be a just-big-enough family.

But dreams cost dollars. Everything did, down to the cartons of formula Jordy could empty in the blink of an eye. Dee gently eased the bottle teat from his mouth and put him over her shoulder to rub his back, nuzzling him with her cheek. It was remarkable how much he looked like Whit, from his slanting eyebrows to the squared-off tips of his fingers. Inside, though, Dee hoped he was filled only with her.

Jordy let out a burp, and she shifted him to the crook of her elbow. In three months he'd gotten so big. He could hold up his head, smile, laugh, and push himself up onto his forearms like a miniature strong man. Sometimes when he slept, Dee leaned down and kissed his perfect bowed mouth, licking her own lips afterward, amazed by the way her baby's breath could cleanse her.

She'd quit wanting to share him with anyone. In the first few weeks after she'd come home from the hospital, she'd been grateful for the way Jo and Claire doted on Jordy. Her incision ached, and she'd had a difficult time doing the most basic things—climbing stairs, sitting up in bed, lowering her ass into the bathtub. And Jordy had seemed so frail. Dee had been worried she'd drop him, or accidentally break him or something, but that didn't happen, and she began to see that she was the one who'd be broken without him. She especially didn't like Claire's habit of scooping him into her arms at every available opportunity and running her index finger down his forehead and the bridge of his tiny nose.

"He's not an arcade game," Dee would snap, and rush to retrieve him. "You don't press a button on him and get a prize." It bothered her even more when Jordy started smiling at the diversion.

"See, he likes it," Claire crowed, and kept on doing it.

Dee would ban Claire from her attic apartment, she decided. And if she ever came into Dee's salon in the future, Dee would shave all that pretty red hair off her.

She didn't even want to share Jordy with Whit anymore. Ever since Icicle's death, she just wanted to get as far away from him and this marsh as she could. Her plan was simple. All she needed was a little bit of money and even less time.

Whit wasn't as rich as he seemed—she'd overheard that from Jo and Claire—but surely he could sell off something in that big house of his—a painting, or how about that fancy car he still drove around in? Even if it was a few years old, it had to be worth something. She'd get Whit alone somehow and ask him. *You can make me go away*, she'd say, drawing her finger across her throat to remind him of what she saw that day when he'd slipped into the barn. *I'll never set foot in this town again. Just write me a check and there will be one less female on Salt Creek Farm you have to worry about.*

Not to mention one less male.

He'd do it, too, Dee thought. A lifetime of child support for a kid he was ashamed of versus a quick lump sum wasn't hard math. Even she could add that total up in her head, and she hadn't finished out her junior year of high school.

Or maybe he'd just kill them both. There was no way to know. For all his hustle and smooth talk, Whit wasn't a betting man. He went after only what he was sure he'd win—first Joanna, then Claire, and then Dee. *He had us all*, Dee thought. *I'm not going to wait around until he decides he wants Jordy.*

She tiptoed back indoors. Around her the house was dark and still, lit only by the moon, and the household clutter seemed even more unmanageable. Once she'd wanted to get to the bottoms of these heaps. Now she didn't care enough. There were the bedrooms with their crammed closets, a collection of dented canisters and tins in the kitchen, and a decade's worth of papers in the writing desk, and none of it had anything to do with Dee.

Without any forethought, she wandered into the parlor and opened the desk, staring at the morass of papers inside. Just as before, ancient catalogs hawked their outmoded goods. Forgotten coupons advertised their specials. And a letter from the bank thanked Jo for her recent payments and reminded her that she wasn't all the way done yet. Dee squinted at the numbers and then pocketed that correspondence. Whit might be interested in something like that, for a price. He sure seemed to want Salt Creek Farm. If Dee had to help him get it, then okay. She would.

She was about to let the lid of the

desk drop when a page of script bearing her name caught her eye in the faint moonlight. Puzzled, she picked it up and examined it. It appeared to be a letter to Whit from her, asking him to meet her in the barn on December's Eve, but the handwriting wasn't quite correct and Dee would never sign her name with a stupid heart next to it. At least not when it came to Whit. She squinted, thinking hard. Jo and Claire were definitely up to something, but what? There was only one way to find out. She'd have to beat them at their own game. She would go to meet Whit herself.

She left the forged letter with her name on it alone and then walked into the hall, where she saw that one of the red pears from the tree in town was propped on top of the piano. It was an ugly thing, speckled, hardly worth taking, but she grabbed it anyway, scooping it into the pocket of her dressing gown, where it rolled against her hip bone. It was getting late in the year for fruit. This might very well be the last specimen of the season. And when someone handed you the last of some-thing, Dee knew, you should reach out and take it, always. *I can do this*, she told herself, climbing the stairs. And if everything worked out, she'd never have to accept the last of anything again.

Chapter Twenty-eight

Claire had forgotten how the end of a summer happened in a rush out on Salt Creek Farm, the season tumbling forward so swiftly she practically had to run to catch it. Thanks to the money from Ida's rings, she and Jo had bought themselves a little reprieve from the bank, but they still owed more on the loan. If they didn't come up with another lump sum soon, Claire knew all too well, Whit would buy the property in foreclosure.

Day after day she and Jo scooped dry salt from the big piles at the edges of the marsh into barrows and wheeled the loads to the barn for storage, even as they still raced to skim the ponds. And then, without warning, autumn fell upon them, hard and fast. The few trees in town began to yellow, and the milk-weed went brittle and pale. The cran-berry bog up the coast turned brilliant red, and the morning air grew confused with intersections of birds—those head-ing south versus the pipers and gulls, who toughed it out over the hard Cape winter. The last strands of summer grasses died back, and the humid haze burned off the ponds, a chill sharpen-ing everything.

Claire had switched from making cobblers to baking spice cake, and in-stead of squeezing lemonade she'd started mulling cider, but no matter how many apple pies she pulled from the oven, no matter how many bacon-and-squash turnovers she folded, she couldn't figure out what to do about Whit or, for that matter, Ethan. One man still had her heart cupped in his open hands, and the other was determined to tear it to shreds, and Claire was left with a hole gaping in the center of her: an empty spot that was dangerous not because of what was missing but because of what it invited.

To her utter surprise, it turned out to be the salt.

By the time she and Jo had gotten it all moved into the barn, it was clear they had so much of it on their hands they were going to have trouble getting rid of it. "I've never seen a season quite like this," Jo admitted, dumping the last barrow of gray salt into a trough. "You better fire up the oven, Claire, and get cooking. That's the only way we're going to use it all up. Not even the fishermen need all of this. Chet Stone's generous, but not *this* generous."

An uncomfortable silence spread between them. Claire cleared her throat. "About that," she said, a blush creeping over her cheeks. "I've been thinking. Maybe it's time to bring the salt back to Prospect."

Jo peered at her. "What are you saying, Claire?"

Claire took a deep breath. "What if

we reinstate the salt for the December's Eve bonfire this year?"

Jo dusted off her hands and considered the idea. "Folks would like that, I bet. And, even better, it would sure rile up Whit. If everyone starts eating our salt again, he'll have a harder time getting rid of us."

At the mention of Whit, an idea started spinning in Claire's mind. She narrowed her eyes and weighed it for a moment. "Jo," she said at last, stretching herself out on a heap of dusty packing crates and trying to keep her voice casual, "what if we told Whit the truth about who you are? He probably deserves to know."

Jo stuck her hands on her hips. "He doesn't deserve to have his head attached to his neck." She was silent for a moment and then frowned. "I don't see what good telling Whit any of this would do."

"Think about it. We could warn Whit that if he doesn't leave us alone, we'll go public with some nasty truths about his mother. We can prove it if we have to. We have Ida's letter. And I bet we could find Father Flynn."

Jo frowned. "I have his address. I got it from Ethan. But I don't know what I'd say after all this time, Claire. I haven't worked that out."

Claire stretched out her open hands, as if weighing the thick barn air. Jo always was a hard sell. "We'll make a trade," Claire said. "If Whit leaves Salt Creek Farm alone, we won't go any further with our story. But if he wants to keep fighting with us, then we'll go public with what we know. Tit for tat. You can worry about Father Flynn later." She folded her fingers back in her lap and waited.

"I don't know, Claire," Jo said. "I reckon we might need more proof than an unsigned letter."

Claire grinned. "I know, but the local papers would enjoy chewing on the story in the meantime, and Whit would sure hate having to share his noble lineage with the likes of us. Not to mention what it would do to Ida's reputation."

Jo snorted. "It wasn't that good to

begin with." Then she paused, thinking the plan over. It was crazy, but it was all they had. "Okay," she finally conceded. "Maybe it could work. But how do we get Whit to listen? It's not like we can have our secretary call his secretary to arrange a meeting."

Claire tried not to look triumphant. "I've thought of that, too. We can have Dee do it."

Jo frowned. "What?"

Claire waved her hands, still spectacularly white in spite of the summer's labor. "We'll write something ourselves but say it's from her. I know what her handwriting looks like. It wouldn't be hard to copy. Think about it," she continued. "If I ask Whit to meet us, he'll just ignore me. If you do it, he'll just laugh, but if he thinks it's Dee—especially if we mention Jordy—he'll think she wants to come crawling back to him, and for Whit the prospect of someone groveling is like sugar set out for a fly. We'll say she wants him to meet her in the barn, but we'll be waiting instead."

Jo scowled. "I'm still not sure."

Claire smacked her hands on her knees. "Do you have a better idea?"

Jo admitted she didn't. And so they planned it. They'd deliver a letter to Whit forged in Dee's hand, telling him to meet her in the barn on the night of the December's Eve bonfire.

"It's perfect," Claire said, narrowing her eyes. "The entire town will be in one spot, and in the confusion no one will notice if Whit's not there. And we never stay. If anything unpleasant happens, everyone will be busy." She thought about the town huddled around the flames, distracted with the return of the salt, their attention focused on what it would say about their futures. Jo eyeballed her.

"What will happen that's unpleasant, Claire?" she asked, as if she knew that Claire hadn't told her the whole plan.

Claire looked back at her with flat eyes. "I have no idea." She stood up, pushed the barrow into a corner, and hung her tools on the wall. "Well, then," she said. "It's all settled." They began walking back to the house. In the distance the ocean seethed. Behind Claire the barn loomed, and as she cast a final glance back at it, she pictured the salt piled inside, coarse and gray, brittle as bone and twice as dry, a heap of possibility waiting for the spark of her touch.

———o-o o-o———

Claire wrote the note to Whit that evening while Dee was upstairs feeding Jordy and Jo was busy fiddling with some old nuts and bolts on the front porch. The only way Whit would come to the salt barn, she knew, was if he believed he was going to get something really good out of it. But what did Dee have to give him? Money? None of them had that—not after paying the bank. Undying love? Claire snorted and chewed on the end of the pen. That's what had led to their all being stuck out here in the first place. That left only Jordy.

Claire wasn't sure how Whit felt about his son. On the one hand, Jordy was definitely an embarrassment for him, a physical manifestation of his moral weakness, no better in his eyes than one of the lowly children he'd refused to consider adopting. On the other hand, Jordy was the son and heir that Claire had never been able to produce, and now that she was gone, wouldn't Whit be desperate for some kind of child to carry on his family name, especially on land he was convinced should be his? Claire would just have to find out.

"Meet me in the salt barn at eight-thirty on December's Eve," Claire scribbled in an approximation of Dee's round, childish hand. *"I'm begging you. Come and see your son for one time. At least give me that."* She picked up the page and scanned her work. The loops of the *G*'s and *F*'s were wrong, but Claire was betting that Whit wouldn't notice. She wasn't even sure he knew what Dee's handwriting looked like. Claire signed Dee's name with a heart next to it.

Without telling Jo, Claire had changed the meeting time slightly. On December's Eve, when Prospect was looking to its future, Claire would be settling the scores of her past. It wouldn't take long. Just an extra half hour. That would be plenty for her purposes. She folded the letter and sealed it into a fresh envelope. Now all she had to do was wait.

———o-o o-o———

The day before the December's Eve festival, Claire headed to Turner House bearing two envelopes—one full of salt, one of deceit.

Jo and Dee were handing out the rest of the salt packets, going from mailbox to mailbox across town. Claire and Jo had agreed that, going forward, maybe it was better if everyone got to throw his or her own packet of salt to the flames. Claire would toss the first packet in, of course, per tradition, but after that, the sisters decided, it was best to let people take their futures into their own hands.

They even had plans to deliver a salt envelope to Cutt at the Lighthouse, and secretly Claire wondered how that would go, if Cutt would receive his daughter and grandson with open arms or, as Claire rather suspected, he would shut the door in their faces. Dee had wondered why Claire insisted on delivering the salt envelope to Whit personally, and Claire had had to think fast to distract her. "Because I want the last thing I give him to be the first thing he knew about me," she said.

Dee thought that over and then wrinkled up her nose. "I guess that makes sense," she said, but she didn't sound happy about it.

When Claire got to the bottom of Plover Hill, she paused under the pear tree. The fruit was knobbier and scarcer than ever. She reached up and plucked off one of the misshapen globes, remembering the hours she and Ethan had spent in the shrubbery under the tree and the day in the dunes when he'd broken her heart, and then she recalled the beat of Icicle's hooves as she'd galloped him to Salt Creek Farm with Dee. A lifetime could pass in a single year, it turned out.

The wind shivered through the tree's leaves, causing one or two of them to detach and flutter to the ground. It was almost as if the thing just wanted to get it over with and die. A year ago Claire might have felt sympathy, but her skin was rougher now, toughened by salt and then made tender again in ways she'd forgotten existed. She'd lost a husband but gained a sister—two sisters, really, plus a nephew of sorts—and she'd reclaimed her home. And if Whit Turner thought he was going to take that away, he had another thing coming.

She headed up Plover Hill, taking longer strides as she climbed higher, until she reached the gates of Turner House, where she stopped. Today she was just a messenger, not an intruder. She opened the mailbox and thrust in the letter and the salt packet, then tipped her head back and regarded the stern façade of the house she knew so well, remembering the things of hers that were still inside—riding attire, clothes, a book about an English heiress she'd been halfway through reading last winter. Cosmetics. Her wedding albums. A framed photograph of her beloved Icicle. More problematic were the intangible things she'd abandoned to the Turner walls. There was her dignity, for starters, hooked together with her pride. Memories. The enviable status that went along with being Claire Turner. And, finally, there were the wisps of her unborn children, the specter of Ida, and the phantom of her youth.

She'd been so god-awful young when she'd married Whit. Being around Dee had made her see that. Dee still liked cherry candies—the kind with the gum in the center. She turned the kitchen radio to pop music and danced when she thought no one was looking, and if Claire and Jo let her, she'd stay in the shower so long there'd be no hot water for the next two hours. Sometimes, though, when Claire watched Dee playing with Jordy, tickling him on the parlor floor, rolling on her back and waving her feet in the air to make him laugh, just as full of puppy fat as he was, she wanted to weep.

Everyone had moments that acted like a prism, Claire believed, breaking up visible matter so you could see elementally what was in front of your eyes. She squinted, her vision coming back to Turner House. She wished she could wad it up with her eyes. When Joanna returned her wedding invitation, Claire remembered, she'd filled the envelope with salt to remind Claire of who she was and where she'd come from. Claire had opened it in the Turner foyer, spilling chunky gray grains across the floor, and as she'd swept them all up, she'd vowed revenge. But what if she'd been wrong all these years? What if Jo hadn't been sending her a curse at all? What if it had simply been her blessing?

———o-o o-o———

The weather on the night of the bonfire was so miserable that Claire was surprised it wasn't canceled, but tradition in Prospect was nothing if not stalwart. In the end she packed Dee into the truck with a box of spice cakes, an urn of hot cider and one of mulled wine, a folding table, and a cash box, and warned her not to abandon her post until the flames were all dead.

"I'm going to freeze my ass off," Dee griped, wrapping her arms around herself.

"Everyone's going to be freezing their asses off, Dee," Claire replied, opening the truck door for her. "That's the point. They'll want something hot to drink. We'll make a killing, and you can keep half the profits." Dee's eyes glowed at that, and Claire suppressed a smirk. Life with Whit had been worth a little something. It had taught her that profit margins made good incentives.

When she went back inside, Jo was rocking Jordy by the fire in the parlor. She looked up at Claire. "Do you have Ida's letter?"

Claire scowled. She had some time yet before she was supposed to meet Whit, and she and Jo had been over the plan twice that day already. "It's upstairs in my drawer. But I don't think it's a good idea to bring it."

Jo frowned and considered. "I suppose you're right. We can't replace it. But what if he doesn't believe you?"

"Oh, he will." Claire was going to meet Whit alone. She and Jo had decided it would be better that way, and besides, the weather was so rotten that someone needed to stay indoors and tend to Jordy. Dee had wanted to go to the bonfire. Privately, Claire was more than happy to serve as the sole messenger. After so many months of being baited by Whit, after what he'd done to Icicle, she wanted to be the one to sink a hook into him and watch him writhe.

There was just one thing she needed to do first, though, before the fire. She kissed Jordy on the top of his head and drew her scarf tighter around her throat. Jo glanced up, her glass eye burning with the reflection from the hearth. The image was disturbing, and Claire looked away. She was supposed to be the one filled with fire.

"Weren't you supposed to go with Dee?" Jo asked. "I just heard her leave."

Claire shivered and buttoned her coat. "I'm walking into town. I'll be there in time to throw the first salt packet," she said. "Don't worry. I just have a few loose ends to take care of first."

———o-o o-o———

When the wind hit St. Agnes hard enough from the north, the whole building hummed, a vibration that started in the roof beams and rattled to the roots of the church. Claire fumbled to light a candle to Our Lady. The hesitant flame trembled and then made a sole point of yellow. Claire cupped her palm around the votive and knelt in front of the faceless Virgin. She thought about how Our Lady had absorbed the pains and joys of the town over the years with calm abundance, and then she thought about Jo and Ida and how some sorrows were too deep to tell. Claire rose and stepped close to the wall, stretching her arms out along the Virgin's. The two of them were almost the same shape and size. She closed her eyes and inhaled the odor of dust and plaster, what bones must smell like after they've been powdered in the grave.

The wind howled a higher tune, and a door banged open. Claire opened her eyes and saw Ethan standing on the far side of the sanctuary. She gasped and pushed herself away from the mural, upsetting the candle at her feet in the process. Ethan hurried over to blow out the flame before it could spread.

"Claire, what are you doing here? I

thought you'd be at the bonfire. Besides, there's a nasty storm brewing." She took the dead candle out of Ethan's hands and looked out the east window of the church. He was right. In the short time since she'd been inside, the clouds had muscled themselves into angry stallions streaming across the sky, and the wind was racing to keep up. In about an hour, there would be a stampede of awful weather. Her stomach knotted. Would the bonfire still roar to life? Would Whit still come to the barn? He had to come. Everything depended on that.

Ethan took her by the elbow and guided her over to the pews. "Are you okay? Your face has gone green." He put a hand up to cup her cheek, then abruptly stopped himself, and Claire turned her head away from him. He was due to leave after the holidays. They'd largely avoided each other since that day at the market back in summer. Ethan didn't know about the death of Icicle, Claire realized, or about what she and Jo were planning. He didn't know that Claire had lost her sister in name and then gotten her back again two times over. Maybe he didn't even know that she and Jo had given the town back their salt.

"I'm fine." She didn't mean for her voice to come out so flinty, chipping the air between them, but once it did, she couldn't stop it. She didn't seem to be able to walk a middle ground with Ethan. She was either fire in his arms or an iceberg out of them. She put her hands up over her face and tried not to sob. "Oh, God, I'm not fine, but I can't tell you why."

Ethan frowned. "Is there anything you want to confess?" Claire shook her head, and Ethan bowed his. "I'm no better than you are, Claire," he said quietly. "If there's something you need to say to me, you can."

She yearned to curve her body against his. He so easily filled all the blank spaces inside her. Close to him she had been able to forget she was a Gilly, cursed by a patch of earth. She clenched her hands. She'd never expected him to come back to Prospect, but here he was, the boy's heart she remembered still beating, the rest of him grown into a man she had no right to love. Was this what Ida—Jo's mother, Claire allowed herself to think for the first time—had endured? Claire turned her face back to Our Lady. The past was always going to sit between Ethan and her like an empty circle, and there was no way to break it.

"I'm sorry," she whispered, standing up and edging her way out of the pew and to the door.

Ethan stood to follow her. "Claire, don't go, not like this."

She turned. For the rest of her life, she would remember the look on his face. "I love you, Ethan," she said. "I always will. But you were right. This all has to end here." Her hand was on the door.

Ethan frowned. "Are you still talking about us?"

Claire flung the door open to the weather. "There isn't any us," she said, letting the wind smack her face, a fitting rebuke. "There never was. There's just a story we were fools to repeat."

———o-o o-o———

The first raindrops were falling fat as grubs when Claire finally reached the barn. She'd left her coat in the sanctuary, and her sweater clung to her like a ruined second skin. A few degrees colder and it would snow.

Her teeth were chattering. She paused. Had Whit even bothered to come? Was she too late? She hadn't worn a watch since she'd come back to Salt Creek Farm, and she had no idea how long she'd spent at St. Agnes. She sniffed. She could smell wood smoke hanging in the air and knew that the bonfire had been lit, but it was okay. She still had some time. She squinted through the darkness and spied Whit's car parked in the distance, and then she saw him approaching the barn, his jacket collar flipped up against the rain, hands shoved in his pockets. Even his walk looked mean.

She sucked in a breath and crouched into a thicket of shrubs, glad for the shadows hiding her. She thought about poor Icicle, felled on the floor of the barn, and it occurred to her that if she could run Whit through with something sharp, she'd do it without thinking twice. She felt around in the darkness for a weapon of some kind, but there was none, and that was just one of the many problems with Salt Creek Farm. It was silted, defenseless land. She reached into her pocket and felt the book of matches. She'd slipped it into her jeans after she'd lit the candle to Our Lady. A crack of lightning clawed the sky, ripping the dark clouds to tatters and igniting Claire's temper.

She heard Whit go into the barn, and then, before she could change her mind, she pulled the matches from her pocket and crept to the structure's back wall. She was sheltered from the wind on this side, and when she put her hand out to the rough boards, they still felt dry in spite of the freezing rain and snow flurries that had started to fall.

The first match fizzled, but the second one flared with sulfur. Claire held it low to where the barn's wood met earth, pinching it as long as she could before her fingers got scorched. One second, two, and finally the wind flickered and the flame caught life, flitting onto the side of the barn.

She stepped back and watched it burn. Another lightning strike scratched the air, and the fire started tonguing its way around the base of the barn, each burst of wind stretching the flames a little farther. She had the impression of something—or someone—rustling past her in the dark. *If I want to stop this, now's my only chance*, Claire thought as the flames turned the corner, but she didn't. She twisted back and walked as quickly as she could through the grass, toward the lane. Behind her she smelled gathering smoke, but she didn't stop. It was done, out of her hands. The past had a tendency to repeat itself, but this time, Claire vowed, her future would be very different.

————o-o o-o————

The bonfire was roaring full force when Claire arrived. She had missed the lighting of it, but it didn't matter. Frankly, the town had been relieved when she didn't cast the salt. Nothing good ever happened when she did.

She pushed her way through the small crowd, scanning faces she recognized. She heard whispers of smothered speech as she passed the trio of Agnes Greene, Cecilia West, and Katy Diamond, but Claire no longer cared what those women thought of her. She nodded to them cordially as she neared them, but they didn't reply in kind, and that was fine. Claire hadn't expected them to. It was enough to see them holding the salt again.

She neared the table that Dee had set up at the back of the crowd, but it was empty, the cash box locked, the paper tablecloth flapping ragged in the wind, fat snowflakes beginning to disintegrate it. "Dee!" she called into the darkness, but there was no answer.

"She left," a gravelly voice said. "Right after the fire began. Didn't even throw her salt. See?" It was Mr. Weatherly, Claire realized. His gnarled finger was pointing to the dampening envelope propped next to the cider.

A fizz of irritation bubbled through

Claire. "Did she say where she was going?" The wind whipped the sharp ends of her hair against her cheeks, stinging them.

Mr. Weatherly shook his head. "Nope. But what about you? Why don't you have a go?" He gestured at the salt on the abandoned table.

Claire remembered the time when she'd thrown her first packet into the fire and how the flames had turned black. The crowd's hush had been so absolute she thought the world might never come to life again. And maybe, for her, it hadn't. She shook her head. "No," she said, an uneasy feeling beginning to crawl up her bones. She knew better than anyone what a tricky business dabbling in the future could be. She was through with all that now. The sooner she found Dee, she thought, the better.

Chapter Twenty-nine

Dee hadn't wanted to, but Jo convinced her to ride into Prospect to deliver the bulk of the salt packets the day before the December's Eve bonfire. Overnight, it seemed, the trees had dropped their leaves and changed to skeletons. Out in the marsh, the wind scratched at the farmhouse's shingles and windows, and veils of frost raced across the ponds and turned the levees white. As they bumped along the lane in the truck, Jordy nestled in blankets on Dee's lap, she couldn't help but think back to the bonfire the previous year, when Whit had given her the locket and made love to her under the pear tree and all she'd known about Gilly salt was the extra saliva it cultivated on her tongue.

Jo turned onto Bank Street, and Dee blinked against the cool winter light, surprised at how narrow the road now seemed. She remembered the hazy dawns when she'd wait by her window for the sound of horse's hooves and a glimpse of Claire's braid and then, later, the sound of Whit's car, idling quietly. She thought that if she really did manage to leave Prospect, how sad it would be to have no one to say good-bye to anymore, for the less Claire and Jo knew about her plan, the better.

Jo pulled even with the diner and slowed the truck. "Are you sure you want to do this?" she asked, but Dee simply thrust Jordy at her and opened the passenger door.

"Just wait here for a minute," she replied. "I'll be right back."

She yanked on the door to the diner, and, as usual, the bells above the door burst into life, making her cringe. Her father was at the counter, stooped over the cash register. He looked a lot older than Dee remembered, and she felt sorry if she'd caused that, but truth be told, she didn't think she had. His ruin was between him and the bottle.

The place had a neglected air to it, as if he hadn't been getting a lot of business. Some of the counter stools were dusty, and several of the light-bulbs in the ship lanterns were burned out or flickering. The menus had turned yellow under their plastic sleeves, and there wasn't anything written on the specials board.

"Hey," Dee said, and Cutt narrowed his eyes at her.

"What do you want?" he asked, and the way he practically wadded up the word and spit it in Dee's general direction told her he hadn't reconsidered his policy of scorched earth. Dee might as well have been an insignificant mouse, scurrying through the walls. She pictured Jordy's wriggling body after his bath and couldn't imagine any crime he could commit that would be large enough for her to want to walk away from him. She tossed the packet of salt on the counter and shoved her hands into her pockets. *Your loss*, she thought. "Here," she said. "This is for the bonfire tomorrow night. Claire and Jo are giving them out to everyone this year." Cutt looked confused, and Dee remembered that he hadn't gone to the fire last winter. Only she had, and only briefly, before Whit had gotten his hands on her.

"I had the baby," she said. "Just so you know. It's a boy. He's in the truck out there with Jo." She pointed through the window at the rattletrap pickup, but Cutt didn't look. "He's doing good."

Dee waited one extra heartbeat to see if there'd be any kind of crack in her father's armor, but there wasn't. His jaw didn't twitch, and neither did his eyes flicker. It didn't even seem like he was really breathing. Dee glanced around at the tables and noticed dishes of salt set out, as if their presence would help stave off Cutt's inevitable ruin.

"It's not really toxic, you know," she said, jutting her chin toward one of the bowls, "but it's not magic either. Jo would tell you the same, and so would Claire. She's a whole different kind of person now."

And so am I, she realized as she breezed back through the door, bells jangling, glass rattling, her bones loose and easy but her heart pounding like a fist in a fight—one she thought she finally might have won.

———o-o o-o———

The night of the bonfire, Claire hurriedly packed Dee into the truck with boxes of spice cake and urns of mulled cider, and then she made her a promise.

"Is Whit going to be there?" Dee probed, and Claire mistook the rise in her voice for anxiety. She leaned through the window of the truck and stared intently into Dee's eyes.

"I swear to you, he never attends this thing," she said, totally oblivious to the fact that last year he'd not only attended but that he'd done so with Dee.

Dee shrugged and slid her eyes away. "Whatever. If you're really sure."

"Absolutely," Claire answered, her voice bright, and for a moment she sounded like the woman Dee had met when she first came to town. Maybe it was the pile of gray clouds lining up on the horizon behind her, or maybe it was all the spices that had been floating around in the kitchen lately, but tonight Claire's hair was as red as it had ever been and her skin as white. She cupped Dee's chin in the vise of her hand and looked hard into her eyes. "You're still so young," she said. "Sometimes I forget that. Don't worry about Jordy," she continued. "Jo will take perfect care of him. Go and have some fun. Shake the dust off of yourself. I have an errand to run first, and I'll be along soon." Her face cracked into an unexpected smile. "You'll be the life of the party," she said. "I guarantee it."

Dee thought that was none too likely, but she didn't dispute Claire. After all, it didn't matter. If everything lined up for Dee this evening, she and Jordy would be long gone, and she would make sure neither one of them ever so much as touched any kind of salt again.

—o-o o-o—

The town's oldest person always lit the bonfire. Dee remembered Mr. Weatherly telling her that once in the diner, and when she arrived on Tappert's Green, she saw that this year Judith Butler had the honor, the torch wobbling in her shaky hand as the town's men finished the last-minute touches to the pyre. Dee watched from behind the plywood table she'd set up, craning her neck to witness the coming festivities. The crowd began to cheer and clap, and from somewhere in the darkness the familiar sound of a flute started up, followed by people's voices taking up the tune.

She allowed herself to relax for a moment, enjoying the crackle of the flames and the smell of orange peel and hot wine floating over Claire's stand. It was one of the few times Dee had been without Jordy since his birth, and though it was exciting to stand bareheaded and alone in front of a hot fire on a cold night, she also felt as if she were missing a limb. She looked around the crowd to see if she could spot Whit, but there was no sign of him, and for that she was glad. Maybe he really was going to the barn after all. Soon she'd have to sneak away.

"I was beginning to think that marsh might have ate you up," a gruff voice said out of the darkness, and Dee jumped. Mr. Weatherly was standing in front of her, his long face grown ghoulish in the flickering light. "Where's the baby, then?"

Dee poured him out a cup of cider and waved away his coins. "He's home with Jo," she said. "It's too cold to bring him."

Mr. Weatherly took a sip of his drink and seemed to accept that.

"Seems like it lit okay," Dee said, gesturing toward the fire.

Mr. Weatherly looked pleased. "It sure did," he said. "It's nice to have the salt back." He took another sip of his cider and regarded Dee expectantly, and then, before she could say anything, he fished in his pocket and pulled out one of his knot charms. "Here," he said, laying it on the table next to the plate of cake slices. "For the baby.

Since you wouldn't let me pay for the cider."

Lying exposed on the oilcloth like that, the string looked anemic and far too ordinary to take on the kind of malice Dee now knew existed in the world. On the other hand, her time on Salt Creek Farm had taught her that anything was possible, and besides, she and Jordy were going to need all the help they could get in their new lives. She reached down and slipped the thing into her pocket.

"Thank you," she said, regretting that Mr. Weatherly wasn't related to her. It would have been nice, she thought, for Jordy to have a grandfather like him—somebody good with a hammer, who knew how to recite limericks and also the best legends. Someone who knew how to take the strings of the past and tie them up safe.

Mr. Weatherly jutted his chin at the packet of salt lying on the table next to the cider. "Well, ain't you going to toss it in the fire and see what the year has coming for you?" he asked.

Dee hesitated. All around her, people

were laughing in the face of the cold wind and tossing their packets of salt to the flames. Flashes of blue, green, and bloodred popped and danced like fireworks. Gangs of preteen girls squealed and flipped their hair when high-school boys paraded by them, and young families huddled in knots, trying to keep their sleepy kids warm.

Dee's heart started beating a little harder. She looked at her watch. Where the hell was Claire? She'd promised she'd be here. Dee could only stay maybe five more minutes before she left to meet Whit in the barn. A burst of wind snagged the bonfire's flames, sending sparks shooting into the sky and scattering people who had gathered too close. Dee pulled her coat tighter. The temperature seemed to have dropped ten extra degrees in the past half hour. More wind screamed over the fire, and people laughed and clutched their hats and scarves.

"If this keeps up," someone said, "we'll all be burned to high heaven." The flute music stopped, replaced by what sounded like a banjo. Out of the corner of her eye, Dee watched someone step up and throw one more handful of salt into the bonfire. She held her breath and waited. The flames sputtered, but from where she was standing, she couldn't see what the future held. She looked at her watch again. It was time to go. She had her own date with destiny.

———o-o o-o———

On the lane to Salt Creek Farm, the weather wasn't just bad; it had turned shit-storm terrible. Dee had left the truck at the bonfire. It would be easier to keep a secret meeting with Whit if Jo and Claire didn't know she was back in the marsh, she thought. She'd get what she needed from Whit, wait until all of Salt Creek Farm was asleep, and then she'd disappear with Jordy. She'd even packed some of their things in an old duffel bag and hidden it out on the lane. She pulled up her hood and started jogging in the darkness, stuffing her hands in her pockets. She passed St. Agnes and was tempted to stop in and get warm, but she had only a little distance left to go and not much time, so she pushed on through the wind and sleet, picking her way along the edge of the marsh, past the graves and around the back of the salt barn. It was a good thing Whit was as stubborn as a mule's mother, Dee told herself, because she wasn't sure how many other men would bother leaving their comfortable houses on a night like this. But Whit would. Surely he would.

She froze as a pair of headlights swung up the lane and Whit's car pulled into view. She was totally exposed where she was standing, but Whit was focused on getting into the barn and so didn't see her. From her spot by the marsh, she watched him unlatch the double doors and let himself into the structure. She held her breath, listening, but heard only the wind and pelting rain.

Fuck it, she finally thought. *My ass is going to ice over standing out here. I'm going in.*

As she pulled open the door, two things struck her. First, she had the impression of something—or someone—

rustling in the dark. She glanced into the rainy air but saw no one, and so she stepped into the barn.

Without Icicle the air in the barn had started to smell different. Not cleaner, the way Dee would have expected, but heavier, sweeter, smokier. She inhaled again and frowned. Where was Whit? She wanted to settle things now. She imagined again the apartment she would rent, just Jordy and her. But now it was getting harder to see, and her eyes were stinging, and then she heard a roar and looked up to see a wall of flames bearing down on her. She screamed and turned, but the darkness had turned to heat, light, and ash, and she realized too late that there was going to be no such thing as a future for her.

Chapter Thirty

If the time had come for truths, Jo knew, then she possessed a black one. She wondered if she could have saved Dee the night she was trapped in the barn with Whit, but there was no way to know for sure. The fire department had declared otherwise. By the time Jo got to the barn, they'd pointed out, Whit and Dee were most likely already gone, but Jo knew from experience that a person could walk through flames if she had to, and she wondered why she didn't do it again that night.

It was the way Claire had entered the

house on December's Eve that told Jo that something was terribly wrong. Claire had come inside far too quickly, slamming the door behind her as if she were shutting out a pack of feral dogs. Outside, Jo heard a crackle and a snap. *The bonfire's wild this year,* she thought, laying a sleeping Jordy down in his bowl and wondering what Claire was doing home so early. *It's strange to hear it all the way out here.*

Over the past hour, Jo had watched the weather whip itself into a snit. Wind had started slapping at the shingles, daring them to come loose, and every now and then evil fingers of lightning reached down from the sky and grasped for the earth like a hand pulling weeds. She waited to hear Claire take off her coat and boots, then stick her head around the corner of the parlor door, hatless, but that wasn't what happened. Instead Claire had come careening into the parlor, snatching Jordy out of the bowl, speechless with terror.

"Where's Dee?" Jo had asked, frowning at the rivulets Claire was dripping on the floor, but Claire had just stuttered, her face turned waxen. "What on earth is it?" Jo asked as Claire uttered the same frantic words over and over: Dee was gone.

"What are you talking about?" Jo said, pushing past Claire out onto the porch. And that's when she saw that in the distance the salt barn was on fire. Jo placed her hand over her heart—or where she thought it might be—and felt it thumping, and then she tore off into the darkness, her slippered feet sinking into the icy mud, her bad leg dragging behind her.

"Dee!" Jo screamed as she neared the fiery structure. She ripped off her robe and tucked her head down, ready to rush through the flames. After all, she'd done it once. She could do it again. But out of the corner of her eye, she saw Whit's car sitting on the lane, and she immediately stopped, straightened up, and put a hand over her mouth.

"Too bad I burned the damn thing down once already," she remembered Claire muttering the night they'd hatched their plan to corner Whit. They'd been closing up the barn after bringing in the salt, and Claire had cast a glance back at the building. "Whit would make perfect kindling."

"Don't get ideas, Claire," Jo had answered. "Whit's not kindling. He's kin."

But Claire had just loped ahead, her long legs outpacing Jo's, leaving Jo to straggle the rest of the way back to the house alone, juggling the uncomfortable fact that while she and Claire might finally be family, they'd never really shared the same skin.

"Oh, Claire," she said now, turning her face from the rising heat. "What have you gone and done?" And then she stood and watched with horror as the roof came crashing down, sending an explosion of sparks straight up into the night.

———o-o o-o———

February 18, 1981

Dear Jo,

Thank you, child, for returning Ida's letter after all this time. You were but a girl when you found it, you say. You came in that day to pray, I remember, after an argument with Whit. Instead you ended up committing a sin. Well, you are not alone in that. What must you have thought of me all these years?

It's true that I loved Ida. I gave her the necklace shortly after I found out she was pregnant with you. I wanted to abandon the priesthood. I even offered to leave town with her and make a new life for all of us, but she refused to let me ruin myself and threatened to tell everyone I'd forced myself on her if I breathed a word to anyone.

What could I do? I was weak to let you be born to this kind of life, but I felt I had no choice, and after so many years lapsed, you seemed so grounded where you were. It never seemed appropriate to reveal the truth. Instead I had to satisfy myself with the small moments I was able to have with you when you came to St. Agnes. I truly regret all this now, but I also consider myself a lucky man that you chose to come to me for answers.

I really was stuck in Prospect during the time when you and your brother were born. Your mother was alone out in the marsh, or so she thought, but she didn't know that Ida had snuck out of the Temperance League with you wrapped in blankets and made her way to St. Agnes to find me. You were just hours old.

She came to the church, but she found your mother instead, defacing Our Lady, her own newborn babe bundled to her chest. They made a pact that night. Ida would remain silent about what she had seen if your mother would raise you as her own. When I returned, Ida was long gone and Sarah had two babies, one with ginger hair and freckles and the other with the eyes of the woman I loved. I never thought Ida would be back. I don't believe she thought so either. Certainly no one ever predicted she would become a Turner.

It's a remarkable and terrible thing which you've told me, the barn burning down like that in a storm with Whit and Dee inside, but I guess once a spark lights, you never know what will happen. The fire department ruled it to be the fault of lightning, you wrote, but the devil sometimes has an unseen hand in these matters, I have found.

In answer to your final question: I don't know if Dee and Whit would still be with us if all this had come out sooner. History will bear witness, I suppose. And in that vein, being family and perhaps needing fewer words than other people, allow me to suggest that now that old truths have come to light, this well may be the time to turn the page and start writing a new and brighter Gilly history. Stay true in your faith and heart, my daughter.

Magna est veritas, et praevalibet,

Patrick Flynn

Jo put down the letter and closed her eyes, trying to do the familial math in her head. Three women and a child tangled around one man. Two sisters and the same man. One faceless woman and a man without a name. A woman with half a face. Any way Jo whittled down the story, she couldn't make it come out even, but how else had she thought things would end? When it came to the Gillys, history was always going to be at odds with itself, and Jo was just going to have to learn to accept that.

It was seven in the morning on Salt Creek Farm. Outside, in spite of the bitter cold, Timothy Weatherly was pacing in the marsh and sketching plans for a new barn. He promised to build it so strong and fine this time that nothing would ever bring it down again—not lightning, not a match, not even the tempers of the Gilly women.

In the kitchen Claire was feeding Jordy his morning bottle and baking a loaf of cinnamon bread. In the past month, Jordy had started crawling and was everywhere now. After the fire Cutt had left town, and no one could find him (not that anyone had really wanted to), so Claire had gotten her wish and gained custody of Jordy. One day, Jo knew, they'd have to tell him what had really happened, but hopefully that was still years away, and by then maybe they'd be able to tell the story right.

Jo walked over and plucked Jordy out of Claire's arms. After the fire Claire's scarlet hair had started developing strings of gray in it, as if ash had settled permanently on her head, but Jo thought the look actually suited her sister. It softened her somehow and took away a little of her venom. Or maybe it was all the fish. After everything, Ethan had decided to stay in town and join his uncle Chet at the docks. At first, racked by guilt, shocked by the loss of Dee, Claire had wanted nothing to do with him, but every day over the past two months Ethan had brought her something to eat from the sea until, to his relief, she decided that salt and fish went together after all and accepted his proposal in the dunes with a solemn nod and a deep kiss.

Jo looked down at the silver locket hooked around Claire's throat. Claire had gone and set it with Ida's pearl. Pasted inside on the left was a picture of Claire and Jordy, covered in flour and laughing, and the right side contained a photograph of Dee cradling Jordy.

"Are you sure you don't want this?" Claire had said when she'd asked Jo for the locket. "The pearl should really be yours by rights. Not to mention the locket."

But Jo refused. "I didn't want it the first time around," she said, "and I don't want it now." The truth was, it pained her to be reminded of Dee. No matter what she did from now on, Jo knew, a part of her would always be lingering in front of the barn as it burned, as trapped as Whit and Dee. And how much worse it was for Claire, she suspected. Bad enough to wear that necklace like a penance, where it thumped and twisted on her chest, with every movement reminding her of what she'd done. Jo reached down and stroked Jordy's nose, so similar to his mother's.

"Are you ready?" she asked.

Claire swallowed and bundled Jordy tighter. "Not really," she admitted.

They said little as they trudged together toward St. Agnes and even less as they approached the faded and chipped painting of Our Lady.

"Are you sure we should be doing this?" Claire asked as Jo opened the rucksack she'd brought and began uncapping pots of paint.

Jo held out a brush and waited for Claire to lay Jordy down. "You know it's the right thing," she said as Claire opened the locket to the photograph of Dee.

Claire took the brush in her shaking hand. "I know," she said, and then added, "I once made a promise to the Virgin that I'd give her a face if I ever had a son." She hung her head, tears forming in her eyes. "I only wish I weren't doing it like this."

"I know." Jo put her hand around Claire's and guided the brush to the wall, smearing fleshy paint on the Virgin's cheek, first by dabs and then in bigger smears.

May God grant her grace, Jo thought as the outline of Dee's features began to take shape, *and keep her soul forever in salt.*

It was only a small prayer—Jo was rusty after so many years of absence from St. Agnes—but it was heartfelt and it was the best she could do. In time, she hoped, it might even be heard.

Chapter Thirty-one

On the face of it, Claire believed, Salt Creek Farm wasn't the kind of place to inspire pilgrims. Marshy and windblown, choked in pickleweed, there were no haloed glories hiding in the barn, no gold-leafed idols to bow down to on the tipsy porch, no charms to be bought or blessings to reap. There were only acres of salt, miles of sand, and Jo, scarred up and down her right side but just fine in the places where it counted.

And yet, miracle of miracles, people chose to travel from as far away as Tokyo and Paris to find the place. Some of the visitors who arrived were culinary specialists. They owned starred restaurants or wrote award-winning food columns. Some of them worked in the food industry, running marketing for giant corporations, and some were taking time off to try to piece together the scraps of their souls again. Most recently a famous chef had arrived in despair because he had lost the sensation of taste. Pastis, bouillon, foie gras—it was all the same to him, he said. The world had turned to a pile of rubbish in his mouth. Jo and Claire spent three days with him at the end of August, the ripest time of year, the last push of the season, and when they were done, he'd not only regained his sense of taste, but also had an entire notebook of fresh recipes.

Not everyone got such fine results, though. Jo greeted each prospective visitor on the porch of the farmhouse with a silver spoon of salt and a list of rules (no disturbing the collection basins, no drinking, no wandering unescorted through the marsh, and above all no mindless chitchat), and then she asked three simple questions: *What is your first memory? Who do you love? What do you think you'll find here?*

Some of the travelers took a quick taste from the spoon and fled, their gums blistering. Some flubbed their answers, and the ones who stayed got to trade in comfortable beds and conversation for lumpy mattresses and long afternoons with only their shadows for consolation.

On the first day of instruction, Claire would spread her different blends of salt on the table in a hodgepodge of bowls and ask her pupils to choose. "Pick the one you like," she would say, for the first hurdle that anyone had to undertake with the salt was an exercise in letting go. When a person stumbled over his tongue or took too long answering, Claire made him pick again until the salt loosened his lips and his words slipped out easily.

"You have to use everything when you work with salt," Claire reminded the students. "You can't pick and choose. If the silt is full of iron and turns the color of rust, you have to learn to work around it."

They didn't know yet that the price of happiness was loss, but Claire had learned that lesson by heart, and she was going to pass it on. Her students couldn't imagine ever being forced to trade their newfound fluidity for a condition of painful solidity, but if they wanted to make salt, they would figure it out. Or rather some of them would. The ones with hearts up to the task. The ones who accepted that breaking their backs and blistering their hands for a scoop of salt, only to watch Claire dissolve it in a bowl for the next newcomer, wasn't cruelty but a kind of poetic progress.

Her second lesson was to take her students out to the graves at the edge of the marsh. Luckily, their curse against boys seemed to have broken when it came to Jordy. Maybe because he was Gilly in soul but not blood, or maybe the curse had run its course. Whatever the cause, Claire was grateful. Here she simply observed. The pupils who cataloged and ordered the graves by date

would do fine but never produce anything startling. The ones who wandered
and ran their fingers over the stones
showed promise, but Claire wasn't so
interested in them either. She was looking for the one or two students who
stopped, put their hands in their pockets, and bowed their heads, struck by
the fact that in a salt marsh time meant
nothing. Those were the students Claire
sent out to scrape the first of the season's salt crystals, for they were the
ones she didn't have to teach a blessed
thing to.

When the visitors left, most of them
drove straight out of town with chapped
lips, aching shoulders, and hands wrinkled from the brine. They motored past
the Lighthouse Diner, sped by the leafy
canopy of the pear tree (which still produced the same gnarled fruit), and totally ignored Plover Hill and Turner
House, which Claire could understand
but which stuck in her craw nonetheless.

She knew that the pursuit of history
wasn't the reason people came all the
way out to this little spit of coastline,

but she still wished they would take a look around. If they did, they might learn a story about salt they didn't know. But then, Claire had chosen to spend her life with the stuff clinging to her lips and tongue. It had become the only tale she could tell, the single thing she was certain she would leave behind when her time eventually came.

———o-o o-o———

Ethan liked to claim that the quickest way to check a person's heart was to look in his eyes, but Claire begged to disagree. "Don't listen to your stepfather. Just feed a person a pinch of salt," she'd whisper to Jordy, "and his lips will tell you what you need to hear."

Jo and Claire had always tried to do that for Jordy. They schooled him well in the history of Prospect, telling him most especially about Turner House and the last man who'd ever lived in it. Just as she and Jo had to prepare the ground before they flooded the marsh, Claire knew, they also had to take care of the foundations of their own line. Jo and Claire had finally gotten around to tidying up the detritus of Salt Creek Farm, and some of the old letters and diaries they'd found were telling. They'd gathered them up, tied ribbons around them, and put them aside for Jordy's eighteenth birthday, which at the time had seemed an eon away. First Jordy crawled, then he walked, and then he learned to talk, but with each new leap in his development Claire's heart would lurch a little as she considered the confession she'd have to make one day.

"You don't have to tell him everything," Ethan pointed out, which shocked Claire, for although he was her rightful husband, she still sometimes thought of him as a servant of the Lord. When he gave earthbound advice, it always surprised her.

Claire shook her head. "No," she said. "I do. He deserves to know. Besides, he'll never really be mine otherwise."

Ethan kissed her cheek. "Nothing is ours in the end," he said, and shuffled off to finish the knitting his uncle had convinced him to take up, leaving Claire rooted on the spot, wondering if the bonds of love were really as frail as all that or if they were perhaps woven for sterner depths than a single strand could reach.

—◦◦ ◦◦—

"Are you ready?" Jo asked, squeezing Claire's hand in the entry of the cottage she and Ethan shared in town.

"One minute," Claire muttered, smoothing out her hair in the hall's mirror. *Where does the time go?* she muttered to herself as she surveyed the ruins of middle age in her reflection. Her torso was thickening, her cheeks were no longer quite so taut, and her red hair, once her glory, was almost all gray now. Some days she almost didn't recognize herself. She turned to Jo, who handed her a thick bundle of papers, and together, being as quiet as they could, they tiptoed' into Jordy's room and woke him.

"What's this?" he muttered as Claire and Jo presented him with the documents—some of them so antique their ink was almost vanished, some crinkled and torn, and some in handwriting

Claire recognized very well, even if it wasn't totally authentic and was signed with a little heart. And then there was the letter penned in her own hand.

"Happy birthday, Jordy," Claire said, brushing the hair out of his eyes the way she used to when he was a young boy. "These are for you. When you were a baby, your aunt and I decided that this is the day you should have them."

He sat up in the narrow bed he still slept in—the same one Claire had slumbered in as a girl—and took the packet out of her hands. Jordy was accustomed to old things—everything in his life from his furniture to his shoes was used, faded, and comfortably worn—but this was an odd gift, even from the likes of Jo and Claire. "What is it?" he asked, untying the ribbons that held everything together.

Claire paused. "It's your inheritance."

Jordy rubbed his eyes, and Claire could guess what he was thinking. Jo gleaned salt for a living, and Claire blended and baked it. As far as Jordy knew, the only things she and Jo had to hand down were old bread rolls and a working knowledge of how to scrape mud.

Claire took the bundle out of his hands and gently pulled the first document from it. "Start with this," she said. It was a legal paper, a deed to Turner House, which had sat empty on Plover Hill since Whit's death, looming over the town like a depressed gargoyle.

Jordy scanned the jargon and handed the page back to Claire. "I don't understand."

Claire looked over at Jo and took a deep breath. "It's your house now, Jordy. Whit Turner was your father." Jordy looked around the room in confusion. An open trunk lay in the corner, half packed, and a suitcase was propped by the door. In a few weeks, he would be going off for his freshman year at Boston College and starting a new existence. Claire bet he wasn't expecting to begin it now. For Jordy's whole life, she and Jo had always told him they didn't know who his father was—the better to protect him—and he had always believed them. Now he was finding out he was the son of an old and prominent family, once the richest in town.

"What am I supposed to do with a house?" he finally asked. "Especially one like that?"

"Oh, it's not for now." Claire folded up the deed and slipped it back in with the other papers. "It's for someday. You'll know when."

"So why give it to me right before I leave?" he said. "Who's been taking care of it all this time?" From the tone of his voice, it was clear he'd been looking forward to tailgating parties and college dances, not roof repairs and domestic chores.

Jo leaned over and patted one of his legs with her scarred hand. "Just read the papers, Jordy, and you'll understand everything. There's a letter in there from Claire, an apology for what happened the night your real mother died." She looked over to the suitcase by the door. "Claire loves you, Jordy. Try not to judge her too hard. She never wanted to tell you any of this. I know it's breaking her heart to do it, but it's the right thing. She loves you enough to risk losing you. Remember that." And with a quiet click of the door, she left Claire and Jordy alone to come to their own conclusions.

———o-o o-o———

Claire often wondered how it must have felt for Jordy to go from being a boy with two parents to an orphan, from poor to a homeowner, fatherless to an heir, all in the reading of a pack of old letters. She wondered, too, what he thought of the story she'd written of his mother's death by fire in the barn, but he never shared that, and Claire never had the courage to ask him about it. Ethan was right, she decided. Sometimes things were better left untouched.

The only way to lay history to rest, Claire had learned, was to keep it alive, and in transforming Turner House into the Historical Landmark Association, Jordy had swept away some of the cobwebs of the place. The house still hulked on Plover Hill, eyeing the village with its menacing rows of windows, but now anyone could walk inside. Anyone could poke through its dusty corners and shout up its tall chimneys, making the walls echo. The Turner insignia was still engraved on every available surface, spiky as ever, but it had been tempered and mixed with the names of Gillys, and in that way maybe softened.

Like the house, Jordy's life was neatly divided, even as it was also a hodgepodge of conflicting elements. He'd departed for college as planned, but Claire knew he'd gone with an altered soul. It was as if he'd gained weight, as she supposed he had. He took up history instead of economics as a planned course of study, then married young, had a daughter, and tragically lost his wife to cancer, leaving Jordy thirty and alone, grieving, and raising a daughter he had no idea what to do with. "Come home," Claire had pleaded with him over the phone, the line crackling like a fire between them.

There was a long silence, and then Jordy had asked, "For how long?"

For once Claire had said exactly the right thing. "Let's let the salt decide."

Starting with the packet of letters and clippings, Jordy had been able to build a collection of memorabilia and artifacts stretching from Prospect's start as a whaling outpost to its current incarnation as a summer haven for the wealthy. St. Agnes was the same as ever, along with Salt Creek Farm, but in the end Claire found it ironic that Whit had gotten his wish in a manner of sorts. Prospect had become a Destination.

Now the bottom floor of Turner House was public, open weekends and every day except Monday. Jordy and his daughter, Rose, inhabited the second floor. They didn't need much—barely a suite of rooms between them—and of course they spent most of their time at Salt Creek Farm. In the summer Jordy gave lectures and tours, and in the winter he was simply Rose's father. One day, he claimed, he might even start a book, and Claire wondered what would happen if their story was ever written down, fixed in black and white.

"Just wait," she always told Jordy when he brought the subject up, for as the salt was something she regularly consumed but didn't truly own, the history of the Gillys and Turners wasn't really hers to give away either. There would come a time when the marsh would pass to Rose, and then, at long last, the strands of the past—Turner and Gilly alike—would be woven into a single neat braid like the one that hung down Rose's back.

But all that was in the future. For now Claire was content to watch Rose through the blurry prism of Salt Creek Farm's windows, her arms moving in sync with Jordy's and Jo's as she learned to rake, while the wonderful smell of fresh bread was rising from the kitchen. If she knew anything, Claire thought, it was simply that though our time on earth was short, our lives were long. They seeped and spread, watery and wide, moving in unexpected directions.

Claire reached up and touched the locket at her throat, her thumb fixed on the pearl. If she had to atone for her sins, she figured, so be it, she was ready, ice pitted in her bowels, frost gathered in her hair, and salt scattered painful beneath the papery skin of her feet—for as it was in the beginning, she suspected, so would it be forever in the end.

Acknowledgments

First thanks go to my agent, Dan Lazar at Writers House, for being an advocate, a friend, and for bringing out the best in me and my work time and time again.

Thanks to Caryn Karmatz Rudy for walking me down the first part of the editorial path and for her continuing friendship. And a spectacular thanks to my editor, Helen Atsma, the fairy godmother of editors, for getting me across the finish line.

It takes a village to put out a book, so thank you to everyone at Grand

Central Publishing: Jamie Raab for running the whole show; Deb Futter for support; Carolyn Kurek, Maureen Sugden, and Celia Johnson for their sharp eyes. And thanks to Catherine Casalino for the beautiful cover.

I think I owe some drinks to the Council of Mental Health and Domestic Crises, otherwise known as Pam, Andrea, Laura, and Lynn. Thank you for always being at the other end of the phone line with open ears and open hearts. And thanks to my dining committee, Jack and Nancy, for testing recipes.

Thanks to the Debs—Kris, Meredith, Eve, and Katie—for keeping up my spirits and always responding so nicely to any e-mail tagged FDEO. Thanks to Joshilyn Jackson for giving public speaking advice and for showing me the authorial ropes.

I have immense gratitude for all the independent booksellers in the San Francisco Bay Area, especially Elaine Petrocelli at Book Passage and Calvin Crosby at Books Inc., for their love of good stories and their care and respect for local writers and readers.

Finally, my family needs the biggest thanks of all. Without my own sisters, Lala and Bella, I wouldn't have inspiration for the relationships in this book, and without the Drever tribe I wouldn't have a cheering section. And without Ned, Willow, Raine, and Auden, my own clan, I wouldn't have anything at all.

About the Author

TIFFANY BAKER is the author of the *New York Times* bestselling novel *The Little Giant of Aberdeen County*. She lives in Marin County, California, with her husband and three young children.